ANN JEFFRIES

Acknowledgments

The Creator

The Ancestors

My Parents

William and Verna Griffis Ward

Jessica Tilles, Project Design, TWA Solutions

Kelley Hazen, Narrator, Storyteller Productions

Laurie D. Willis, Editor, Laurie's Write Touch!

Members of the Carolina Forest Authors' Group

Carolina Forest Public Library, Horry County, S.C.

Faithful family, friends, and fans

The journey continues and the struggle for literary perfection shall never end

I remain faithfully yours,

Ann Jeffries

All that is gold does not glitter,
Not all those who wander are lost;
The old that is strong does not wither,
Deep roots are not reached by the frost.
From the ashes, a fire shall be woken,
A light from the shadows shall spring;
Renewed shall be blade that was broken,
The crownless again shall be king

John Ronald Reuel Tolkien

3 January 1892 – 2 September 1973

CHAPTER 1

"Samantha?" a woman's voice called out in the well-appointed, private, Adventurer Executive Airline (AEA) waiting room. "Samantha Montgomery?" Others in the jetport suspended their conversations and turned their heads to watch.

Samantha's head came up to look away from the soft, yellow, and grey blanket she was absently knitting. Her velvety brown eyes focused on a young woman coming toward her who she hadn't seen in many years. After frowning and shutting off the audiobook novel she was listening to, she pulled the earbuds from her face. "Paulette? Paulette King?" Samantha questioned, surprised. Paulette's face had filled out to the point that she was a bit overweight and almost unrecognizable from the young girl she remembered.

"It's me," Paulette King acknowledged as she moved forward. She bent and awkwardly hugged her former private-school chum and then sat beside her. "I wasn't sure it was you because I called your name several times. You've cut your hair, and you seem so different. Wow, you look like that actress, Halle Berry. I apologize if I interrupted you. Were you on a call?"

Samantha capped her knitting needles and put her work and cell phone aside in the oversized canvas bag at her feet. Then she focused on the woman who had once shared her most closely held secrets and betrayed her. "Uh, no, Paulette. I wasn't on a call. I didn't hear you. I was listening to my sister's guy friend's novel, *Rising Eagles*."

"Oh, yes, I saw it on the Best Seller's List, but I haven't read it yet. I hear that Tina Justice and her company, Sweet Justice Productions, optioned the story for a movie. According to the trades, Bill Chandler will be the executive producer, and Miguel Menendez-Gaza will take the leading male role. King Advertising is competing for the contract to do the marketing for the movie. They're not quite ready to take meetings yet, though. They're still looking for a female star. The novel is by Simon Wilde, isn't it?"

"It is, yes."

She furtively looked around them, winked, and conspiratorially whispered, "Simon is such a hottie, but I didn't know that he was dating one of your sisters. Which one?"

"Geneviève. They've tried to keep their relationship low key." She needed to change the subject, so she did. "Wow, it's been years since I've seen you. How have you been?"

Paulette shrugged. "Fine, but not as well as you, I hear."

"I have no complaints," Samantha tentatively smiled. She wasn't exactly sure about her relationship with Paulette…or her former friend's family.

"I saw on the world news that you've been on the continent with your textile show."

Samantha sighed, slowly coming to grips with her discomfort. It appeared that she was going to have to carry on a conversation. Her only other option would have been to get up and move to another seat, but no matter what, her parents taught her to be kind even to those who were not kind to her. *Hopefully, she wouldn't have to wait long before her flight was ready to board,* she thought while trying to assure herself that she could hold out for a few more moments. Inwardly, she sighed and put on a professional smile to get her through this uncomfortable experience. "I have, yes, and I'm finally on my way home. Madrid is my last stop on the tour."

"I can't get over how much you seem to have changed. You look so stylish, chic, and sophisticated. Your look is marvelous. You seem to have changed so much compared to when you played tennis on the amateur circuit back in high school. You set records which no one has been able to break," Paulette gushed.

"Thank you," Samantha offered, knowing her appearance was the result of having a sister, Linda, who is a prima ballerina, and an aunt and close friend, Angelique, who is one of the top supermodels in the world. Samantha and all of her sisters were taken under Linda's and Angelique's wings and taught first how to take care of their bodies and faces to perpetuate a healthy glow. Then they learned how to use makeup, style their hair to their best advantage, and dress for success. Those lessons came in handy when she went away to college at the University of Washington-Seattle and had to learn how to take care of herself away from home. She ate junk food and drank sugar-filled sodas from time to time like everyone else in college and grad school, but never to excess. She kept to a healthy diet and a strict exercise routine. For an energy outlet, she took up racquetball and found that she liked it. "Now, enough about me. What are you up to these days?"

"I'm working for my brother in our family's advertising agency." Paulette looked up and around as if searching for someone. "There he is over there." She waved at someone at Samantha's back.

Samantha tensed again and thought, *If she turns around right now, like Lot's wife, she might become a pillar of salt.* She didn't want to look back at her Sodom, otherwise known as Paulette's twin brother, Samuel King, or Sam the Slugger to his multitude of tennis fans.

From their early days in a Georgetown private elementary school academy in a fashionable section of Washington, D.C., his tennis prowess was clearly evident. Sam and she had been close for all of the years they played tennis together. She had shared her first of many kisses with him up until high school graduation. They used to joke that Sam and Sam went together like M&Ms. However, on prom night, she prepared herself mentally and emotionally to go beyond kisses, but he never came to escort her to dinner and the dance. Instead, the next day it was all over the academy school campus that Samuel escorted Pamela Halstead, another classmate, to dinner at a posh restaurant and then to the prom. Now it was Sam and Pam instead of Sam and Sam. Nine months later, the newlyweds, Samuel and Pamela King, welcomed a son into their hasty marriage.

Being dumped on the night of the prom, she supposed, wasn't as bad as the possibility of being left at the altar on some future wedding day. She could philosophically assure herself of that now looking back to yesteryear. Still, she braced at the thought of seeing Sam again and was glad she was sitting. The disappointment of that singular event irrevocably changed the trajectory of her life. Although she, too, had a promising career as an athlete, she gave up the game and rarely played tennis now except on occasion with her siblings.

"Look who I found," Paulette chirped up all grins and giggles.

Sensing someone behind her, Samantha galvanized her emotions against the impact of seeing Sam, stood, plastered a polite smile on her face, and turned to face her past. "Hello, Sam—" she began and then faltered.

Quentin King noted the momentary hesitant expression on Samantha Montgomery's gamine face. It was a face he hadn't been able to get out of his head for too many years. She was a cute preadolescent, a pretty teen who was a bit on the shy side, and now a lovely, sophisticated-looking young woman. Because of her poised personae, he sensed that over the intervening years since last he saw her, she developed style and grace. Now, she was simply breathtakingly gorgeous. He felt that she embodied a kind of vivacity and enthusiasm, an effervescence found only in a rare, choice sparkling wine.

As he gazed at Samantha, he thought she had changed so very much since those early years when she and his younger brother, Samuel, played tennis together. They teamed up and won nearly all of their mixed-doubles tennis matches throughout high school. Quentin expected Samuel and Samantha would continue in the same way in college if his father, Quentin King, IV, hadn't stepped in to break up their relationship. Quentin didn't want to think of the past now. Seeing Samantha again was a pleasure in and of itself.

"Hello, Samantha." He took the hand she offered before it went limp.

"Quentin." Momentarily, she got caught up in his dark chocolate, Morris Chestnut-like gaze. *His hair has always been ebony-colored, healthy-looking, and wavy, but have his eyes always been so mesmerizing?* she wondered. *If so, how did I not notice that before?* Well, he and his younger brother did look alike, and back in the day, she only had eyes for Sam.

Dismissing the errant thought and summoning a brighter professional smile, she affected a warm, two-handed shake. "It's good to see you, Quentin. I trust that the rest of your family members are well." *When he drew me into a loose embrace...the hug was a surprise, too,* she thought. They had never been that familiar with each other.

He held her for a brief moment longer than necessary so that he could draw in more of her enticing scent. Before releasing her, he noticed his brother and nephew, Samuel Junior, approaching from behind her. Quentin didn't know whether Samantha had residual feelings for Samuel, but he hoped not. Even when Samantha was a teen, and he was in college, he enjoyed her sweet and somewhat shy personality. He was friends with her older brothers at the prestigious, exclusive, private school they all attended in the Georgetown area of Washington, D.C. When he graduated and went away to college and grad school at UPenn, they hadn't kept in touch. Although Samantha's older brother, Brian Montgomery, was an underclassman at UPenn while he was a senior, they didn't run in the same circles or renew friendships. Everyone in Samantha's family knew how Sam betrayed her in a way that was not easily forgotten or forgiven.

Similarly, when their father forced Samuel to dump Samantha, her relationship with Paulette also came to an abrupt halt. According to their father, Samantha's background made her undesirable as future marriage material for Samuel. However, Pamela Halstead, a member of the über-wealthy Halstead family of Northern Virginia, was considered to have an impeccable pedigree. *What an error in judgment that had been,* Quentin thought as he watched his younger brother and nephew draw nearer.

"Hi, Aunt Paulette and Uncle Q," piped up a little person.

"Hi, Sammy," Paulette acknowledged while smiling down at the youngster. "Do you know who this is?"

"Nuh-uh." The little boy curiously peered up at Samantha. "She's pretty."

"She is," another voice reverently added to the conversation. *She is even more attractive now than he remembered*, thought Samuel King. When they first met, she had a Princess Dianna sweet shyness and innocence about her. Even in his preadolescent years, he wanted to be her friend, and they became very close. Throughout high school, they shared a love of the game of tennis and teamed up to help improve each other's skills and abilities on the tennis court and circuit. No matter when or where the events, they made efforts to attend each other's singles matches and were always teamed together for mixed doubles.

Their closeness led to other more intimate encounters, but not to sex. Still, they believed their relationship in the future would ultimately result in marriage. However, it was not to be. His parents forced him to break off his bond with Samantha in the most cruel and unforgiving way, an experience he sorely regretted. Since he had not seen or talked with her since high school, he didn't know what type of reaction to expect from her.

Years ago, on the night of their high school prom, as he was preparing to leave to pick up Samantha, his parents stopped him. He and his sister, Paulette, were forbidden to see or speak with her again. Their parents made it clear that she would not be welcomed into their home or their family. Instead, they arranged for him to escort Pamela Halstead to the prom because they determined that his future would be with her instead of Samantha.

Well, his parents got what they wanted but got duped in the process. So, too, did he. The only good thing to come out of the marriage to Pamela was their son Sammy. Much to his regret, he and Pamela were still husband and wife but had not lived together since their son was born. Sam could only think about how different things might have been if he and Samantha were permitted to stay together.

Awkward was an understatement for what Samantha felt, but the little boy with a smooth Hershey-colored complexion and dark-brown, wavy hair—the spitting image of his father at the same age—was too handsome to ignore. It surprised her to see that he wore a diamond stud in his left earlobe like the one she gave to his father. His hair was thick, not as long, but tied with a rawhide at the back of his neck, again, just like his father's. She sat down to engage the child in conversation and give herself a moment more to settle before facing his father. "I think you're pretty handsome, too. You must have all the young ladies' attention. Where do you go to college?"

His grin is lethal, Samantha thought. *Again, just like his father.*

"I'm six. I don't go to college yet."

"No?" With wide eyes, she feigned shocked surprise. "I thought you had to be at least sixteen."

"Nuh-uh, but I'll be seven, and I'm going to have a big birthday party. My daddy said I could. You can come, too, if you want. I might even get a puppy this time." With that last revelation, he slid his gaze up over his shoulder to his father before looking at the pretty lady again.

"Why, thank you, kind sir. I'll put it on my calendar." Samantha offered her hand for a shake before standing again. She hoped she was ready to face his father after getting over the shock of so suddenly being in his company. She turned and faced Sam for the first time in nearly eight years. There was that face that had lived in her memory; it seemed like forever, but he had lost all of its boyish charms. His eyes were black and sharp, his face more narrow with a noticeable five o'clock shadow on a strong chin, which went well with the dark slash of eyebrows and curtain of long lashes. His hair was thick, liquid-asphalt black, naturally wavy, and tied in a bushy tail at the nape of his neck.

A diamond winked at her from his left earlobe, and she briefly wondered whether it was the same one she gave to him on his sixteenth birthday. She also gave one to Paulette and wore a companion one in her left earlobe until he dumped her. Somehow, he seemed taller now than before, so that she had to adjust to look up into his face. "He's a real joy, Samuel." She looked briefly into his eyes but then down and shared a smile with his mini-me. "You must be very proud of him."

"He's my best pal." Sam ran his hand over the boy's wavy hair, smiling down at his son's upturned face.

"Ms. Montgomery?" a voice intruded.

"Yes?" Samantha turned to the uniformed pilot, Glen Kennard.

"If you're ready, you may board now."

"Thanks, Captain Kennard." She reached for her carry-on luggage and was grateful for the intrusion. It spared her from having to continue conversing with the King family. *Old familiar pains*, she thought, *die hard*.

"I'll take that for you." The pilot stepped forward, taking the canvas bag from her hand, and stood by waiting.

Paulette gave Samantha a quick farewell squeeze.

"You're still living with your parents, right?"

"I am, yes. We're living at the ranch in Maryland, not the Georgetown brownstone in D.C."

"Good. May I have your cell phone number? I'd like to contact you and arrange to get together over lunch or dinner." Paulette offered her cell phone to Samantha.

"Certainly." Samantha was reluctant to take it, but keeping in touch would likely be limited to a lunch date or two before Paulette and the rest of the King family would again disappear from her life. So, she accepted the cell phone, entered her business contact number, and sent Paulette's info to her cell phone. Then she handed Paulette's phone back to her. "It was good to see all of you. Take care and have a safe journey." Samantha impersonally shook Quentin's hand and then Sam's, before running her hand over the youngster's shoulder. With a little wave, she turned to join the captain, who put a guiding arm around her to escort her to the departure gate.

CHAPTER 2

"Samantha?" Quentin spontaneously spoke up and then moved closer to her before she could get too far away. She stopped and turned around to face him as he moved toward her. "As I understand it, you're heading home. Is that correct?"

"Yes, that's right."

"We're heading back to the states, too, but our flight hasn't arrived yet from Brussels. It's been delayed for a few hours because of heavy weather in that area. Sammy is a real trouper, but he's a little tired of the long hours of travel. Would you mind if we caught a lift with you?" He knew he was putting her on the spot. Still, he would have done almost anything to spend more time with her, and he didn't even question the reason why. He was also curious about the possessive nature of the pilot's arm around her.

There was something about the way Quentin looked at her, which had her blood uncharacteristically warming. Momentarily non-plussed, she frowned at the sensation. "Uh, let me check with my pilot to see whether there are other passengers scheduled for my flight." She forced herself to turn away and look at Glen. Sensing his need to consult privately, she stepped closer to him into his personal space and looked up into his eyes. "You're concerned?"

Glen passed off her canvas bag to the steward who stood at the ramp door, which led to the jet. He turned his back to the Kings and looked into Samantha's upturned face. *She is so absolutely lovely,* he thought, but quickly got his mind back on business. "Yes, I'm concerned because we have strict instructions about your safety.

Richardson Security allows joint travel accommodations only when the parties, other than your family, have been vetted. Purposefully, there aren't any other passengers scheduled for this flight. However, you know we're slated to land in Maryland, not D.C." He began to dial the secured line.

"I know the rules, Glen. We shouldn't have a problem with security. I've known the King family since I was a child. If they are clear to fly on another AEA flight, they should be okay to join me. However, if you can't get clearance to land at Reagan National in D.C. temporarily, I suggest there be a car waiting once we land in Maryland to take them into the city."

"You're directing me to do this?"

Taking his free hand in hers and a deep breath, she nodded and continued looking up into Glen's concerned expression. She had to admit to herself that she had a soft spot for children. Sighing, Samantha couldn't believe what she was about to do, but she clearly understood why she was going to do it. She remembered what it was like to be young and caused to suffer. "I'm *asking* you to do this, Glen, yes, for me. There is a child who needs to rest. If we can accommodate the King family, then I want to do this."

He sighed and briefly squeezed her hand. "Yes, ma'am. You know the protocol. What is the safe word?"

She went to her toes, leaned in, and whispered it to him. He nodded, then put the phone to his ear to answer the security dispatcher, but never broke eye contact with Samantha or released her hand. He knew that his call would get priority treatment when he repeated the safe word and his personal code. If Samantha felt threatened or under any type of duress, she would have given him a different stress word. While he waited to connect and was still looking into her eyes, he absently said, "We've got snow and sleet in the forecast at the county municipal airport in Maryland. We'll have to see what's what when we get within an hour or two of landing. However, I'm going to have to check in to ensure that the Kings are authorized." He then said into the phone, "Dispatch, security check on four members of a King family waiting for an AEA flight from Brussels, Belgium, slated for a pickup in Madrid, Spain, to Washington, D.C., ..." and continued with the security protocol while still looking into Samantha's eyes. "The flight is still on the ground in Brussels." He informed her and continued. "Heavy weather has all flights from there grounded for several more hours."

She nodded her understanding, broke eye contact, turned, and released his hand to walk back to the King family.

Paulette frowned. "Is there a problem, Samantha?"

"I don't think so, but there are a few security measures which have to be cleared before we take off. Due to heavy weather, your flight is still on the ground in Belgium and it will likely be several more hours before it can resume its schedule. It shouldn't take long to get clearance for you to join my flight. I'm the only passenger scheduled, but we would have to add your names to the flight manifest and alert your original flight of the change." Just then, she noticed Glen give her the thumbs-up sign when he ended his phone call. She nodded to him and then turned back to the group. "Are we all here, or are we waiting for someone else?" Seeing Samuel again was enough of a shock. She sincerely hoped that she didn't have to brace to see his wife, Pamela, too.

The silence was surprising, but then Quentin spoke up. "No, it's just the four of us."

"Okay, then if you're ready, I'll have the crew load your luggage, and we can board."

The King family moved toward a stack of luggage just as the flight attendant emerged from the ramp leading to the aircraft. That's when Samantha noticed that Sam seemed to be moving with a certain degree of difficulty. She turned away, concerned, but not feeling as if she should intrude on his privacy about his physical condition. Feeling someone take her hand, she looked down into Sammy's smiling, upturned face. "You're such a gentleman. Are you sure you're not twenty-six?"

"Nuh-uh." He beamed that megawatt smile and proceeded to skip along beside her pulling his one piece of luggage and following the flight attendant to the door, which led to the jet. "I will be one day and we can be boyfriend and girlfriend."

Heaven forbid, Samantha thought. *Been there, done that with your father, and I have the heartbreak to show for it.*

The Cessna Citation X was among the smallest aircraft in AEA's fleet, but one of the fastest, even with the extra bodies and additional luggage weight. It would be a bit snug, too, so Samantha hoped they wouldn't face any headwinds or other turbulence so that the usual eight-hour flight would go quickly. Still, it had a restroom where she could sequester herself if necessary. Since the seats converted to comfortable single beds, she could always claim that she was weary and sleep during the flight. Frederick Canton, the steward, always kept the galley kitchen well-stocked with seven-course meals. To avoid carrying on a conversation, she might just consider taking a nap after the evening meal.

To keep to their flight schedule, they quickly sat and buckled in. Within moments, they were on the runway and lifting off from the airport runway in Madrid, Spain, headed to the United States. Samantha found herself sitting beside Quentin and facing Paulette across a polished oak table. She wondered how that happened. Sam sat across the aisle on the other side of the fuselage next to his son, preparing to entertain him by reading a few books to him.

When the flight leveled off to cruising altitude, the steward offered drinks and lite snacks and took their dinner orders. Samantha and Paulette struck up a conversation about people they knew or remembered from their private school days.

Quentin reviewed and sent text and email messages and listened to his sister's conversation with Samantha. He was particularly interested when Paulette asked whether Samantha was dating anyone special.

Samantha laughed. "Frankly, Paulette, I simply haven't had the time. However, recently Glen and I've joked that we've been dating for months."

Paulette grinned. "The hunky pilot? I noticed that you two were holding hands."

"Really? I didn't notice. We've been on the move for over four months. Glen usually ends up accompanying me to events when I'm exhibiting or meeting with buyers, so we've had the odd meal together. I suppose we've become friends and familiar with one another. Nothing formal or structured between us, though. It's more for grins and giggles."

For his own reasons, Quentin wanted to engage Samantha in conversation directly so that he would have an excuse to look at her. "So, you design furniture?"

"I have, yes, when the client's décor needs something I can't find on the market. More often, I design the patterns for fabrics used for upholstery, curtains, drapery, carpets, and rugs."

"Did I read that you've started a line of linens?" Paulette asked.

"I have, yes. It's called The Pleasure Series. It's the second season that I've done linens. I premiered the collection at the start of my tour this season. I'm thinking of adding other comfort pieces to the collection for next season."

"Who handles your ad campaign?" Paulette wanted to know.

Samantha chuckled. "My brothers, Roger and Ryan."

"The twins? I thought they were still playing professional baseball."

"They are, but they enjoy dabbling in electronics, the technical aspects of audio and film production, and social media platforms. So, in their, *ha-ha*, spare time in the off-season, they designed my website and created on-line advertising campaigns for me," she joked. "It's all automated and runs several different ads daily. They create new campaigns every month. They plan to do something with communications and media as a second career once the cheering stops."

"Are they involved with special women?"

Samantha laughed. "Yes, often and continuously. Usually twins. They go to these conventions all the time for people who are twins. They even convinced Vincent and Geneviève to attend a few times. Don't tell me you still have a crush on Roger and Ryan."

"Well, half the women in the world love to see them suit up for professional baseball games. So do I."

"Oh, no, don't say that loud enough for them to hear you. My brothers' egos are big enough as it is." Samantha shook her head and giggled.

She has the most infectious laugh, thought Quentin, *kind of light and genuine*. It amused him to hear it. Her voice was on the lower register with a Téa Leone quality with a little huskiness that is as sexy as hell. After the steward served dinner, Quentin continued to half-listen to the conversation between his sister and Samantha and occasionally interjected a question or comment. He noted, now that his nephew was asleep, Sam showed an avid interest in everything Samantha had to say.

Quentin knew that his brother never quite got over his infatuation with Samantha, but Samuel adhered to his wedding vows, although his wife, Pamela, did not. What kept Sam grounded in the marriage was his son, Sammy. As recently as last week, Sam asked Pamela for a divorce, and she laughed in his face. No way was she giving up being the wife of the world's top tennis pro or the money and the notoriety his status brought her. If he even attempted to see other women and word got out to the media, she threatened to take their son away from him. Because his life was in a constant state of limbo, Quentin felt empathy for his brother. Yet, where Samantha Montgomery was concerned, it was a winning scenario for him. It appeared that Samantha was free, single, and disengaged. For all intents and purposes, so was he and he intended to press his advantage with her.

CHAPTER 3

They were well into hour five of the nearly eight-hour flying time. Thankfully, Paulette had talked herself out and moved to another seat where she could watch an in-cabin movie and recline the seat into a bed for a nap. Both Sam and Sammy were asleep on the other side of the cabin, but Quentin was still awake, working on his laptop.

She was awake, too, listening to her cousin's novel and knitting a blanket for the baby boy of her brother and sister-in-law, Brian and KiLe, who would be born next month. Samantha wanted to finish it before the baby shower in two weeks. Considering this was their second child and also an unplanned pregnancy, this was such an important time. They were discussing names for the new baby but hadn't settled on anything specific yet.

Samantha hoped this would help lift KiLe's spirits because her parents essentially disowned her. They did so because she refused to marry one of the men they selected for her, a Japanese man she never met before. Her sister-in-law learned that the men her grandfather chose were like him, a member of the Yakuza criminal syndicate. What made it even more untenable, she was unexpectantly pregnant with Brian's child at the time. Her parents, Japanese traditionalists, couldn't have been more harsh toward their only daughter, declaring KiLe *persona non grata* in their lives.

Although KiLe's parents and grandparents stayed in the United States for the impromptu wedding, they left immediately after the ceremony without speaking to the new bride and groom. KiLe hadn't heard one word from anyone in her family after they left the states. Samantha and her family wrapped their arms around KiLe, welcoming her into the Alexander and Montgomery families.

Although Brian's and KiLe's wedding, held during the Juneteenth holiday celebration, was rather spur-of-the-moment, it certainly was a joyous occasion. It came together later in the afternoon on the same day as the wedding of their cousin, Whitney Alexander, to Tucker Cavanaugh. Since the family gathered for the traditional Juneteenth family reunion held annually in Goodwill, Summer County, South Carolina, literally, a thousand people were there to wish Brian and KiLe well.

Despite her pregnancy, KiLe, a student at Georgetown University, was working on her graduate degree, starting with a summer internship. Initially, she was reluctant to begin the program because her parents withdrew their financial support. Still, Brian insisted that she accept the opportunity to participate in the advanced studies science and technology program conducted under Mensa's auspices.

The whole family was proud of KiLe's accomplishments and didn't want her to miss out on this wonderful opportunity. This internship counted toward the completion of KiLe's chosen master's degree program. It also guided her doctoral study, which she had just started in the summer.

Initially, KiLe was so dispirited by her families' rejection; it took all of Brian's love and trust to convince her to accept his financial support. After all, they were husband and wife. He was a multi-millionaire and loved KiLe to distraction. Samantha was happy for them and hoped that one day she too might find a man as special as her brother, Brian, or their father, Chuck Montgomery. She had many positive examples of notable and special men in her family. Her fervent hope was to find a man with whom she would be able to share a happy life.

Though they were not related by blood, they were cemented together by love. Samantha didn't know who her parents were and frankly didn't care. When she and her multitude of siblings were adopted a second time by Chuck and Vivian Alexander Montgomery, she had all the family she wanted or needed. She missed them while she was on tour and couldn't wait to get home to see them.

Samantha thought of her brilliant sister-in-law as she continued to knit the blanket for her new nephew.

"You're smiling," Quentin interrupted.

Samantha looked up and stared at Quentin, not sure he had spoken to her. His voice was smooth and soft, almost as a purr. "Sorry, did you say something?" She removed an earbud from her right ear.

"I said you were smiling. Was there something in the novel that pleased you?"

"Novel?" she frowned. Then it dawned on her that he was talking about her cousin's novel, which had ended. She had not removed the earbuds. "Oh, no, the audio book ended a while ago. I was thinking about my brother, Brian, and his wife, KiLe. They're expecting again." She smiled at the thought.

"I didn't know that Brian had married. When did that happen?"

"June 19, a few years ago." She told him about the wedding without mentioning that it had been necessitated by KiLe's pregnancy and the loss of her student visa privilege. Under ordinary circumstances, after graduation from Georgetown University, KiLe would have had to return to Japan, where she would receive no support from her family.

"I see," Quentin nodded. "I remember that your family holds those reunions annually, correct?"

"Yes, that's correct. It's tradition on the Alexander side of the family to hold the reunion for ten days around Juneteenth. We had four weddings during the last reunion this past summer. The younger members of the family, who are still matriculating through school, from daycare through post-graduate studies, gather in Atlantic Beach, South Carolina, around Labor Day to reinforce their determination to do well academically."

"I imagine it's convenient to have several weddings when the family is already there."

"It is, yes. It takes a lot of the pressure off of those planning the wedding when you don't have to decide on a venue, date, or food service. Then we need only to focus on the guest list, housing for the guests, events such as the showers, and the theme. They are all such lovely and unique occasions." Smiling, she continued to knit.

"Is that where you want to have your wedding ceremony?"

"Of course." Samantha's response was automatic. "The groom's family and friends are invited to attend the whole ten days of activities. My family lives and works on hydroponics farms in Summer County, where they grow fruit, vegetables, and flowers. There are also traditional farms and fisheries, so there is always plenty of fresh food. We have several great chefs in the family and more than enough hands to help. It's an exciting time, and I look forward to it each year.

"Then around Labor Day, all of the young people who are still in school gather in Atlantic Beach, South Carolina, to re-commit to working hard during the school year. When I was still a student, we slept in tents right on the beach in front of our great-grand Aunt Hannah Ivy's house. We'd shop for school clothes and shoes at the outlet malls in Myrtle Beach before we left to go home."

"So, you have someone in mind?" Quentin's curiosity was getting the better of him, he knew, but her answer was vitally important to him.

Confused, Samantha beetled her brow and asked, "In mind for what?"

"To marry at the family reunion next year."

"Uh, no," she slowly shook her head, still a bit confused about how or why the conversation reverted to her getting married.

"You seem confused."

"I am."

"Okay, you mentioned to my sister that you were dating the pilot and that you would like to get married at your family's annual reunion."

"That led you to think my marriage was imminent?" Confusion still covered her face.

"Well, yes," he said and watched the humor build in her lovely eyes as she laughed.

"Uh, no, I'm not in love with Glen. He's been my constant companion along with his co-pilot, Cameron Diaz, and the steward, Frederick Canton, while I was on tour. I'm not sure that what we were doing could be considered 'dating,' especially since there were usually four of us wherever we went. Glen is from Texas and generally flies the international charters and routes because he speaks several languages. We would have meals together with his co-pilot and attendant. We stayed in the same hotels in every city, so it was convenient to hang out. They helped me with the setup or takedown of my display for each occasion. We were usually scheduled to fly to another locale after each event."

"Interesting." Quentin was pleased that an opportunity to get better acquainted with the grown-up Samantha hadn't just slipped through his fingers.

That one word confused Samantha even more. She decided to change the subject. "You didn't say why all of you were in Spain."

"Oh, I thought you knew." Quentin was surprised that she wasn't keeping up with a sport she avidly played as a youngster. "Sam played in the Spain Open, and this year's tournament was a record thirty men's singles Grand Slam final."

"Uh, no. I didn't know. That's wonderful. Although I remember that Mutua sponsors the Madrid Open and is a professional tennis tournament played at the Park Manzanares in Madrid, I haven't been keeping up with sports these days. I've been on the road."

"It's the 22nd edition of the event on the Association of Tennis Professions World Tour. Sam played brilliantly for the ATP World Tour Masters 1000 event. You'll remember that it's the premier mandatory event on the tour. This was the final professional tennis tournament for this season's players.

"Don't you still play?"

Samantha shrugged. "Not much, no."

That is even more surprising and disappointing, Quentin thought. Samantha showed as much talent and promise in the sport as did Sam. He was beginning to believe that her long-ago breakup with his brother must have had a traumatic impact on Samantha. Maybe there were still vestiges of that incident which rendered her unable to trust men. If so, that wouldn't bode well for his intentions where she was concerned.

Feeling a little uncomfortable with the direction of the conversation, Samantha put away her knitting. "If you don't mind, I think I'll nap for a while." Samantha reclined her chair into the sleep position, turned her back to him, and pulled a blanket over the length of her body.

"Yes, rest well." Quentin watched her get comfortable beside him. He was generally much better at holding a conversation with a woman he desired in preparation for a one-night stand. However, it was different with Samantha. With her, he was interested in something more involved and more long term. He needed time with her and a way to feel her out about the possibilities. As he, too, put away his work, he reclined his chair into a sleep position. He turned on his side to face her, closed his eyes, and let his agile mind conjure up ways and means of insinuating himself into Samantha's life while the opportunity was present.

CHAPTER 4

"Ms. Montgomery?" the steward quietly questioned.

Samantha slowly woke from her nap. "Yes, Freddy?" She stretched and covered her mouth as she yawned.

"We're an hour and a half away from landing. If you're ready, I'd like to serve breakfast to you and your guests now."

"Thanks, Freddy." While she stifled another yawn, she activated the mechanism which brought her chair to an upright position and repositioned the footrest. Peering at her watch, she noted that they were making good time. While the steward began to awaken the others to take their orders in preparation for serving breakfast, she slipped into the small restroom to take care of her needs and splash water on her face. When she peered at her eyes in the mirror, she could see the weariness there. Samantha promised herself that she'd get a full facial, a massage, and body scrub at her first opportunity.

Fortunately, the spouses of several employees, who worked for her parents on their ranch, opened a physical therapy and spa facility right across the single-lane road from her parents' Maryland Alex-Mont property. The physical therapy office was her dad's idea to accommodate his patients. The spa was the newest addition. Their father's medical office was in the same group of buildings with an old-fashioned country store where they sold produce from their hydroponics farm and fishery. There was also a barbershop and now a beauty and nail salon. Her brother, Brian, managed the shopping area and the ranch in the Maryland countryside and their ranches in Monroe County, Pennsylvania, and Summer County, South Carolina.

The Maryland ranch was in an area that was rural on a seldom-traveled back road and off the beaten path of larger developments. Yet, they were within thirty minutes to an hour of larger shopping venues in Baltimore and Annapolis, Maryland, and Washington, D.C. It was country living at its best, and she was eager to get home to enjoy it.

After breakfast and the dishes were cleared away, Glen asked Samantha to join him in the cockpit.

"As I mentioned to you before, we have heavy weather blanketing the landing area. The major airports are closed, but because the municipal airport near your home has heated runways melting the snow, we can still safely land there. Reports from the county and state indicate that the road crews are having difficulty keeping roads clear. I'll have to helicopter you to your home because of the heavy snowfall on the back roads. Fortunately, we don't have blizzard conditions with high winds yet, just heavy snowfall. I'm confident that I can get you there safely. The airport will have a Sikorsky H-34 available so that I can fly you and your guests to the ranch. Your parents, Richardson Security, and Brian have been notified and have granted permission for the King family to stay at the ranch until the weather emergency ends."

"Aren't you and the crew going to stay at the ranch, too?" Samantha's concern was evident in her troubled expression.

"No." He shook his head in regret and appreciated her concern for him and his crew. "As soon as you're in situ, your team and I are off to Texas for a mandatory crew-rest period. So, when we land in Maryland, we have to make it quick, getting you loaded onto the helicopter for the ten-minute run to the ranch. You'll have to leave your samples, trunks, boxes, and tour set up in storage at the airport. We can take you, your guests, and the luggage. However, the rest of your equipment and products will have to wait for when the weather breaks. Once we reach the ranch, handlers will be waiting to unload you and your guests."

"I'm concerned, Glen. If the weather is as hazardous as it seems, maybe you and the crew should stay in the area for your mandatory downtime."

"I couldn't, even though I appreciate the offer and would like to take you up on it. This is one of only ten jets this size in the AEA fleet which can reach Mach speeds. It's been out of service to anyone but you for the duration of your tour. It's got to earn its meat and potatoes like all of the others." He smiled at her.

"Oh, I didn't know." Samantha shook her head, surprised.

"Your Uncle Gregory put it exclusively at your disposal. That's why we were able to stick with you for all of your shows and appearances. He does that for each of your tours. Do you know now when you're going out on the road again?"

"I haven't worked it out yet. I have several local shows and speaking engagements to attend. I'll work with my agent, Bill Chandler, on the next tour. Otherwise, I probably will be here in Maryland until Thanksgiving, when we'll all go to our home in Goodwill, South Carolina, where my factory is located. I'll spend time with the Alexander side of the family for a quick vacation. I have a few short business trips before the holidays. This year, my family will enjoy Christmas at our home in the Pocono Mountains with the Montgomery side of the family before returning for the New Year's Eve party at home in Maryland until the end of winter. I'll probably start the new season again in the spring."

"If it's okay with you, I'd like to sign on to be your pilot again for your next tour."

Her smile is beatific, Glen thought and wished he didn't have to leave her for the next six or so months. They joked about "dating," but he wanted to make it the real deal. He had grown to like and respect the woman she was, but he knew his schedule wasn't conducive to sustaining an intimate relationship. Technically, she was also his boss during the tour. He didn't want to confuse their business relationship with sharing the pleasure of her time and attention away from work.

However, at the next mandatory crew-rest period, he'd make it a point to return to the area and ask Ms. Samantha Montgomery out on a real "date." At least, then, she wouldn't be his boss.

"Of course it's okay, Glen. If I have any influence with my uncle Gregory, I'll weigh in on having the same crew I have now. We'll hit the big textile shows in New York City, Chicago, Denver, Seattle, San Francisco, Los Angeles, and San Diego before we take my show on the road to Hawaii, Japan, and all the big towns in Asia and Europe."

He laughed with her because of her enthusiasm. "Don't forget you wanted to include Africa and Australia this next time."

Conspiratorially, she winked at him drawing closer and speaking of the rigidly precise English butler Frederick Canton, who they teasingly called Freddy. "I especially want to do Seychelles just to see Freddy in a speedo."

Glen hooted a laugh. "You are wicked."

She gave herself a self-satisfied nod and then sobered. "I can't tell you how much I appreciated your guidance on this tour, Glen. You and the guys were the best travel companions anyone could ask for. Thank you."

"Speaking for all of us, you're more than welcome, Samantha." He smiled at her and very much wanted to kiss her delectable mouth. However, this was neither the time nor the place. He'd make sure his schedule would permit him to return to her area soon.

When she stood from the co-pilot's seat, she leaned in, giving him a warm embrace before she went through the cabin door. She gave the co-pilot, Cameron Diaz, a similar hug as he passed her in the narrow passageway on his way back to his seat in the cockpit. She'd miss these three guys and would give her uncle a call to tell him how great they were as travel companions and to ensure that she'd see them in the spring for her next tour. For now, she'd return to her seat and try to avoid thinking about Sam.

Samantha knew her parents would be hard-pressed to allow Samuel King and his family into their home, but she also knew that they would rise above their latent feelings. Her family felt the King family's disrespect as gravely as she did. As children, Sam and Paulette were in and out of the Jackson-Alexander Georgetown home all the time. They were great pals in their youth. They ate meals with them and even stayed over some nights if they had early tennis practice the next morning. She and Paulette often had slumber parties and playdates. Her mom made sure that Sam and Paulette could come and spend time during the summer with them. It was such an idyllic time that she couldn't have conceived of a time when they wouldn't have been close friends…and later she and Sam, lovers.

Her dad, more so than her mom, was furious about how Sam treated her. Chuck wanted to go to the King family home in the Rock Creek Park area of Washington, D.C., known as the Gold Coast, and give the patriarch, Quentin King, IV, a piece of his mind. However, her mom convinced him that it wouldn't help make her pain any less devastating. Her brothers and uncles wanted to suit up and escort her to her prom, but she didn't want to show up with a bunch of guys who had murder in their eyes. What made it worse, she was a part of the senior class who worked on the plans for the prom. She arranged to have Changelings, the hottest new band, and sensational new singer and movie star Miguel Menendez-Gaza perform for the event.

When Miguel, a long-time family friend, heard what had happened, he and Changelings refused to perform until she came to the prom. She was already in the McCoy Grand Hotel, where the dance was being held in one of the ballrooms, so she had no choice but to go. Her mother told her to hold her head up, keep her back straight, and be the better person they all knew her to be. Miguel and the band came to her suite and personally escorted her to the prom. They serenaded her all the way. Once there, they never let her sit alone. A band member or Miguel would dance with her even as they sang their most popular songs. At the conclusion of the evening, the band members and Miguel formed a circle around her and sang a cappella while passing her from one band member to the other for the final dance of the evening. It was so achingly sweet, and she appreciated everything they did to make the best of a bad situation. With so much attention focused on her by Miguel and the other handsome male band members, she was the envy of all the girls at the prom. Her notoriety at school lasted for the succeeding weeks until graduation.

Hopefully, those family members who witnessed her humiliation wouldn't be at the ranch when she arrived. Otherwise, she wasn't sure of the welcome the King family would receive.

CHAPTER 5

Glen hovered the big, piston-engine AEA helicopter over the landing spot dissipating the snow until he could see the round edges of the landing pad. As soon as the wheels touched down, a group of Alex-Mont workers hurried out of the mansion to retrieve the luggage and assist Samantha's guests. With his handsome face aglow, his cheeks pinked from the cold, her brother, Brian, was there to help her down to the ground. Then he pulled her into a big happy-you're-home hug. He moved to assist Paulette and left the King men to climb down on their own. Since they were not dressed for the snow and cold temperatures, they hurried to the mansion's closest side entrance. Before entering, Samantha stopped and turned to wave to Glen as he lifted off. He saluted her and smiled before he headed the big helicopter back to the airport.

The warmth enveloped them as soon as they were inside the wide, long hallway, which led past the ballroom and into the great room, the mansion's central cavernous area. There, Samantha saw streamers and balloons heralding her return. Though a smile grew on her face, tears of joy and happiness leaked and overflowed. Her fatigue instantly fled when she spotted all of her siblings and her parents waiting for her with open arms, tight hugs, warm smiles, and many kisses.

At nearly seven-feet tall, her dad, Chuck, dwarfed most of her immediate family. Still, her mother, svelte and nearly six-feet tall, though visibly pregnant, completed their picture of unadulterated love and happiness. She went into her parents' arms, squeezing them as tightly as they hugged her. More kisses and hugs abounded as she went from one sibling and in-law to the next, down to the baby boy, the youngest, Charles Patrick Montgomery, Junior, who she called Patty Cake because he liked to play that game with her.

There were clamors for her to recount the details of the places she'd been and what she saw. So, for the next hour, she gave a running commentary and answered a myriad of questions about every aspect of her tour. Fortunately, she had videoed much of the trip and sent snips via text home to her family. Daily texts and emails from her siblings arrived, which made her feel as if she was still at home with all of them. The twins, Roger and Ryan, videoed her homecoming to add to all of the segments they captured starting from the day she left on tour. They would show the film during the nightly show-and-tell session through the dinner hour. Her family was big on memorializing family events, but they weren't the only ones who seemed riveted when she looked into Quentin King's eyes.

Unbelievable, Quentin thought when he looked up at Samantha while she did a thirty-minute travelogue on her recent tour and another thirty answering questions. He didn't want to appear too obviously enthralled by her, so, thru part of the Q&A session, he looked up three stories in the great room to see a massive skylight. Modern chandeliers hung down, casting beautiful filtered light on the walls, and large fans silently turned slowly, moving the palm fronds strategically placed throughout the space. A polished wood-frame and wrought-iron railing circumnavigated the balcony on each level where flower boxes hung and overflowed with greenery and fall foliage perfuming the air. A hint of moisture made the vast space feel cozy instead of dry and cool. Warmth filtered from the heated, hardwood floor. He could see what must be communal areas interspersed with open bedroom doors. Corridors or wide hallways angled off the great room like spokes on a wagon wheel with bookcases lining each one.

The furniture was large and looked very comfortable in complementary colors. Groupings were arranged for conversation areas but didn't overwhelm the space. The salon reminded Quentin of a fine hotel or country club, but the Montgomery children sprawled everywhere, some even sitting on the warm Brazilian cherry hardwood floor to talk.

It always amazed Quentin how the Alexander-Montgomery family managed to contend with so many children of different ethnicities. There were many age groups and skin tones, from ebony to ivory. When he met for the first time the wealthy young widow Vivian Alexander Jackson, a black female attorney, it was shortly before her famous husband died suddenly of a massive heart attack. He was the former basketball great, Derrick "Dunk and Jam" Jackson, a black man who later became a noted pediatric surgeon after enjoying a sterling sports career. Dr. Jackson had developed some type of medical treatment that revolutionized pediatric medicine. His invention caused his celebrity as a surgeon to be as stellar as his career as an iconic basketball player. A dramatization of his life still played periodically on individual television networks, particularly during the basketball season and Black History Month.

Mrs. Jackson and the original twelve children she and her late husband adopted were living in a large, stately, four-story brownstone home at the edge of Rock Creek Park in the prestigious Georgetown section of Washington, D.C. All of the Jackson rainbow coalition of children, Linda, Brian, Ryan, Roger, Vincent, Geneviève, Dena, Andrew, Darren, Spencer, Samantha, and biological son Derrick Jackson, Jr., were enrolled in the private academy enclave. It was located in the Embassy Row section of the city where he and his siblings were also enrolled. It was the most prominent and celebrated international private school in the city and pricey for one child. Still, the children of foreign dignitaries, future government leaders from different countries, captains of industry, and the famous attended. It is the best place to cement networks of future global connections.

Years later, Mrs. Jackson, who became a U.S. Federal Court judge, married another stellar basketball star-turned medical doctor, Charles Patrick Montgomery, a white man. Their number of United

Colors of Benetton children grew to astronomical proportions, including four natural-born children to the interracial couple and more adopted children from as far away as Iraq and Japan. According to the introductions, the Montgomerys must have added six to nine additional young children whose parents were friends and died in a tsunami.

For some reason, Quentin remembered the media reports about the American doctor, Raymond Phillips, and his wife Denise Harris, a nurse, killed in Indonesia. The story played in the local news media because they had once been working together at Georgetown Medical Center in Washington, D.C.

According to the news reports, the Tsunami left their six children with various degrees of injury. Dr. Montgomery and other U.S. aid workers flew to the affected region to lend aid and to bring the Phillips children back to America. Quentin also recalled a few other American children who lost their parents because of the Tsunami. So, Dr. Montgomery must have brought them home, too. Apparently, the Montgomerys kept all nine of them together and raised them as their own.

Quentin didn't know of any two people more selfless than Charles and Vivian Alexander Montgomery. Certainly, as multibillionaires, they could afford to provide for the additional children. Still, it is their altruism that impressed him. He also knew other people who could afford it but wouldn't even think of bringing orphaned children into their home. His parents could well afford it but never would have considered it. They barely gave charitable organizations donations unless advised to do so by their tax accounting firm to avoid paying taxes.

Quentin was introduced to the eleven-year-old Raymond Phillips, Junior, and the rest of his stair-step Phillips' five siblings, the youngest of whom is only five.

In addition to the Phillips children, there were a plethora of twins in the Alexander Montgomery family. Some were from

South America, but all of the children initially needed extensive and, therefore, costly medical treatment. Most were abandoned as babies by their parents and ensconced in orphanages, which were ill-equipped to deal with the high medical treatment costs for severe illnesses.

Now, as Quentin looked at the ones he knew growing up, he never would have believed any were ill or had physical ailments a day in their lives. He knew their stories and immediately recognized the black female, Linda Montgomery, the eldest daughter. She was orphaned when her father died in Iraq, and an automobile accident killed her biological mother and younger brother. The accident left Linda broken and unable to walk. Due to Derrick Jackson's medical prowess, Linda, the first patient to use his invention, in later years, became a beautiful, world-renowned prima ballerina and figure skater.

Quentin remembered seeing the newspaper articles announcing Linda's marriage to baseball great Will Hamilton. They lived in New York City and, from the looks of it, had two young sons who, although toddlers, gravitated toward Sammy with the other Montgomery tender-age children. Linda produced and directed a long-running SRO show, Goodwill, on Broadway. He and Paulette took Sammy to see the show in New York City. The show was so profound that the boy still talked of that experience. Although Paulette urged them to renew acquaintances with Linda while at the show, Quentin never would.

Linda's husband, Will Hamilton, owned INDULGENCES, an exclusive athletic sports club in Manhattan. A colleague of Quentin's with a membership in the club invited him to come as a guest. He accepted and found the facility was everything it was touted to be and more. Still, he never divulged that he knew and went to school with the wife of the owner.

Then there was Brian Montgomery, the eldest adopted son, a white man who graduated summa cum laude from UPenn's Wharton School of Finance four years after Quentin. Brian, apparently, used his degrees to manage his family's sprawling Alex-Mont properties. He was now married to the petite but very pregnant and pretty young Japanese woman who looked as if she should still be in high school.

Standing almost protectively beside her were the tall twins, Roger and Ryan Montgomery, the current baseball phenoms batting record-breaking scores for a major league team that won the World Series the year before. Paulette was grinning from ear to ear, chatting them up like old friends would want to do.

The second set of many sets of twins, Vincent and Geneviève Montgomery, were born in some South American country. Despite having been conjoined at the hip and unable to walk, they grew up to stand straight and tall. Years of surgery followed them into adolescence. Geneviève, whom everyone called Eve, had always been a beautifully exotic-looking female. Apparently, the white guy Quentin recognized as the award-winning investigative reporter and novelist, Simon Wilde, shared his opinion. Quentin observed that Eve and Simon had kissed more than once since Samantha entered the room. They were smiling at one another as if they had a guilty secret. Actually, Quentin had just finished reading Wilde's best-selling, military suspense novel in a Wilde Wolf series. This novel had an Academy Award written all over it. That was why King Advertising was vying for the opportunity to do the ad campaign for the movie when it was shot.

This, under ordinary circumstances, would have been an ideal opportunity to press for Wilde's support. The producers, Tina Justice at Sweet Justice Productions and Bill Chandler, Esquire, at Alexander, Carter, Chandler, Charles, Lightfoot, and Towson, PA, were Vivian's law school, honors program chums. Tina and Vivian Alexander Montgomery were in undergrad together at Spelman College, and Bill Chandler and Vivian were partners in her law firm before she became a judge. Yet, Quentin didn't feel it appropriate to use this social occasion as a business opportunity.

Quentin continued to study his other former school mates and the other fifteen or so children who came behind them in age. A female friend, Miranda Bazemore, mentioned that she had recently toured a new and innovative academy built and operated by Alex-Mont Ranches in this rural area. She was invited on the tour by one of her sorority sisters, Dr. Roslyn Hunter Greenfield, the dean of the same type of school in Baylor Plaza Park, an intriguing new community in far North East Washington, D.C.

Vivian Alexander Montgomery noted how the adult King family members seemed reluctant to respond to her children, all except little Sammy King, whose effervescence was a joy to observe. He had no filters about his open and eager acceptance of instant friendship. Paulette was enthusiastically renewing acquaintances with her twin sons, Roger and Ryan. However, Quentin, the eldest son of the patriarch, seemed a bit reserved, while the culprit of her daughter's teenage disappointment of her life, Samuel King, stood and appeared to be in major discomfort.

Her husband, Chuck, must have thought something wrong, too, because he moved in Sam's direction. As an emergency room doctor, her husband spent most of his medical career quickly identifying a person's malady and efficiently finding a solution. Since Chuck was leading Samuel away, Vivian decided to invest a little time talking with Quentin. She hadn't seen him in many years. He had grown into a very handsome but somewhat reserved man.

"Hello, Quentin. I was surprised to hear that you were in Spain," she reached out to hold him in a brief embrace.

"Judge Montgomery," he acknowledged rather stiffly, he realized, as he found his arms briefly around the tall, shapely, and attractive pregnant woman, Samantha's adoptive mother. *I've always felt her warmth radiate like sunshine in her presence. Heavens, the woman never seems to age,* Quentin thought. *If I didn't know better, I'd believe that Judge Montgomery and Samantha are sisters instead of mother and daughter. True, Judge Montgomery, a U.S. Supreme Court Justice, was still in her early twenties when she and her first husband, Derrick Jackson, who was over thirty, adopted Samantha. Their adopted daughter was already in preadolescence, but given the number of other children Vivian raised alone after her first husband's death and later with her new husband, her face is still remarkably youthful and wrinkle-free.* "Yes, we were a bit stranded when Paulette spotted Samantha at the airport. We would still be in Spain had your daughter not agreed to let us piggyback a ride to the states with her. It's good of you to permit us to intrude."

"Nonsense. There is no intrusion. We're happy to be able to offer anyone a port in a storm," Vivian joked. "As you may remember, we always look for any reason to celebrate every special event. Samantha's exceptional success is just such an occasion. Everyone made an effort to be here to welcome her home." Taking his arm, she walked to a cluster of seats away from her children's noisy, excited voices for a more quiet area to chat.

"You have a lovely home. It's enormous. It could have been the prototype for the Downton Abbey series. When was it built?"

Vivian chuckled. "Around the early eighteen hundreds, I believe it was constructed. Perhaps the right century, but it's built more in a southern antebellum style, not an English castle. From the historical records we found, the initial footprint was a very large farm owned for several generations by the Norman White family. Each generation would often add on to the basic and expanded floor plan for no apparent reason that we could find. Around April of eighteen eighty-nine, the Whites and their eleven children visited family in Johnstown, Pennsylvania. They were there when the infamous Johnstown flood occurred and killed all of them and their relatives. This house went into receivership until Chuck, Stacy, my sister-in-law, and I stumbled across it while taking a back route from Baltimore to Washington. By then, it was in shambles, a really hot mess. Pigeons and other woodland creatures had set up housekeeping everywhere inside the building. We believe no one wanted to take on the extensive project to restore it because the property was off the beaten track, and the state required that it remain a working farm. The house and the shopping area across the road are a part of the White family's estate. They are both registered as historic sites."

"It must have had great bones to be able to restore it to what it is today. The workmanship is incredible."

Vivian nodded. "Chuck bought this place and enlisted the help of his brothers and sisters, who are all in the building trades. He's the youngest male of eleven siblings in his family. For over a year, they restored this house, the outbuildings, added new structures as necessary on this land, and remodeled the shopping area across the road. Of course, he made changes to modernize the properties and bring them up to current codes." She chuckled. "My husband was born and raised on a farm in the Pocono Mountains of Pennsylvania, and he wanted to own a ranch. So, we call this property a ranch instead of a farm to satisfy his dreams of being a cowboy.

"After Chuck and I married, we renovated even more of the spaces. For example, we believe that the third-floor rooms were, at one time, in the 1800s, the servants' quarters. They were much too small for comfort. Chuck and I are both from large families, and we have a substantial number of close friends. We're isolated out here in the rural area. So, when our relatives and friends came for visits, we wanted to make sure that we had enough space to accommodate everyone. To accomplish that goal, we hired Roderick and JaiHonnah Hawkins Baylor, of Baylor and Baylor Design and Development, to do a top to bottom renovation to fit our needs and the needs of our immediate growing family. Thank goodness Samantha helped to appease everyone's taste in furnishings and décor. It's not easy to mollify the diverse tastes of a family this large. We think she succeeded brilliantly. We're all very proud of her. She's receiving the notoriety and world acclaim she deserves."

Quentin looked around at the furniture again. It was comfortable, and the colors and fabrics perfect for the setting. It amazed him that this was an example of Samantha's handiwork. It was so different from what he remembered about the pretty but shy young girl she had once been. Here, what she created was bold and beautiful. "So, this is the original footprint of the property?"

Vivian shook her head. "We've expanded the footprint of the initial floor plan to include a breakfast room, lunchroom, indoor-outdoor swimming lagoon, barn garage, and an exercise facility. Although the two levels below ground were already there, the next level down has been converted into a sound and video studio where we play music and record video greeting cards for friends and family. There are other rooms or salons on the lower levels created for various functions, like a theatre room."

"You've also added a helipad," Quentin noted.

"Yes, several of our children have a pilot's license. The helipad certainly came in handy today," Vivian smiled as they continued to chat.

At the same time that his wife was chatting with Quentin, Chuck leaned back against a desk in his in-home medical examination room. He folded his muscular arms over his broad, firm chest, relaxed, and regarded Samuel King. "What have your doctors told you?"

The younger man sat up and slowly swung his long legs over the side of the exam table. "I've learned that what I have is a form of osteoporosis. It means that my life is over even though I'm years away from my thirtieth birthday. By the time I reach thirty, I'll be in a wheelchair and unable to walk."

Chuck shook his head in frustration. "Look, Sam, yes, your situation is grave, but your life is not over. Bone loss is a disease that causes your skeletal form to become brittle and more likely to fracture. With your degree of osteoporosis, your bones lose density. I'm sure you understand that bone density is the amount of bone tissue in your skeletal frame. A diagnosis of osteoporosis means you are at risk for bone fractures, even if you do not have a severe bone injury. Your body needs minerals, calcium, and phosphate to make and keep healthy bones.

"During your life, your body continues to both reabsorb old bone and create new bone. Your entire skeleton is replaced about every ten years, though this process slows as you get older. As long as your body has a good balance of new and old bone, your skeletal structure stays healthy and strong. Bone loss occurs when more old bone is reabsorbed than new bone is created. Sometimes bone loss occurs without any known cause. Some bone loss with aging is normal for everyone. However, you're too young for that. Other times, bone loss and thin bones run in families and the disease is inherited. That appears, from my brief examination and x-ray, to be the case here. Your bone loss is inherited from someone in your genealogy. Brittle, fragile bones can be accelerated by anything that makes your body destroy too much bone or keeps your body from making enough new bone material."

"That's what the doctors in Switzerland told me, although they didn't make it as clear and understandable as you have. Bottom line, they gave me no hope of reversing the condition. Although I shouldn't be, I'm somewhat surprised that you immediately spotted my condition. Yet, Samantha always said she had the best two doctors in the world as fathers; you and Dr. Jackson."

"She was right about Derrick. He was my best friend and a helluva pediatric surgeon, which brings me to something you may want to consider. Derrick developed a webbing system for babies and children to help their bodies reabsorb minerals, calcium, and phosphate from their bones to make them stronger and prevent stress fractures.

"For someone like you, who is currently ranked number one in men's singles tennis by the Association of Tennis Professionals, bone strength is critical. You've won a multitude of Grand Slam singles titles, the most in history for a male tennis player since Roger Federer many years ago. You've held the world's number one spot in the ATP rankings for a record total of three hundred fifty weeks and ranked number one a record number of consecutive weeks since you turned professional right out of high school."

Sam looked up at the tall man, surprised.

Chuck noticed and nodded. "Yes, I've followed your career. Although your behavior toward my daughter was reprehensible, your skill as an athlete is laudable. You've also won a record number of Wimbledon titles, Australian Open titles, a record six consecutive U.S. Open titles, and two French Open titles. You are among a very few number of men to have captured an impressive number of career Grand Slams and have reached a record number of men's singles Grand Slam finals, including several in a row from the Wimbledon Championships to the U.S. Open. Many players and analysts consider you to be the greatest tennis player of all time."

Sam mirthlessly laughed. "To me, those are just meaningless stats. The ones who gather that data and report it didn't understand that I had nothing else except my son in my life." He looked up into Chuck's surprised expression. "My life went on a downhill spiral the day I was forced to take Pamela to the senior prom instead of Samantha, whom I fiercely loved at the time. To receive the financial support I needed to play professionally right out of high school, I had to agree to dump Samantha, marry Pamela, and get her pregnant. That was the only way I could exercise any control over my life at that point. Except for the birth of my son, every day has been a struggle to survive the mistakes I've been forced to make. The only way for me to exorcise my demons is to smash a little furry ball back over a net and keep it in bounds. That's been my single focus. You can't imagine how limiting that is in one's life and career."

"Forced? Someone forced you to hurt my daughter and to marry someone you didn't love?"

"Yes, my parents and Pamela's. You see, the marriage was a bargain struck by our parents. Regrettably, I participated in it for selfish reasons. So, I cannot, in all honesty, place all of the blame on Pamela's parents or mine. I didn't want to go to college, and I needed the financial support from my parents to travel and continue to participate in high-purse competitions. I was a kid and wanted the quick thrill of joining the professional tennis circuit. I struck that bargain with my parents, and now I'm married to a woman with whom I haven't slept since my son was conceived. After that happened, I discovered that she's a lesbian.

"Her family is ashamed of who she is, and they forced her into the marriage to save their reputations. She never cared about our son or me. We hardly ever spoke over the many years that we were in private school together or after we were married except to arrange to get her pregnant. Though we are estranged, and because her parents hold the purse strings, Pamela refuses to give me a divorce. She shows up for the necessary photo ops, but otherwise, we don't see one another. Rather, Pamela lives under a pseudonym in Europe with a string of lovers but denies me the companionship of a woman for fear that the truth about our non-existent relationship and sham marriage will get out. If the news that Pamela is a lesbian were ever to become public knowledge, her parents would disown her and cut the purse strings. So, I may have accomplished a number of sports-related feats, but nothing other than my son has made me happy since I was in love with your daughter in high school."

Chuck was surprised at Sam's candor about his life. He should feel sorry for the guy, but where his children were concerned, his sympathy was unavailable to anyone who caused his sons or daughters pain. However, he took a medical creed, which says that health care is a fundamental human right. He swore to the Hippocratic Oath, The Physician's Oath, Declaration of Geneva, Oath of Maimonides, Osteopathic Oath, and many others that he would do no harm.

It was a risky business, but he had the means to help this young man avoid the rapid advance of his illness. It would also prolong Sam's career on the tennis circuit.

Although infusing bone with the minerals, calcium, and phosphate is a painful procedure, Chuck had used the treatment to relieve pain in his knees. He also arranged for several of his children to undergo this treatment when they were very young. Even more recently, when his daughter, Linda, a prima ballerina, began to exhibit stress fractures, he subjected her to re-treatment after she gave bone marrow to her biological half-brother to save his life. It worked, and although she no longer has such a grueling schedule, she teaches dance at her school and figure skating to students. However, Linda retired from competitions for prizes and stage presentations. Chuck wondered whether Samuel was at a point where he might be ready to consider a different lifestyle that didn't put a great deal of stress on his bone structure. So, he continued to engage Samuel in a discussion about his plans. He was also keen to ensure that Samuel's plans did not include resurrecting a relationship with his daughter, Samantha.

Chuck knew that he could help this young man; the question was whether helping him would put Samuel back in his daughter's life and cause her more pain. He'd have to speak with his wife and his daughter about that before he went any further. After all, as a Supreme Court Justice, Vivian was accustomed to weighing the pros and cons and arriving at an unemotional conclusion. As he did with every significant issue, he discussed it with Vivian. She added the balance he needed in his life. She was his center, his north star, the love of his life, and his best friend.

CHAPTER 6

Samantha sat on the warm, Brazilian cherry hardwood floor in the great room with Patrick on her lap, his back to her breasts. He was forcing her to clap her hands together for his favorite game of patty cake. His grin was maniacal, prominently showing all four of his teeth. Once he got her hands going, he bounced and clapped his own hands together as she sang the song to the rhythm of his hand motion.

"Pat-a-cake, pat-a-cake, baker's man.
Bake a cake for me as fast as you can
Pat it, and roll it, and mark it with a 'P'
And put it in the oven for Patrick and me!"

At the conclusion of their play, Patrick turned in her lap, clasped his hands to her jaws, and demanded, "Kizz."

She laughed and puckered up to deliver his kiss. He said, "ah," and smacked his lips as if he tasted something delicious, making her roll with laughter. She thoroughly enjoyed being home again and briefly squeezed him to her, rocking him in her arms from side to side while stealing kisses.

Patrick then crawled out of her lap and waddled away to find someone else to play with and found a willing victim in the arms of their sister, Dena, and her guy friend, Drew Hamilton, Will's younger brother. While she had time, Samantha just sat on the floor tailor style with her back against the sofa and watched her family members' dynamic interaction. They were a noisy bunch, energetic and demonstrative, but they never failed to be attentive to one another, always learning to appreciate each other's points of view.

Then it dawned on her that, after she was at home with her family, she hadn't given the King family members another thought. She looked around to find Paulette monopolizing her brothers' Roger and Ryan's time while thoroughly enjoying their undivided attention. Sammy was all grins and in animated conversation with her younger siblings Eden Ann, Scott, Connell, and Nelson, and with the Phillips' kids, who were all around the same age. Her mother was conversing with Quentin King, but she didn't spot Samuel though she visually searched the room. Her father was noticeably absent, too. That made Samantha wonder whether her father diagnosed the difficulty Samuel seemed to experience with his mobility. She noticed that Quentin had to help Sam down the few steps to the ground when they climbed out of the helicopter. It would be just like her father to check out anyone who seemed to be experiencing physical distress. As an emergency room doctor, Chuck would be in a position to spot an ailment quickly.

"Who are you looking for?" questioned her sister, Linda, as she, too, came and sat tailor style on the floor next to Samantha.

"I don't see Dad or Sam King in the room and wondered."

Linda nodded. "Yes, Sam left the room with Dad a while ago. Initially, I thought Dad just wanted to vent and resurrect his angst over how Sam treated you in high school. Then I noticed how Sam had difficulty moving around. For a top-ranked tennis pro, he wasn't moving very well. So, I'll bet Dad took him into his medical suite for an exam and chat."

"That's what I thought, too. Samuel seemed to have difficulty with his mobility when I saw him at the airport in Spain and when the helicopter landed here. His brother had to help him down the steps to the ground."

Linda moved closer, turned toward her sister, and placed her arm on the seat cushion, supporting her head on the palm of her hand. "Are you okay with seeing the King family again?"

Samantha shrugged and turned toward Linda so that they could speak quietly. "I'll admit that initially seeing them, seeing him so suddenly, gave me a jolt." Samantha and Linda linked hands, and Linda gave a comforting squeeze as they continued to talk. "Although I didn't have to, and despite my discomfort, I made a conscious decision to allow them to travel back to the states with me. Sammy was the pivotal factor in that decision. Fortunately, Samuel and I had limited contact on the flight from Madrid. I spent my time talking with Paulette and Quentin."

Linda did a quick observation of Quentin across the room, talking with her mother. "Sam has always been drop-dead gorgeous with a level of animal magnetism few men possess, but Quentin certainly turned out to be quite appealing."

Samantha briefly turned her head to look at him, too, and shrugged before looking at her sister again. "I guess, in a very conservative Morris Chestnut sort of way with a full head of shiny, close-cut, wavy hair. He's wicked smart, but, as I recall, he's always been that way."

"He runs the King Advertising Agency now, doesn't he?" Linda released Samantha's hand, leaned back against the sofa, and continued to periodically eye Quentin.

"I really don't know. I limited the amount of conversation I had with Quentin on the flight home. Paulette mentioned that she worked for him, but I didn't delve into what he did for the advertising agency. I haven't had a reason to keep up with the King family since I graduated high school and went away to college and grad school."

"Who are the King family?" asked KiLe as she eased her pregnant body down to sit tailor style on the floor on the other side of Samantha. "I've never heard of them before."

"Long story short, Samuel King and Samantha used to be an item in their younger days," offered Linda.

"I presume it didn't end well?" KiLe surmised. "Brian is not happy about Samuel being anywhere near you. Are you okay, Samantha?"

Samantha smiled at KiLe and wrapped an arm around her sister-in-law. "I'm fine, KiLe. What happened is old news."

"Maybe not, considering how often Samuel's brother, Quentin King, has checked you out," nodded KiLe, "you may not be done with the King family yet."

Samantha snorted an unladylike laugh. "Get real, KiLe. Quentin's not paying any attention to me."

Linda shook her head. "I don't know, Samantha. I think KiLe has a good eye. I noticed him checking you out, too."

KiLe motioned another Montgomery sister-in-law to join them. "Let's ask Geneviève. She's a cop. I'll bet she noticed it, too."

"What's up?" Geneviève Montgomery sat on the floor with the growing circle of her sisters.

"Have you noticed Quentin King tracking Samantha's movement?"

"Like a heat-seeking missile, yes," Geneviève acknowledge *sotto voce*.

"See, I told you so," KiLe assertively nodded.

Frowning, Samantha looked up and right into Quentin's eyes. Their gazes held for a moment before she turned to her sisters, her brows rising in question. "I don't know why he would do that," she offered, confused.

Three pairs of eyes looked at her with surprised astonishment until she had to ask, "What?"

"You're gorgeous, sister mine," nodded Linda, with KiLe and Geneviève nodding in agreement.

"You have that kind of classic-style like the movie star from the fifties, Dorothy Dandridge."

"You're my sisters. You're supposed to say things like that to me on my first day back home."

"Hey, as long as you give me new linens from your collection, I'll say it twenty-four-seven," joked Geneviève, purposefully changing the subject.

"Did you have anything left from your tour?" Linda wondered aloud, following Geneviève's lead.

"Not one thing. I completely sold out of all of my stock. I don't even have samples left, but I'm back in my studio later tonight and tomorrow. If I feel sufficiently rested, I plan to start the design of my spring collection. So, don't be surprised if you get sheets, pillowcases, bed skirts, curtains, draperies, and/or comforters for Christmas. You can be my focus group and let me know what you think."

"Works for me," they chorused, giving each other high fives.

KiLe piped up. "Could I put in a bid for one of those bed seats?"

Samantha frowned. "You mean a wedge pillow? One stuffed with arms so you can sit up in bed?"

KiLe nodded and rubbed her distended belly. "That's the one. It would give me someplace else where I can nurse this little one. Is it too much to ask?"

Samantha shook her head. "Not at all. In fact, I was thinking of adding wedge pillows with memory foam to the new collection. I'll make it a priority and work on that concept."

"That sounds great, Samantha. Although I don't have a baby, Simon and I like to read in bed. So, add two for me to the list." Geneviève's statement had their other sisters chiming in.

"What colors are you going to use for the new collection?" Linda wondered.

"That's a secret. You'll have to wait until Christmas morning." She laughed.

"It couldn't come too soon." KiLe continued to stroke her motion-filled belly.

"Are you comfortable sitting on the floor like this, KiLe?" Samantha worried.

KiLe took Samantha's hand and placed it on her belly. "I'm fine. This little rodeo star is riding a bucking bronco just like his daddy. Sitting like this is one of the positions where I feel comfortable."

Wonder lit Samantha's face as the active baby tossed and turned under her hand. She wondered whether she would ever find someone to love, respect, and trust as her sisters had. KiLe had Brian; Linda had Will Hamilton, and although they weren't married yet, Geneviève had Simon Wilde. Samantha hadn't thought much about a happily-ever-after for herself until she saw Sam again. She had loved him so completely once. Now, after all these years, her feelings of love for him were only a distant memory, overshadowed by the pain he caused her. At least she didn't have to regret sleeping with him for the first time on prom night.

"Stop thinking about him," cautioned Linda.

Samantha looked up into her sisters' faces and gave them a wan smile. "I'm okay. He's only someone I used to love."

"Good. Save your love for someone who deserves it. Maybe that drop-dead handsome pilot?" Geneviève teased. "You were together for months. What's the four-one-one on him? Did you tap that hunk?"

Samantha laughed and whispered. "I can't say I wasn't tempted because Glen Kennard is something to behold in swimwear."

"So, you didn't—?"

Samantha shook her head and shrugged.

"One day," Linda commiserated.

When Samantha hugged her sister, she looked up into Quentin King's eyes again. *Is he really watching me?* she wondered.

CHAPTER 7

For a moment, Quentin held Samantha's stare. He wondered what the four sisters sitting on the floor together had been talking about. From time to time, he caught one or two of them looking in his direction. He didn't know the pretty Japanese woman. So, maybe the sisters were explaining who he was and perhaps giving a little background information about Samantha's history with Samuel. That was only to be expected, he supposed. Although most didn't share blood ties, they were an extremely close-knit family.

He dismissed the thought when Judge Montgomery excused herself to tend to a call she received. Then, his cellphone vibrated in his pocket. "King," he automatically answered.

"Hello, Quentin. Are you back in town?" Miranda Bazemore asked.

"Hello, Miranda. Yes, I landed in the states earlier today, but I haven't gone to King Manor yet. The weather is preventing local travel."

She sighed audibly long and deep. "Really, Quentin, isn't your driver capable of navigating a little precipitation from the airport to your home? If not, you should fire him and hire someone else."

Obviously, this was going to be a longer conversation than he intended. He got up, looked around, and spotted a comfortable-looking salon. It was adjacent to the great room, and he could see through the wood and bevel-glass door that a fire burned in the hearth. The salon appeared to be empty when he entered and closed the door. Since he was alone in the room, he engaged the speaker app on his phone. "I don't expect my driver to risk his life or mine in this weather, Miranda."

"We had plans for this evening, Quentin. Did you forget?" Her tone was impatient and testy.

He hadn't forgotten—cocktails and dinner with Jonah and Rosemary Cleveland. The event was on his calendar as there were many other things he wouldn't be able to attend to because of … Well, actually, at the airport in Spain, everything on his schedule went out of his head at first sight of Samantha Aretha Montgomery. Truth be told, he planned to have lunch with Miranda to call off their relationship. They had a liaison of sorts for the last fifteen months, but he didn't see it going beyond this point. He was not inspired to keep the relationship going because of the seemingly endless number of engagements and events they attended together.

Miranda was a nice enough person, but as Dean of the Political Science Department at Howard University, she had an inordinate number of social events to attend. She was also considering a run for a position on the D.C. City Council. That created other events where she needed to be seen. He didn't want to get caught up in the political arena and felt that it was time to pump the brakes on where their association was going. "No, I had not forgotten, Miranda. However, considering the weather conditions, I don't know whether the Clevelands are still going to be able to host a party tonight for you to test the waters for an election bid. You should check with them to confirm. Regrettably, even if they are still planning to hold it, I apologize, but I won't be available to be your escort."

"This has been on the calendar for months, Quentin. Road crews are out in full force in the city. You should be able to make it home from the airport with only a short delay." Her tone was reserved, but he sensed the anger which lay beneath the apparent reticence.

"I'm aware of that, Miranda. We need to talk, but not over the phone. I will contact you as soon as possible, and we can arrange to get together. Again, I apologize for my inability to be your escort this evening."

"This is unacceptable. What will I tell your parents, Quentin? They are expecting us to be at the party together. After all, they are just as invested in my run for the city council as I am. They believe that in a few years, I'd be a shoo-in to run for mayor."

Heaven forbid, he thought. "I'll contact my parents and explain the circumstances. I'll talk with you soon."

The dial tone was the next sound he heard and shook his head before he unnecessarily clicked off. He didn't mean to anger her, but he was fed up with her histrionics when he didn't conform to her directives or something else didn't go her way. That would all be over soon.

He turned at the sound of the tap on the wood-and-glass door. When he spotted Samuel through the beveled glass, he motioned him to enter.

"I apologize for the interruption. Were you talking with Miranda?"

Frowning, Quentin nodded. "Yes, how did you know?"

"You get these frown lines whenever you speak with her."

He hadn't known that, but it must have been true since he was more and more annoyed of late when speaking with her. He didn't want to discuss Miranda at the moment. "You disappeared for a while. Are you all right?"

"I'm as good as can be expected given the circumstances. I've been talking with Dr. Montgomery."

"Oh, about what?"

"My current health crisis. Dr. Montgomery told me about a procedure that may be beneficial to me. Do you have a moment?"

"Sure. Let's sit down." His brother looked about ready to drop, so they moved to a couple of comfortable dove-gray, deep, leather chairs in a conversational cluster beside the lit fireplace.

Over the next fifteen minutes, Samuel told Quentin about the physical examination Dr. Montgomery performed, the test he administered, and the possible procedure which might prove beneficial. "He also told me that his daughter, Linda, had the procedure when she was a preteen. She was in a car accident that killed her biological mother, younger brother, and left her with leg and hip fractures so severe that she was unable to walk. As you know, Linda scored Olympic gold as a preteen in figure skating and became a world-renowned prima ballerina. She retired from the stage last year after she married and had a son with Will Hamilton."

"The baseball phenom. Yes, I was introduced to him when we arrived. Linda doesn't look as if she's in any discomfort."

"According to her father, she was beginning to experience stress fractures and underwent the procedure again after her son's birth. It seems that carrying a child can impact a woman's calcium. Since then, she's had a second son. Dr. Montgomery says that she's fit enough to go back on the stage, but instead, she opened a school of dance in New York City."

"Yes, I know about that. While you were on the tennis circuit last season, Paulette and I took Sammy to see the Broadway show *Goodwill,* which Linda choreographed and produced. It's a show by and about young children growing up in an idyllic world. It's already considered a classical ballet and it's still running on Broadway.

"So, Dr. Montgomery believes that the treatment Linda had could help you?"

"He does, yes. Other children in the Montgomery family, like the twins, were conjoined at birth and underwent this bone-strengthening or bone-replacement procedure, all with great success. Ryan and Roger, as you know, play professional baseball. Vincent and Geneviève ran track in high school and college. Laurel and Laura, although preteens now, had the procedure when they were four-years-old. They show no signs of distress when they walk. They don't even have a limp. Even Dr. Montgomery had the procedure on his knees. As you know, he is a famous basketball player and nearly seven feet tall. He retired because he was beginning to experience painful stress fractures and joint pain. What's more important, though, is that Dr. Montgomery asked me what my plans were when the cheering stops. He faced the same decision when he stopped playing professionally. He still plays with a team of medical personnel called The Body Snatchers."

Surprised, Quentin sat forward in his chair, hands clasped together, with his elbows resting on his knees. "You do know that you're at the top of your career. If you chose to retire now, no one could say that you're not making a sound decision. You've broken every conceivable record in the sport. You don't have anything else to prove except more of the same."

Samuel nodded. "I'm glad to hear you say that. If this treatment can help my physical health, then I'm ready to leave professional tennis."

"Then what?"

"I'm still young. I'll do what Linda has apparently done so successfully. I'll open a school and teach. However, I don't want to do it here in this area."

That surprised Quentin even more. "Then, where?"

"I'm not sure yet, but I don't want to live at King Manor any longer. I want to take my son and move somewhere father and mother will not be able to influence my or my son's life anymore. They believe that my name recognition will bring in new clientele for the advertising agency, particularly new clientele in my age group. I don't want to be a sales and marketing magnet. If I don't leave, they will demand that I enter the family business with you and Paulette. I don't want to do that. They forced me to marry a woman I couldn't love and to hurt a woman I once loved very much." He shook his head; his misery was evident. "I can't blame them because I chose the direction I wanted to go with my career. Still, going forward, I'm done with letting them or anyone else dictate the steps and stages of my life. I'm no longer a kid. I should have moved years ago."

"Maybe you and Samantha—."

Sam shook his head before Quentin could suggest that he rekindle the relationship with Samantha. Sadness covered his face. "I won't do that to her. This is the first time I've seen her since we graduated high school. When she spotted me at the airport, I saw in her eyes how much I hurt her. I look at her now, and I see how sophisticated, chic, warm, and lovely she is, and I can only regret what I was forced to do to her.

"She's grown so much beyond the young girl who was once so shy and vulnerable. She doesn't need someone like me, but I've noticed how you've looked at her. You see her not only for who she was as a sweet kid but also as a strong, capable woman now. You've always thought she was special. You told me on prom night not to dump her and that I would regret it if I did. You were right on both counts. She is exceptional, and I will regret what I did to her for the rest of my life. However, if I sense what you feel for her is much more than what I felt, I hope you'll help her forgive me."

Astounded, Quentin sat back in his chair, crossed his right leg over his left knee, and steadily regarded his brother.

Little did they know that stretched out on a sofa on the other side of the room, listening to every word, was Samantha's twelve-year-old sister Eden Ann Montgomery.

"So, what should I do?" Eden Ann asked her parents later.

Chuck frowned at her. "Were you purposefully eavesdropping on them?"

"No, I promise I wasn't, Daddy. I was in there listening to an audiobook for my school homework when Mr. King came in. At first, I wasn't paying attention because I was wearing earbuds until I heard the door close. His back was to me, and the potted plants next to the chair shielded me from his view. Maybe I should have gotten up then and left the room, but I thought he would be in there for only a short time to finish his phone call. So I didn't say anything and went back to listening to the story. However, he had the speaker on, so I heard both sides of his conversation with a woman named Miranda. She was really steamed with him. When he ended that call, the other Mr. King came in, and they started to talk. I felt silly jumping up then, so I stayed quiet until they left. That's when I came to find you and Mom to tell you what I heard.

"Did Mr. King really dump Samantha on her prom night?"

"I'm afraid that's true, babe." Vivian pulled her daughter to her side for a quick squeeze.

"Well, he sure is sorry that he did that," Eden Ann sagely proclaimed. She yawned. "I won't say anything unless you think I should tell Samantha that the other Mr. King really likes her."

"Save it, pumpkin. You've got a good head on your shoulders. You decide what the best course of action is where your sister is concerned."

Eden Ann beamed a smile up to her parents. She was the oldest of the siblings her parents gave birth to after they were married. It made her tummy feel funny because they always treated her like she had working brain cells. She loved her parents and all of her brothers and sisters so much. Nodding and hugging them both, she left them in her mom's office, no doubt to talk. She'd decide whether to tell Samantha or not and, if so, what to say. In the meantime, she'd go back to the chapter book she had been listening to before the drama started. They'd be called to lunch soon, and she'd have another chance to see how the two Mr. Kings acted around her sister. Plugging in her earbuds, she went off to find another cozy nook to get comfortable.

When Eden Ann left, Chuck pulled Vivian into his arms, flush against his body, her head tucked under his chin. She kissed the space on his neck, where his pulse beat mimicked her heartbeat. "What do you think we should do, Annie?" He used the pet name Annie Oakley, he continued to call her because she was so feisty from the first moment they met. She was still in law school then and he was in the midst of his medical residency program to become an emergency room specialist. They were both Georgetown University students, though in different departments. Vivian was still so young, barely into her twenties while he was over thirty. Yet, the first time he saw her in Chicago's O'Hare Airport, her smile captivated him. It still did now when she looked up at him. He smiled at her impish expression. "Don't look at me like that or I'll be forced to take you back to bed to make love with you for the rest of the day." He leaned forward and kissed her mouth.

"Oh, babe, I wish we could, but we'll have to save that particular pleasure until a time when we don't have to keep an eye on our daughter and the King family." She sighed into her husband's warm embrace.

"Samantha is strong, Viv. I believe she will handle this situation. She's not the vulnerable kid you and Derrick adopted when she was still a baby. We've seen her grow, stretch her wings, and fly. She's still young, yet she's grown into her skin, and she's comfortable there."

"That's because you've made it possible for all of us, yours, mine, and ours, to reach for whatever made us feel complete. You're the one who keeps us all on an even keel, and our lives together a dream come true. Because of who you are, I am so much in love with you. I love you more today than I did yesterday and not as much as I will tomorrow. You, Charles Patrick Montgomery, complete me." She went to her toes to secure herself to his nearly seven-foot height, looped her arms around his neck, and smiled into his eyes as she kissed him.

Her eyes widened in surprise. She felt how long and thick he was through his jeans. Reaching down and running her right hand between his muscular thighs to fondle him, she grinned.

Her words of love were always his undoing, and then she gave him that sexy grin of hers. "Annie," he warned and then grunted as she unzipped his jeans. She reached inside to find him hard, hot, and heavy in her palm. "*Christ*, Annie, at least let me lock the door!" Lifting his very pregnant wife while she wiggled out of her jeans, panties, and shoes wasn't easy. Still, he managed to make it to the double doors of her office and lock them before she dropped his jeans down around his booted feet.

With her back against the door and her legs free and chained around his waist, Vivian took her very virile husband's member in hand, and with her eyes locked on his, guided him home. "There's no reason we can't have a quickie before lunch," she grinned, causing him to laugh. She stripped off his T-shirt and attacked his nipples with teeth and tongue while they made love against the door like randy teens for another thirty minutes.

CHAPTER 8

Quentin admitted to himself that he'd never experienced anything like mealtime in the Alexander-Montgomery household. They were in a glass-enclosed salon in full view of the still falling snow. It was an amazing backdrop to the winter wonderland in full view unfolding outside the glass accordion walls. It was amazing to watch the snowfall on the grounds and the trees. However, inside the glass walls, the floor was a heated, herringbone-style tile, and the room, although large, seemed cozy and comfortable.

A four-foot high, perpetual aquarium ran completely across a back wall with various colorful schools of fish swimming in the bright, clear water. He couldn't imagine how many gallons it took to fill such a massive aquarium. The aquaculture was reminiscent of natural habitats he had seen on dives off the Florida Keys. He recognized some of the beautiful freshwater species, like barbs, tetras, rasboras, danios, and rainbowfish, as peaceful, community fish. However, others were even more beautiful and were new to him. Ingenious rock formations, white sand, and a healthy array of water plants added to the scenery's beauty. Still, it was as mesmerizing and calming to watch the schools of fish moving back and forth in their underwater world as it was to watch the snow falling on the landscape.

When he was able to pull his gaze away from the aquarium, he noted that lunch was being set up buffet-style at different stations in the room. Enticing aromas permeated the air, and nice music played in the background. There were healthy-looking, live plants hanging unobtrusively from the ceiling trusses and placed around the salon. Round tables, beautifully dressed with colorful and festive table cloths, napkins, silverware, and crystal, sat at least twelve in comfortable chairs.

One, several-tiered table contained a variety of salad greens and toppings on display. Not only fresh, leafy greens, but also a carrot-and-raisin salad, a Waldorf salad, a cucumber salad, and even a white potato salad. In another section was a soup station with four different options, including his favorite, French Onion. The sandwich bar had sliced cold cuts and a variety of cheeses artfully displayed with fresh-baked small loaves of bread and rolls in baskets. Then for those with serious appetites, there was the hot-food station with strips of tender, melt-in-your-mouth London Broil marinading in hot *au jus* with onions and Shiitake mushrooms. Baked potato-and-cheese puffs sat beside savory baked chicken, sweet potato fries, and hot salmon cakes.

This, to him, was more like an event, but the family members seemed as if this were an everyday occurrence. Once assembled, one of the children Quentin didn't recognize read a Langston Hughes poem while heads were bowed in reverence or concentration. The older children then helped the younger ones select what they wanted from the buffets and then ushered them to age-appropriate seating. His brother and sister, having been close friends with the family, chimed right in. Sammy had no trouble whatsoever following the protocol, with several of the same-aged Montgomery children acting as escorts. The two oldest children at each table poured whatever drink the person requested before sitting down to eat. As they ate using the proper utensils, fun and frivolity shown on the young faces while they talked, ate, and listened.

It was an amazing sight to witness in a pleasing atmosphere. However, a bit overwhelmed by what appeared to be controlled chaos, Quentin found himself standing, not quite over the sheer size of the offerings and environment.

Vivian caught Samantha's attention and nodded toward where Quentin stood, seemingly rooted to the spot.

Knowing her duty, because the Kings were essentially her guests, Samantha acknowledged her mother and then went to stand beside Quentin. "Aren't you hungry?"

"Starving, but I don't quite know where to start."

"How about starting by taking off your suit jacket and tie and rolling up your sleeves?"

He looked down at himself dressed for business and then at everyone, even the Supreme Court Justice and her husband, a doctor who owned a hospital, dressed in jeans and T-shirts. "I guess you have a point." He slipped out of his jacket while Samantha loosened his tie, opened the top buttons of his hand-tailored dress shirt, and pulled it up out of his slacks. As she performed the tasks to make him more comfortable, his eyes remained on the crown of her bent head as she reached around him to snap his shirt down his hips.

"Now, doesn't that feel better?" She looked up at him, took his jacket and tie, and placed them in a closet near the lunch salon entrance.

"Infinitely." He watched her walk back to him, enjoying the view while he removed his cufflinks, slipping them into his pocket, and rolled his sleeves to his elbows. "Now what?"

"Now, you can go through that door to the restroom where you can wash your hands. I'll wait right here until you return." When he rejoined her, she took his arm, a bit surprised by the strong, firm muscle she found under her hand, and led him to the table where the lunch platters were stacked. Handing one to him and taking one for herself, she smiled winningly. "Now, we begin to select your first course of delectable delights."

They went from station to station until their platters were filled to capacity. Then they found two seats at the same table with Samuel and Paulette and Samantha's twin brothers Roger and Ryan, the twins, Vincent and Geneviève, and her guy friend Simon Wilde, Dena, and her guy friend Drew Hamilton, and her teenage brothers Andrew, Darren, and Spencer.

Quentin vaguely remembered the last three as youngsters, but they were now in their mid-to late-teens. Time certainly had flown.

Quentin forked up another bite of salmon cake with an interesting flavor to the cocktail sauce. "This is really good. It tastes fresh."

Andrew nodded. "I braved the weather to get the fish this morning. It was my turn to make the run."

Quentin frowned. "This morning? You caught fresh salmon this morning?"

"Sure. I had to go only a quarter-mile to the fishery."

"A fishery?"

Andrew laughed. "Well, it did take me longer to catch them. After all, they can be slippery suckers."

Darren laughed at his brother. "He makes it seem harder than it is. He had only to trap them in the water trough and then scoop them up in a net."

"You breed salmon on a cattle ranch?" *This is new*, Quentin thought. As he recalled when he knew them years ago, they bred horses and cows.

"Sure," Spenser chimed in. "Alex-Mont Ranch has the largest indoor aquaculture in the state. My brother Brian built it." There was unmistakable pride shining in his grey-green eyes with Nordic features and Scandinavian skin tone. "We also raise and harvest other fish, crustaceans, mollusks, aquatic plants, algae, and aquatic organisms. Brian and I aren't particular fans of the snails, but the restaurants pay big bucks for them to make Escargot."

Andrew added: "Our facilities cultivate both freshwater and saltwater crustacean populations. We have to be very careful and keep them under stringently-controlled conditions."

"You three seem to know a lot about it. Is that what you're studying at the Georgetown Academy?"

Darren shook his head of silky, long, black hair, his Indigenous American heritage evident in his high cheekbones and golden-bronze skin tone. "Oh, no, we don't go there anymore. Brian and our parents built Alex-Mont Academy on land we own here in the county."

Spencer added: "We get to ride our horses to school now because it's not that far away, and we don't have to cross any public roads. However, to answer your question, Brian lets us work with him. He and KiLe also teach a class at the Academy on aquaculture and business. We use the fishery as a classroom, too. Our cousin, Donald Dixon's wife, Cecile, and their oldest son, Donald Junior, are both oceanographers. They live near our ranch in Summer County, South Carolina. Still, she and Donald Junior teach us via Zoom about the chemistry of ocean water, the geology associated with the ocean, the physical movements of the ocean water, and even the life that calls the ocean its home."

Darren nodded. "She and Donald Junior take Spencer, Andrew, Petra, Stephany, and me on expeditions with her to places around the world. On our second rotation, we went to Seychelles to dive. Dr. Noah Mikasi from Operation Uplift was there, too. He knows absolutely everything about that part of the world. He's brilliant. Like me, he's also part Indigenous American, but he's from the north on the border between the United States and Canada.

"He and Cecile showed us how the Seychelles plateau, together with India, Madagascar, Africa, South America, and Antarctica, formed Gondwana about one-hundred-sixty-five million years ago. Together with Madagascar and India, Seychelles drifted away from Africa and left Madagascar behind about eighty million years later and followed India to the north. It stopped its voyage about fifteen million years later."

Darren picked up the conversation. "We learned that during this period, one of the greatest volcanic eruption events in world history took place and dominated Seychelles and the whole region. The volcanic remains at Pointe Zeng Zeng and Pointe Ramasse Tout are the only evidence of this volcanic activity in the earlier Seychelles."

Andrew swallowed a bite of his foot-long, monster hoagie and continued. "We dived in that area. Cousin Cecile said that it's one of the most interesting and unexplored ocean areas, and she is right. She told us that some theorists believe that the catastrophic impact causing an end to the dinosaurs' era should have placed Seychelles forming the Amirante Basin. For the moment, it is only half a circle, but at that time, Seychelles and India were still together. So, the other half drifted away," he finished with a self-satisfied smile and nod. Then he devoured another bite of his hoagie.

Samantha noticed how impressed Quentin seemed to be with her teenage brothers' depth of knowledge and intellectual prowess. She turned her head away from him to look at her plate of food, a little grin on her lips. Even though her brothers didn't share an ounce of blood between them or with her, she was still so proud of them.

Stunned, Quentin stopped eating to concentrate on the three teens. "You said you did this on rotation? What's that?"

Darren wiped his mouth before he spoke. "Oh, that's when school is in session. You see, we study one subject, like science, all day every day for six weeks. Then we're out of school for two weeks before we return to school to start another rotation and study a different subject, like math or languages, for another six weeks."

Frowning, Quentin continued to engage the teens. "So, you went diving off the coast of Seychelles for six weeks for class study?"

They all nodded and chorused, "yes."

Fascinated, Quentin continued. "In that region of the world, I imagine that you have to be a strong swimmer."

Andrew nodded. "Yes, we are. All of us had to qualify not only as lifeguards but also as divers. Dad and Mom started swimming lessons for us when we were all still in diapers." He laughed. "Then we advanced to diving. We do that often, particularly when we go to Bimini on vacation."

"Eve and I went with them," offered Simon Wilde. "I never dived that region either, but it is as fascinating as Andrew, Darren, and Spencer said. Eve and I plan to go again the next time Cecile takes a group on an expedition in that area. I think it's scheduled for late February."

Samantha turned her head toward Quentin to look into his eyes. "Do you dive?"

"I do, yes, but I haven't done Seychelles."

"It's a beautiful area, Seychelles," offered Roger.

Darren suggested, "You might enjoy diving in the various areas of the basin before corporations start drilling for oil and spoiling the natural beauty of the undersea world."

The other two teens nodded in agreement as they continued to eat lunch. As teens were prone to do, they kept rising to refill their plates.

Intrigued, Quentin began eating again. "What's your next rotation?"

While Dena Montgomery rose to go back to the buffet, her guy friend, Drew Hamilton, answered, "Dena teaches at MIT. She's bringing the class up for their next rotation to participate in her math classes for six weeks. She's a mathlete and sponsors mathematics competitions for school children, teens, and young adults."

Dena shrugged as she returned to the table and sat down. "I thought I was giving them interesting facts about math and how it impacts our daily lives, but they took it to a whole new level the last time they came. I enjoy having them in my classes. This time I'm working out more challenging things for them and my regular students to do."

"Yeah, boyeee! Bring it on, sister mine," Andrew teased and high fived his brothers, who apparently also enjoyed the challenges their sister created for them.

Even more astounded, Quentin looked across the table at Dena. She was much younger than he was. Her Ph.D. was from Massachusetts Institute of Technology, MIT, and she was already a professor teaching there, he wondered. He remembered when Dena was a rodeo star as a preteen. She was prone to dress in western regalia all the time like her father, and from the looks of things, she still did. She was wearing what looked like an authentic Western buckskin jacket with strings and tassels, riding boots, a chambray shirt open midway her breastbone, and low slung, snug jeans with a big rodeo buckle. Several long, cascading silver chains and one gold chain that read **FAMILY** hung around her neck. There were an array of musical silver bangles on her wrists, several large, hooped, silver earrings climbing up her earlobes, and silver, intricately designed rings on every finger, including her thumbs. Her dark brown hair was loosely contained in a fat braid curling over her right shoulder and down between her breast with a rawhide tie at the end. She had a pouty mouth and a straight, narrow nose. Her skin was a satin-looking, smooth light, butter-brown biscuit complexion, and she had the most unusual, luminous, crystal-brown eyes he'd ever seen. Her facial features conjured images of the renowned African actress Omotola Jalade-Ekeinde.

Boy, did my parents have it wrong or what about children who are adopted from disadvantaged and medically-challenged situations? Quentin thought. He surmised that every one of the Montgomery children who was not theirs by blood was certainly theirs by love. They were unique in every way but fit together like a jigsaw puzzle to form a perfect picture. To the best of his recollection, the Montgomerys never made a distinction between their children. It was the formation of this tight bond that Quentin felt was absent from his own family. It was one of the reasons he believed that Sam wanted to move far away from their parents. Paulette, as Sam's twin, would no doubt want to follow him to help raise Sammy.

Samantha noticed the shift in Quentin's degree of attention to the table discussion. From the vertical lines in his brow, something disturbed him. "I'm going back to the buffet for seconds. May I get something for you?"

Quentin shook off his troubling thoughts and looked up at Samantha as she began to rise and reach for his empty plate. "Oh, uh, I'll take that, and I think I'll join you."

"Okay, we'll place our plates here," she indicated a station with other soiled plates and utensils and proceeded to gather clean dishes and silverware. "So, what would you like to try next?"

"This time, I'm going to try a cup of the tomato and basil soup with a teriyaki chicken and horseradish cheese sandwich. I didn't get the carrot-and-raisin salad before, but I'd like to try that this time."

"Would you like a chilled white wine with that?"

"I would, yes. What would you suggest?"

"Zinfandel or Moscato?"

"You choose. Surprise me."

Nodding, she went in one direction as he went in the other. After pulling a Moscato from the tall beverage cooler in the anteroom, she turned and came face-to-face with Samuel.

CHAPTER 9

It took a bit of courage to approach Samantha when she went into the butler's pantry anteroom, where the beverage coolers were lined against three walls. No one went in after her, and he didn't think anyone else was already inside. He didn't know what his reception would be, but he needed to apologize for the past. He also needed to know that if he took her father up on his offer to help with his medical problem, having him and his son in the area wouldn't cause her more pain or distress.

She was so achingly kind that it hurt his heart that he made her, a young woman, his best friend in their youth, suffer so much pain and embarrassment. He was surprised that she came to the prom after what he had done, but being escorted by the popular, young movie actor, Miguel Menendez-Gaza, and members of the sensational new band, Changelings, made her the envy of all of the girls at the prom. She held her head up even though people openly talked about how he had dumped her in favor of Pamela.

Some of the people from their graduating class still talked about that incident. After all these years, they focused mainly on how he and Pamela married so quickly after graduation when they hadn't been an item in high school. Yet, Samantha moved on and, after college, made a name for herself in the textile industry. Now, facing her, he was nearly at a loss for words.

Shaking his head, he took a deep breath before speaking. "I need to apologize for what I put you through in high school. What I did was unspeakable. I won't ask for your forgiveness or your friendship because I don't deserve either. I've learned a valuable lesson, though."

"Which is?"

"I was selfish because I wanted so desperately to play professional tennis. I sacrificed my relationship with you to make that happen. I played for Olympic gold. I now know that all that glitters ain't gold. I was young and dumb, but those excuses don't fly now. Still, even after how I treated you, your father has offered a possible medical treatment to me. He will also allow Paulette and my son to stay here at your ranch with your brothers and sisters while I undergo the procedure. I won't do it if our being associated with your family will cause you one moment of pain or discomfort."

"You are right, Samuel. What you did hurt and humiliated me, but my parents taught me that whatever doesn't kill me makes me stronger for having overcome it. So, although your rationale for what you did escaped my understanding back then, I can forgive you for what happened, but I will never forget it. It was a valuable lesson in trust and respect. However, I recognize that I wouldn't be the person I am today if you and I had continued. I like the person I see in the mirror each day. I don't wake up with regrets.

"Just as I would not have stood in your way in high school, I won't stand in your way now. I don't hold grudges, so if my father believes he can help you physically, let him. You couldn't be in better hands. I will not belabor the point *Ad infinitum.*"

He nodded his appreciation, "Thank you," and smiled tentatively. "*Ad infinitum.* You are your mother's daughter. I remember she'd say things like that to us when we would fuss over a disputed call on the tennis court when she refereed our practice matches. I didn't know what it meant, but I would always remember it, and then as soon as I could, I would go online and look it up." Looking up into Samantha's eyes, he shrugged. "I haven't had the courage before, but I plan to apologize to your mother for hurting you and embarrassing your family. I've already apologized to your father."

"You must have forgotten who Vivian Alexander Jackson Montgomery is. She doesn't hold grudges either, Samuel. My mom is slow to anger, but we, her 'unguided missiles' as she calls us, are the better for it. However, 'The Judge' also doesn't suffer fools lightly, but her heart is always open. So, you need not fear approaching her.

"On the other hand, with my dad, all bets are off. Although I know that he loves me fiercely, if he is willing to help you with your medical challenges, he will never do you any harm. My parents are people I love, trust, and respect. My siblings and I desperately try to emulate them, but we're not always successful. I love my family without question or forethought, and I know that they love me even more. They are the reason I got beyond my hurt and disappointment. They are my best friends and support system. So, just as I have no reason to be against my father helping you, I also have no reason to be against my mother opening our home to your son and Paulette. If that's all you need to say to me, don't fret. I'm fine, but I need to get back to my lunch. I wish you well, Samuel. I always have, and I always will." She was able to walk away from her former best friend and potential first lover without regret.

His heart literally disintegrated with the wholly impersonal way Samantha looked at him and called him Samuel instead of Sam, the way she used to in their youth. The closeness Sam and Sam developed is now officially a thing of the past. The loss of their intimacy hurt most of all. He knew that he would never find anyone better than her in his entire life again. He resolved that whoever made her broke the mold.

Quentin watched as his brother followed Samantha into the butler's pantry, where beverages were kept. He knew that Sam looked for an opportunity to speak privately with her, considering Dr. Montgomery's offer of help. Quentin wanted his brother's health to improve, so it was his fervent hope that Samantha would accept Sam's apology even at this late date. He also recognized that he, too, had mixed feelings about his brother and Samantha being in such close proximity. He didn't know whether she had latent feelings for Sam, and if so, how deep those passions ran.

As she left the pantry to return to the table, she gave no hint of what transpired between them or what she may have been feeling. One of her younger siblings stopped her and asked her to help tie her shoelaces. Placing the bottles on the table, Samantha stooped to help guide the little girl's fingers while looping laces and then securing them together to form a bow. Then they grinned at one another, rubbed noses, and kissed before Samantha stood, retrieved the bottles, and continued to the table.

She has such grace and style not many women can pull off, Quentin thought. Slender, but not skinny, she had pronounced curves evident in her casual wear. The wine-colored sweater set she wore complemented her skin tone and formed nicely around her breasts, tapering to her narrow waist and subtly flared hips. Her legs were long in her hip-flattering slacks and ankle boots. When she tilted her head to one side in question, he realized that he had been staring at her for too long.

"Something wrong?" Samantha passed the junior-size wine bottle to Quentin, sat at the table, and wondered why he was intently watching her.

"Uh, no. Sorry. Just thinking how much you and your siblings have changed since the last time we saw each other."

"Same goes. You were much different back then than you are now. As I recall, you were on the swim team at the academy. I thought that you would do something related to swimming as a career. However, you've taken on quite a different task as president of King Advertising. Your cell phone hasn't stopped beeping or vibrating since we met at the airport. Is your work rewarding?"

"It's a living. We're constantly running advertising campaigns for our clients in different markets and on different media outlets, like television, radio, magazines, newspapers, and outdoor media."

"Outdoor media?"

"Yes, billboards, reader boards, mobile ads, including panel trucks and buses."

"Okay. I didn't think of those venues for ad campaigns. They are things I rarely think about when I see them. Come to think of it,

Alex-Mont Ranch is displayed on all of our utility vehicles. However, I think Brian doesn't spend a lot of advertising dollars on anything other than newspapers."

"We place a number of our ads through Simon Wilde's family's Wilde Star Media Group." He nodded toward Simon, who was in conversation with Samantha's brother, Vincent, a pediatrician nearly finished with his pediatric surgery residency program. "They're one of our largest outlets. Simon's sister, Meara Wilde Standish, is our liaison with the media group. She heads the Advertising Department for Wilde Star.

"There are so many outlets for ads that lately, I've spent a great deal of time getting up to speed on the new platforms. Our advertising executives are a bunch of young, energetic professionals who compete to bring in new business. Our public relations workers spend most of their time helping existing clients improve their share of the marketplace. It's a competitive business, and our managers handle multiple advertising executives and public relations specialists with loads of clients and portfolios."

"I imagine that for an agency the size of King Advertising, which serves as a liaison between the client, its market and customers, handling and coordinating ad campaigns for clients involves marketing, promotions, and creative designs, too."

"That's true. Our advertising executives are required to know their customers' markets, as well as our customers, do, if not better than the clients. They have to do that in order to understand how to meet their needs and objectives. Before embarking on a campaign, the account exec must determine who the target audience is for that product or service. Then the exec is responsible for forming a team and multiple game plans which address the marketing strategies and opportunities for the client."

"Then, as president of King Advertising, you have to know everything that your people know about every client's market and decide whether it all makes money for the client and the agency."

"You must have been listening in on our leadership conferences," he deadpanned, an irony in his tone.

"Paulette mentioned some of what she's been doing for your agency. As I understand it, she's more on the creative design side of your business. She and her department have to develop the storyboards and jingles to capture the audiences' attention. She mentioned that you might be embarking on political advertising."

Shrugging, he poured some of the wine into a goblet and sipped, approving of the flavor. "That's more where my father and mother want me to steer the company."

"From your demeanor, I gather that you're not so inclined to adhere to their wishes?"

"We're at odds over the strategy at the moment. In my view, adding a political component would necessitate adding an entirely new arm to the company. We may even be forced to take a particular political position. I'm not in agreement with that perception of the agency's brand. Because your aunt is Senator JeNelle Towson Alexander, you're probably aware, in politics, campaign advertising is used to influence a political debate, and ultimately, voters. I would have to bring on political consultants and campaign staff familiar with the field. As they say, all politics is local, and we would have to vet the candidates and their organizations in fifty different states, regions, and locales before agreeing to take them on as a client. That would require in-depth investigations, which are costly and take an excessive amount of time.

"Political messaging has become very important, and the wrong messaging could cost millions, which could leave King Advertising open to lawsuits and protracted legal fees. Last year, I had lunch with David Carter, your mother's former law firm's managing partner. He gave me some pointers but confirmed that their law firm was not interested in getting into the political arena to represent clients like our advertising firm. He suggested several other firms which might be interested. For the most part, those firms were lobbyists. There doesn't seem to be any way to exercise strict control of messaging through these channels, often out of campaign managers' hands. I'm averse to the risks and the extraordinary costs. Despite the inordinate amount of resources candidates spend on their campaigns, I don't see the benefit of moving the agency in that direction the way my parents do.

"I understand the need to expand the business. If we don't, we'll become stagnate. That's why I was abroad meeting with foreign entities who are looking at expanding into U.S. markets. Over the next year or two, I plan to move King Advertising into the international arena and cultivate relationships with foreign clients."

"I noticed that you didn't answer my question. Is what you do rewarding?"

He had to think about that question for a moment. No one had ever asked him that before…not even his parents. Indeed, no woman he dated cared enough about whether he was happy or even content with his life. Most were not even sufficiently astute enough to carry on a conversation and understand his work.

Upon first acquaintance, women would ask what he did for a living, but their eyes would glaze over within two minutes of the description. Conversing with Samantha was refreshing. "From a very young age, I was groomed to join the family business and take a leadership role. After all, I'm the fifth generation to head the agency. So, it was never an option of whether my work would be rewarding. It simply would be what was expected of me, just as it was of my father, grandfather, and great grandfather. It's the King legacy."

She nodded sagely. "Now I understand." She didn't mean to comment aloud.

"Understand?"

Okay, "in for a penny, in for a pound," as her Nana Sylvia Benson Alexander would say. "I understand why you seem uncomfortable here."

Shaking his head and frowning, he questioned, "Uncomfortable? You've stripped off my coat and tie and pulled my shirt from my slacks. Believe me, Samantha, I'm comfortable."

"Not in that way, but you could lose the dress shoes and —."

"*Whoa*, I'm not doing a striptease for your family's entertainment." He was surprised at the merriment he saw shining in Samantha's luminous eyes before she looked away.

While shaking her head, a smile rimmed her mouth. "Now that I think about it, my family might be willing to pay to see that, but before we go too far down *that* road, I meant you seem uncomfortable with the chaos which is my family when we get together in one space."

"Oh," he elongated the single syllable and nodded his understanding. "Perhaps. There are a lot of you."

"This?" She opened her arms to encompass those members of her family still in the lunch salon. "This is a drop in the bucket, so-to-speak. This isn't even the tip of the iceberg. There are—." *His laugh is full and rich*, she thought, *and transforms the angles and planes of his rather austere expression into manly perfection. Funny how I never noticed that about him before.*

"Enough with the platitudes and colloquialisms." He laughed. "I get your point. Initially, I considered it controlled chaos, something to which I'm unaccustomed. Meals at King Manor are sedate events where we barely converse. Your family enjoys talking with one another. They seem to be capable of conversing on any number of topics and never lack for interesting conversation. I learned many thought-provoking facts in a short time, things I never knew about before. On the surface, the discussion might appear to be chaotic; however, it is anything but anarchic." Then he looked up and around the salon. "Where did everyone go?"

Samantha shrugged and looked around the nearly empty lunch hall. "My brothers and sisters, who are still in school, have classes to attend. They took the morning off to welcome me home, but it's a school day for them. Everyone else is probably scattered about doing whatever comes to mind." Focusing on him again, "What would you like to do?"

The question surprised him, and he was tempted to tell her exactly what he would like to do—with her. Wisely he didn't say aloud what he was thinking. "Well, if I'm not going to audition for the Chippendales, what would you suggest?" That got a laugh out of her; he noticed and liked it. He found her to be easy and comfortable to converse with.

"If you brought swimwear, there's the pool. If you want some exercise, there's the gym. If you'd like table challenges, there's the game room. If you want to binge on movies or television shows, there's the movie theatre. If you have work to do to answer your many text messages, there is a quiet room or your suite. What appeals to you?"

You do, he thought, but wisely, didn't say that aloud either.

CHAPTER 10

Samantha thought that there was something unusual in the way Quentin was looking at her. Whatever vibe she was picking up from him had her a little breathless and twitchy. So, she decided it was time to part company. "Come with me. We'll take a walk and see what you might find interesting to do this afternoon, but first, do you have casual clothes and shoes with you?"

"No, not really. I was in Europe to attend to some business. Paulette came along to take Sammy to see his father play in the masters' tennis matches. That didn't leave a lot of leisure time, so we packed light, just for what we had to do."

"Okay, I'll show you to your room and find something for you to wear. Then we'll roam until we find something to entertain you for a while until dinner at six. Sound like a plan to you?"

He nodded. "It does, yes."

After retrieving his jacket and tie, he followed her through a long hall to a set of elevators, one of which took them to the third floor.

"This is quite a place, your home. Two elevators? I saw on the elevator panel that they also go down two levels."

"They do, yes. The elevators are a relatively new addition. My parents had them installed on both the east and west sides of our home several years ago. Just after Mom had Patrick, she couldn't walk up and down the steps, particularly not while carrying him. Then Dad twisted his ankle playing basketball and had to be on crutches for weeks. It wasn't fun watching a nearly seven-foot man climb two flights of stairs on crutches. One or more of us would break something and not be able to climb the stairs, so we'd have to be carried. All of us have our bedrooms on the second level. Dad and Mom's master bedroom is on the second level too. Our grandparents or elderly members of our family, like our great-grand uncles, aunts, or cousins, would come to visit for various events. They are still so independent, but it was difficult for them to navigate the stairs to the third level where the guest rooms are located. We also enjoy having extended family members stay in our home with us. So, instead of building a bunch of cabins, Dad and Mom decided to install the elevators to access the guest rooms on this level. Two birds, one stone," she grinned.

When they stepped off the elevator, Quentin could do nothing but stop to stare. The balcony was wide, overlooked the second-floor balcony, and the great room below on the ground-floor level. Initially, from below looking up, he thought the flowers in the boxes attached to the railings couldn't be real, but they were and were very healthy-looking plants, too. He stepped forward to get a better look. Now he could see that the massive chandeliers hung at different levels, as did the large fans. He also noticed the quiet. He could see that the bedroom doors on the second level were open, but even for a house full of children and young adults, all was quiet. There were full bookcases between the opened bedroom doors and little spaces along the walkway, like book nooks, ideal for curling up with one of those books to read. Live plants were strategically placed everywhere.

Samantha let him look his fill before she interrupted him. "This way," she moved to her right, slowing as he seemed reluctant to take his eyes away from the view. They turned the corner to the left, and midway the balcony, they turned right into a bedroom suite with open, double doors. "Here you are, and your luggage should be in the closet." She opened the closet door and stepped in. "Yes, here they are. If you want to unpack and get comfortable, I'll be back in about fifteen minutes."

"Make it twenty. I'd like to grab a shower."

Nodding her understanding, she left, closing the suite doors behind her. *Why was she thinking that she wouldn't mind scrubbing his back in the shower for him?* She shook off the troubling thought and went to the closet where they kept new clothes that their family friend, high-fashion model, and movie actor Bill Chandler gave to them each season from his *Stallion* and *Risqué* clothing collections.

Quentin stepped out of the generous shower and took a thick, rug-sized towel from one of the shelves in the four-piece ensuite. It was a nicely decorated king-sized bed with linens he hadn't seen on the market. Of course, he didn't decorate his space at King Manor, but the spacious bedroom and bath here at the Alex-Mont Ranch were just as comfortable as his rooms there. The double French doors, which led to an exterior balcony, had attractive seating and strategically placed potted plants. He couldn't see much of the grounds through the heavy snowfall, but he imagined it had stunning views from this elevation. When he left the bedroom, he walked around an opening in the wall that led into a sitting area complete with a gas fireplace with a flatscreen television above, a sofa and occasional chairs, a desk, and a coffee table. The suite wasn't overly large but had a vaulted ceiling, nicely appointed, and comfortable furniture. He particularly liked the linens, no doubt from Samantha's collection.

On the coffee table was a stack of clothes with the tags still attached. Samantha must have come in while he was still in the shower and left the clothes. Frowning, he looked at the labels and wondered how she guessed his size. He removed the towel from around his waist and began to dress. He shouldn't have been surprised, but everything fit perfectly, including a pair of low-cut, comfortable tennis shoes and athletic socks. They were all from the Bill Chandler Stallion Collection.

Quentin recalled that Chandler was one of the founding members of the prestigious Washington, D.C. law firm, Alexander, Carter, Chandler, Charles, Lightfoot, and Towson, PA. Bill Chandler and

Vivian Alexander were classmates in their law school's advanced scholars' program. After they graduated, Vivian opened the law firm with Bill and others whose focus was on diversity and inclusion to support the country's future leaders in reaching their goals. That was when she was still a practicing attorney with others from their law school class.

Quentin was well aware that Chandler was still an exceptional, high-powered attorney for movie stars and sports figures in the entertainment industries. He was also a high-fashion model himself and an in-demand movie actor with a high Q rating. The trendy magazines, *Risqué* and *Stallion,* both of which had high-fashion clothing lines with an international flair, were owned and operated by Bill Chandler. *Neither has been my style,* Quentin thought now, looking at himself in a full-length mirror, *but I can't deny the quality and fit aren't perfect.*

Quentin also read somewhere that the law firm recently expanded and opened a relatively new international law office in Landstuhl, Germany.

At the knock on the door, he turned, expecting to see Samantha poke in her head. Instead, it was his sister Paulette. He was a little disappointed but covered it with an acknowledgment for her to enter.

"Wow, Quentin, you look—," she gestured with her hands, indicating his attire and smiling broadly, "I don't know, really lit."

"'Lit'? Is that something good?"

"It is, yes. It means radical or lit up in the most popular and positive way. Like a rock star. I don't think I've ever seen you in anything approaching sportswear like that before."

"I don't have time for lounging."

"You should make time. You work all the time and never take a break or go away for a real vacation. Any trips, like this last one, are always related to business. You worked the whole time we were in Europe and never took time to rest or relax. You didn't even take clothes to relax in. You look really nice now, though."

"Thank you, I think. Did you need to speak with me about something?"

"Yes, could we sit for a moment?"

He checked his watch and sat in one of the occasional chairs across from where Paulette sat on the sofa. "I suppose. Samantha will be here shortly to give me a tour of sorts."

"Uh, yes, she told me. I ran into her in the hall when she was delivering the clothes to you. She said that you were in the shower. My suite is right next door to this one, and Samuel's suite is on the other side of yours. He's in there now, resting. Because I needed to speak with you, I told Samantha that I'd bring you to her after you and I talked." She looked tentatively at him. "Is that all right?"

He frowned. "Yes. What is it that you want to discuss?"

"Father and Mother have been trying to reach you to see why we are delayed arriving at King Manor. You spoke with Miranda Bazemore earlier? She seems to be in a lather because you told her that you're not going to be her escort at some political shindig this evening. When father couldn't reach you, he called Samuel. He didn't answer his cell and turned it off because he is exhausted and he's trying to get some rest, so Father called me. He asked me where we were, and I didn't want to lie to him. So, I told them the truth, that we ran into Samantha at the airport in Spain, and because our flight was delayed, Samantha let us fly back to the states with her. Needless to say, Father and Mother are not happy that we're here at Alex-Mont Ranch instead of trying to make our way back to King Manor. I explained that the snowfall here in the rural area seems heavier than in town, and road crews are having difficulty clearing the roads. That didn't go over very well with Father. I've been directed to instruct you to call them immediately and make arrangements to come to King Manor before the party tonight at the Clevelands'."

Quentin stood, dug his hands in his pockets, and paced to the French doors. He shook his head as he looked into the still falling snow. "Did you notice that you never said the word home?" Turning, he looked at his younger sister. He wasn't surprised that she wasn't confused about his non-sequitur.

She nodded. "I guess you're right. I have lived at King Manor all of my life, but I don't believe that I ever thought of it as a *home*. It's a very large plantation house listed on the National Registry of Historic Homes. However, it reminds me of a museum. It sits on acres of land in the Gold Coast Region of Washington, D.C. I'm very proud of the heritage it holds. However, when I think of a *home*, I think of Ms. Vivian's house in Georgetown on the edge of Rock Creek Park, where Samuel and I spent a lot of time with Samantha and her sisters and brothers. Miss Anna, she's the majordomo of the Alexanders' Georgetown house. She would gather us up in the kitchen and let us make cookies, cakes, and cupcakes. You can imagine what a mess we made, but that never mattered because she taught us how to clean it up. We also made all kinds of pizzas, too." She smiled to herself. "We had crazy fun, and it was always off the chain good times when their grandparents, cousins, aunts, and uncles visited. They would hug us up and find fun things to do with us.

"However, that wasn't the case at King Manor. There we were always cautioned not to run around on the property or get our clothes dirty. If we went outside, we had to sit in the chairs and be quiet. We weren't allowed to socialize with the house servants or even go into the kitchen. Then I think of this place, Alex-Mont Ranch, where we were encouraged to run, play, and explore. It didn't matter how dirty we got. We would always shower before dinnertime and wash our clothes." She smiled warmly at the little remembrances she told Quentin about. "That lasted only until Mother found that announcement in the newspaper that Ms. Vivian was going to marry Mr. Chuck. Then everything changed."

As she talked, Quentin could see the light of excitement in his sister's eyes and a smile on her face he hadn't seen in years—since she was in high school. He remembered, too. His parents heard the very young Vivian Alexander speak at a Congressional Black

Caucus Week event when she was still in law school. That speech garnered a standing ovation from thousands in the crowd. They vetted her and found that she is the daughter of an educator, Dr. Bernard Alexander, and his wife, Sylvia Benson Alexander, a registered nurse, both Howard University alums. That's when his parents invited her to attend certain events to determine how she would behave in public around their friends and acquaintances.

Of course, people in the service industries, like teachers and nurses, weren't acceptable in Quentin and Ashanti King's higher echelon class of people. To garner their time and attention, one had to be among The Talented Tenth, a leadership class of African Americans who owned the means to effect social change. They were of the notion of social progress or sociocultural evolution, the philosophical idea that society moves forward by evolutionary means.

The fact that Vivian scored Olympic gold in basketball, while she was a dean's list student at Spelman College, didn't impress his parents, but it did impress many of their guests. Still, Vivian was added only to the B-List of the King social register. Even when she graduated at the top of her law school class at Georgetown Law Center, her position in his parents' societal circle was not solidified. His parents believed that Vivian would have received a better education at Howard University because it is one of the oldest law schools and the oldest historically black college or university law schools in the United States. Their parents criticized Vivian for attending a school with a history of enslaving nearly three hundred people of African descent.

However, even while still critical of Vivian, she was elevated to the A-List when it was discovered that her brother, Kenneth Alexander, an engineer and inventor, did his undergraduate work at Morehouse College, another historically black school. He also owned and operated a successful telecommunications firm in Silicon Valley, California. Another one of Vivian's three brothers, Benjamin Alexander, was a U.S. Air Force jet fighter pilot. Her younger brother, Gregory Alexander, is an icon in the NBA, a gold medalist known as Alexander the Great on Wall Street.

Vivian didn't accept many invitations, but his parents doubled their efforts to entice her to come to their events when she married the multi-billionaire, Derrick Jackson. They eschewed the fact that he was a legendary basketball player choosing to highlight the fact that when Derrick left the sport, he became a noted pediatrician and pediatric surgeon. He was also a social activist, which appealed to his parents. Many of his parents' group tried to get their children under Dr. Jackson's medical care. Although they could always count on Derrick and Vivian giving support to the private school where the children they adopted were enrolled, his parents couldn't understand the Jacksons' propensity for bringing "foundlings" into their home.

When the Jacksons adopted children who were not Americans of African descent and enrolled them in the prestigious academy, his parents spoke to the school administration in an effort to have some of the Jackson children excluded from enrollment. That ploy went nowhere fast when Dr. and Mrs. Jackson showed up at the academy with the Dean of Georgetown Law Center and promised a colossal lawsuit if any of their children were excluded on the basis of race, creed, or color. They also threatened the immediate withdrawal of financial support for the school's coffers. Instead, wisely the school's administration invited his parents to withdraw him, Samuel, and Paulette from the academy with a full refund of tuition. His parents backed down from that fight. Still, with the growing popularity of the Jacksons, his parents continued to curry the Jacksons' favor.

Then, Dr. Jackson died suddenly of a massive heart attack on the day his and his wife's only biological son, Derrick Junior, was born. His parents redoubled their efforts to ingratiate themselves with the wealthy young widow by introducing her to as many of their single male friends as they could find. They were frustrated because Vivian Jackson went on with her life and raising alone what were eleven, health-challenged children by that time and her healthy biological son. To his parents' certain knowledge, she didn't even date during the next five years after her husband's death.

However, in the newspaper's society pages, the wedding announcement that attorney Vivian Alexander Jackson would marry Dr. Charles Montgomery, a white man and former basketball icon with Olympic gold to his credit, rocked his parents' foundation. As a result, Samuel and Paulette were forbidden to communicate with Samantha and her siblings ever again.

His parents' racism was rooted in their abhorrence of the slave stock their ancestors had once been. They were zealous on the subject of race as their forefathers had been and counted no one with a drop of Caucasian blood as their friend. They allowed only people of color into King Manor and would not socialize with anyone other than people who thought and believed as they did. It was probably causing his parents no little amount of animosity to know that he and his siblings were in the home of a woman they considered a traitor to the race of Americans of African descent.

"Quentin?"

"Yes." His sister's voice dragged him back from his thoughts and he turned to face her. "Don't worry about this situation, Paulette. You're enjoying the renewal of old acquaintances, so enjoy your time with them."

"I plan to, and, if I'm not mistaken, you seem to be enjoying Samantha's renewed acquaintance as much as I am. Am I right?"

"I've always thought that she was special. That's nothing new."

"I remember, but the King family has caused her a great deal of pain. According to Samuel, she's risen above it, but unless you're seriously interested in her, please don't cause her any additional heartache."

He frowned at his sister. "Why would you say that?"

"Well, although we've known her for much longer, you're involved with Miranda Bazemore, aren't you? I mean, you've been her escort for the last six months or so. I overheard father and mother say that they expect you to propose marriage to her around Valentine's Day and have the wedding sometime next spring."

"Ha!" his laugh was sharp and without mirth. "Yes, we've dated, but I have no intention of marrying Miranda."

"I believe that she thinks otherwise. So, you didn't ask for any advice, but if you had, I would say to lightly tread where Samantha is concerned—unless or until you clear up your status with Miranda."

He nodded his agreement. "It will be the first thing on my agenda when we get back to King Manor."

"Uh, about that, Quentin, I'm not going back. I've spoken with Dr. and Mrs. Montgomery and with Samantha. They have agreed to let me stay here to take care of Sammy while Samuel is hospitalized. While we're here, we're going to talk about Samuel's retirement from professional tennis and look for someplace where he can start a tennis school, preferably somewhere with year-round good weather like San Diego, California.

"Samantha said her Uncle Benny still has a four-bedroom, three and a half bath, bi-level condo there that her family uses because Benny and his wife are still stationed in Japan. If Samuel and I decide to move to San Diego, Samantha said that she'd speak with her uncle and aunt to see whether they'd be willing to lease their condo to us until we can find something permanent."

"Us? You're planning to go with Samuel and Sammy when he is released from the hospital?"

"I am, yes. I'm not a child anymore, Quentin, and as long as I live under the King Manor roof, Father and Mother will dictate my life for me. They've vetted several of their friend's sons they want me to date. I don't think I can live that way anymore. Samuel and Sammy will need me, at least until Samuel gets back on his feet, and they get situated and settled. I want to be there for them. Can you understand?" Her voice was a plea.

"I do, yes. I thought you might want to go with Samuel, but I didn't expect you two to act so swiftly."

"If you want, I can still remotely work until you hire or promote someone into my position. It doesn't have to be right away. I know you'll be inundated once you get back into your office. If we move to San Diego or wherever we decide to go, once Sammy is in school, I can still help whenever you need me."

"I appreciate that, but I think you'll need a clean break from King Advertising. Maybe you'll find something to do that you really like."

She smiled, but her eyes were moist, she knew. "Thank you, Quentin." She stood and thought about hugging him, but they didn't do that type of thing in their family, so she took his hands in hers and squeezed lightly. "If you're ready, I'll take you down to the pool where initially Samantha planned to be."

"Yes, I'm ready, but before we go," he took her into his arms for a tight hug, and the dam burst. She hugged him tightly and he realized that he had never hugged his parents or siblings before. It felt somehow sad but liberating to be holding her now...and to be held. So, he let her cry while he held back his own tears.

CHAPTER 11

"Oh, no, you don't, brother mine," Samantha teased, "a bet is a bet. You lost and I won. You have to take my duty work tonight after dinner."

"Ah, come on, sis," Roger wheedled. "I'll trade you—"

"No reneging, son," Chuck chimed in before palming Roger's face and pushing him back into the pool. "Your sister beat you fair and square. You know she's a better swimmer with the backstroke than you are, but she's not supposed to beat her dad," he pushed Samantha into the pool with her brother.

"Mom," Samantha whined, aggrieved when she surfaced. "Did you see what Dad did? That's not fair. We raced doing the backstroke, and I won."

"No, babe, I didn't see it, but you're right. It's not fair. Chuck, go jump in the pool," Vivian ordered from her position, reclining on a chaise lounge and relaxing with her eyes closed.

Chuck huffed in adherence to his wife's edict and jumped into the deep end of the pool. That brought on a spate of laughter that rose to the glass dome from those relaxing in the lagoon-like space where lush tropical plants grew in abundance.

"If I hear anyone else laughing at my husband's plight, everyone will find themselves taking an unscheduled dip in the pool."

That quieted the laughter for about half a minute. When the music changed, the pool cleared, and all were on their feet dancing.

When Paulette led him to the glass doors, Quentin was surprised to see people in swimwear energetically gyrating poolside to something called the *Rockin' Pneumonia and the Boogie Woogie Flu*. It was a hilarious sight to see fifteen or so people wringing and twisting to the beat. Quentin cast his eyes around the group and landed on Judge Montgomery dancing with her daughters, one of whom was Samantha in a peach-colored bikini. Her swimwear seemed to almost disappear against her skin. She swiveled her hips as did her sister Geneviève, who Quentin learned from his sister on the way to the pool was a former Coast Guard helicopter pilot and officer, and currently a D.C. police lieutenant. Her brother, Brian, was now the general manager of the Alex-Mont Ranches. Will Hamilton was dancing with KiLe while his wife, Linda, the world-renowned prima ballerina and figure skater, danced with Simon Wilde. Dena danced with her brother, Roger, while Drew Hamilton danced with one of his sisters-in-law, Petra. Vincent, the pediatrician, seemed to be free-styling, something that looked like salsa. Then Vincent grabbed his mother's hand and twirled her into his arms. Vivian giggled and effortlessly followed her son's footfalls.

Quentin had been taught ballroom dancing from an early age but didn't know anything about the dance moves any one of them was emulating. Still, they seemed to be enjoying it. It was rather incongruent to see snow falling outside the glass walls while inches inside people were frolicking in a warm indoor lagoon in swimwear. It was the same type of scenic view as they had in the lunch salon, except this space had a profusion of beautiful and fragrant tropical plants and trees. Outdoor furniture was placed in abundance on the thick Zoysia grass that surrounded the perimeter of the lagoon.

"Ah, it's the wacky-song contest," Paulette squealed delightedly.

"The what?" Quentin frowned and bent closer to his sister to hear her explanation over the loud music.

"Someone has to come up with a wacky song that makes everyone get up and dance. I've never heard this song before, but it's funny. See, everyone is up dancing. Whoever chose this one wins."

Samantha did a little bootie shake and danced around her father to dance with her brother, Brian. He was the best dancer of all of her brothers, although Andrew was trying to be a contender.

"Ah, you know you can't handle this, sister mine," Brian teased as he swung his arms up over his head, snapped his fingers, and provocatively swiveled his hips to repeatedly bump Samantha's hips in a rock-steady motion. "I can go Bruno Mars on you in a finger snap." He proceeded to do just that. His white skin still showed a hint of the bronze tan he recently received from a three-week, part business, part vacation trip that he and his pregnant wife, KiLe, took to Argentina's southeastern coast. They went there to celebrate her birthday and buy thirty wild horses from family friend Tina Justice and her husband, Nico Collins, at their winter retreat.

"Oh, no, brother mine, you don't know what I'm working with. Let me show you a little somethin' somethin'." She snaked her body as if she taught Beyoncé how to move.

"Now you want to go *Single Ladies* on me, sister mine?" Brian joked, finding two more of his sisters, Dena and Geneviève, with Samantha using the *Single Ladies* dance routine on him. They learned that sequence of steps and body movement years ago and hadn't missed a step in their performance in the intervening years.

"Let me take some of your light work." Ryan danced his way into the ring.

When the music ended, they all laughed and applauded Will Hamilton, the former baseball star, for coming up with that recording.

He took his bows, laughing, and wrapped his arms around his wife's body from behind. "Hey, I used to live at 124th and Lenox Avenue, right down the street from the Apollo Theatre in Harlem, New York. My grandparents and parents used to groove to that music when we were kids in short pants."

"Okay, brother-in-law, you get to pick the music for the rest of the afternoon," teased Samantha as she high-fived him. When she turned, she was breathless from the energetic workout and facing Quentin and Paulette.

"Ooops! Sorry." Samantha laughed, fanned herself, and took a step back from Quentin's personal space. "I didn't see you two come in. It's more humid in here than it usually is, so you may want to lose some of those clothes. Otherwise, they'll be sticking to your body like glue in no time."

"I think you're right. I'm going to go change into a bathing suit." Paulette sprinted for the door.

Quentin was fixated on Samantha. Her hair was natural, without chemicals enhancing her multiple shades of brown to bronze. It was wet and slicked back from an engaging face that was also free of any enhancement. In a word, her face was breathtaking. "I'm beginning to wonder why you're continually attempting to undress me."

"Would you believe that I'm a good hostess who wants visitors to be comfortable?" she challenged.

"Without question, I would believe anything you tell me."

"Smart man," Brian interjected. "Let me take you to where you can change out of those jeans."

Quentin followed Brian out of the pool area, but he had a feeling that he knew what was coming. They walked into a wood-paneled room that resembled a combination of a high-end haberdashery and boutique filled with women's and men's clothing neatly arranged on shelves or hanging in sections according to size. Brian picked up and then handed a couple of pairs of swim trunks to him for his selection.

"Look, Quentin, we were never enemies, and the fact that we're both Phi Beta Kappa weighs heavily on your side where I'm concerned. To me, it means that you're not stupid. However, society brother or no, I love my sister, and if you or any of your family hurt her again, understand that there will be hell to pay."

"I have no reason to want to see your sister hurt, Brian. It's not my intention, but I am interested in her on a personal level. So, understand this: If she tells me to go away and not contact her again, I won't like it, but color me gone. However, unless or until I hear that from her, I'll be around."

Brian nodded sagely. "Samantha is a grown woman who makes her own decisions. So, if she wants you gone, her family will ensure that she won't have to ask you twice. Now, change your clothes and let's go get some exercise. We'll see who can win the endurance races."

Although he was on the swim team in high school, college, and still swam daily for exercise, Quentin had the feeling that the "endurance races" Brian mentioned had nothing to do with water sports.

Samantha sensed that everyone knew why Brian took Quentin to the dressing room closet. It was tantamount to being taken to the woodshed and having a can of whoop-ass unleashed on the unsuspecting. Her family was circumspect, but she could feel their arms metaphorically around her, even at a distance. She loved them all the more for it. There was no way to get them to stand down and not worry about her. Her family wasn't built that way. Admittedly, if it were one or more of them in the same situation, as it had been for Geneviève several years ago when she had a bad experience with a guy, Samantha felt that she would react the same way. They were, as their dad branded them, a posse—all for one and one for all.

So, Samantha was pathetically grateful when Brian and Quentin returned, and neither sported a black eye or bloody nose or split lip. Brian breezed by her kissing her cheek. He moved on to go to his wife, sitting on the edge of the lagoon, talking with Dena. Samantha turned back just as Quentin approached. Paulette also returned, making a beeline for the section of the lagoon where the twins, Ryan and Roger, played volleyball. They were in an area near the pool's deeper end by one of the waterfalls while others floated in the lazy river stream.

Well, hell, Samantha thought when Quentin continued toward her looking as if he could pass for a black version of the Greek god Poseidon.

"Got a minute?" Quentin asked.

She shrugged and frowned but let him guide her out of the pool area.

They went inside the dressing room closet. Quentin, with his hands on his hips, his head down, paced away from her and then back several times. Then he finally stopped in front of her. "I'm socially involved with someone, a woman, but I don't have feelings—-I mean that I'm not in love with her or anything near that. However, she is under the mistaken impression that I want to marry her. I don't, but, apparently, I need to make that clear not only to her but also to my parents. Am I making myself clear? I mean, are you following me so far?"

Brows beetled, she shrugged nonchalantly. "O-kay?" Her tone was uncertain and a bit dismissive. She had no idea why he was sharing this type of personal information with her.

Seeing the confusion clearly evident on her face, he released a frustrated breath. "I'm not good with interpersonal relationships. In fact, I rarely get it right, and I tend to miss all of the nonverbal cues about how a woman feels. So, let me be clear and to the point—oh, the hell with it." Frustrated, he took her upper arms and pulled her close for a thorough kiss of that delectable mobile mouth of hers. When she didn't act to push him away, he changed the angle of his kiss, sinking deeper into it.

At the beginning of the sweet but electrifying assault on her senses, Samantha's arms had been trapped between her body and Quentin's. When he changed the angle of the kiss, her hands flattened on the hard plane of his warm, broad chest. Her fingertips grazed over his raisin-sized nipples under the white, soft T-shirt, eliciting a needful groan from him. So, testing, she did it again and found herself pulled even more flush against Quentin's body with a hard, vertical ridge evident between them. Tentatively, her arms went up and wrapped around his neck as she went to her toes to play hide-and-go-seek with their tongues.

Physically shaken, Quentin promised himself that any moment he would end this madness that had overtaken him with the breathtakingly appealing Samantha Montgomery in his arms. Yet, this kiss spun out into another hemisphere when her arms circled his neck. Of their own accord, his hands slid slowly down the sides of her ribcage to settle on her impossibly narrow waistline, pulling her closer. She perfectly fit chest to breasts and hip to hip against him. All of that smooth, exposed skin in the damp bikini was electrifying under his palms. Gradually, he took hold of her forearms again, releasing the hold she had on his neck. That move stopped him from taking more of her into his arms. "Okay. Okay, we have to stop this," his forehead pressed against Samantha's.

"We do? Why?" With her eyes closed, she asked nonsensically, her tone bordering on aggrieved. "We were just getting to the good part, weren't we?"

Quentin laughed mirthlessly, tucked the crown of Samantha's head under his chin, and held her securely in his arms. "For one thing, we're standing in a dressing room in your parents' home. For another, we reconnected for the first time less than twenty-four hours ago in a different time zone after more than seven years of not seeing one another. Your brother just warned me that if I hurt you, there will be hell to pay. I take him at his word because we are frat brothers. I imagine that there are places on this ranch he knows about where my cold, dead body would never be found."

She leaned back and looked up into his eyes. "Brian would never hurt you so badly that he'd kill you." She shrugged. "My father, on the other hand, just might, with his bare hands. My mom would just make you feel as if you wanted to die rather than face off with her. She can do more with one look than most people can do with a tongue lashing." She took a deep breath; all humor was gone from her tone. "What are we doing, Quentin?"

"Something that I wanted to do from the time you wore your hair in two long ponytails as a teenager. I didn't know or understand what my feelings were about back then. You were my younger brother's best female friend, his girlfriend. The only girl he talked about all the time was you. After Samuel was forced out of your life, I never acted on my interest in you because you were too young. If I touched you, that contact could have been considered statutory rape. I was already in college when I would think about you. That was particularly true while your brother, Brian, was a freshman, and I was a senior or in grad school. Sometimes you would come up to visit Brian on campus for a weekend or when he played on UPenn's lacrosse team. I would see you with him having fun, but I wasn't sure how you felt about the King family at that time. So, I didn't get in touch with you."

"'Forced out of my life'? Who would force Samuel to treat me that way?" She took a step back, putting space between them, and defensively crossed her arms.

Quentin palmed his face dragging his features down with the moisture on his brow. "My parents forced the twins to stop seeing you."

"Why would they do such a thing? I don't understand."

"They did it because your mother wouldn't conform to their way of thinking."

Confusion was even more evident on her face. "My mother? What did my mother have to do with my relationship with Samuel and Paulette? She was always kind and loving with your family."

"My parents believed then and still do today that a Black woman of prestige and prominence, like your mother, a U.S. Supreme Court Judge, should not marry outside of her race and particularly not to a white man. They do not trust anyone who is not of African descent. Historically, their families suffered under unfathomable circumstances and believe in the motto do unto others as was done unto them. Their racism is extreme and borders on irrational, but there are members of their ancestry who were strange fruit on many trees. One such man, a relative of ours, traveled from Baltimore, where his troopship landed after World War II, to go to his home in Florida. He was found hanging from a tree in Georgia. He was still wearing his uniform with all of his medals for bravery above and beyond the call of duty. No one was ever investigated for his murder. He was still in the military, but they didn't even bother to look into it.

"Before that, around the early 1800s, a woman, much like Sally Hemmings, was repeatedly raped and forced to bear fourteen of her slaveholder's children, sometimes twins or two children in the same year. According to the 1870 Census, the first time he raped her, she was ten years old. This atrocity continued long after the so-called end of slavery. She died at age thirty-two after giving birth to another child. He never acknowledged any of his children with her and was never brought up on rape charges. My mother is a direct descendant of that last child.

"There are many other affronts and atrocities which have been recorded in my parents' family histories. They've sworn an oath never to forget that a total number of African deaths directly attributable to the Middle Passage voyage is estimated at up to two million people. A broader look at African deaths directly attributable to the institution of slavery from 1500 to 1900 suggests up to four million African deaths. All of those who survived until today have their blood tainted with European blood. The majority of Americans of African descent with varying amounts of European blood did not receive it through consensual relationships.

"My parents keep meticulous records of all of the modern-day atrocities that occur and plan to publish an encyclopedia of names, dates, places, incidents, and atrocities. They've been working on the volumes for years. That's why my father turned over the presidency to me earlier so that he and my mother would have ample time to complete phase one of the project.

"They also want to cleanse the blood of their offspring and future generations. That's why Samuel was forced to marry Pamela. Her DNA shows that she has little if any European blood in her ancestry. However, clearly, you do have some European blood. It was drilled into us by my parents from a very early age never to have close, personal relations with people who are not of our race.

"On the other hand, your family celebrates diversity, multiculturalism, and working for the common good. I see the rainbow coalition that includes your sisters and brothers in your parents' posse and the cohesion among all of you. Just as Caucasians form race-based hatred groups, my parents and people like them are just as vehement on the opposite end of the spectrum. They are angry every day of their lives. That hatred spilled over and affected your relationship with Samuel and Paulette."

"I imagine the fact that I don't know anything about my parentage or heritage didn't help."

"You're correct, but neither Samuel nor Paulette gave a damn about that. Your skin tone indicated to my parents that you are a mixture of races, in addition to African. Still, it infuriated our parents that the twins defended you so vehemently. Disobedience is not acceptable behavior in King Manor. If Samuel didn't start dating Pamela Halstead, my parents threatened to take away their financial support for his desire to play professional tennis after high school graduation instead of going to college. Pamela's parents threatened to take away all financial support if she didn't get pregnant and marry Samuel. They didn't care in which order those two events came to fruition. You see, Pamela is a lesbian, and her parents believed that having sex with a man and having a child would 'cure' her. If there is something our parents hate as much if not more than having relationships with someone not of our race, it's people engaged in a same-sex union."

Shocked at the revelations, Samantha shook her head in disbelief. "That's why Pamela wasn't with you in Spain?"

"That's correct. Samuel has asked for a divorce, but if Pamela agrees to it, her wealthy parents will cut the purse strings, and she'll forfeit any right to inherit from them. He has offered to buy her out of the marriage, but he can't match or even come close to what she would inherit when her parents pass away. Pamela is their only child. She plans to have a sex change using any inheritance she receives. For now, she lives lavishly with her lovers and hasn't ever seen Sammy. She gave over her parental rights before he was born and has had nothing to do with him. Her parents, however, use him for photo ops. They play the dutiful grandparents' role, and Samuel can't deny them the opportunity to spend time with him. Other than that, they have little or nothing to do with him."

"He's a sweet little boy," Samantha anguished. "How could anyone not love him?"

"I agree with you, but Samuel has been his only parent, and he's fiercely protective of his son. Because we live in King Manor and Samuel is often traveling, he leaves Sammy at home with us. My parents have tried to mold Sammy into their dogma, but Samuel has fought them every step of the way. As a result of his illness and his son's welfare, he's decided to retire from professional tennis. If your father's treatment is successful, Samuel will move away from this area."

Samantha nodded. "Yes, I know. Paulette told me that Samuel has a severe form of osteoporosis. She's planning to go with him regardless of the outcome of the medical therapy. My dad is an excellent doctor. I can only hope that all goes well for Samuel and his son. Paulette also said that, should something happen to him, Samuel has signed over custody of Sammy to you and Paulette."

"Yes, I know. He doesn't want my parents to get custody of Sammy. I share your hope that there is a good outcome for this medical treatment so that we won't have to argue the question of Sammy's custody in court. I don't know how I would stack up as a father figure for Sammy."

"You'll have to think about their indoctrination if or when you marry this woman your parents want you to marry and have children with."

He looked at her askance. "Not funny, Samantha. If the way I tried to swallow you whole moments ago didn't tell you something about my intentions, buy a clue."

"Hey, just sayin'," she shrugged and then stepped into his personal space. "The way I *let* you kiss me, touch me, said handle your business, Ace, or there won't be any more of those kisses from me." Winking at him, she stepped out of the dressing room, leaving Quentin determined to do just that—handle his business in several areas of his life.

CHAPTER 12

After dinner, Samantha escaped to her studio to catch up on several projects she had no time to deal with while on tour. Before leaving the dining hall, she ensured that all of the King family members were engaged in doing something entertaining. As she opened several new bundles of fabrics, her excitement grew as she began to visualize what could be used for her spring collection. There were a lot of cloths she hadn't worked with before, but she believed she might be able to create wall or ceiling murals using some of the colors for her spring collection. She was thinking about new furniture pieces to create to meet more advanced decors.

Leaning back in her chair, she propped her bare feet on the desk and pulled a stack of fabrics into her lap. Closing her eyes, she ran the cloths between her fingertips, getting a feel for the fabrics' strength and texture. She was beginning to see it in her mind's eye—something bright and happy. She was so done with colors in the grey family, light to dark. She had done blues two years ago and green last year while everyone else was thinking about orange and brown for the fall.

People tended to use darker colors in the fall and winter and lighter colors in the spring and summer. She preferred to mix or reverse that age-old trend. When people went for the traditional red for the Christmas holidays, she had gone for maroon and silver, blending it with a royal blue for the New Year. Her collection will be gold with a prism of bright fall leaf colors across the spectrum this Thanksgiving. Christmas would be purple and light lavender with snow-white for New Year's. She wasn't sure about it, but it would settle for now.

"Were you looking for me, babe?" Vivian asked as she came into the salon studio to sit in a chair beside Samantha. She lifted her long legs, put her feet on the workbench, and leaning her head back, closed her eyes.

"I was, yes. You and Dad disappeared right after dinner. Were you busy?"

"Not really," she yawned and kept her eyes closed. "Laurel and Laura had a meltdown."

Samantha sat up straighter and looked at her mother, her brows beetled with concern. "Is something wrong?"

"Separation anxiety."

"Oh," Samantha relaxed again. "I forget that the twins will be thirteen next month. You brought them home when they were what, about five years old? They were the first ones you and Dad adopted after you married. I believe that I was in my last year of high school."

"They were four going on five, yes. It was the first time the girls could move without being conjoined. They hadn't learned how to move separately yet. They did everything together."

"Where has the time gone? I remember when you gave me my own bedroom when I became a teenager. I cried and cried because I thought I would be so lonely without Linda, Dena, and Geneviève to talk with after the lights went out at night." She smiled at the memory. "Then you told me to decorate my space to suit my dreams. My love of color and textures exploded from those dreams. That was huge for me. I developed my own style and individuality. It was a turning point in my life. You and Dad encouraged me to be whoever I wanted to be. Having a bedroom of my own was such a simple thing, but crucial to my life's growth, steps, and stages. I'll never be able to thank you and Dad for all that you helped me become. I'm still a work in progress, but I'm happy with who I am when I look in the mirror each day and where I am in my life. Because of you and Dad, I don't wake up with regrets."

"I can remember how you behaved before that. You've come such a long way from that battered and abused child the police found in an alley. You were so near death that Derrick feared he wouldn't be able to save you. Then, he worked so hard to address your needs. You were so traumatized that you would not speak to anyone. Derrick stayed with you until you were off the critical list. Now, look at you. He would be so proud of the young woman you've become, as are Chuck and I."

Samantha reached out for Vivian's hand, and they linked their fingers. "I was so afraid whenever Derrick finished his rounds and left the hospital. I kept thinking that he would never come back, but he did every day. Sometimes he'd come back twice a day, particularly when new patients were admitted to the children's wing of the hospital from the orphanage. Then one day, Derrick brought you with him for Linda's birthday party in the hospital ward. Because I was the only one who didn't join the party, you came to my bedside, sat down, and began to read a story to me. Then you came back every day, too. Even if it was just for half an hour, I felt as if it was special. You didn't try to force me to talk, but you always made a get-well card with a special poem or verse for me every time you came. I saved every one of those pieces of paper. I still have them in the scrapbook you gave to me for my birthday. You told me to put my counted joys in it, so I did. I look at it sometimes and remember that long ago time."

"I remember that one day when I came into the hospital early in the morning before breakfast, I intended to spend only about half an hour with you. However, you crawled into my lap, laid your head on my shoulder, stuck your thumb in your mouth, and fell asleep while I was reading to you. I had a class later that morning that I should have attended, but I couldn't leave after that monumental breakthrough."

"I remember that day, too, Mom. I think it was the day I learned to trust. I felt safe with you and Derrick. Then after you two married and adopted Linda, Brian, Dena, and the others, you asked me whether I wanted to come to live with all of you and be a family. I didn't know what adoption meant until you held the adoption ceremony. Then I began to understand that I was loved, and I had a family to love and protect.

"When Derrick died on the same day that Derrick Junior was born, April Fool's Day, I was so afraid that you weren't going to be able to keep all of us, but you did. You made it clear to us that we were still a family and would always be a family no matter what."

Vivian turned her head toward her daughter and squeezed her hand.

"That had to be so hard for you, Mom, losing Derrick so suddenly," Samantha continued, "but that's when I learned what family really is and why we wear these gold chains around our necks. These chains bind us together. All the uncles, aunts, grandparents, and cousins wrapped their arms around us to get us through the worst of losing Derrick. Yet, you wouldn't let us wallow in grief and despair. Instead, you just kept moving forward and did whatever came next. You were just a little over twenty years old when you headed your own law firm and raised us, teaching us, challenging us to explore and meet life head-on. You put a tennis racket in my hand when I was barely seven-years-old, and we began hitting a ball back and forth over the net. I could barely see over the net." She laughed.

Vivian smiled at the memory. "You were such a shy waif, afraid to come out of your cocoon. Yet, I could see that you had great hand-eye coordination. Once you got your confidence up, you could compete against children older than you. That's when you began to shine. Your confidence grew, and in no time you were traveling the world, playing and winning your tennis matches."

"You and my family were right there with me every step of the way. When you married Chuck, we adopted him as our father, and he adopted all twelve of us as his children. We were so happy to add Montgomery to our names, and then the family got bigger."

"I look at where you came from, and I couldn't be more proud of you, of all of you. You are my joy. So, babe, tell me what's bothering you."

Samantha shook her head and smiled. "I don't know how you do that."

"Do what?"

"You always know. I mean, it never fails. You can read all of us as if we're yesterday's news."

Vivian smiled, too. "I have excellent teachers in Bernard and Sylvia Benson Alexander. If you think you can get around me with a diversionary tactic, remember I'm a mom, a lawyer, and someone who loves you fiercely."

Samantha nodded in agreement. Her maternal grandparents were the absolute best, and her mom was even better.

"So, stop stalling and spill."

So, Samantha told her mother what Quentin said about his parents and their influence when they were in high school.

After Samantha's commentary, Vivian shook her head and sighed. "From the very beginning of my acquaintance with Mr. and Mrs. King, they seemed to want to direct my life. They are closer to my parents' ages, and I was taught to respect my elders. The first criticism came from Mr. and Mrs. King because I was a black student at Georgetown Law."

"Why would that bother them?"

"Around 1838, the Jesuit priests owned and operated Georgetown University and enslaved nearly three hundred men, women, and children. The enslaved were sold to the West Oak and Chatham Plantations in Louisiana to pay the university's debts. The terms directed from the Catholic Church leadership in Rome included that there be no familial separation, that the proceeds not be used to pay debts or the operating expenses of the college, and that the religious practice of the enslaved people be supported. Of course, the Jesuit priests did not meet any of the terms directed by the Pope. Because of the school's terrible history, Mr. and Mrs. King railed against the university and any student of color who chose to attend the school in any of the university's departments, including medicine and law.

"You already know that Gus Fahey is a Georgetown alum, a former California senator, and my faculty advisor while I was in law school. He is still one of my most trusted counselors. You've met him, and you know that he's not Black. He was incensed over the treatment of the Black students by Mr. and Mrs. King and their cohorts. As a result, he arranged through his Congressional contacts for a number of Black students he mentored to speak at a Congressional Black Caucus weekend event. Of course, that led to other allegations against him by Mr. and Mrs. King, using very derogatory terms. The fact that we Black students wouldn't leave the law school or any of the other departments in protest for what the Jesuit priests had done in the early 1800s caused the rift to deepen.

"Back in April 2019, two-thirds of the Georgetown student body voted to establish a semesterly fee to fund reparations for descendants of the enslaved people. The non-binding resolution was presented to the university for the approval of its board of directors."

"Still fighting those issues, are they?"

"I suppose. When Mr. and Mrs. King invited me to come to their social events, it was to introduce me to their society. It wasn't that I was not cognizant of racial injustice. I really didn't have time to devote to other peoples' emotional insecurity and negative baggage. I couldn't afford to attend a lot of extra activities. I supported those causes and I believed I was serving the common good without reference to race, color or creed. I was in law school, volunteering at a family homeless shelter, and clerking for Professor Fahey. I also volunteered with the Police Boys and Girls Club in an economically challenged part of the city. I was an assistant coach for the girls' basketball team. They were identified as at-risk students and required a great deal of time and attention. Some of their home environments put them at risk of mistreatment. I intervened in several situations acting as guardian ad litem on behalf of a child and investigating the circumstances for the court. When necessary, at my request, Professor Fahey found Child Services attorneys to argue the court cases. With so many activities, I barely had time to sleep. So I turned down more invitations for social events than I accepted.

"I made time in that schedule, in my third year in law school, for Derrick and a social life with him. I was shocked that he asked me to marry him, but the Kings didn't think he was good enough because he came from an economically challenged Philadelphia neighborhood. As you know, Derrick's father, your grandfather, was a former Mississippi farmer and an enlisted Marine. Your paternal grandmother was back then a beautician in a disadvantaged community. The Kings believed that anyone of color who wasn't academically superior or prominent wasn't worth their time. They were selective in their snobbery, particularly when Derrick created the webbing system, which revolutionized pediatric medicine. Then he was all right with them despite the fact that he made his initial millions from bouncing a basketball better than anyone else." She shook her head again.

"When Derrick died, the Kings wanted to take over my life and my social calendar. When they learned who my parents are, they stepped up their approach. Again they tried to parade eligible men of color they vetted in front of me, but I had even less time to attend their events than I had before. However, the proverbial shit hit the fan when I married Chuck. I became *persona non grata* to the Kings, and they labeled me a traitor to the race. I ignored it and them, but I didn't anticipate that they would take their animosity out on you or any of my other children because of who I decided to love and marry."

"Until Samuel dumped me, but you wouldn't—"

"No, babe, you can't slap lipstick on this pig and call it pretty. I've taught you to turn the other cheek when life slaps you in the face, but I didn't teach you to be anyone's punching bag. You're a strong woman, Samantha, so own it. Don't let what happened in the past wreak havoc on your future. You would disappoint yourself and me if you did. That's not what both of your fathers and I raised you to do."

"Not to worry, Mom. It helps to know why this happened to me, but you're right. I'm able to handle this now."

"Good." Vivian lifted her feet off the table and stood with her hands on her lower back, and stretched. "I'm off to see what other mischief I can get into before the evening ends." She leaned over Samantha, squeezed her, and kissed her head. "Are you going to work late?"

"No, Mom, most of this can wait. According to the weather reports, we're in for a pretty bad, slowly moving snowstorm. The road crews are still having a hard time getting the roads clear. So, it looks like we'll be socked in for the next few days. I'll have plenty of time to spend on this. There are a few more bundles of new fabrics I want to look at, and then I'll find the rest of the offspring for some quality family time before bed."

"I think it's your father's turn to pick a movie. So, head for the theater when you're done. We're all likely to be there. Do you want a game of racquetball in the morning?"

"I'm battling jet lag, but Linda and I are going to play at five-thirty."

"Okay, I'll pick on Roger." She laughed. "Love you, babe."

"Love you more, Mom." Absently, Samantha continued to go through the fabrics that arrived from various textile mills while she was away, but her thoughts were on what her mother told her about the King family. When she was a preadolescent, she didn't have much interaction with Mr. and Mrs. King. Of course, she had met them, but they didn't interact. She certainly didn't know what type of people they were, but to force Samuel and Paulette to sever long-held friendships because her mother married Chuck; she was glad that she didn't have to mingle with them.

She was so embedded in her thoughts that she almost missed the knock on the double doors. "Come," she absently called out as she continued to review the samples and make notes.

"*Wow!*" Paulette breathed, astonished as she stood just inside the studio door, her eyes wide as she looked around.

Samantha smiled. It was a little intimidating she knew for someone to see fabric everywhere hanging on the walls, on tables, shelved, and on desktop mockups. She had some new ideas for designs pinned to a wire that spanned the studio. "Hi, Paulette. Come on in."

"Thanks, Samantha. I noticed that you disappeared after dinner. I asked where you were, and one of your younger sisters led me here. I forgot how big this place is. I hope I'm not interrupting." She wandered around the room, feeling the fabrics and seeming awed by the sheer kaleidoscope of colors and textures.

"No, I'm just going through the mail that accumulated while I was away. What do you think?" she held up a particular fabric where the colors appeared to move like a fjord on a canvas."

Paulette came forward and took the fabric Samantha held out to her. She rubbed it between her fingertips and smoothed it along her cheek, closing her eyes. "This is like heaven. The colors seem just to move and swirl on this fabric." Handing the fabric back to Samantha, she looked up and around before wandering the room again. "I would never leave this studio. Now I see where your inspiration for things you design comes from."

"Actually, my inspiration comes from my travels. While I was on tour, I took side trips to see parts of the countryside in several countries. For example, I hooked up with my aunt Aretha and her guy friend, Russell Greene, in France's Rhône Valley wine region. My uncle Gregory is a wine connoisseur, and I'm always on the lookout for wines he may not already have in his collection or wineries that are for sale. My pilot, Glen Kennard, knows the region, and he's a wine connoisseur, too. He's familiar with my uncle's collection. Glen said that the area had so much to offer from a cultural perspective, with Lyon being one of the UNESCO World Heritage Sites."

"UNESCO?"

"Uh, yes, the United Nations Educational, Scientific and Cultural Organization is a specialized agency of the United Nations based in Paris, France. Its stated purpose is to contribute to the promotion of international collaboration in education, sciences, and culture. My cousin, Whitney, practices international law in Germany for my mother's former firm. She told me that UNESCO does that to increase universal respect for justice, the rule of law, and human rights along with fundamental freedom proclaimed in the United Nations Charter. Whitney is an affiliate of the program."

"Wow! I remember Whitney Ivy. Her parents had two sets of triplets, I think. I used to think her dad, your uncle Benny, was so hot! Especially when he wore his Air Force uniform." She fanned herself. "Ooh La La! You say that Whitney Ivy is an attorney now? Shouldn't she still be in college? She was a little younger than us. She was living in Japan with her folks, wasn't she?"

Samantha laughed at Paulette's memory of her uncle, but she agreed nonetheless. Actually, she thought that all three of her mother's brothers, Kenneth, Benjamin, and Gregory, were smokin' hot. She sighed a little, too, and smiled at Paulette. "Yes, Whitney's parents, my uncle Benny and aunt Stacy, are still in the military and deployed to Japan. Whitney Ivy finished college at Temple University's Tokyo, Japan, campus, and then came to America to go to law school. She was still young and brilliant with a high IQ. So, she finished her education far ahead of where the rest of us mortals did." She decided not to mention that Whitney graduated with honors from Georgetown Law. "She met a great guy and married two years ago." Mentioning that Whitney married a Marine physician, who happened to be white, didn't seem to be necessary to their conversation, so she simply moved on. "As I was saying, Glen was right. The Rhône Valley wine region of France was fascinating and beautiful. I took a lot of pictures, bought cases of wine to ship to my uncles and aunts as holiday gifts, and gained a lot of inspiration for my spring collection."

"I've seen Russell Greene's art, but I haven't been able to get my hands on anything of his. His art seems to get snapped up as soon as he has a show. However, your textiles here seem like art people can hang on a wall. This is fabulous work, Samantha."

"Thank you, Paulette. I enjoy what I do."

"You do it well." Turning from the fabrics on display, she studied Samantha. "Did you ever imagine that you would do this as a career option when we were in art class in high school?"

"No, I didn't. I enjoyed the creative process, but I thought I would spend my life playing tennis. I envisioned being the next Ora Mae Washington, Althea Gibson, Zina Garrison, Venus or Serena Williams on the tennis circuit."

"You were certainly headed in that direction. You were ranked in the top one hundred in high school. Both you and my brother were magic when you played mixed doubles tournaments."

Samantha shrugged. "Then I decided to go to college instead of following the circuit. I believe that I made the right choice."

"At least you had a choice. My parents didn't give me an option. I was forced to attend Howard University. Don't get me wrong," she hastened on. "I enjoyed my years there, but I would have liked to have had a choice. Both Quentin and Samuel found ways to avoid following our parents' directives. Quentin went to UPenn, and Sam avoided college altogether. On the other hand, I had to get my undergrad and graduate degrees at my parents' alma mater in preparation for working for King Advertising. I did get to put my artistic interests to use designing the visuals for ad campaigns."

"You aren't happy with that role?"

Paulette slowly shook her head as she surveyed the studio holding her arms wide to encompass the room. "*This* would have made me very happy. Doing what you're doing is where I wanted my career to lead. You have an opportunity to use all of your creativity in a field you love."

"Well, it's not too late to follow your dream."

Paulette's brows beetled. "I couldn't—"

"Yes, you can," Samantha interjected with emphasis. "We aren't even in our mid-twenties yet. So, if you want to take your life and career in a different direction, get on that pony and ride."

As she studied Samantha, Paulette's facial expressions moved from denial to the possibilities. "I'm already planning to leave King Advertising so that I can help Sam and take care of Sammy. Your parents have been kind to my siblings and me by allowing me and Sammy to stay here while he's hospitalized. Would you…?"

"What? Let you work with me?" She nodded in the affirmative. "Yes, I'll be here at the ranch most of the time anyway. So, yes, I'll help you get acclimated to textile design. Then after you leave here, if you want to continue working remotely, that's doable."

Tears sprang into Paulette's eyes.

Concerned, Samantha put her feet on the floor and stood to embrace her former friend.

"You're the best, Samantha. I've missed you and our friendship," Paulette cried. "After our friendship ended, I was never able to develop a close relationship with anyone else; neither did Sam."

"Hey, it's okay. We're okay, Paulette." She held Paulette in a loose embrace, rubbing her back. "I've come to understand that what happened all those years ago wasn't your doing. We're different people now. We'll get to know each other again, and maybe we can get back some of what we had as children." She handed tissues to Paulette to dry her eyes. "We'll work on it, okay?"

Paulette took the tissues, nodded, and offered a shaky smile.

Samantha returned the smile. "Okay, let's go get some hot buttered popcorn and sodas. I think we're going to see a Miguel Menendez-Gaza movie which Uncle Bill produced and Ryan and Roger worked on before their baseball season started last year."

"Can we add hot sauce to the popcorn?"

Samantha linked arms with Paulette as they went to the door. "Is there any other way to eat it?" she joked, turned out the light in the studio, and then closed the door as they laughed the way they used to as young girls.

CHAPTER 13

Quentin didn't think that anyone in the household would be up at five in the morning; however, he soon learned that wasn't the case. With only the low lighting to guide his steps, he chanced to remember the route to the pool, and just as he found his way through the corridor that led to the pool, the teens, Darren, Spencer, and Andrew, were just leaving. They seemed to hang together a lot, Quentin noticed, and they never seemed to run out of conversation. They greeted him but kept up a running commentary while going toward a hall where he hadn't been before.

Brian was in the pool, as were Simon and Will. They were getting in their laps for exercise before breakfast. Quentin joined them for fifty laps. He was then invited to sit at a small, round table poolside to enjoy flavor-filled coffee, ice-cold orange juice, and hot scones. They laughed and talked of world events. Sometimes serious, but often funny, each bringing something interesting to the conversation. Quentin admitted to himself that he hadn't experienced this type of camaraderie with people he could enjoy.

Of course, he had meetings with business people, but not a group he could call friends. There were his fraternity brothers he knew well enough to gather and have a drink with, or he could talk over a project with his alums, but he rarely had time for their larger confabs. It was a command performance that he attend his parents' soirées with the families of their close friends, people his own age, but in all the years that he had known most of them, he hadn't developed close alliances with any of them.

He sensed that what seemed to come so easily to Brian, Simon, and Will, two white men and one black man, was a level of closeness he had never experienced. Moreover, it was clear that these guys were head-over-heels-in-love with their partners, KiLe, Geneviève, and Linda, respectively. Yet, it was apparent that if he wanted to be in Samantha's life, he had a high learning curve to accomplish to achieve the level of intimacy these guys seemed to share.

When the men dispersed, and upon hearing sounds coming from a different hallway that he hadn't explored before, curious, Quentin moved in that direction. He came upon Linda and Samantha in a glass box involved in an energetic racquetball game. Their toned bodies gleamed and glistened with sweat, so, obviously, they had been at it for a while. The ball ricocheted from wall to wall at lightning speeds, causing them to sprint up and down the narrow court to return the volleys.

From his observation seat on a five-tiered bleacher, he and several of the sisters' siblings watched and cheered enthusiastically. Quentin got the impression from those around him that the sisters had played often. Of course, Linda and her husband, Will, lived in New York City and were in town only to welcome Samantha home from her tour, so it must have been a while since they played. Yet, it was clear to him that Samantha's years of playing in amateur tennis tournaments gave her a slight advantage over her sister, who was a prima ballerina and scored Olympic gold as a champion ice skater. Still, the battle often hushed the onlookers until the end of the match. The two sisters breathing hard, hugged, and laughed as they left the box to the cheers of their siblings. Two more of the Alex-Mont kids geared up and replaced Linda and Samantha on the court.

Surprised to see Quentin sitting in the bleachers at nearly six in the morning, Samantha offered a "Well, good morning."

"Good morning. I see that I'm not the only early riser."

"No, not in this family." She huffed out a breath, wrapped a towel around her neck, and used the ends to wipe the moisture from her face.

"You're an outstanding racquetball player."

She smiled and shrugged. "Thank you. You were in the pool?"

He noted that she quickly changed the subject. "I was, yes. Brian, Simon, and Will were there before me, as were your brothers, Darren, Spencer, and Andrew before them. We had a snack after, and we were just leaving. I was trying to fight off jet lag."

Samantha nodded. "Me, too. It slows me down and it takes a while for me to get used to being home again. Getting back into my routine here helps. Are you going into the gym?"

"I was exploring when I came across your match with Linda. I haven't been in this part of your home before."

She looked at a clock on the wall and decided to join him. "Yes, if we want to get ahead of everyone else, we start early. My mother and brother, Roger, beat us to the court. I saw Darren, Spencer, and Andrew heading for the pool when Linda and I were on our way to play. The exercise gets us going to wake up the brain and clear away the fog of sleep. It helps to burn off some of that overabundance of energy for the younger ones so that they can buckle down to study. However, today is a snow day. Breakfast will be served at seven instead of six. I have time before I need to shower and dress. So, let's continue down this way."

They went through a couple of double doors into a multi-purpose gym where some of Samantha's older siblings and parents were shooting baskets. Lines were painted on the floor, indicating that basketball, tennis, and volleyball were played here. A rubberized running track circumnavigated the space hugging the perimeter of the wall where several people were taking advantage of the indoor track. Three people were in various places on the climbing rock wall, while others worked out on spin bikes. As his eyes passed over those in the space, Quentin spotted Sam sitting on a section of bleachers watching his son learn to dribble a basketball.

"Good morning," he nodded to Samantha and Quentin as they came in out of the way of the runners to stand by the bleacher where he sat.

Samantha acknowledged him and walked away to grab cold water bottles from a concession space.

"How are you feeling this morning?" Quentin climbed up a few rungs from the floor and sat on the bleacher next to Samuel.

"Pretty good. The long rest helped, and Dr. Montgomery gave me a shot of something called ketorolac. It's apparently used for the short-term treatment of moderate to severe pain. Dr. Montgomery said that reducing the pain will help me recover more comfortably so that I can return to nearly normal daily activities until I'm stable enough for the surgery. This medication is a nonsteroidal anti-inflammatory drug that has taken the edge off of my pain."

Quentin nodded. "You do look better this morning."

"I feel better. I was able to work out in the pool earlier this morning for some hydro resistance training. Darren, Spencer, and Andrew came in when I was finishing up in the pool. I'm looking forward to the medical procedure as soon as the weather breaks and we can get into Dr. Montgomery's hospital. It's also good to see Sammy having such a wonderful time."

Samuel and Quentin looked across the court to where four of the kids in Sammy's general age group were bouncing balls to one another in a circle. The level of concentration and joy on the little boy's face when he smiled was evident, even from across the room.

"He told me this morning that he didn't want to have his birthday party at King Manor. He wants to have it here at the Alex-Mont Ranch."

"What did you tell him?"

"That I'd see what I could do." He looked into Quentin's eyes. "That made him so happy that his face just lit up. So, I've asked Judge Montgomery whether that's all right with her, and she said yes. I remembered that they hold a big birthday party on the first weekend of each month for the children born in that month because they have so many children. Sammy's birthday will be celebrated with the other children on the next occasion."

That made Quentin wonder what was the date of Samantha's birth. He figured that his brother and sister knew but wouldn't ask either of them. Instead, he asked his brother, "What should I buy for Sammy?"

Samuel shook his head. "I'll take care of that. In the Alex-Mont household, the children make cards and gifts for birthdays and contribute to one gift that each family member wants. For example, a gift could be a week of sweeping the kitchen floor when it's the birthday person's turn or raking leaves or dusting the books. You see, each sibling has duty work, which changes with every season of the year. So, they make trades as birthday gifts. Others outside the immediate family may contribute specific gifts or money to a jar for each child, and the child decides where to donate the money and the gifts. Sammy will have a donation jar, and we'll decide where the donation should go or what to do with individual gifts. I know that he wants a skateboard and a puppy. I'll get the skateboard for this birthday. Brian has a new litter of Labrador puppies that are only four-weeks-old, out in one of the barns. He'll let Sammy pick one from the litter."

Quentin nodded. "He'll enjoy that."

"He's enjoying this family the same way I did when Paulette and I were about his age. We relished being in the Jackson-Alexander household when Dr. and Mrs. Jackson started adopting children who were once Dr. Jackson's hospital patients. That was way back when they lived at The Watergate. We were all in awe of Dr. Jackson because he was such a famous basketball player, but when we got to know him, he was just a regular guy and a lot of fun to be around. He and Mrs. Jackson used to arrange play dates with those of us who were at the academy and other children in the neighborhood. Linda was first, and then Brian, the Kelso twins, Roger and Ryan, Vincent and Geneviève, Dena and Samantha, and the others followed or were in the process of being adopted when Dr. Jackson suddenly died.

"Paulette and I felt that loss as profoundly as did the Jackson-Alexander family, but then Dr. Jackson's and Mrs. Jackson's families and friends stepped up and were there carrying on the closeness we all experienced before Dr. Jackson's death. I particularly remember Mrs. Jackson's law partners teaming up on weekends to do something special with all of us. We went places like the zoo, bike riding through Rock Creek Park, or sailing on the Potomac River. They took us to baseball, football, and basketball games. There were trips to the museums, particularly the African American and Native American museums. There were outings to shows at The Carter Barron Amphitheatre, and William H. G. FitzGerald Tennis Center, where Samantha and I often had tennis matches, and much more.

"I plan to do the same thing for Sammy once we find a new place. With Paulette's help, we'll spend quality time exploring the area and making new friends for him."

Surprised, Quentin nodded. "That's a great idea. You say that's the way they've always celebrated by receiving and giving a gift on their birthday?"

Samuel nodded. "That's how it's been since Samantha, Paulette, and I met as children. They haven't changed anything since we've known them. There used to be only twelve siblings, so there seemed to be at least one birthday party a month. It's just that there are so many more of them now, nearly three times as many than there ever were before."

Quentin nodded. "Sammy will need that support system. I'll make every effort to visit."

To give gifts to others seemed such a selfless way to raise children to appreciate what they have and to remember those who are the have nots in society. It further underscored how differently he and the twins were raised in King Manor. Their birthday parties were catered, seven-course, sit down events. Gifts were never opened during the dinner. Instead, they were opened after the guests left, and certain gifts were discarded as unworthy or unacceptable. Those gifts went into the trash rather than be donated to worthy causes.

As he looked around, he knew that wouldn't happen here in this family. They respected people and themselves. He didn't realize that his heart could break a little over how life already robbed Sammy of a warm and loving existence. His mother wanted nothing to do with him. His father was constantly on the road playing in tournaments. The rest of his immediate family was benignly absent and emotionally unavailable. Yet, as he watched the smile bloom on his nephew's face, he hoped that his future going forward would not be as desolate as it had been.

"Water?" Samantha offered to Samuel and Quentin.

"Thank you," they both spoke, accepting the bottles she held out to them.

Then she settled on the bleacher beside Quentin to watch the activities.

Leaning forward to get her attention and pointing across the gym, Samuel asked, "Sam, —-, uh, I mean, Samantha, who are the children teaching Sammy to play basketball? The taller one is very skillful."

Hearing Samuel call her "Sam" brought back an instant flashback from their youth, but she shifted her focus in the direction of Samuel's son. "They are Dr. and Mrs. Phillips' children."

He smiled. "Wow, I remember Dr. Phillips. He and your father used to play basketball on a hospital team, uh, what was the name?" He snapped his fingers.

"The Body Snatchers."

"Yeah! That's it! It's a mixed team, right? Both men and women played on the team."

"You're right, yes. Dr. Phillips and his wife, Denise Harris, a charge nurse, used to play with other hospital personnel on the team."

"'Used to?' Don't they play with the team now?"

"Uh, no. Dr. and Mrs. Phillips were killed in Indonesia during a tsunami. They were working in one of the hospitals when the tsunami hit. The building collapsed, killing most of the medical personnel. The Phillips had six children, stairsteps all. Raymond Phillips Jr. is the oldest. He was nine at the time. The children were in school in a location miles from the devastation, but the earthquake damaged the school, too.

"My dad was among the first American contingent of medical doctors and nurses to reach the affected region. He arranged to bring all of the American children and the bodies of the American medical workers home for burial. My parents were already godparents to the Phillips children. They had spent the summer before the tragedy here at the ranch for two weeks. Although they had some other relatives, none wanted to take on the responsibility of raising six children. Dad and Mom didn't want them separated, so they and four other American children who lost their parents at the same time suffered similar fates. They, too, were essentially orphans. So, our family grew by ten, seemingly overnight."

She didn't mention that her father, Chuck, used to date Denise Harris before she married Dr. Phillips and her dad married her mom. So, Chuck had a particular affinity toward Denise and her children, as did her mom. Samantha remembered that they were all close friends back in the day. That's why her parents were asked to be the Phillips' children's godparents.

Another act of selflessness, thought Quentin, as he listened to Samantha and Samuel converse until bells chimed. "What's that?"

"Thirty-minute warning." Samuel laughed. "Some things never change. Thank God."

Samantha nodded and stood. "Breakfast will be served in the breakfast room shortly, and everyone is expected to be on time."

"Okay, I presume that the breakfast room is different than the lunch or dinner areas?"

"You're right. After I shower, I'll show you the way." Samuel climbed down the bleacher and waved to get his son's attention.

As he looked around, Quentin noted that everyone stopped whatever they were doing, put away the balls or other equipment, and headed for the doors on either end of the gym. Samuel followed

Sammy while he and Samantha took the stairs to the upper floors. She peeled off on the second floor while he continued to the third.

Paulette was just coming out of her door when he approached his suite. "Good morning. You decided to sleep in?"

She yawned. "I did, yes. After the movie last night, Samantha and I went back to her studio for a few hours."

His brows beetled. "Studio?"

She nodded. "Samantha has a studio on the lower level where she designs textiles for her collections. It's a big space with a high ceiling and lots of shelves. She has fabrics she collects from countries around the world. She shared some of what she's done with me and agreed to let me work with her on new projects. I'll tell you more about it, but I volunteered to help set up this morning for breakfast, and I don't want to be late. I'll see you later?"

"Yes, I'll be down after I shower and shave."

She waved and was gone hurrying down the stairs.

He shook his head and entered the suite to the sound of his ringing cellphone. He looked at the display and decided to let this call from his parents go to voicemail…again.

CHAPTER 14

"I'm glad to hear that you made it safely to Texas, Glen." Samantha wandered around her studio, talking on her cellphone and shelving fabrics according to her strictly ordered cataloging system. She knew that without it, she would lose sight of where she kept certain fabrics.

"We did, yes. I see that the storm system still has you housebound." Glen Kennard sat bare chested on attractive outdoor terrace furniture. He was at his lakeside, double garage two-level townhome in Dallas not far from the airport with his bare feet on an adjacent hassock. The terrace, which overlooked the lake and parts of the city beyond, had warm sunlight and a light breeze bathing his toned body.

"Not likely. I think my siblings are gearing up to do some cross-country skiing."

"You're not going to join them?"

"Remember what happened when I tried to stay out and ski for hours while we were in Italy? I had what looked like freezer burn all over my face, and I had a show to do in two days."

Glen's laugh was hardy. "Yes, you were not quite ready for prime time. However, practice makes perfect."

"Yes, but I don't have to be perfect. I just have to stay warm and keep my face camera-ready for when I do interviews. I haven't been able to arrange to have a facial. My blood isn't thick enough yet to battle the cold. I'm going to spend time laughing at my sibs when Roger and Ryan show the video of their misadventures this afternoon. I'll set up the hot chocolate for when they finish freezing their faces off. It's below twenty degrees here. I hear it's seventy degrees where you are."

"Seventy-three and no humidity." He laughed. "I just got back from a five-mile run. I'm on my terrace soaking up the sun and having a breakfast frappé. I'll have a tan in no time."

"That's just mean, Glen," she feigned cruelty.

He laughed again. "You're welcome to join me."

"If I could get out of the house here, I just might take you up on that." She laughed and then realized in an instant how provocative that might have sounded.

"If I weren't on mandatory downtime, I might just fly up there and bring you back here."

"Another time, perhaps. I need you to be safe for when I start my next tour." She also needed to be careful here because she wasn't sure what might have developed between them. "I spoke with my uncle Gregory. He's agreed to let me have my same team for the next tour."

"Yes, I saw the orders come through, allowing me to block out the time once you've locked down the dates. If you prefer the same jet, I'll schedule it for the tour or at least one like it. AEA is adding new jets to its fleet. We can schedule one that's right off the assembly line for your exclusive use. By the way, I'm scheduled to fly one of the new jets on a triangle route from here to Miami. It will put me in New York City for four days, three nights just before Christmas. Any chance you'll be in the area around then?"

"I'm not sure what my plans will be, but I do have a request to dress one of the windows at the McCoy Department Store in Times Square. I should be in the city for five to seven days after Thanksgiving, around the first week of December. That might work if our stars align," she joked. "My family will gather in Monroe County, Pennsylvania, for the Christmas holiday. We usually spend New Years' Eve here in Maryland because my parents always have a New Year's Eve party."

"When you have time to check your calendar, will you let me know?"

She stopped wandering the studio and leaned her butt against a table, legs crossed at the ankle, and with her arms across her breasts. "Glen—" she began.

"No pressure, Samantha. Separate rooms, if you like," he interrupted. "I thought we might do some sightseeing, have a few dinners, and see a show or two on Broadway."

"I, uh. That sounds lovely…"

"Do I hear a but?"

"I'm not sure, Glen. Can we table this discussion until I have time to sort it out?"

"We can, yes. I'll let you go for now, but not forever."

Though he could not see her, she closed her eyes and nodded. "Be safe. We'll talk again soon."

"Okay, I'll look forward to hearing from you when you know your plans. Goodbye for now."

"Goodbye, Glen." Samantha stood in contemplation for a humming moment before she pulled the headset away and turned to place it on the table. She was brought up short when she noticed Quentin leaning against her open door with his hands in the pockets of his jeans. "I, uh, didn't hear you come in."

Steadily he looked into her eyes as he approached her. Taking her into his arms, he kissed her mouth and then slowly let her go until they were only a breath away. "You were on the phone, and I didn't want to interrupt you."

She looked up into his eyes. "It wasn't a business call. I was speaking with Glen Kennard."

"Yes, your pilot. I overheard a part of your conversation. You had it on speaker. I understood you told Paulette that you weren't dating. Has that changed?"

She shrugged. "It's not clear at this point. However, it's not a topic I want to discuss."

He nodded. "Understood, but I'll say one more thing before I leave the topic. I'm interested in having a relationship with you,

Samantha, an exclusive relationship. You've, apparently, had months to get to know your pilot. I'd like to take advantage of the time between now and your potential date with him for you to get to know me."

"I'm not opposed to that, Quentin, but unlike before, when I was a youngster, I don't know you well enough to decide whether I should commit to something exclusive."

"I intend to leave no doubt in your mind about what my feelings are and what we could have. After this initial period, I trust that we'll have all the time in the world to become reacquainted."

"This isn't some type of sibling rivalry, is it? I mean, some type of competition between you and Samuel?"

Frowning, Quentin shook his head and, hiking a hip up, sat on the table, facing her at eye level. "Is that what you think?"

"It's crossed my mind."

He took her hands in his, drawing her closer between his open legs and kissing her mouth. He looked directly into her eyes. "Dismiss the thought. Admittedly, I've been interested in having a relationship with you for many years, but initially, you were too young, and my brother was crazy about you."

"However, your parents weren't...crazy about me, I mean. At least, not in a good way. I don't imagine that their feelings toward me have changed."

"That's true, but I didn't then, and I don't now allow my parents to dictate who I choose as friends or who I choose to date."

"If we do decide to become more than friends, you'll learn that I do invite my parents, grandparents, siblings, aunts, uncles, and cousins into decisions in my life. They are my best friends and never fail to have my best interests at heart. They don't make the choices, but I value their opinions."

"I understand. I've always suspected that you're a very closely-knit family. I can only hope that you'll give a relationship with me a chance to develop without the emotional baggage from the past."

"I can do that, Quentin, but I won't put my heart at risk. I know how a broken heart feels, and I don't relish the idea of going through that experience again. I also don't do multiple partners."

"That's good to know. I can pledge fidelity in the relationship, too. I don't have the time or inclination to date multiple women at the same time."

"However, you are in a relationship now."

He nodded and gently squeezed her hands. "Yes, but, as I said before, it's not one that I intended to lead to marriage. It was more of a business-related liaison, but, yes, it included sex. Nevertheless, I will clear that up once I get back to town and on schedule."

"Until then, let's table the relationship discussion."

"Reluctantly, I'll agree for now. I would like to pick this up again in a week or so."

"Agreed. Now, were you looking for me or just exploring?"

He looked up and around the well-appointed studio before he released her hands and stood. "A little of both. There are a warren of interesting rooms and spaces in your home. Paulette mentioned that your studio was on this level. I've been wandering around. I passed the theatre room and the music room and just kept going. However, I didn't imagine that this space was so large. That's what, a ten or twelve-foot ceiling?"

She looked up, too, and frowned. "I guess it's taller. Those carpets and canvases hanging from the ceiling rack against the wall are all twelve feet by nine feet."

He walked toward them and began shifting them apart to look at the designs. "You created these?"

She nodded as she leaned against a table and watched him go from carpet to carpet and canvas to canvas, which hung back-to-back on individual racks. "I did, yes. Some were done in the early years after college and then grad school. Others are more recent."

He briefly looked at her over his shoulder and then continued to study her work. "You're very creative. Each one is uniquely different.

This one looks like an abstract of the Golden Gate Bridge in San Francisco."

She smiled. "That's where the inspiration came from, which led me to create wall-sized murals like this one." She moved aside several rugs to reveal what looked like a painting but was actually made of many fabrics like a quilt, but not entirely. Tiny penlights lit at strategic points in the mural, making the Golden Gate Bridge seem to come to life in a nighttime scene. Miniscule car headlights and taillights made it appear that cars were crossing the bridge. "This is a gift for my uncle Kenneth and Aunt JeNelle for their next wedding anniversary. This view is from Scoma's, a restaurant they love in Sausalito." She moved to turn off the overhead lights to see the full effect of the lit cloth mural.

"It's hypnotic," Quentin moved the other rugs and canvases further away and then stood back to appreciate the work. "You're referring to your aunt, who is the junior senator from California, right?"

"Yes. Aunt JeNelle is serving her third term. She and my uncle have homes in Marin County, and Santa Barbara, California, and Goodwill, Summer County, South Carolina. There is a space on one of their walls in Goodwill, where I think this mural will fit nicely. They built a California ranch-style home with ultra-high ceilings there many years ago. They've asked me to help them and their nine children to redecorate it."

"This is a statement piece that doesn't need anything to compete with it."

Samantha turned on the ceiling lights again, surprised at Quentin's insight. He was exactly right about the canvas. It was a standalone piece and would be a focal point. It would also inform the rest of the interior décor.

He moved on to other pieces she had hanging and stopped at one that appeared to be race cars on a track. "This is unusual," he commented.

"Uh, the inspiration for this came from watching Adam Hawkins race his cars at the Grand Prix in France last year. It was an attempt to capture the speed of the cars on the track. They moved so fast that they seemed to blur. That's why I did this in a kind of streaking watercolor but using primary colors. It's unfinished. I had to put it aside when I left on tour. I'll pick it up again when time permits. There is no hurry to finish it. It's just an inspiration piece."

Quentin couldn't take his eyes away from the mural. "I'd like to buy it from you exactly as it is now."

"Really?" She frowned, surprised again at what interested him.

"Yes. I'd appreciate it if you'd autograph it for me."

She shrugged negligibly. "I can do that. I can also have it stretched over a frame and delivered to your home."

"I'd appreciate that, too, but hold off on the frame and delivery. The frame should fit the décor. I'll give you an address in a week or so."

Surprised again, Samantha shrugged. "I never would have imagined that you're into abstracts."

He turned to smile at her. "That's only the beginning of what I hope you'll be willing to learn about me. Tell me, do you also do interior design?"

"I have, but it's not my strong suit. More often, I do interior decorating. As you're probably aware, that's an entirely different skill set. I'm not into taking down walls or designing closet systems. Why do you ask?"

"I have a project in mind; actually, a few of them. However, based on what I've seen here, there are several pieces I think will fit into my plans."

"Sure, but understand that this is my design studio. The manufacturing arm of my operation is in Summer County, South Carolina. I usually do only one-of-a-kind designs. However, my new collection of linens and towels will be mass-produced."

"That'll work for me. Do you mind if I keep browsing?"

"No, go ahead. Let me know whether you see anything else you want. I'll put a hold on it for you."

He grinned at her. It surprised her to see that expression on his face and the gleam in his eyes.

"Yeah, no, I walked right into that one, didn't I?"

"You did, yes. However, I'm not letting you off the hook, Samantha."

She had a feeling he meant those words sincerely. He wanted her, and she wondered whether the emotion would be mutual.

CHAPTER 15

The next day, after noon, Samantha knocked on Quentin's door. When he answered, he was talking on his cellphone and motioned her inside. She rolled in a cart and positioned it beside the round table by the French doors, which led to the snow-covered balcony. When she started to leave, he stopped her but continued his conversation.

"Yes, that's correct. Jamerson is out with the flu. Filmore will pick up the Clairmont account for you. Yes, my best to your wife and new baby. We'll see you back in the office at the end of your paternity leave. We will talk more if the need arises, but I believe, for now, all of your accounts are covered. Goodbye." He clicked off the phone, closed his eyes for a brief moment, and just breathed. "Something smells great. What did you bring for me?"

"A little of this and a bit of that. You didn't make it down for breakfast or lunch, so I brought a combination of the two meals for you to select from."

"Thank you. I am hungry, but I had so many calls and text messages to return that I couldn't break away." Just as he said it, his phone chimed again. He looked at the readout—his parents again, he noted—and sent the call to voicemail. When his laptop beeped, he shut that down, too. He held a chair for her to sit with him. He held a chair for her to sit with him before taking a seat on the opposite side of the round table. "I did get in a swim early this morning. I had a snack with your brothers after my swim. Vincent said that you were on Patrick patrol this morning for breakfast. I hope you'll join me for lunch." He opened the dome-covered tray of foods and, smiling, dug in, enjoying each morsel.

She shook her head. "Yes, I claimed my sister's rights this morning and won Patrick's company away from my parents. So, I've already had breakfast and lunch with the posse." She looked at her watch. "I'm meeting Paulette in my studio shortly."

He nodded. "Yes, she stopped by earlier before lunch to tell me that she was going skiing again with your brothers and sisters. Did they make it back already?"

He continued to eat while Samantha opened a carafe of wine and poured it for him.

"Yes, they're back. They didn't go far and were out for only about three hours. The snow has finally stopped, but it's frigid out. My sibs went skating on the pond that's in front of the house. They had a great time, but they were freezing when they came in for lunch."

He hadn't noticed that the snow had stopped and turned his head to look out of the balcony doors. "No school today?"

"Change in rotation. School's out for two weeks. This early snowstorm will keep my siblings in the area. Usually, my parents or the teens make plans for their school breaks, but with the birthday weekend coming up and this snow event, they've had to alter their plans."

"I have the impression that your siblings are not idle for long periods. What will they do now that they're out of school for a while?"

"That depends. Usually, between rotations, Dad and Mom would have planned for us all to visit a foreign country or two for the two weeks. However, because Mom is pregnant, Dad doesn't want her to take long trips. Plus, Mom has a hectic court schedule. The court just started on the first Monday in October. Dad has an excessive number of conjoined twins at his hospital to see to and your brother's procedure. So, if the posse can manage to get up to Monroe County, Pennsylvania, most will spend a couple of weeks with our grandparents, Stephen and Harriet Jackson Montgomery. They'll go downhill and cross-country skiing with the Montgomery uncles, aunts, and cousins. There's plenty of snow for both in the Poconos and bigger lakes where they can ice skate. Linda promised to teach her two boys and the younger sibs to skate.

"Some may decide to visit our other grandparents, Bernard and Sylvia Benson Alexander, in Summer County, South Carolina. There they can ride horses and, if it's warm enough, they'll find plenty of outdoor activities. The Oktoberfest should be going on there this time of the year. We have scads of family members in that area, too. All of the school-aged kids in Summer County are on the same educational system schedule at Summer County Academy as my sibs are here. The dean of the school in South Carolina is Dr. Jefferson Logan."

"The diplomat emeritus? He and his second wife, the heiress, LaiLoni Skai Hawkins, were prominently discussed in the international news and financial media while we were in Europe."

She nodded. "Yes, I know. Dr. Logan's former father-in-law, Tyler Montrose, recently died in prison. Dr. Logan's eldest son, Jefferson Junior, who is my age now, inherits the rest of his maternal grandfather's entire Montrose fortune. When he was a preteen, he inherited the first half of Montrose Global when his biological mother died in a car accident."

"'Car accident?' That's putting it diplomatically." He snorted a laugh. "As I recall, she was high on drugs and riding nude on the hood of a Stutz Bearcat sports car in the Georgetown section of Washington, D.C. She fell off the hood, hit her head, and the man driving the car, who was also high, didn't notice until he ran over her body."

"Well, yeah, there was that." Samantha shrugged. "However, Jeff Junior and his brothers, Miles and Steven, are close family friends. So, we don't purposefully talk about hurtful events from the past."

"You're better people than my parents. They used that incident to support their premise that nothing good comes from a black man with the stature of Ambassador Logan, marrying a white woman, like Felicia Montrose. They see him as a traitor to the race. That is to perpetuate the negative connotation that he was bought, like a slave at auction, for his stud fee. His wife was one of the wealthiest women in the world at the time of her death."

Finished with his meal, Quentin relaxed, enjoying the last of the wine and Samantha's company.

"As I understand it, she was bipolar, which had nothing to do with her skin color. According to my parents, Ambassador Logan and Felicia Montrose met in college at Harvard and began dating. They had an unguarded moment, she became pregnant, and he did the honorable thing. He didn't marry Felicia Montrose because she was white or because she was wealthy, but to be a responsible father and give his son his name." Samantha huffed, incensed. "I consider Jeff Jr., Miles, and Steven among my closest friends. Despite their wealth, they're good people. So are their parents and younger siblings.

"Dr. Logan is responsible for many acts of bravery in war-torn countries. He brokered many peace agreements and settled long-term disputes in the Middle East and African countries. He is celebrated, particularly for saving and sheltering twenty young African girls from being forced into becoming child brides or sold into the sex trade. Those girls' prominent families were slaughtered in Africa. They flourished here and have grown up to be fine teens and young adults."

Quentin nodded. "I agree, Dr. Logan is a fine example of the type of diplomat we need representing this country. Unlike my parents, I don't consider it any of my business who Dr. Logan chooses to marry. I'm just surprised that he's the dean of a school instead of the Secretary of State. His profile seems much larger than his role as an educator. I didn't realize that he left the diplomatic corps."

"Actually, he still keeps his hand in international events, but he does so on a much lower profile. In addition to his three sons with his former wife, he has four tender age girls; two he fathered with LaiLoni Skai, and two he rescued from Africa. So, he and his wife travel much less than they did before. I usually see the Logan family when I go to visit my grands in Summer County for Juneteenth."

"His wife is an Indigenous American, right?"

"Half Navajo and half American of African descent, yes."

"If my memory is correct, one of her brothers is Adam Hawkins, a Formula One race car driver. Is that how you know him?"

"Actually, I met Adam through his other sister, JaiHonnah Hawkins Baylor. JaiHonnah and my mom were in undergrad together at Spelman College. Adam used to visit the campus a lot because he had a crush on my mom. Roderick or JRock, as he was known in his stellar days on the basketball court, and both of my fathers, Derrick and Chuck, were close friends. They played together on the Olympic teams. Derrick introduced Mom to Roderick, and they became close friends and business associates, too. Later, when Mom was still a practicing attorney, he and his company were among Mom's first corporate clients. She represented J. Roderick Baylor and Baylor Design and Development in the early days of his company. When JRock was looking for an architect and engineer for Baylor Design and Development, Mom suggested that he hire JaiHonnah. She introduced JRock to JaiHonnah, who had studied architecture and engineering at one of the most prestigious schools in Italy, earning her doctorate in both disciplines. JaiHonnah returned to the states to work for JRock.

"Then, as they say, ball game. JRock and JaiHonnah fell in love and were married a few years later. Adam used to come to visit JaiHonnah, and because he was still crushing on Mom, we got to see him. Adam and JRock stuck to us like glue, particularly after Dad died, and they helped us through that tough time.

"If I'm near where Adam is racing, I make a point of going to observe. He's like another uncle to us, just like he is to JRock and JaiHonnah's children. We all grew up together. I saw much of the Grand Prix, and that inspired this mural." She laughed. "However, every year JaiHonnah and her family, friends of my mom's from Chicago, Nico and Tina Justice Collins, and our family compete in a regatta in South America. They sail the *OUTLAW JUSTICE*. JaiHonnah and her family sail the *NAVAJO PRINCESS*. Dad and

Mom commissioned a new, larger sailing ship, *HOOP DREAMS*, because our family has grown. However, we still have *THE VIVIAN LYNN*. That's the yacht my first dad, Derrick, named for Mom. Adam joins us when we get into the Gulf of Mexico near Texas. He sailed the *SKAI HAWK* and came in second last year in America's Cup Regatta in Buenos Aires, Argentina.

"You didn't ask for all of that history, but," she shrugged. "There it is. Members of the Logan-Hawkins family are very close to our family."

"You're passionate about people, particularly close family friends. It helps me to know you better. You've traveled extensively, something I haven't done as much as I'd like to. I'm enjoying seeing the world through your eyes, though. I imagine you speak several languages."

"Not fluently, no." She shrugged. "As I said, my parents would take us to other countries on vacations three or more times a year. Months in advance of each trip, we had to learn things about the country we were going to visit. Things like its climate, culture, cuisine, customs, and some of its phrases. Some we absolutely had to know were: 'it's a pleasure to meet you' or 'how do you do, my name is ...' or my personal favorite, 'where is the closest restroom.' I can probably say those phrases in twelve different languages. My sister, Geneviève, however, is the linguist in the family. She is a former Coast Guard Officer and can curse like a sailor in any language." Samantha laughed, and Quentin smiled. "I usually don't have to use a lot of foul language to get my point across. So, I use the app on my phone that translates spoken English into whatever language is necessary. When the person speaks, the app translates it into English for me."

"I could have used an app like that while I was in Europe. I had to depend on interpreters. Where did you get the app?"

"My uncle Kenneth's company, CompuCorrect, created it. It's standard on all of the telephone equipment he manufactures."

"Ah, another Silicon Valley company."

"Yes, how did you know?"

"In the advertising industry, there is a list of the top one hundred companies it would be considered a coup to sign. Your uncle's company is on that list. Some of my sales staff have gone after contracts with CompuCorrect. However, the company has its own internal advertising and marketing department, which is headed by one of your uncle's business partners, Tom Jenkins. They don't outsource their sales and marketing functions."

"My uncle believes that they have better control of the messaging if it's generated from within the company by someone who has skin in the game."

"He's right. However, his company is still considered a premier account for anyone successful enough to get it."

"Ha!" she laughed. "My cousin, Kevin Alexander, is working his way from the ground up through the sales and marketing department. His twin, Kenny, is working his way through the engineering and innovation side of the company. They are Uncle Kenneth and Aunt JeNelle's oldest children, a year or so older than me. The next set of twins, Justin and Jerritt, are right behind them, working on the business model. So, the company will likely keep a lot of their business practices in-house for at least the next few generations." She looked at her watch and rose from her seat. "I've kept you from your work long enough. If you're finished with your meal, I'll take the cart back to the kitchen on my way to meet your sister in my studio."

He rose as well, stepped around the cart, took Samantha in his arms, and kissed her. With his forehead pressed to hers, he closed his eyes and just breathed her in. "Thank you. Please, interrupt my work anytime you're free. I enjoy relaxing with you. That's never happened to me before. These new counted joys spending time with you are adding up."

She gave him a little squeeze before stepping back. "Next time, maybe we'll find less heady subjects to discuss."

"I'm just glad that there will be a next time."

She smiled and left. However, she thought, *If he is still involved with another woman, there may not be another 'next time' for us that includes his addictive kisses.*

"Is everything all right, Samantha?"

Samantha snapped out of her malaise and turned to answer Paulette's question. "Yes, sorry. I'm fine. I'm just a little distracted."

"I should say. Your phone has been vibrating on the table for a while now."

"Really?" With her brows beetled, she unearthed the phone from beneath a bundle of cloths and ran through several missed calls and text messages. She stopped on one and immediately returned the call. "Hi, Uncle Bill. I apologize. I missed your call."

"I'm glad that you called me. My office has been inundated with calls from groups who want you to give lectures and exhibit during your next tour. Here are a few of them: Tier & Technik, St. Gallen, Switzerland; Fabric Show Gent, Antwerp, Belgium; Bielefeld Fabric Market, Bielefeld, Germany; Quilt Craft & Sewing Festival, Pomona, California; R & T Asia, Shanghai, China; Fabric Spectacle, Luxembourg, Germany; Kassel Fabric Market, Kassel, Germany; Fashionista, Aurangabad, India; Tribal & Textile Art Show, San Francisco, California; Fabric Show, Barneveld, Netherlands; and Tex Style Expo, Chéraga, Algeria.

"There are more coming in every day, but these are the biggest ones who want to get in an early bid on your participation. So far, these are also the ones that seem possible to fit into your next tour. Their proposed contracts all have the same inducements; a full ride on transportation and accommodations, your required speaking fee, and prime display spots on the exhibit floor. It's pretty much what was offered for your last tour with higher signing bonuses."

"I definitely want to do the ones in Germany. Hopefully, I can work in some time to spend with my cousin Whitney and her husband, Tucker, in Landstuhl. I also wanted to spend more time in Africa and South America, maybe Australia, too. I've received samples from textile companies in those countries, which may inform my collection two years from now."

"Okay, Germany is definitely doable. I'll have my staff look for opportunities in those other countries. I'll submit the possible choices for vetting and security checks and reviews. I saw the notice from Gregory about your travel team. I'll copy Glen Kennard on the schedule as it develops."

"Thanks, Uncle Bill."

"You're welcome, babe. Look for more email shortly, but don't work so hard. Remember, this is your rest and recuperation period. If you decide to include even half of these engagements on your next tour, it will be more grueling than the last one."

"Okay, I'll take it easy, Uncle Bill. *Ciao.*"

"*Ciao.*"

"Wow, that's awesome." Paulette came to sit beside Samantha. "I didn't know that Bill Chandler is your agent. He is so delicious. I still have pictures of him from when he lived in your home in Georgetown and was one of your mother's law partners."

"Yes, he's my agent and my attorney. He also still lives at the house in Georgetown when he's in the area, but he travels so much that he's barely around. He also produces movies and stars in some. In his last movie, *The Golden Guys*, he used some of my fabrics in the shots." She laughed. "I got new business just from that product placement in Bill's bedroom scenes."

"Anything to do with Bill Chandler and a bedroom will get a lot of notice." Paulette fanned herself dramatically. "Your next tour schedule seems to be filling up fast."

"It does seem that way, yes. The problem is trying to avoid flying back and forth between the U.S. and other countries. If we can work the schedule to make equitable stops and hops along a reasonable route, then it all works. I usually start in the U.S. to hit the trade shows and then move west and end in a European country—"

"Like Spain," Paulette interjected.

Samantha smiled and nodded. "Yes, like Spain. Then it's not so hard on my pilots and steward. Most places have handlers who help with the setup and takedown for my exhibits, but Glen and his crew knew my equipment and how I liked it set up. They were my right and left hand everywhere we went and managed to keep me fed and on schedule, too."

"Well, they do get paid for their service."

"They do, yes, but they do a lot of extra without asking for or expecting compensation. For them, it's not about the money. Still, I make sure that their bonuses reflect my appreciation. We have a lot of fun together and enjoy each other's company. That's why I've asked for the same team to be my escorts for my spring and fall tours."

"That hunky pilot would be my sole purpose for making the trip."

Samantha laughed. "Yes, Glen is a woman's fantasy, but he's not just good looks and a great body. He's a fascinating man with a great sense of humor. He's wicked smart, too."

"You like him, don't you?"

Samantha nodded. "I do, yes. Don't you have someone special in your life?"

"Other than your brothers Roger and Ryan, uh no," she joked. "I've dated men I've met professionally, but my parents never seemed to approve of the ones I liked. They parade their friends' sons in front of me, just as they do when they parade women before Quentin. Women seem to latch onto Quentin, but he doesn't latch onto them. This most recent woman thinks she's going to be his bride in the next few months. Boy, does she have a rude awakening coming?"

"Really? Why would you say that?"

"Because I've never known Quentin to be interested in any woman as much as he seems to be attracted to you. He's on every eligible bachelor list, but my brother is not the type of man who is out and about often and continuously. The majority of his time is spent working to continue the King Advertising legacy. I wouldn't call him a social misfit. He just doesn't pay a lot of attention to women in his sphere. He never has, but around you, he seems different. He actually lights up when I've noticed him talking with you. Believe me, that hasn't happened with any other woman he has been with. I think you're stacking up to be a very important element in his life."

Counted joys, he called it, Samantha remembered. *That is a warm and wonderful way to feel about someone as if time spent together is counted as joyful. It is the way she felt about the little cards her mother made for her every day and gave it to her while she was hospitalized as a child.*

CHAPTER 16

No sooner had Quentin entered King Manor than the vitriol began. He hadn't even gotten his coat off and handed it over to Mr. Casey, the house servant, before his parents started their harangue.

"Exactly, where are your brother and sister?" demanded his father, Quentin IV.

"Can we not stand here in the vestibule for this discussion?"

With a quick look at Mr. Casey, hovering nearby, his parents turned on their heels and headed down a long, wide hallway. Larger-than-life portraits of ancestors hung high on the African grass cloth-covered wall with wainscoting made of polished African Ipe wood along the bottom. They turned into the double-door library where books were shelved nearly to the domed ceiling and wrapped with kente-cloth covers. The hardwood floor was spotted with African weaved mats and colorfully covered seating. Even the painting over the fireplace and figurines on the mantle were Africa-inspired.

Quentin had lived with the décor for so long that he failed to notice it anymore. After being in the Alexander-Montgomery household for nearly five days, coming into his home of more than thirty years seemed somehow incongruent. Yes, Samantha's home celebrated multiculturalism, but it didn't ascribe to a single focus. There was a natural flow carried on throughout each common area of the Alex-Mont mansion. Still, he discovered on his wanderings that each space was unique. No matter the interior décor or venue, the mansion inspired a warm and comfortable vibe,

He hadn't bothered to identify his own tastes, even in his wing of the manor house. Now, as he studied the library, he realized that despite its relationship to generations of his heritage, it didn't suit his taste in the least. Still, he had more heady issues to contend with.

"Junior! You haven't answered me!" his father thundered. "Where are the twins?"

"They decided to stay in Maryland. Tomorrow morning, Samuel will undergo a surgical procedure at Physicians Hospital, which, if successful, may delay the advance of his osteoporosis and strengthen his skeletal structure. Paulette decided to stay with him to take care of Sammy."

"Nonsense!" Ashante, their mother declared. "There is no reason for Samuel to submit to any medical procedure other than what is prescribed by his doctor, Perry Harrison, at Howard University Hospital. He's looked after this family since you were a boy. I demand that Samuel and Paulette should come home this instant and bring my grandchild with them," her voice shrilled.

"That's not going to happen, Mother. You may be the dean of the Student Affairs Department at Howard, but you're not a medical professional. Dr. Harrison is your colleague, but he is in his eighties. He doesn't keep up with medical science as it's practiced today."

"He has taught medicine at Howard since I was a student there, and he has a whole staff of doctors on his service."

"Since I had business abroad, I accompanied Sam to Europe before his tournament to see the specialists in Switzerland. They didn't hold out much hope of a treatment. Sam needs specialized medical treatment, which Dr. Harrison doesn't offer, and his students and doctors aren't familiar with what he needs. I should know because I called them to discuss this procedure. They hadn't even heard of it. Several of the doctors and students wanted to observe the surgery. With Sam's permission, Dr. Montgomery agreed."

"Montgomery? Who is—? You don't mean that white man, do you? The one from the Ozarks or whatever, do you?"

"Dr. Charles Patrick Montgomery is the current owner and head of Physicians Hospital and the former chief of emergency medicine at Georgetown Medical Center. He was born and grew up in Monroe County, Pennsylvania. Not the Ozarks. I checked with other medical professionals I went to school with and know personally. They are frat brothers of mine, and all were aware of the procedure. Each and every one of them holds Dr. Montgomery in high esteem."

"Georgetown? Haven't your mother and I taught you about the Jesuit Priests who once owned that hospital and enslaved our African people?"

"Yes, Father, I'm fully aware of this hospital's history. However, Dr. Montgomery didn't work for the hospital when that atrocity occurred."

"Don't be flippant with me, young man!" Ashante demanded. "Your generation is too liberal and willing to forgive and forget. That's unacceptable behavior from you, and I will not tolerate it in this house! You've been obstinate for far too long!"

"I have not forgotten what our people have suffered. I'm mindful every day of what we are striving to overcome and to achieve. Don't mistake my tolerance for blindness to this country's ills. However, you're right, Mother. You don't have to tolerate anything from me. That's why I've decided to move out."

"What?" his father demanded while his mother went silent with shock.

"I should have done this years ago, but better late than sorry. A van should arrive shortly to pack and remove Samuel's, Paulette's, Sammy's, and my personal property. Once I'm settled, I'll provide my new address. The twins and Sammy will be living with me. When Samuel is sufficiently recovered, he and Paulette plan to leave the area. If you want to see him before the surgery, you know where to find him. If not, I believe either Samuel or Paulette will let you know—"

A knock on the library door interrupted their conversation.

"Yes? What is it?" Ashante demanded.

Mr. Casey cautiously opened the door and announced that there is a truck at the front gate requesting permission to enter.

"Do not let them in! Their services are not needed here! Send them away!"

"Mother." Quentin exhaled a frustrated breath before turning to the manservant. "Thank you, Mr. Casey. They are here at my request. Please admit them to the property, and I'll be there in a moment to show them to the rooms above stairs."

Seemingly confused or unsure of his ground, Mr. Casey looked to his employers for any counter instructions, before saying, "As you please, sir," and backing out of the door and closing it firmly behind him.

Quentin waited a beat before he turned back to his parents. Before he could speak, his mother's voice rang with censure.

"That Vivian Alexander woman has something to do with this, doesn't she?" Ashante stormed.

"No, Mother, Judge Montgomery has nothing whatsoever to do with our decision to leave home. We're all adults and over the age of twenty-one. It's long overdue that we move out on our own."

"Then perhaps it's time for you to leave the firm, too!" Quentin IV sniped.

"That's your call as chairperson of King Advertising's board of directors. However, as you're aware, I was voted into the position unanimously by the full board. You can call an emergency board meeting to discuss my position. However, I am not planning to leave the position as president of the company and a member of the board. Nor am I planning to leave this family unless you force me into it. That is also your call."

With one last look of regret at his parents, Quentin left the library and closed the door on his past and uncertain future. However, his steps were somehow lighter. He directed the moving men to where they would begin packing his siblings', Sammy's, and his clothes, shoes, and other personal items.

Quentin stood three hours later in the midst of a four-bedroom, four-and-a-half-bath, furnished, single-level condo in the Watergate

Hotel and Condo building. The iconic building overlooking the Potomac River in downtown Washington, D.C., was made famous by the major federal political scandal involving the administration of President Richard Nixon that resulted in the end of his presidency. The scandal reminded Quentin again why he didn't want to bring King Advertising into the political arena on any level.

It had been less than three days since he tasked his administrative assistant, Ms. Carmen, to find accommodations for him and his siblings. She was superefficient, asked no inane questions about moving out of King Manor, but got the job done in record time. When she met him at the concierge desk, while the moving van waited, she and the Watergate manager took him on a tour of the Kingbird restaurant, where views of the Potomac River surrounded the lively bar and elegant surroundings. The spacious and stylish brasserie had a festive setting. It was open daily for breakfast, lunch, and dinner. The menus featured seasonally-inspired Mediterranean cuisine with a French Riviera twist. On weekends, guests could enjoy brunch and afternoon tea. The Kennedy Center was right next door, convenient for times when he wanted stellar entertainment.

In the lobby, Quentin was drawn to the soft amber glow of The Next Whisky Bar, where he had occasionally met with clients and shared a meal. The Top of the Gate rooftop bar and lounge had unrivaled 360-degree panoramic views, with Georgetown's charming waterfront in one direction and the Washington Monument in the other. A crystal blue oasis awaited in five lap lanes and a dedicated aerobic area in the indoor pool on the lower level. The heated pool was available year-round. The wet area included the pool, sauna, and steam room. The fitness areas were outfitted as well as his private club. It wasn't quite as homey as the Alex-Mont lagoon, but nothing could be.

Still, when it came to residences in the Georgetown area of Washington, D.C., the Watergate Condo facility didn't disappoint.

Finally, they showed a seventh-floor condo to him. One walk-through was all it took to convince Quentin that this was the right move for now. The lease agreement was ready for his signature, a cashier's check was prepared to cover the first six months' rent, and the moving men placed the boxed clothes in the designated bedroom suites.

He had been standing at the balcony door with his hands in his pockets for some time. However, since the moving people and his executive assistant left, he had been doing nothing but thinking while staring into near space and ignoring his cell phone and laptop. He had not really observed the snowy scene outside or the world-famous Washington, D.C., buildings, architecture, and skyline visible from his condo. For the time being, he had his things arranged in the bedroom walk-around closet. He would tackle his siblings' and nephew's things next. It would help to prepare for the period to come during Samuel's convalescence. Until then, Paulette and Sammy would be guests of the Alexander-Montgomery family. With that issue behind them, they could decide what to do next.

Because of the snowstorm, schools weren't opened yet. Still, Sammy would be able to attend his school until the end of the fall term. Also, getting to and from the King Advertising offices for Paulette and him from this location would be convenient.

Walking away from the balcony doors, he moved toward the open-concept kitchen area. The cabinets, refrigerator, and walk-in pantry were empty, and it dawned on him that he didn't know where to begin with providing food. However, the building had twenty-four-seven concierge services. He hadn't eaten since breakfast and was about to call for a delivery when his phone chimed. When he checked the readout, he noted that it was Miranda calling. *Good*, he thought, *two birds, one stone,* as Samantha was fond of saying.

"Hello, Miranda. I'm glad you called. Are you free for a late lunch?"

"Yes, of course, Quentin, but what is this foolishness your parents have told me about you moving out of King Manor? Have you gone daft or something?"

"I'll explain over lunch. Would you meet me at this restaurant?" He rattled off the name and address.

"Yes, yes, all right!" she huffed testily. "I can be there in thirty minutes.

"That's fine. I'll see you shortly." He disconnected and heaved a breath of relief.

"What do you mean we shouldn't see each other socially anymore?" Miranda demanded so loudly that others in the restaurant turned and focused on them. The waiter, who had started in their direction likely to remove the dishes, did an awkwardly abrupt about-face and retraced the steps from which he had come.

"This relationship has been moving on a course I had not contemplated."

"That's not what you said before you went to Europe three weeks ago when you were in my bed between my open thighs!" She knotted her cloth napkin and slammed it down on the empty plate on the table before her. "I expected you to propose marriage to me today. Why isn't that going to happen?"

"I'm not in love with you, Miranda. I believe you know that. From the very beginning, we agreed that there would be no strings attached. You agreed and said that you only wanted to be friends with sexual benefits. You also needed a plus-one for certain events."

"Is that why I'm the one who always had to call you to arrange to get together? Because you were sticking to the rules we originally discussed? Didn't our sexual encounters change your mind? You didn't once say that you didn't want to see me. You spent very little time with me, but I thought it was because you're always so busy. I had to book you weeks in advance to go to an event. However, over the months, you never said no when I wanted to sleep with you. You led me to believe that we had a future together."

"If that's true, it wasn't my intention. Until my sister mentioned that you were expecting a marriage proposal, I continued to think that we were on the same track. Friends with occasional benefits."

Miranda sat back and crossed her arms tightly over her breasts, malevolently eyeing him. "What's really going on here, Quentin? You would not allow me to accompany you to Europe when I offered to go with you. Once you returned, you refused to take me to a planned event because you claimed you couldn't get there through the snow. Then you drop off the grid for nearly a week with no communication with your parents or me. Then, this morning, your parents call me in a lather to tell me that you abruptly moved your siblings' and your things out of King Manor. Your parents and mine have been putting together preliminary plans for our wedding, and now you tell me that we shouldn't see each other anymore? What's up with that?"

"I don't know how much more clear I can make this. All I can say is that I apologize for any misunderstanding. If you felt that our relationship had somehow changed from what we said it would be at the beginning, I wasn't aware of it."

She continued to scrutinize him before she leaned forward and braced her arms on the table. "Look, Quentin, if this is about the fact that I'm older than you or you're going through some type of mid-life crisis…" she halted a beat. "Why are you laughing?"

"I'm not that old, Miranda. I'm not even in my mid-thirties yet. I'm not having some type of out of body experience either. I'm making strategic changes in my life that suit my current needs."

She moved in closer and whispered, "I notice that you don't kiss me on my mouth. When we have sex, you may kiss my cheek, neck, or breasts, but you never go down on me. You give me only vanilla sex. Are you one of those brothers who is on the down-low?"

He burst out laughing again. "Uh, that's a definite no, Miranda. I'm not gay or bisexual. I want to sleep with only women. I have no inclination to be with a man. Sex has nothing to do with my decision to end our relationship."

Leaning back in her chair again, she frowned. "Then, I don't understand. My parents sit on the King Advertising board, and our parents have been good friends for years since they were in college together. We're compatible sexually, matched intellectually, and from financially comfortable backgrounds. What is it that you believe is missing from our union?"

"How about love, Miranda?"

"Love? What's love got to do with anything?"

"It has everything to do with what I want. I also want to marry a woman who wants to have a family."

"You mean children?"

"Yes, children are included in a family."

"You never mentioned wanting a child." She said the word child as if it were foul, her expression pinched.

"We didn't have that type of relationship. We weren't looking at the possibility of marriage, or, at least, I wasn't, so children didn't come up in conversation."

"Why should it now? We're a power couple, Quentin. We're movers and shakers. We make things happen. We don't need to have a child."

"Perhaps that's true for you, but not for me. I do want to marry and have not just one child, but several."

"Oh, for heaven's sake, Quentin! Forget that foolishness. Running for office on the city council is all we need to focus on for now. It will take all of your skill at advertising and marketing to put me on the city council and, in a few more years after that, into the mayor's office. Your parents can mold your brother and then later, your nephew, into taking over King Advertising's leadership. Your brother can stop all of that globetrotting foolishness and bring in more business from his age group. He can also train his son to carry on the King legacy. They don't need another King offspring from you."

"Have you heard anything I've said, Miranda?"

"Of course, I have, but whatever this foolishness is that's going on with you will just have to wait to burn itself out. You and your parents just need to patch up this snit—. What are you doing? Sit down, Quentin! We haven't finished working this out yet!"

"Goodbye, Miranda." He tossed some bills on the table, stood, and walked away. He could hear her calling after him, but he didn't give a good damn.

CHAPTER 17

"Mmmm," Samantha moaned long and deep, "that feels soooo good."

"Your muscles are as tight as a drum," said Sofee Carter as she continued to massage Samantha's body. "Samantha, did you see much of Dr. Paris McAllister while you were abroad?"

She lay naked and face down on the thickly padded table. "No, we never did catch up with each other. We planned to get together in London, England, but the lecture he was there to deliver ran late, and I had a flight scheduled for Germany to keep later that night. We talked via phone a few times, but our schedules didn't link up again where we were in the same city at the same time."

"His sisters, China and Capri, came in a few weeks ago with Paris for facials. They were all here to celebrate Capri's twins' birthday. Capri is pregnant again, don't cha know? Her husband is on another mission to SPACEHOME, the space station. I watch them on television every chance I get. It's so fascinating to know that they're floating around in outer space, working while we watch them from Mother Earth. He's due to be home next month. Paris mentioned that he hadn't seen you lately. So, I told him that you were away on tour in Europe and Asia."

"Yes, I know. He told me…oh, yes, right there, Sofee. Your hands are magic."

Sofee laughed and continued to work her hands up and down Samantha's body, kneading her tight muscles. "That's what my husband says all the time. By the way, I hear that your sister Geneviève is going to marry that wonderful man, Simon Wilde, next summer."

"Finally, yes," Samantha proclaimed. "He regularly asked her to marry him, but he ultimately wore her down and boxed her in long enough for her to take his proposal seriously. They announced their plans during show-and-tell the other night at dinner."

"I can't wait to get my hands on him. I'll have to send an invitation to them to do a couples' massage session. I heard that the whole Wilde family came to dinner that night."

"They did. Simon and Geneviève said that they wanted to wait to announce their engagement and have the engagement party until after my welcome home party, but before everyone scattered. We waited until the snowstorm was over and the roads passable so that his family could be there. There are a lot of Wildes and Hendersons. Simon's father is the head of Wilde Star Media, and his mother is a U.S. Senator from Virginia. The Wildes are Irish, and Simon's mother's family, the Hendersons, are Scots. It was a laugh riot the whole evening.

"We're gearing up for the wedding. If the number of Simon's family members who attended the engagement party is any indication, this wedding is going to be huge. As the bride's family, we're going to have to plan for at least another hundred mobile homes just to accommodate the Wildes and the Hendersons in Summer County. As I understand it, so far, there will be five other family weddings celebrated during Juneteenth in addition to Simon's and Genevieve's. Linda and KiLe are the Matrons of Honor, along with Simon's sister, Meara. The rest of us and Simon's other two sisters, Catrina and Lanae, are bridesmaids. Simon selected his pal Congressman Arnold Graves and Genevieve's twin, Vincent, as his Best Men. His two brothers, four brothers-in-arms, and the rest of our brothers will be groomsmen. The little ones in our families will be flower girls and ring bearers."

"It sounds like the wedding party alone will be huge."

"That's what it looks like to us, too. Linda, Dena, KiLe, and I will meet with Simon's three sisters to lock down the number of save-the-date announcements we have to get in the mail. We won't even present the plans for approval to Simon and Geneviève until all of the details are worked out. If we don't have our act together, those two will hop a flight to Las Vegas and be done with it."

Sofee laughed. "True that. I'll have to get them in here for the works on a Couples Pamper Day. Since you already know when and where, have they decided where they are going on their honeymoon?"

"Connemara, Ireland. Believe it or not, during the engagement party, they spun a world globe, closed their eyes, and with their hands joined on the count of three, they pointed to a place and stopped the spinning globe. Their fingers landed on Connemara."

Sofee laughed. "That is so like them to do something like that."

"Exactly, right. I half expected my sister and Simon to go to the airport, pick a flight going somewhere interesting, buy tickets and just leave so that no one would know where they went. Dad said that Geneviève would more likely schedule to take one of the AEA jets and take off for parts unknown. This was better. They plan to be away for two weeks."

"Next, it will be you or Dena making wedding plans."

"Dena, maybe, because she's been dating Will's brother, Drew, for a few years. However, I don't even have a guy to date."

"Turn over." Sofee held up the warm cover while Samantha slowly turned on the massage table. "Don't you think it's about time to find your one true love? You know what they say, 'Gather ye Rose-buds while ye may, Old Time is still a-flying: And this same flower that smiles today, Tomorrow will be dying.'"

Samantha laughed. "That's what I get for giving a set of classic novels and poems to you for your birthday. The next time, I'll give you toffee."

Sofee laughed, too. "Now, now, you mind yourself, Ms. Samantha. You've let a number of good catches slip through your fingers. Paris McAlister would make any woman a good catch."

"He usually does, often and continuously, and then he slips the net and swims away."

"He just hasn't found the right woman yet. Now, I'm done. I'll put these cold cucumber slices on your eyes. You just rest, and I'll send Wilhelmina in to do your facial."

On a windy sigh, Samantha yawned. "Thanks, Sofee. I feel great. You're the best. Tell Mina to take her time. I'm quite at my leisure."

"Oh, oh, I know where that's from." She said excitedly, closed her eyes, and searched her memory. "Uh, uh, Louisa May Alcott, *Little Women?*"

"Close," Samantha laughed. "Jane Austen, *Pride and Prejudice.*"

"Yes! You have always been so good at this. Even when you were a little bitty thing, you were so studious. You read any and everything put into your hands. Maybelle Tyson had no trouble getting you to sit still while she did your hair because you always had earbuds stuck in your ears, listening to one story after another or reading a book. Then you'd be up and out on the tennis court beating up on a defenseless tennis ball and sweating out your pretty hairstyle. Lands sake, you were a caution."

She had been, Samantha remembered, when she wasn't much more than a toddler. Before the ink was dry on her adoption papers and she was sufficiently well enough, Derrick and Vivian took her into their home and introduced her to the world through books. Before that, when she lived on the street, she could neither read nor write. She couldn't even count to five. They read to her every night before sleep overtook her. Before then, she didn't remember much except living in a cardboard box covered with a sheet of plastic in an alley with other young kids. When the police came, she and the other children would scatter like flies. Until one day, she just couldn't make her feet run anymore. It was icy cold and snow was piled up everywhere. She had only sandals, which didn't even fit her feet, and no coat. The sundress she wore was filthy and torn. She felt as if someone took a hammer to her head, as her teeth chattered, and the pain throughout her frail body was so great.

She must have passed out, because the next clear thought she had was of Dr. DJ, or that's what everyone called him. Dr. Derrick

Jackson was a really tall man, taller than anyone else in the children's ward of the hospital or in the orphanage. He was so kind to her when he came to examine her. She suffered from a severe case of tetanus, pneumonia, malnutrition, dehydration, and other deadly infections from untreated wounds. Without a clear memory of who she was or where she came from, she couldn't tell the police, social workers, or medical professionals anything, not even her name. The other children who took care of her just called her Baby. She used to have flashbacks, but over time, even those recollections faded and were replaced by daily visits from Vivian Alexander. She never knew when Vivian would come, but she began to trust that no matter what, Vivian would be there and read to her every day.

Samantha later remembered being in Derrick and Vivian's wedding as a flower girl in a pretty dress and shiny new shoes. Her hair was freshly done and she wore a crown of fragrant flowers. She walked down the aisle of the big church with Linda, Dena, and Geneviève, dropping rose petals from her sweetgrass basket on the white carpet. Come to think of it, she still had that basket and scads of pictures she was in during the event. They could barely believe the number of people who came to the church and to the picnic in the park for the reception. She must have been all of five or six at the time, but no one could determine when or where she was born. When Derrick and Vivian took her into their home at the Watergate, it didn't matter to her where she came from. She was where she felt safe and where she wanted to be.

As she slipped deeper into a twilight sleep, Samantha knew that she was still where she wanted to be, despite what the King family thought of who she was...

Whoa!

"Relax, Samantha. It's just me, Wilhelmina James. I'm preparing to give you a facial. You must have fallen asleep. I didn't mean to startle you awake. I see on your chart that you're scheduled for the works today: a full body scrub and a massage. Now, a facial, a mani-pedi, and then a haircut and style. I hope you're doing all of this for someone special."

Samantha laughed. "Yes, for me." Though, somehow, Quentin King slipped into her mind or at least his parents did. Thoughts of them were what startled her awake. They must have come to mind because Samuel's medical treatment was underway at Physicians' Hospital, but his parents had not put in an appearance. Quentin and Paulette were both there when Samuel was wheeled into the surgical theatre at six-thirty that morning. She sat with them as long as she could, but she had purposefully made her pamper day appointments to coincide with the date and time of Samuel's treatments. She left the hospital so that she wouldn't intrude on Quentin's and Paulette's vigil.

Clearing her mind, she allowed herself to drift while Wilhelmina worked her magic. It gave her time to think about Glen's invitation to join him in New York for a few days and about Quentin's kisses. She wasn't quite sure that she was ready for a relationship. However, the recent slumber party she shared with her sisters over Geneviève's decision to accept Simon's marriage proposal had her wondering about her own life. She hadn't felt the need to bond with a man since she was in high school. That had been such a terrible disappointment that she didn't date much while she was in college and grad school. Her interest in men didn't awaken again until she spent time with Glen Kennard while on tour, but she hadn't acted on her feelings where he was concerned. Though they had plenty of opportunities for over three months, they hadn't even kissed.

Then came Quentin King, and, after not seeing him for many years, within forty-eight hours, they had kissed multiple times. What was that about? He wasn't even the type of man she believed suited her. He may have made a perfect Mr. Darcy. Inwardly, Samantha laughed at the analogy. Obviously, thoughts of him as a modern-day Mr. Darcy were brought on by Sofee's and her reference to the classics. Still, there were inklings of his character she would never have ascribed to him. He always seemed so uptight to her back in the day. She believed him to be maybe five or six years her senior, but very reserved for someone so young.

She preferred men like Glen Kennard. He was wicked smart, but a smile was his default expression. He made a great companion and an essential part of her tour support system. He encouraged her to think outside the confines of her set routine and always made excursions into unknown areas an adventure with loads of fun. She enjoyed his spontaneity. He never let her sit idly in her hotel room but instead found exciting places to go and things to do in every city they visited. She learned so much just being in his company, but that was the problem. He was a much in demand airline pilot who was always on the go except for mandatory crew rest periods. His schedule didn't bode well for a sustainable relationship. That was something she would have to consider going forward.

On the other hand, Quentin King was right there, literally in her home area, and didn't travel often. He, too, was wicked smart, but she noticed that he rarely smiled. Austere was *his* default expression. There was also the complication of his existing relationship with another woman. Still, for some unexplained reason, she did want to get to know him. He asked her to come to his condo to consult on his furnishings and interior décor. She hadn't done interior decorating for anyone other than members of her family and close friends in quite a while. Still, he gave her *carte blanche* to reimagine the interior décor. She enjoyed challenges like that. So, she agreed to meet with him and take him on as a private client.

Paulette and she planned to collaborate on this project. After all, Paulette knew her brother as well as anyone. She, Samuel, and Sammy would be living with Quentin for a while until Samuel was sufficiently strong enough to leave the area and move to California. To keep the agreements between all parties strictly business, she had Paulette and Quentin sign contractual agreements. She charged Quentin her usual fee for this service and then shared a portion with Paulette.

CHAPTER 18

A few days later, Samantha and Paulette got out of Samantha's Lexus LX SUV under the *porte cochère* in front of the Watergate. A porter hurried out and began to load the bags and boxes from the trunk onto a dolly. When finished, a valet took Samantha's keys and drove her SUV away, while she and Paulette followed the dolly into an elevator.

When they reached the seventh floor, Paulette hurried ahead to open the double doors to the condo. "Thank you," she offered once the dolly was unloaded. She tipped the porter as he removed the dolly, closed the doors, and left.

Samantha wandered around the spacious condo taking mental notes about the décor she wanted to institute in each space. Although it was fully furnished, it was a blank canvas to her. She wasn't surprised by how roomy the condo was. Her mother still owned one with a similar layout on an upper floor. It had been where her first father, Derrick Jackson, already lived when he and Vivian met and later married, and the first real home she had outside of the orphanage. Although Linda, Dena, Geneviève, and she shared a room with bunk beds and a bath, it had all of the amenities four little girls could dream of and was the exciting beginning of their family. Brian, Roger, Ryan, and Vincent shared another spacious bedroom and bath. The third bedroom and bath were being outfitted for Andrew, Darren, Spencer, and their new baby brother Derrick Junior. While plans were underway to remodel a bigger home in the Virginia countryside on farmland, their father unexpectedly died on the day Derrick Junior was born.

Losing Derrick was hard on everyone. Though her mom tried to hide it, she was angry with Chuck because he knew that Derrick had a serious heart condition, hypertrophic cardiomyopathy, but said nothing about it to her. The heart ailment was particularly dangerous for athletes. When Derrick learned that he had the condition, he told only Chuck and swore him to secrecy. At the top of his game, Derrick retired from professional basketball and went into medicine.

Derrick and Chuck were long-time best friends since puberty pimpled their skins. They were as close as twins in a womb. They happened to fall in love with the same woman—Vivian Lynn Alexander—but that didn't destroy what years of friendship created. Chuck could have revealed Derrick's condition to Vivian and perhaps caused a breakup in the relationship, but he didn't. Derrick knew what it meant to ask Chuck not to tell Vivian the truth, but Chuck kept Derrick's secret, thereby risking his relationship with a woman he loved in favor of his relationship with his best friend. Samantha and her siblings were caught in the middle. They loved Chuck as much as they had loved Derrick.

A month after Derrick's funeral in the Pennsylvania Poconos, Vivian moved the family out of the condo and into the Georgetown home she once shared with her law school pals and Anna and her two children, Angelique and Miguel. Although all of her mother's friends were now attorneys and partners in her law firm, everyone had moved out of the brownstone, except Bill Chandler. The house was a much more spacious three-level mansion which provided more bedrooms and bathrooms and a four-bedroom, three-and-a-half-bath apartment on the basement level where Anna and her children once lived. Eventually, Anna married their next-door neighbor, Fenster Jones, a middle-aged, renowned concert violinist. Anna remained the majordomo of the mansion, and Bill stayed, too. He and Anna helped Vivian raise all of them. By the time Vivian went back to work, they were all settled into their new home and were enrolled in school, and accustomed to a daily routine. Samantha smiled at the memory.

However, Vivian remained angry with Chuck for five years. They had to sneak around behind Vivian's back to visit with Chuck. Their subterfuge was aided by Bill, Anna, and both their maternal and paternal grandparents. It worked until Derrick Junior's fifth birthday when he let it slip that Chuck bought a pony for him and that he would receive it at a birthday party on Chuck's ranch. They thought that Vivian would skin them alive, but she didn't. She actually loaded all twelve of them up and drove to Chuck's ranch in the Maryland countryside. Chuck was shocked to see them. However, as promised, Chuck hosted Derrick Junior's fifth birthday party, and he received his pony. The next thing they knew, Vivian and Chuck buried the hatchet and were planning their wedding for the Juneteenth celebration that same year. It was devastating to be dumped on her prom night, but Chuck and Vivian's wedding was a wonderful memory for her to assuage her sorrows.

After their marriage, Chuck and Vivian continued to adopt health-challenged, abandoned children from the orphanage as well as have children of their own. It warmed Samantha's heart that Chuck and Vivian never made a distinction between those they legally adopted or the ones to whom Vivian gave birth. Neither did anyone in any of their extended families.

"You really must have something on your mind."

Samantha smiled at Paulette. "Just a few memories. Mom still has her condo here. She and Dad come here if they are in town for an event, if they work too late to drive home or on their date nights several times a week. I was just remembering those early days when we lived here after Derrick and Mom married."

Paulette looked up and around. "I remember them, too. I hadn't thought of it before, but your parents' condo has a similar layout to this one." She looked at Samantha and smiled. "Do you remember that we met on the first day of school when your parents enrolled you in the academy? There were a lot of you, your sisters and brothers, who were enrolled on the same day, but you came and sat beside me."

"We became fast friends right away." Samantha nodded at the sweet memory. "Then it was a bunch of sleepovers, play dates, outings to the theatre, the zoo, horseback riding in Rock Creek Park, picnics, bike rides—."

"Do you remember when your mom took us all on the horse-drawn barge up the Chesapeake and Ohio Canal—?"

Nodding with a big smile on her face, Samantha joined in, pointing at Paulette. "We got off the barge at Great Falls, Maryland, and had a picnic."

"Then we rode our bikes back here to the Watergate," Paulette finished. "Your mom had a big surprise birthday party waiting here for those of you who were born in that month and she included Sam and me."

"It was so special and we didn't know what she was up to. Our cousins, grandparents, uncles, and aunts were there and yelled surprise as soon as we came into the condo." Samantha smiled. "As busy as she was with her law firm and everything, Mom always did special things like that for us.

"That's the type of mom I want to be when I grow up," Samantha joked.

"I'll bet you'll be just like her," came a male voice from across the room.

Samantha and Paulette turned to see Quentin leaning against the wall at the end of the wide vestibule.

He looks handsome in his haute couture business suit, designer shirt, and Hermes Windsor knotted tie, thought Samantha.

"Wow, I didn't hear you come in." Paulette looked at her watch. "Is something wrong?"

He straightened from his leaning position against the wall, and, with his hands in his pockets, strolled toward his sister and Samantha. *She looks even more lovely than she did when Paulette spotted her in the airline terminal's waiting room*, he thought. He couldn't determine whether she was wearing makeup to give her such a creamy glow, but whatever it was, he could hardly take his eyes from hers. "No, nothing is wrong. I knew that you and Samantha would be here today to evaluate the interior, so I ordered lunch and blew off a chunk of my day so that I could join you."

"Wow, Quentin, you've never done that before." Paulette noticed that her brother's eyes were riveted on Samantha. Then when she looked at Samantha, she was looking intently at Quentin. Rolling her eyes, she was glad to exit the room when the doorbell sounded.

"You look…incredible." Quentin moved closer when Paulette left to answer the door.

She shrugged. "Thank you, and you look…" she dropped her eyes and looked at him from the bottom up, "like someone who needs to get comfortable." They stared into each other's eyes while she removed his tie and jacket, tossing them aside. Then, she moved in, pulling his shirt from his slacks and straitening it down around his narrow hips.

He stood still, looking into her eyes and breathing in her enchanting scent while she made him more comfortable. "Uh, since you seem to enjoy undressing me, you don't have to stop there. Keep going."

She grinned. "Okay." She took his strong wrists in hand one at a time, removed the cuff links, and rolled up his shirt sleeves, never breaking eye contact with him. "Now, don't you feel more comfortable?"

"Decidedly, but you didn't have to stop there either."

"I know." She turned as the waiter rolled in a cart and set up buffet style in the open-concept space's dining area. She recognized him and smiled. "Hello, Kyle."

"Hi, Samantha. I didn't know that this order was for you."

"It wasn't. Mr. King ordered it."

"That's interesting because it has all of your favorites."

"Really?" she looked from the waiter to Quentin.

He shrugged. "I called the restaurant and told the maître d' that I wanted to order foods that you liked."

"How did you know to do that?"

"Brian. I called him. He said that you and your family like to eat at Angelique's Place whenever you're in the city. He called ahead to the restaurant and then told me who to speak with. I followed his instructions."

"Well, let's see how well you did." She moved to where Kyle was lighting the last Sterno and lifted the first lid. "My, my, we have spanakopita… fried okra… and grilled artichoke hearts." Lifting lids as she went down the row, she smiled when she lifted the lids over the beef and lamb meat, lemon potatoes, green beans, and warm pita bread. "So far, so good, and what do we have here?" She lifted the lid off the last container sitting in crushed ice. "Bingo! A Greek salad with a choice of feta cheese, tomatoes, cucumbers, extra olives, onions, and peppers. Yum!" Rubbing her hands together, she grinned. "Well, it looks like I'm all set for lunch. This is just enough for me. Gee, Quentin, what are you and Paulette going to eat?" she deadpanned.

He laughed, delighted with her, and then watched her take a picture of him before he sobered.

"Well, I'll be. You really do know how to smile. See? I have the proof right here." She shared the picture she took of him and then associated it with his cellphone number in her phone.

He did the same, taking a picture of her while she gave him a cross-eyed, frog face. He laughed, even more enchanted.

"Come on, you two. I'm hungry." Paulette grinned, grabbed a warm plate, and began to serve herself from the buffet.

Quentin handed a plate to Samantha and followed her down the row as they filled their plates with the great Mediterranean food while Kyle filled goblets with Greek wine.

After lunch, Kyle cleared the dishes and took away the cart with the empty serving containers. Paulette and Samantha made the beds with linen from Samantha's Pleasure Series Collection, while Quentin placed the new dishes and silverware in the dishwasher. He was about to add the new pots and pans when Samantha stopped him.

"Those pots don't go in the dishwasher, Quentin. They have to be washed by hand."

He looked at the array of pots and pans on the quartz countertops, which he had just removed from their boxes. "There are a lot of them, but if that's the case, they certainly won't get much use in this place."

"True that," Paulette agreed. "Considering that none of us know how to cook, maybe you'll want to take this set of pots and pans back to the store."

Surprised, Samantha frowned. "Okay, so what are you going to do about eating if you can't cook?"

Quentin and Paulette looked at each other and shrugged. "Go out to eat?" Paulette offered. "There are at least three places to eat here at the Watergate, and they deliver."

"Or we could order in from Angelique's Place or other restaurants in the area?" Quentin shrugged. "As you probably already know, there is a twenty-four-hour concierge service here."

"Maybe we could hire a cook." Paulette looked to Quentin for confirmation. "In any case, we will have to hire a cleaning crew, too."

"Okay, give me a moment." Samantha took her cellphone from her pocket and dialed. "Aunt Althea? Hi, it's Samantha. Would you put together a package for four and charge it to my business account? It's for my clients, the King family. Yes, two adult men, one adult woman, and a seven-year-old boy." She nodded. "Yes, that's three full meals a day and snacks…Yes, send it special delivery to this address." She recited the relevant information. "Yes, they'll supplement with fresh fruits and vegetables here locally…Yes, thank you, Aunt Althea. I love you, too."

She sighed. "Okay, in a few days, you'll receive your first order of Mountain Fresh Meals. It will contain full-meal samples for you to try. Once you decide what you like, go online and make your selections. Every two weeks after that, a food package will arrive packed in dry ice with instructions on how to prepare the meals. You'll need to put the food in this industrial-size refrigerator and separate freezer as indicated on each package. You'll have to select what you want to eat, place it in the microwave, which is this device right here or in this wall oven here, set the temperature and the timer, and wait."

Paulette laughed. "We do know what kitchen appliances look like and what they do. We simply haven't had to do anything in a kitchen before. The staff at King Manor took care of all of those things."

"Okay, I imagine you're not familiar with grocery shopping either. We'll go to a grocery store to buy other things like fresh fruits and vegetables."

"Or I could have those things delivered once a week by Roger or Ryan from the produce grown at Alex-Mont Ranch," Paulette suggested with a wide grin.

Samantha shook her head. "Uh, sorry, Paulette, but the delivery service would interfere with my brothers' cooking lessons. Then, after the holidays, they'll be off to spring training camp for the next season."

Paulette laughed while Quentin nodded, impressed with Samantha's quick wit. "You know how to solve problems. I could use your skills and abilities at King Advertising."

"Thanks, but no thanks. I have my hands full with Alex-Mont Textiles. Okay, Lesson one: never go shopping on an empty stomach. Now that our stomachs are full, who's up for a foray to a neighborhood grocery store?"

"Not me. I have to get back to your family's school to pick up Sammy and take him to see his father in the hospital." Paulette gathered her coat and purse, waved, and was gone.

Samantha turned, regarded Quentin with her arms akimbo, and grinned. "When was the last time that you did something for the first time?"

He sighed heavily, pulled his phone from his pocket, and dialed his assistant while gazing at Samantha's provocative pose. "Hello, Ms. Carmen. Would you reschedule anything on my calendar for the rest of the day and evening, please? Yes, I'm fine. I'll be in early tomorrow morning. Yes, I assure you that I am well. I am not ill. There is no need for concern." He clicked off and waited. He didn't have to wait long.

She grinned at him. "Okay, now you can change out of your work clothes while I search for the closest grocery store in the area. Do you have a car?"

He frowned. "Yes, and a driver. Do you want me to call him to pick us up here?"

She shook her head and gave him a pitying look. "Never mind. I have my car here. If there is no grocer within walking distance, we can take that, if necessary."

"Walking distance? Now, really, Samantha, I could call and have anything we need delivered…" he trailed off, his words falling on deaf ears. "Okay," he sighed.

She grinned. "Now, hurry. We're burning daylight."

He returned her grin. "What if I need help changing my clothes and selecting something to wear?"

She rolled her eyes at him and pointed an arrow-straight finger toward his bedroom suite.

He saluted her and marched away to change his clothes…alone.

CHAPTER 19

Quentin and Samantha strolled the Capitol Harvest on the Plaza at 1300 Pennsylvania Avenue near the White House. It was within walking distance of the Watergate, so they didn't have to drive her SUV or call for his chauffeured car. Amicably chatting while filling cloth bags with fresh produce from the various vendors who populated the Capitol Harvest Farmer's Market, they were having a good time.

"I don't imagine that you do this type of thing often," Quentin commented as he watched Samantha scrutinize a head of lettuce. Maybe it was actually a cabbage. He wasn't sure. There were a number of foods he didn't recognize in their natural form. Some had labels, but not all. He recognized some items because Brian had taken him on a tour of the Alex-Mont hydroponics farm buildings and the fisheries. It was no small operation. He was receiving an education because he didn't know how to judge the quality and the price. Apparently, Samantha did know as she moved to another vendor and selected the lettuce or cabbage without much scrutiny.

"Before we left puberty, all of my siblings and I were taught how to shop for a good deal and how to make basic meals. We've all taken turns laying out a menu, cooking the meal, and cleaning the mess we made. Everyone is proficient, even my dad. However, my mom," she shook her head, remorsefully, "is a total disaster in a kitchen. Boiling water is a challenge for her," Samantha deadpanned.

Quentin shook his head. "No, I can't imagine that there isn't anything Judge Alexander Montgomery cannot do blindfolded with her hands tied behind her back." He accepted a large bag of greens that Samantha handed to him. He didn't know what they were, but he put them in the canvas bag with the other things. He did recognize the beets but didn't realize that they came on longs stalks. It was amazing to know how much he didn't know about the simple things in life. The turnips looked like round potatoes, and he couldn't tell one bunch of green leafy vegetables from another.

"Under those conditions, if Mom is able to speak, she can order any one of us to make a meal." Samantha shook her head again. "My maternal grandparents, Bernard and Sylvia Benson Alexander, taught all of my Alexander uncles and aunt how to burn in a kitchen. They are off the chart when we all get together, but though she's been known to try, Mom never got the hang of it. My paternal grandmother, Harriet Jackson Montgomery, is an excellent cook, too. Even my paternal grandfather, Chuck's father, Steven Montgomery, can grill like a master." She selected fresh squash, green beans, and fat turnips and added them to her bags. "Thank goodness, Anna Menendez-Gaza lived with us. She's an excellent cook, and when we moved back to the brownstone in Georgetown, she gave all of the original twelve of us and her children, Angelique and Miguel, cooking lessons. She took us shopping with her so we would know what to buy.

"What do you see that you like?"

Quentin gave her a once over and raised his left eyebrow in silent answer. She got the message, rolled her eyes, and moved on down the rows, teaching him as they went. She had to learn to stop giving him those easy intros. Three hours later, they were back at his condo laden down with staples, fresh produce, and a block of wood containing an array of professional sharp knives and other cooking utensils. She had given his credit card a workout, but he enjoyed every minute of it.

"Now, wash your hands, and we'll get started." Samantha sat at the long, wide, quartz-topped, center-post island and opened her laptop.

"Get started?" Quentin questioned.

"Yes. You're going to make dinner for us."

"Am I?"

"Yes, you are. Nothing complicated. Now, put the stopper, yes, that thing, in the sink, place the collard greens, yes, those," she nodded when he pointed to the greens, "in this bar sink and fill the bowl with cold water. While the water is running, sprinkle a healthy amount of baking soda over the greens. You're doing this to clean the fresh produce. Yes, that's right." She pulled several bottles of red and white wine from one of the sacks, opened one of the reds, and poured the globe glass half full.

He accepted the wine she handed to him. "All of this is a little intimidating for a novice like me. Couldn't we go out to one of the restaurants in the building or in the area?"

She shook her head. "Nope, sorry, son, but we've bought all of this food for a reason. Since I have time before I meet with my sisters later tonight, we can have a cooking lesson. So, always begin by washing your hands. You're going to make one meal for tonight and prep for two more meals you'll have during the week. Your first order of Mountain Fresh should arrive by then."

She took him step by step through the process with explanations of why he was doing each task. She had him taste testing fresh seasonings and learning how much to add to whatever he was preparing. For Pete's sake, he was beginning to enjoy what he was doing and relished, even more, taking instructions from her. She never got up from her barstool seat to assist him. Rather, while he worked, she rose to measure different condo rooms with some type of hand-held electronic device. Then she'd return to her stool, observe his efficiency with following instructions for the preparation of each meal, and then revert to whatever she was doing on her laptop. It took a while, but eventually, the space blossomed with the pleasant aromas of good food.

"Okay, lower the flame under your sauce, and add a cap full of olive oil to that pot of water before it begins to boil. Then come over here so I can show this to you."

Quentin did as instructed, washed his hands, and joined her at the bar, sitting down beside her.

"What do you think?" She had several panels open on her laptop in a type of collage.

As he went from scene to scene, he became fascinated with the décor and furniture depicted in each panel. He went through them again more slowly while they sipped an excellent wine. "Unbelievable," he breathed the word. "You've captured what is in my head. How did you do that?"

"The inspiration came from one of the murals you purchased from my collection, the one that is unfinished. That one piece informed all of the plans for each of the common areas in this condo. Also, remember, I had you select samples of the colors and textures that appealed to you. Paulette added what she thought would be pleasing for Samuel, Sammy, and herself in their bedroom suites and sitting areas."

"I like the style of furniture and the colors you've selected here for my bedroom and bath. They flow well with the ensuite and sitting area. Are you sure that you can do all of this?"

She nodded, took another sip of wine, and headed to the gas range. "I'm sure, yes. Most of these furnishings I have in my storage facility here in the area. I'll have to order what I don't have or design what I think will fit. Give me a week, and you can have this furniture put in storage. I need a day or two for the painters to come in. After that, your new furniture, rugs, linens, and decorations can be installed. It shouldn't take more than a day and a half to get you all set up." She lifted the lid on the boiling water. "Now, your water is ready for the angel hair pasta."

He was reluctant to leave the pictures on her laptop, but he got up and searched the now well-stocked pantry for the box of pasta.

"You'll need only about a half a box since Paulette is going to stay to eat dinner with Samuel and Sammy at the hospital. That's a good enough amount for the two of us. Now, break the pasta in half and slide it into the water. See, it's got a good rapid boil going. Reduce the flame and cover the pot. Give your meat sauce a gentle stir. Very good." She smiled broadly with her praise, her eyes alight. She held his wrist while she sampled the sauce on the wooden spoon he held.

When her tongue captured sauce from the spoon, and her eyes again lit with approval, her gesture went straight to his loins. She held the spoon to his mouth, and he took his turn, testing the sauce, never taking his eyes from hers. It was surprisingly good, but he dumped the spoon in the sink full of soapy water and gathered her in his arms for a thorough kiss of her mouth. He tasted the wine and sauce on her velvet-like tongue and wanted to take her to his freshly made bed, but something chimed, causing her to break the kiss, a smile on her kiss-swollen lips.

"Your hot buns are ready," she grinned at him.

"I'll say," as he released her and put on a mitten to remove the bread from the wall oven.

"That was very good for your first experience in a foreign land, like your kitchen."

Quentin poured the last of the wine into her glass and his. Raising his glass to touch against hers across the candle-lit dining table, he nodded. "Yes, it was, thanks to you."

"You'll keep it up?"

He nodded. "Now that I see the instructions on Mountain Fresh's website, I should be able to do some damage in that foreign land. With the preparations for the means for additional meals in the refrigerator, dinner at Chez King shouldn't be a problem for the next few days. You're welcome to come to dinner to critique my progress. You've gone well above and beyond, Samantha, on so many levels. Thank you."

She inclined her head. "You're welcome." Then she looked at her watch. "Uh, oh." She pulled her phone from her pocket. "Hi, Linda. I'm not going to make it home in time for our meeting. I'm at the

Watergate. I'll Zoom the meeting from here. Okay, hugs." She ended the call. "Wow, time flies and all that jazz. I still have about fifteen minutes. Are you good for the cleanup?"

"I am, yes. You had me cleaning up most of my mess, including the new pots and pans, as I was preparing dinner. I only have to put these dishes and utensils in the soapy water and then into the dishwasher. Do you really have to go? I hoped we'd be able to talk more about the décor and other plans I have."

Her brows beetled. "More plans?"

"Yes. I understand that your family is familiar with Baylor and Baylor Design and Development."

She nodded. "JRock and JaiHonnah? Sure. My parents and the Baylors are besties. JRock and both of my dads played in the NBA at the same time. JaiHonnah and my mom were roommates as undergrads at Spelman College. I have a contract to work with them on interior décor for staging their model homes and businesses. Why?"

"I'd like to build a home here in the city. I understand that they're among the best, but it's hard to get an appointment with them."

"It is, yes, but the person you want to talk with is Wesley Greenfield. He's the general manager for the construction side of Baylor and Baylor Design and Development."

He frowned. "Greenfield? Isn't he the one who owns and operates Greenfield Brothers, the bakeries, and coffee and tea houses around the city? They are also caterers, aren't they?"

"That's his brother, Isaac Greenfield. They're partners, and both are excellent cooks, but Wesley spends most of his time on Baylor and Baylor projects. He's also a native Washingtonian. If anyone knows the best place to buy or build in the city, it would be Wesley. Baylor and Baylor cornered the market on building homes and businesses by repurposing shipping containers and building green."

"Yes, that's what I've read. I understand that they can build almost anything out of those steel containers."

"They have, yes. If what I think you have in mind is in homage to the future, then you should definitely speak with Wesley. He has a wealth of established floor plans he can show to you. If nothing he has suits your taste, then he'll elevate the project to one of the architectural teams for a custom design. Ultimately, it would be reviewed and receive the final approval from JRock and JaiHonnah."

"Do you have his contact…"

Samantha was already speed dialing his number. "Hi, Samantha," Wesley answered. "What's up with ya?" His voice came out clearly through the speaker.

"Hi, Wesley. Two things. First, did you hear that Geneviève finally said yes?"

"Whoa, get out! Wait until Roz hears this." He called out, "Hey, Roz, come here a moment, please, babe." Then more quietly, "I'm putting this call on speaker, Samantha. Simon has been on bended knee since forever. So, the wedding is next Juneteenth?"

"It is, yes, in Summer County. You, Roz, and your family are on the guest list."

"Hey, that's great, but tell whoever is making the plans that I'm doing the wedding cake. Just tell me how many different flavors they want. If the wedding is going to be on the grounds at The Summer House, please let your cousin, Satarah, know that I'll come down early. I'll need her kitchen for several hours to prepare the wedding cake."

"Isaac and his family are also on the guest list, so you guys will have to work it out between you for the wedding cake. You should know that between Simon's Wilde and Henderson families, this wedding is going to be huge. You and Isaac will definitely want to fire up your mobile homes and come down early to get a good spot on the farmland. By the way, several of the other cousins who are also getting married during Juneteenth asked whether you or Isaac would be willing to create their wedding cakes."

He laughed. "Okay, I'll give my brother a heads-up. We'll bake grooms' cakes, too. What's thing two?"

"I have someone who is interested in buying a lot and building a home in the city. Could you make time to meet with him?"

"Him? Please tell me that you finally picked a guy so that my son will stop posting pictures of you on his wall." He laughed.

"Geeze, Wesley, Cole is too young for me. He's only in his teens. I'm not a cougar in training yet."

Wesley laughed. "Wrong son. Cole has a thing for your sister, Petra. You're the pin-up fantasy for Marcus."

"That's even worse, Wesley. Is he out of puberty yet?" She laughed.

"Not yet, so who's this guy?"

"His name is Quentin King."

"King Advertising? Isn't his brother a top tennis player? Didn't he just win some important tournament in Spain?"

"Yes. You've heard of him?"

"I have, yes. His fiancée is a soror of Roselyn's. Her name is Mariah, no, Marisha. No, that's not right. It's Miranda something. So, he wants to build a home before they marry?"

"I don't know the details about his marriage plans," she grinned at Quentin with tongue planted firmly in her cheek, "but he's here listening and wants to speak with you."

"Okay, hello, Mr. King."

"Uh, hello, Wesley. Please call me Quentin. You're right. My brother, Samuel, is a tennis pro. However, let me clear up something else: Miranda Bazemore and I were associated, but we were never engaged to be married. She and I have severed our relationship permanently. The home that I'm planning to build will not have her in the picture."

"Hello, Quentin. I'm Roselyn Hunter Greenfield, Wesley's wife. I came in while you were explaining your relationship to Wesley, and I overheard what you were saying. You should know that as recently as last night at a soror mixer, Miranda was still claiming to be engaged to you and your mother, Ashante King, was there, too. Miranda was sporting an engagement ring that your mother claimed was in your family for generations."

"Damn that! It's not true!"

"Well, the rumors are spreading, but that won't put a stop to my husband working with you on a property. Any friend of the Alexander-Montgomery family is a friend of ours. Samantha wouldn't have called if you don't have her respect and trust."

"Thank you, both. Wesley, what's your schedule like?'

"I'm flexible. I can make time tomorrow."

"That's perfect. I'll call you early tomorrow morning."

"That'll work."

"Roz, I'll call you with bridal shower plans for Geneviève. Wesley, we'll need several cakes for that occasion, too. Do you think you can do it?"

"Yes, I can. Just tell me the date and time. I'll contact your head cook, Melvin, to arrange to use your kitchen."

"Great. Good night."

"Good night, you two."

When she disconnected the call, Quentin was pacing the floor with his phone to his ear. "Yes, thanks, Simon," he nodded and then immediately dialed another number. "Hello, Meara. Quentin King here. I apologize for calling you after business hours at your home. I hope you don't mind. Your brother, Simon, gave your number to me. Are you still interested in doing an in-depth interview with me for Wilde Star Media's Video Society Page? Great. How soon can you set it up? Really? That'll work. I'll clear my schedule for tomorrow at eleven in the morning. Yes, thanks, Meara. Good night."

He disconnected but continued to pace.

He wasn't in a very good mood, so Samantha began to pick up her things in preparation to leave. She had only a few moments left before she had to be on the Zoom call.

Quentin stopped pacing and stood before her. "It's not true, Samantha. I met with Miranda and ended our relationship the same day I moved out of my parents' home and moved in here."

"You and your parents had words over your decision?"

"We did, yes. I'm going to clear this up before this goes any further."

With her coat on her arm and her laptop in hand, she moved toward the front door. "If I'm going to make this meeting, I really need to leave now and go upstairs to my parents' place. I'll be in touch after you and Wesley have time to talk. Thanks for dinner, Quentin. You did well. It was very good for your first time making a meal. Goodnight."

She was out the door and gone before he could get in another word. He wasn't sure what he could say to her other than he wasn't lying about the dissolution of his relationship with Miranda. He threw up his hands in frustration. He could only hope that his mother's and Miranda's subterfuge didn't destroy the headway he hoped he was making with Samantha. After all, he had a tight deadline to win her time and attention before she met with her pilot for a few days in New York City.

CHAPTER 20

Although he had lived here in the city all of his life, Quentin didn't recall ever being in this part of Washington, D.C. It was far northeast and, years ago, it wasn't a part of the city where it was wise to visit. Now, as his driver parked at seven-forty-five in the morning in a lot in front of what looked as if it had once been a public library, he was intrigued by the homes and businesses he saw in the area surrounding them.

When the car door was opened, he stepped out and caught what looked like a brief grin on his driver's face. "Mr. Dillard, is there something on your mind? You're not concerned about being in this neighborhood, are you?"

"No, sir. There's no problem."

Quentin buttoned his suit jacket, shrugged, and proceeded to the front double door that Mr. Dillard opened for him. When Quentin walked in, he could hardly believe the architectural wonders before him. Skylights bathed the wide-open space in clear, warm light. Water features were spotted here and there, with strategically placed plants and flowers growing everywhere in a type of indoor garden. There was an attractive sitting area situated around a cheerfully burning fireplace. A stone reception desk centered the room where two people, a young man and a young woman, spoke quietly using phone headsets. Behind the desk was a scale model of the northeast quadrant of the city, complete with streets, homes, and businesses.

Fascinated, Quentin wanted to study the layout on what must be a rug-sized table, but the young man at the desk spoke to him, taking his attention away from the display.

"Welcome to Baylor Plaza Park. I'm Jemar Hubbard. How may I help you?" the male assistant at the desk asked.

"Thank you, Mr. Hubbard. I'm Quentin King. I have an appointment with Wesley Greenfield for eight o'clock."

The young man's fingers flew over a clear glass desk panel, and then he nodded. "Yes, I have it here on his schedule. Wesley is in his office. Chester, you know the way. Would you escort Mr. King to Wesley's office?"

Chester tore his gaze away from the pretty teenage girl working at the front desk. "Sure, Jemar."

Quentin noticed the smile the young girl gave to Chester and was surprised when his driver acknowledged the task. Reluctantly, it seemed to Quentin, Chester began to lead him around the display table to a set of doors at the rear of the building. As Quentin looked around, it was clear to him, based on the number of books on the shelves and pictures on the perimeter of the walls, that this building had once been a public library. On a feature wall, Quentin spotted what he believed had to be one of Samantha's murals. When they entered a set of double doors, a young man looked up, smiled, and stood.

"Hello, Mr. King." He extended his hand, "I'm Coltrane Greenfield, but people call me Cole. I'm Wesley's son. Dad is ready to see you." He turned to another set of doors, knocked, and then opened the door. "Dad, Mr. King is here."

"Thanks, Cole." Wesley smiled, stood, and then came forward. "Hi, Chester."

"Hi, Mr. Wesley. I'll wait for you out here, Mr. King."

"Thank you." Quentin accepted Wesley's hand. It struck him that although Cole and Wesley had similar features, they didn't look like a genetic match. He dismissed the thought, assuming that perhaps the teenager resembled his mother. He was a tall, gangly teen who Wesley said had "a thing" for Samantha's sister, Petra, who was also a teen of about fifteen. "I appreciate you for making time to see me on such short notice. You have quite a place here."

"You're welcome. As my wife and I said, any friend of the Alexanders and Montgomerys is welcome. May I offer you anything to eat or drink?"

"No, I'm fine, but do you mind if I wander around your office? These images are fascinating."

"No, go ahead. These are Baylor and Baylor projects currently underway or recently completed."

Quentin frowned and pointed. "This looks like London, England."

Wesley nodded. "It is. It's the Berkshire project. It's the conversion of an old normal school and campus into a condo village. It should be completed in the summer of next year."

"I didn't know that your company took on projects outside the country."

"We do, yes. We offer a quality product at a low cost because we build using abandoned shipping containers. We can find those containers in any port city around the world for a nominal fee per unit. For example, here," he pointed to another project, "a four or six container build can produce a four thousand square foot home or low-rise business. This one we built for the Chase Brothers, Elias and Jackson Chase, along the Chesapeake Bay in Mitchell County, Maryland. They took an old fisherman's wharf and converted it into a Farmers' Market with restaurants, fresh seafood shops, handcrafts villages, and a walkable, low-rise, low-density condo community. The Farmers' Market sits on the newly built docks on the Chesapeake Bay. Patrons can have meals prepared on-site by the farmers. There are entertainment pavilions and a crafts village where you can actually learn the technique, including a boat-building business where you can watch boats being built. If you want a lesson on building a boat, you can be hands-on. It's an inspiring place with condos, villas, and townhomes with impressive water views. There are other shops, too, like a unisex hair salon, massage spa, and convenience stores. My brother and I have a bakery and two coffee and tea shops in the village. All of the structures were built with shipping containers and distinctive façades. It's a new, very unique project in every way.

"My family and I enjoy going to lounge there, seeing the sights and sounds at the dance pavilion, paddling boats in the summer, and ice skating on their human-made lake in the winter. Samantha picked up a number of interesting pieces of handmade crafts for the homes Baylor and Baylor build or remodel, stage, and flip. Fishermen and women unload their daily catches there, and it's a real education to watch the crab pickers and clam shuckers work. My children are seafood fanatics, so we go there often to one of the all-you-can-eat seafood restaurants where we can watch the food being prepared. It's what passes for an interesting entertainment area short of driving to Annapolis, Baltimore or here in Washington, D.C., on the waterfront.

"They already had nearly enough abandoned containers to build out their project. What they didn't have, they bought from the Patapsco River Shipyard in Baltimore, Maryland. Once welded together, all of our homes and businesses are insulated and include AC and heating units, plumbing, and wiring. Each home is also equipped for hookup to city drainage or to greywater and blackwater tanks for off-grid living. Here in Baylor Plaza, twenty-one-hundred-square-foot, single-family homes start at less than one hundred thirty thousand."

Surprised, Quentin stared at Wesley and then back at the changing images on the light boards. "Why haven't I heard more about this? Which advertising firm do you use?"

Wesley laughed. "None. We don't advertise. Most of our projects come from word of mouth connections. We have more business now than we can reasonably handle. Because we don't need a large advertising budget, it helps to keep down the cost per unit.

"This is one of our older projects." He moved along the wall to point to another light board. "Gregory Alexander purchased an old rat and roach-infested motel and adjacent buildings several years ago in the SoHo section of New York City. We converted the properties into three-to-five-bedroom high-end condos. He recently revamped the rooftop to add an exercise facility, pool, and lounge. We used prefabricated shipping containers we built off-site to accomplish this. In two days, a crane lifted the completed segments into place. The job was completed in under seven days, thereby saving valuable time, money, and resources.

"This is the Wilde Star Media Headquarters' building in Tyson's Corner, Virginia. We built it several years ago, long before I met Simon or his father. Since then, we've built several properties for Wilde's extended family members. You see, we, Baylor and Baylor Design and Development, train our construction workers and send them to where the projects are located. We have an extensive number of specialists we trained in our facility, but we're careful about the number of jobs we accept. Using our own in-house workers, we're assured of a quality product each and every time we accept a project. As I said, people usually hear about us by word of mouth, especially when we do large projects like the expansion of the headquarters of Sweet Justice Productions in Chicago, Illinois."

Wesley sat on the edge of his desk and folded his arms across his muscular chest. "Initially, I planned to operate as General Manager for only five years to complete the Baylor Plaza Park project because it's the neighborhood where I grew up with JRock. I went to junior college to train as a cook, and I planned to open a soul food restaurant here on my old stomping grounds. I used to own and operate the community center in Baylor Plaza Park, but JRock tapped me to do this job for him. You can imagine that it was a steep learning curve for someone with my background and limited experience to step into this role, but," he shrugged, "when my best friend asks for a favor, I can't turn him down. After all of these years, I still want to open that restaurant, but between doing this job, working with my brother at Greenfield Brothers Catering and Shops, and my family, I'm done. My wife, Roselyn, doesn't permit anything to interfere with quality family time together." He laughed.

"I saw the display in your reception area. Is that Baylor Plaza Park?"

"It is, yes. Let's take a walk out to the display." They left the office and passed by Cole and Chester, who both seemed to be studying. When they reached the display, Wesley took a light pointer to identify aspects on the table. "We started with the demolition of all of the dilapidated housing. Then we began with the park's construction in the center. We removed the old and installed the new underground systems like the spokes of a wagon wheel. Then we fanned out to include the homes, community centers, and businesses. We saved, as historic buildings, what we could retrofit and reuse. Next, we increased the green spaces and restricted cars to the alleys and garages. Most of our residents use electric-powered golf carts to get around the community while others walk. We're self-contained and don't allow gas-powered vehicles into the neighborhoods. As a result, the air quality is noticeably cleaner in Baylor Plaza Park as compared to other places around the city. Through a study conducted by Roselyn and some of her science students, we've learned that we now have far fewer illnesses in Baylor Plaza Park than in other parts of the city.

"Further evidence of this phenomenon is found due to the decrease in pollution and an increase in the number of trees, which absorb carbon dioxide, increasing the clean oxygen levels. Roselyn's students have established an in-depth, long-term scientific study to monitor the levels of pollution and trade winds around the community. Several universities are interested in the results and the students who are working on the project.

"We have fresh food markets in the area, and we stress healthy living through regular exercise at our community centers. We have strict security measures so that our residents feel safe. As a result, it's a very walkable area. Once a month, the residents participate in a clean-up day and picnic in each area. The cleanup usually involves tending to the weeds in the community gardens and yards. We have trash receptacles everywhere and daily refuse removal." He moved along the table, pointing out views of the park and its venues.

"For entertainment, we have regular Summer in the Park events, like outdoor movies and dances for all age groups. Because we cleared away dilapidated, rat and roach-infested buildings and substantially increased the green space, the community has a golf course, equestrian riding park, and baseball, football, and soccer fields. It also has an indoor-outdoor Olympic pool and indoor basketball.

"In the community center, which was formerly a three-story junior high school, there are table games, a daycare center, party rooms, and other forms of entertainment and commerce. Since the community borders the Anacostia River and its estuaries, we have boating, fishing, water skiing, and ice skating when the river freezes. As we continued the buildout, we included the academy school campus, where Roselyn is the Dean of Baylor Plaza Park Academy. We serve all age groups at the academy for academic pursuits."

"I recently visited Alex-Mont Ranch in Maryland. I understand from Brian Montgomery that it is one of only four academies in the country of its kind and that its students routinely score in the ninetieth percentile globally."

"That's correct. The flagship academy was started by Vivian's father, Dr. Bernard Alexander, in Goodwill, South Carolina. When he became a state senator, he turned over academy operations to Dean Jefferson Logan. Dr. Logan has taken it to an international level of competition. In Chicago, Illinois, Tina Justice's nonprofit Sweet Justice Foundation operates the academy. They currently have the largest number of students, more than all of the other academies combined. Of course, in Mitchell County, the newest school is operated by Alex-Mont Ranches, and Dr. Paris McAlister is the Dean. We're very pleased with the success of the students in these academies. Now, how can I help you?'

"I'm interested in buying or building a home in the city." Quentin began to describe what he was looking for as they headed back into Wesley's office.

Wesley sat at his desk, took notes, and asked questions. "From what you've told me, I have a few things in mind." He keyed into his computer, and a large monitor on a wall lit, displaying a map of the city. With a few more keystrokes, the view adjusted to reveal what looked like a dilapidated fire station.

Quentin frowned at the image, and Wesley noticed. "Doesn't look like much, does it?"

"No, it doesn't. It looks like an old fire station."

"It is. It was built around the turn of the century. Let me show you what it *could* look like." With a few more keystrokes, a very fashionable fire station came into view as a side-by-side image. "This is Gregory Alexander's home in the SoHo section of New York City. This was twice the size and in worse shape than the fire station here when he bought it. It was a disaster, and a complete gut job, just as was the motel he purchased a few years later in the same neighborhood. He rehabilitated both properties, which spurred the redevelopment of the entire section of the city. This is what the interior of the fire station looks like now." The image changed to appear to be walking through the building on four levels."

Frowning, with unbelieving eyes, Quentin was intrigued. He stood and walked closer to the large wall monitor. "Is that an enclosed rooftop pool and deck?"

Wesley nodded. "It is, yes. We added this level to the building using shipping containers just so that Gregory would have an outdoor space and pool. We planted grass, trees, and shrubbery on this top level of his home. The glass panels are operable, so the space is usable year-round. His home is completely off the city services grid and creates all of the utility resources needed for its operation. It's a self-sufficient home. The panels provide solar energy, and underground systems provide geothermal energy. The spa and pool are heated. There are water-barrel and filtration systems that provide potable water and propane gas for cooking. It's what we call in the industry a green build.

"Green construction or sustainable building refers to both a structure and the application of processes that are environmentally responsible and resource-efficient throughout a building's life cycle.

That is from planning to design, construction, operation, maintenance, renovation, and demolition. All of Baylor and Baylor's projects are green builds designed by JaiHonnah and built by JRock to be self-sufficient."

"You believe that you can do something similar to what you built in New York City with this firehouse here in D.C.?"

Wesley nodded. "Yes, I know we can. The fire station has been abandoned for years. Because of its age, it would likely be a complete gut job, as was Gregory's New York home, but it's got good bones. It's not a corner building like Gregory's, but it's of sufficient size and sandwiched between these other structures so we can give you a large enough home to accommodate your needs. Let me show you what I have in mind."

As Quentin looked on, Wesley redesigned the spaces in the old fire station from the bottom up. Wesley also added a flat, rooftop garden space with grass, trees, and flowers. The rooftop provided a spectacular view of the Washington, D.C, skyline. As they continued talking and refining the spaces according to Quentin's tastes, he began picturing himself in this home. He added an exercise pool on the rooftop, similar to the one in Gregory Alexander's New York home.

"Before we finalize aspects of this arrangement, I want you to see what these spaces look like and the quality of work we can deliver for you. I'll set up an appointment with one of our sales agents who can walk you through several models at Baylor Plaza Park."

When he got back into his car, Quentin carried the plans for the firehouse conversion. Although Wesley showed other places and spaces to him to build or renovate, the fire station appealed to him most of all. It was in the right location and would allow the maximum amount of space for what he needed to do. He signed the contract to purchase the property from the city and initialed the budget for the construction. Other decisions would wait until he viewed the model homes. He looked forward to the project and felt good about this move, which would take about six months to complete. Now he could contract with Samantha to do the interior décor. He would address that plan later in the week. For now, he was curious about something else.

"Mr. Dillard, I noticed that you seem to know several people at the Baylor showroom."

He nodded as he drove through the late morning traffic. "Yes, sir. Those guys in the showroom office and I grew up in the neighborhood before it was called Baylor Plaza Park. Our fathers were the ones who stayed in the old community and rebuilt it with JRock Baylor. Although we're all in college now, we still live in the community and work for the businesses that are located there."

"Does that include this car service?"

"Yes, sir. A group of our fathers went in together to start the business. Ms. Vivian's brother, Gregory Alexander, the former basketball star, is a venture capitalist now on Wall Street in New York City. He's a partner in Compliant Trading and Investment. CTI created the business package and loaned the start-up capital to help buy the fleet of cars."

"I didn't know that you're in college. What are you studying?"

"Landscape architecture. Or at least that's where I want to start."

"Really? How did you decide on that as a career? Is it what your father does?"

He laughed. "When I was a kid, I cut lawns in the spring, summer, and fall to earn money for things I wanted. I'm still doing that, and I learned how to make mulch from yard waste and use it as fertilizer in the spring. I bag the fertilizer that I've made and sell it at the community flower and garden home store. I rake leaves and clean up yards in the fall, and shovel snow in the winter. I like flowers, bushes, and trees, so my father suggested I try landscaping as a career. Wesley hired me to work as a groundskeeper in the park.

"I also do work on social media sites and create websites to make pocket change. I drive for the car service when time permits, like now when the ground is covered with snow, but I don't want to do this type of work forever."

"What does he do? Your father, I mean."

"He's a social worker by trade, but he took over the operation of the community center from Wesley."

"It sounds as if you're industrious and a jack of many trades."

He nodded. "My dad told me to keep trying on different things to see what fits and what makes me happy. He said that if I like what I'm doing as a career, I won't feel like I've worked a day in my life. Along the way, I will have learned several different trades to keep a roof over my head, clothes on my back, and food in my stomach. When I graduate from college, I want to travel to see more of this world, not just my neighborhood. Then I'll come home, settle down with a woman, and raise a family."

"It sounds as if your father is a wise man."

"Yes, sir. We're best buds."

When Quentin's phone rang, he answered without looking at the readout. "King."

"Junior, I see you're not in the office again today. What is the meaning of this?"

"I was in the office at six this morning. I had outside appointments. I'm on my way to another appointment now. I may be back in the office later today. Did you need to speak with me?"

"Yes, I do. Your mother is distraught over your behavior, and so is Miranda. You need to speak with them and resolve this foolishness between you."

"Father, did you need to speak with me about King Advertising business?"

"Well, yes. Some of the board members are concerned that you're planning to leave your position."

"I haven't spoken with any of the board members. So it's not clear to me how they would have concluded that I might leave the company."

"Well, of course, Miranda's parents, the Bazemores, are members of the board. Miranda mentioned our discussion to them. They may have discussed it with other board members."

"Unless you call a board meeting, I'll give my regular monthly report during the next meeting and answer any questions at that time. Otherwise, I'm not going to give oxygen to the rumors of my imminent departure."

"Junior, your behavior of late is unacceptable. We need to discuss this as soon as possible at home. Your mother demands that you and the twins move back to King Manor."

"I can only say that it's regrettable you feel that way about my behavior. However, neither the twins nor I will return to King Manor to live. When Samuel is well enough, we can get together to discuss family matters if you want. He should be at my home in a few more weeks. I'll let you know. If you need to speak with me about King Advertising business, I will let you know when I'm in my office. Goodbye."

As he was being driven through the city, Quentin marveled at the dichotomy of the lives of both he and Wesley Greenfield. They were both native Washingtonians, but their backgrounds were vastly different. He grew up in a mansion while Wesley grew up in an economically challenged part of the city. Yet, the connecting tissue between them came from a member of the Alexander and Montgomery family…Samantha, who at one time straddled the fence between the two realities. He was also in awe of how her family encouraged her to seek a career that pleased her, just as his driver's family supported the young man's aspirations. Quentin wasn't given that option…to seek his own interests. He was expected to take over as the head of King Advertising and live in King Manor his whole life. Any children he had would also be expected to assume a leadership role in the company and live in the mansion down through generations to come. Now, Quentin wondered what he would have chosen if offered a choice.

CHAPTER 21

Samantha placed the soft yellow and grey baby blanket, matching booties, and the cap she knitted into the box with pretty multicolored tissue paper and put the gift in a colorful, drawstring cloth sack. The family was holding the baby shower for KiLe and Brian after lunch. Instead of moving back to their timber-frame cabin on the ranch in the woods, the couple and their young son were staying in the main house. Brian commissioned the construction of three additional bedrooms, two full and one-half baths, and a playroom to be added to the two-bedroom, one-bath timber-frame cabin. With KiLe pregnant and with a toddler son, it was safer to have her to stay in the main house where there were more hands to help, rather than have her isolated in their pretty cabin while the work was underway.

Although the cabin was within walking distance of the main house, Brian usually left before dawn to begin his workday. He came in to have lunch whenever he could, but he'd likely be out and about on the ranch or in town on business until dinner at six. They would spend time with the family, bathe their son, Cord Montgomery, read a bedtime story to him, and put him to bed.

Brian had the ranch properties in Pennsylvania and South Carolina to look after, too. Because of her advanced pregnancy, it wasn't wise for KiLe to travel with Brian when he had to leave the area on business. Of course, KiLe was working on her doctorate. So, much of her time was spent researching and writing her dissertation. The closer they came to their second son's birth, the more time Brian tended to spend nearer to home where he could frequently check on

KiLe. When he could, he took his son with him, strapped to his body in a harness, while he worked.

Satisfied, Samantha set the finished gift aside to go through her checklist for the next few days.

Later, in the late afternoon, it would be the official start of the birthday weekend festivities. She contributed to the gifts for Ronnie, Nelson, and Scott and for the twins, Laura and Laurel, and Craig and Petra. They were also celebrating the birthdays for two of the Phillips' children, Raymond Junior, who they called Ray, and his younger brother, Harrison, who was Sammy's age. Sammy King's birthday would be included in the festivities also. She brought gifts back from her travels for everyone but came up with additional gifts for the ones with birthdays this month. As was the tradition in their family, they handmade gifts and birthday cards with special sentiments or sayings. Since so many places were still digging out of the snow, her parents and the birthday committee had to go to Plan B for the birthday party bash, but it still promised to be memorable.

Samuel would be released from the hospital today in time to join the luncheon and baby shower. Paulette told her that he was also looking forward to the birthday party and planned to attend. He, Paulette, and Sammy would be at dinner tonight and at the ranch for the next two days. Her father wanted to continue to evaluate Samuel's post-operative condition for a while longer. Quentin would be here, too, for the celebration tonight and, then in a few days, he and his siblings would leave to go to his Watergate condo.

Fortunately, everything went well in the condo with the removal and installation of the new décor. Paulette filled in for her to ensure that all of the pieces were placed as she had instructed on the floor plan. Quentin called her because she wasn't at his place when the work was completed. He wanted to show his appreciation by making dinner for her to celebrate what he described as a "spot-on" creation of the vision he had in his head. He also wanted to discuss his plans for a new home. He asked her to accompany him to see model homes at Baylor Plaza Park. However, after hearing about the disagreement he had with his parents over Miranda Bazemore, Samantha simply didn't want the drama and purposefully declined to go with him.

Samantha felt that she had to get through only the next couple of days, and the house would be "King free." She and Paulette would continue to work on new projects while she shut down her work with King Advertising. The collaboration on the re-imagined condo space had inspired Paulette to consider taking interior decorating classes once she and her twin and nephew were settled in San Diego. Samantha's Uncle Benny and Aunt Stacy gave the green light to a six-month rental agreement for the Kings to lease their four-bedroom, three-and-a-half-bath condo in San Diego. Paulette indicated that Quentin would accompany them to California and stay for a week to help them settle in.

Then, after an early Sunday supper, the teens would be packed and on their way to Boston for their next rotation starting on Monday at MIT with Dena. Will, Linda, and their boys would be leaving with them, heading back to New York with Will's brother, Drew. Simon and Geneviève would return to Simon's home in the Georgetown area of D.C. on the edge of Rock Creek Park. Simon was writing his next novel, and Geneviève would return to working the night shift as a Lieutenant for the D.C. Police Department's Major Crimes Division. Geneviève's twin, Vincent, would return to D.C., too, to finish his training as a pediatric surgeon and his duties as a pediatrician on the night shift of the Georgetown Medical Center. After Geneviève moved out of her two-bedroom condo and in with Simon, Vincent took over the condo because it was within walking distance of the hospital.

All of the children, including the toddlers, were in school for most of the day. With her parents out of the house during the business day, she and KiLe were pretty much the only family members left at home. Even so, they didn't see much of one another because they both had their own work to complete.

Check! Check! Check! Samantha thought as she went through her mental To-Do list. It felt good to be getting back into her routine after being away for so long. She was finally getting a handle on all of the correspondence that accumulated in her absence. She might have to hire one of the preteens in her family to scan her correspondence and file it away. She'd have to talk with her sister, Eden Ann, to see whether she was interested in taking on the task.

"Samantha?"

"Yes, Mom?"

Vivian came to the open studio door. "Your things from your tour have arrived from the airport."

"Thanks, Mom. They're right on time. More of the gifts I brought back from my travels are in those trunks and crates. I'll go up and have them brought down."

"I've already seen to it. They're loading your props on the elevators. It will take a couple of trips. I wasn't sure whether you wanted them in here or in the storage room."

"In here, I think. I need to go through the collection and then decide whether to create a different display for the new season."

"I didn't know that you were still at home."

"Since I was going to be in the office for only half a day, I decided to work from home instead. After breakfast, your dad and I took the little ones to school on his way to the hospital. Then I walked back here. Chuck is doing early rounds this morning at the hospital, but he didn't schedule any office appointments today. He should be home in time for the luncheon. He's bringing Samuel here with him. So far, Samuel's prognosis is good, but your dad is being very cautious. Are you ready to see Sam again?"

"Not to worry, Mom. Being around Samuel isn't a problem for me."

"Then it's his brother, Quentin, who has you sequestering yourself."

Samantha looked into her mother's concerned expression, shook her head, and smiled. "It seems to me that I'm the reason you blew off a day in the office to check on me. I knew there had to be a reason because it's so unlike you to take a day off. You usually keep office hours from seven in the morning to five in the afternoon."

Vivian shrugged. "Could be, but I'm not going to let you withdraw from life because of a tough road ahead. So, let's go up and have a nice cup of tea, and you can tell me what's going on."

"Tea? Since when?"

Vivian huffed a frustrated breath and dug her hands into her jumpsuit pockets. "Since your father instructed that I can't have even decaf coffee. He has ordained that I can have only herbal tea."

Samantha laughed at her mother's mutinous expression. She gave the workmen instructions for the placement of her props. Then she and Vivian linked arms and walked up the steps. Each got a small pot of her favorite tea in the kitchen and a snack tray of fresh fruit, assorted cheese and crackers. In one of the salons on the first floor, Samantha lit the fireplace and they settled.

"I really haven't been sequestering myself, Mom. I have a lot to catch up on, and I'm busy with Geneviève and Simon's wedding plans. I need to get as much done for the wedding as I can. My tour will begin before spring, and it appears I won't return until just before Juneteenth and the wedding. Uncle Bill called me a couple of times to collaborate on the schedule for the next tour. I asked him to look for other venues in Africa, Australia, and South America, where I can speak or exhibit. He's found some interesting ones, so he wanted my okay to fit them into the tour route."

"Yes, I'm aware of that. I spoke with Bill on another matter."

"I'm also gearing up for a few presentations I'm scheduled to deliver in D.C. before Thanksgiving."

"I saw the announcement. Your Aunt JeNelle is scheduled to return from the Veterans' Day Congressional break this weekend. She's helping to spearhead this year's Woman's Agenda Convention."

"You're going to give the presentation on the need to select more females for consideration for judgeships?"

Vivian nodded. "I am, yes. It's the luncheon keynote address on Thursday."

Samantha laughed. "The President is really going to love hearing that from you, considering the fact that he nominated you for the Supreme Court."

"Actually, he told the First Lady to encourage me to take up the cause. He has recommended a record number of women for federal judgeships, but Congress has been slow to act on his recommendations because he's a lame duck. He's not pleased with that, so he's stepping up the pace to bring the inequity to public scrutiny. I had a conversation with Simon. I believe his current notoriety over his best-selling novel with a female secret agent might help the cause. He plans to investigate whether there is an overt pattern underway in the US Senate to deny women opportunities to become judges. If he finds a correlation, then he'll put it on the air and name names. He'll also fashion one of his upcoming novels around that story."

"That will certainly shake up the recalcitrant U.S. Senate to get off their duffs."

"It will, yes. Now, tell me what happened between you and Quentin."

"Mom, it really isn't 'a thing' between us," but as Vivian just sat waiting her out with silence, Samantha sighed and continued. "I was at Quentin's condo and called Wesley to arrange a meeting between them. During the conversation, it was revealed that Quentin's parents are supporting a woman, Miranda Bazemore, to be his wife. He has had harsh words with his parents over the situation. Quentin told me that he is interested in having a relationship with me and that he severed his relationship with this woman. If there is one thing I don't need, it's drama over a man. Especially not over another King. Been there, done that, and I've got the heartache to prove it."

"Tell me, honestly, how do you feel about Quentin?"

She shrugged. "I'm interested, but I don't know whether it's because Quentin is so opposite from the men I find intriguing. He's so pragmatic, cut, and dry. It's either black or white. There are no gray areas for him or colors to change his sometimes dour view. He isn't spontaneous. I can almost predict how he will react in any given situation."

"You want to 'fix him.'"

"Well, yes and no. I want to be surprised and for the man I decide to spend intimate time with to be a creative thinker. I don't want to be the only one in the relationship who has a zest for life and living it to the fullest. Quentin is so laced up and buttoned-down that I want to loosen him up. That could be the reason, but I do *feel* something when he kisses me."

"Frankly, from your text messages and email, I thought you might strike up a relationship with Glen Kennard."

"I'm weighing that option, too. Glen invited me to join him in New York City for a few days. He has a short layover there, and I've agreed to dress one of the McCoy Department Store windows. That project will take about a week to complete. I'll leave the Monday after Thanksgiving and fly to New York with Will and Linda." She turned to face her mother. "Glen is fun, spontaneous, adventurous, and wicked smart. I enjoy his company because he challenges me, keeps me entertained, and puts a smile on my face. However, because we were in an employer-employee relationship while on tour, I believe he was reluctant to take our contact to another level. He's a consummate professional and always respectful. I think that's why he wants to get together in December, outside of a working relationship, to determine whether there is a reason to step up. He wants to pilot my next tour, so what happens or doesn't happen between us will inform that connection."

"Of course, you've known Quentin King longer."

"Longer, perhaps, but not well, Mom. I mean, yes, Quentin was around when I was still a kid. He would deliver or pick up Samuel and Paulette when we got together for events, but we barely talked. Now it's been over seven years since I've been in his company. I don't know him except to the extent that Paulette tells me about him or from what I learned directly from him. I do have to admit that his taste in furnishings and décor is a surprise. I would never have pegged him for the fashion-forward selections he made."

"I was surprised that he's a diver."

Samantha nodded and selected a slice of apple and a wedge of cheese to nibble on. "I remember that he competed in swim meets at the academy, but I don't think I attended many of his races. Brian said that Quentin was an NCAA all-star at UPenn who might have made the Olympic swim team, but his parents didn't support him by coming to any of his contests. When he graduated summa cum laude, his parents were there in full force."

"His parents wouldn't like the optics. A black man or woman known for athletic prowess, even their own son, wouldn't be viewed in their world as having a brain to go with the brawn. They acknowledge or applaud only Mensa-level talent."

"Well, he has both. Paulette told me that Quentin swims nearly every day. It's how he clears his head and relaxes. Although his cell phone rings constantly, I don't get the impression that he has 'friends' he pals around with during his off-hours. Paulette told me that he doesn't even have a sportswear wardrobe."

"He appears athletically fit, but I think you're right. He seems to be a loner and a workaholic."

"That's it! That's exactly it!" Samantha pointed at her mother. "For some unknown reason, I want to introduce him to having fun. To teach him to take off his work personae and just enjoy life. To do things that are new to him or things he wouldn't think of doing on his own."

"To fix him."

Samantha nodded. "I guess you may be right, Mom, but that's a helluva task to take on. I'm not sure that I want that challenge when I could spend time with someone like Glen. He's excellent at what he does, but he knows how to shut it down and enjoy himself. I learned so much from being with him, but his career would mean that we wouldn't have much time together."

"Say the word and I'll talk with Gregory."

Samantha shook her head. "No, Mom. You and Dad put your estates into a blind trust, and you don't exercise direct control over any of it because of your position as a Supreme Court Justice. I don't want you to do that now, even for me. If Glen wants to change the location of his home base, he's the kind of man who will speak up and ask for the change. I think that will depend on whether we connect in December."

Vivian took a sip of her tea and frowned. "*Yuck!* If your father insists that I drink this stuff, I may have to trade him in for a new model."

Samantha burst out in laughter at her mother.

CHAPTER 22

"That's a wrap, Mr. King." Kellen Stark, the award-winning host of the top-rated *Let's Talk About It* Sunday magazine show for Wilde Star Media, extended his hand.

There was applause from those in the studio, including Simon Wilde and his sister, Meara Wilde Standish.

Quentin breathed a sigh of relief to have that over with. He had often been the catalyst for having a client interviewed by the media, but he hadn't faced a camera on purpose until today. "Thank you, Mr. Stark." He accepted the man's hand for a farewell shake and then turned toward Simon and Meara as they approached. "Thank you, too, Meara. I appreciate this."

"Believe me, Quentin, it is our pleasure to have someone of your stature as a guest on our show. You make a very appealing guest, frank and honest about the advertising industry and your reasons for keeping King Advertising's brand clear of the political arena. The news that your brother is considering retirement from sports to open a school eclipsed the sports industry news."

"I have Samuel's permission to make that announcement. He's taking a well-deserved respite to consider his options, but he'll make his final decision soon."

"We'd love to have him on *Let's Talk About It* when he's ready to announce. Anything you can do to encourage him to use us would be appreciated." They began walking toward the exit. "You handled that bit about your personal life with finesse. You're one of the most sought-after bachelors in the area. To hear that rumors you're engaged are total fabrication was another blockbuster announcement. After seeing this interview, we've decided to pull the show we planned to air on Sunday and replace it with this show. It will air at our regular time in the early afternoon and repeat in primetime at eight o'clock."

"Thank you again, Meara." He and Simon left the studio.

"Do you want to get lunch?"

"Thanks, Simon, but I have another appointment." Quentin usually would have dropped the conversation there but found he wanted to get together with Simon again. He genuinely liked the guy. "Could I get a rain check?"

"Sure, that's doable. Vincent and I are getting together for dinner next week at *Déjà Vu,* a restaurant and bar in Georgetown. We'll likely go to Café Citron, a salsa club within walking distance of the restaurant, after dinner. If you can make the time, you're welcome to join us. If Brian can break away from work, he may join us, too."

Amused, Quentin frowned. "Salsa? I'm not much of a dancer."

"It's fun. You'll see."

"Okay. Text the details to me, and I'll join you."

With a tip-of-the-hat gesture, they parted ways and climbed into their respective cars.

Chester Dillard held the car door open. "Where to now, Mr. King?"

"The model homes at Baylor Plaza Park. I have an appointment with a Ms. Jenkins."

"Yes, sir." He closed the car door and got behind the wheel.

Thirty minutes later, they parked in front of the first of ten uniquely different homes in a wide *cul-de-sac.*

Awed, Quentin stood and looked from house to house until a woman came out of the first model home and approached Chester Dillard with a warm embrace before extending her hand.

"You must be Quentin King. I'm Rochelle Taylor Jenkins. You're early. I wasn't expecting you for another hour, but this is good. Let's begin the tour here." She led him up a few steps to a wide covered porch that spanned the entire front of the two-story structure. "This is our Southern Exposure model. It's country living at its best. Notice the extra wide porch with a nice porch swing like the ones you see down south. Just perfect for sitting on a nice afternoon with a Mint julep." She turned to regard the well-landscaped grassy area, disturbed only by the parking lot. "As you can see, we have an abundance of green space. Chester helps to keep it looking nice. Cars and trucks are restricted to the rear of each property. There is room for guest parking there, too." Turning back to the front door, she opened it and led him inside.

"The kitchen comes with all of the necessary appliances, including a microwave and a desk with a computer. All of the homes have computers so we can communicate with other residents concerning events or emergencies. In the model you select, you may have an island or a bar. It can be designed to accommodate a fairly large kitchen table against that far wall as a booth or a long bench. Each home is situated to take advantage of the bright sunlight. We tend to have our own gardens, so the sunlight is essential. For those who don't have a green thumb, we have a hydroponics farm and a fishery in Baylor Plaza Park in the area where we have chickens and a Farmers' Market. It's not as large or fancy as the Capitol Harvest Farmers' Market on the Plaza near where you live in Foggy Bottom South West at the Watergate, but we're pretty self-sufficient here."

The open-concept floor plan was spacious and stunning, Quentin immediately noticed. It created a wow factor with just one glance. The staging for each room was creative and perfect. The further she led him through the four-bedroom, three-and-a-half-bath model home with her running commentary, the more impressed he became. It had a large eat-in kitchen, a full, finished basement, and attached garages, which could be entered only from the rear of the property off of an alley. Even as large as it was, it wasn't the largest model home to choose from, but the cost was far below what he would expect to pay if the house were located in a different part of the city or in the suburbs. Homes of this size would hold their value and appreciate well in the future. *Amazing,* he thought.

"May I offer you something to drink?"

"Yes, thank you. Bottled water, if you have it."

"I'll get it." Chester moved to the refrigerator in the kitchen, retrieved the water, and handed it over.

"Thank you. This is a nice home. It's hard to believe it's constructed out of shipping containers."

"They're the best building blocks in the business. The containers are made of steel with corrugated steel walls, floors, and ceilings. As Wesley likely explained, these homes and businesses can be plumbed, wired, and insulated, just like any stick-built home. However, nothing you build with sticks will match or be superior to a home built with steel."

Quentin nodded. "You know your trade. I'm in sales and marketing, too, so I know a pro when I see one. How long have you been in the sales and marketing business?" He uncapped the bottle and took a mouthful of water.

She tilted her head, her brows drawing together as if searching her memory. "I used to give blow jobs for ten dollars a pop while I was in high school. Then I became a professional hooker right after graduation. I think I've been selling something for most of my life. Back in the day, it used to be my body." She shrugged nonchalantly. "A stud muffin, like you, rarely crossed my path."

Quentin choked and coughed out the mouthful of water. Chester thumped him on his back and handed a few sheets of paper towels to him. However, Rochelle kept walking and talking, showing off the property as if he weren't trying to cough up one of his lungs.

"Well, that is until I graduated from streetwalker to being a call girl," she went on. "That's when I started getting a better class of clientele. I moved on from being a call girl to being a kept woman before Kelley Baylor, JRock's sister, asked whether me and twelve other prostitutes wanted a change in our careers. We all took her up on the prospect and went to school to become real estate agents. So, we went from selling our bodies to selling properties. I'll tell you, it's a lot easier than giving blow jobs on our knees in an alley, and the commissions are a lot more lucrative.

"As you can see, this model has four bedrooms and three baths on this level. All of the rooms are spacious. These two rooms are connected with a Jack-and-Jill bath. The other bedroom accesses the bathroom in the hall. There is also a spacious laundry room on this level. Now, let's go downstairs to the basement." She continued talking as they walked down the steps.

"Fred Jenkins, the man I was shacking with at the time, loved this model. He wanted us to buy it together, but he was stingy with the long green. So, he put a ring on it because he was afraid when I started making long, stupid money in commissions I'd leave him. He was a good old boy, but he was overweight. He walked like a penguin, and his penis was short but thick like a fat sausage. It didn't take much to make him blow like a Roman candle on the fourth of July. After I married him, I told him that he had to take better care of himself or we couldn't buy a property together, but did he listen? Not a bit. I was giving him a blow job, and he came and went all at the same time. Keeled over dead right there on the sofa, he did. I don't give blow jobs anymore because I'm considered a lethal weapon by the other girls and the men I used to service.

"Now, down here in the basement, you can see that it's unfinished. There is roughed-in plumbing for a full bath and enough room to add another bedroom. You can decide what you want to use this space for. Most people want to use it as a recreation or entertainment room with a big flatscreen. Since there's already a fireplace in the family room upstairs, we can add a fireplace here on this wall and one in the master bedroom suite, too. Now, let's move on to the next house."

She is a pro, all right, Quentin thought, as he was being driven back to his office. She took him through each one of the ten model homes, pointing out the differences in each floor plan and how they were achieved. According to her, no two homes would be alike. The brochures she gave him chronicled the construction process from inception to completion. Purchasers were able to select their preferred exteriors and interiors from a wide array of offerings. A full-page ad in the brochure indicated that each interior décor was designed by none other than Samantha Montgomery of Alex-Mont Textiles. She was so versatile, and the interiors fit perfectly in the different styles and types of homes. He was impressed with Samantha's skill and the Baylor and Baylor Design and Development team's high quality work. Yet, he didn't desire to live in the planned community. He still preferred to have the fire station converted, but, based on the quality of what he saw, he felt sure Wesley would deliver exactly the home he wanted no matter the location. The tour gave him ideas he hadn't considered before, like a sleek, modern fireplace on each level, particularly in the bedroom. He liked that it would be a unique and extremely spacious home on all four levels. He just had to ensure that it would accommodate a wife and children…and maybe an ample studio space, should there be a need for one.

When he arrived at the King Advertising office building, Mr. Dillard opened the rear door and Paulette exited the building carrying a large wrapped package. Her car was sitting at the curb.

"Hello, Quentin. I wondered where you were today."

"I had a number of outside appointments. Where are you off to?"

"KiLe and Brian's baby shower. In fact, I'm running late. I had to pick up additional gifts for the birthday people."

"That's at six tonight, right?"

"Cocktails at five, dinner at six, but the party officially starts after dinner around seven."

"Okay, I'll be there. Should I bring something?"

She shook her head. "I've taken care of it and a gift for Dr. and Judge Montgomery for their hospitality."

"Good idea. I should have thought of that."

"Not to worry. You'll be there tonight?"

"I will be there on time."

"Good. I'll see you later. By the way, Mother is upstairs in Father's office. So, beware." She rolled her eyes, hopped into her car, and sped away.

Quentin looked up the twenty-floor office building and shook his head. He was having a really good day and didn't need to include another showdown with his mother. He turned to Mr. Dillard. "I think I'll work from home, and then you're free for the rest of the day."

"Fine, sir, but you have the trip to the Alex-Mont Ranch on today's schedule for later."

"Yes, that's okay. I'll drive myself."

"Uh, sir. Do you know the way?"

Quentin frowned. "Why do you ask?"

"Well, sir, you won't find the ranch via GPS. It's a security measure, sir. You kinda have to know where you're going, and it's not that easy to find, particularly after dark."

Quentin reconsidered. "Okay, if we leave at four-fifteen, can we make it by five? I want to be on time."

"Yes, sir. It's during rush hour, but I believe we can make it on time. I'll pick you up at the Watergate."

Quentin got back in the car. Mr. Dillard closed the door and got back into the driver's seat. He was about to start working on his laptop again when something dawned on him. "Mr. Dillard, is there a Stallion or Risqué men's clothing store near here?"

Chester grinned. "Yes, sir. Both stores are on the corner of L Street and Connecticut Avenue."

"Good. Let's go there before you take me to my condo."

Two hours later, Quentin and Chester walked out of the conjoined stores loaded down with a completely new wardrobe. Two store clerks followed with more purchases. Quentin thought that he had completely lost his mind, but he was satisfied with each piece of clothing and pair of shoes Chester Dillard helped him select. There wasn't a tie or cufflinks in any of the bags. The dilemma came when he stood in his dressing room trying to decide what to wear to impress Samantha and what to pack. However, he did enjoy it when she undressed him.

Mr. Dillard was right, Quentin thought as they joined a line of cars pulling to the gate at the brightly-lit entrance. By five-forty-five, it was fully dark, and the back roads were pitch black with no lights. He hadn't paid attention the week before when he was driven from the ranch to King Manor, and he would never have found his way back to this place on his own. There was still evidence of snow on the expansive field, but Quentin's focus was on the mansion bathed in pearl white light, which sat on a rise far from the entrance. It was a magnificent old mansion with eight large, white pillar posts stretching up three levels to the driveway's portico roof. With its huge verandas on three levels and big double doors and windows, the structure reminded him of the mansions of the old antebellum south. Trees lined the driveway like sentries, their big limbs spread like arms providing a canopy welcoming all to enter someplace special.

Their car was checked by security and a K-9 corps when they entered the gates. It was hard to believe that there might be people with criminal intent to cause anyone of the Alex-Mont Ranch family harm. Still, Quentin understood the necessity for security measures—especially if those measures protected Samantha. Not that she seems to need protection. He believed her to be quite capable of taking care of herself...and those she cared about. When their car passed the security checkpoint, Mr. Dillard drove off to the left under a *porte cochère* with two other vehicles unloading passengers and luggage.

When Mr. Dillard popped the trunk latch and got out of the car, someone else opened the rear car door for him.

"Welcome to Alex-Mont Ranch, sir. I'm Gary Bouchard. I believe that you're Mr. Quentin King of King Advertising?"

"Yes, I am. Let me guess. You grew up in the Baylor Plaza Park neighborhood?"

His grin was broad. "Yes, sir, I did and I still live there."

"Your family operates the valet service for the Alex-Mont Ranch?"

He laughed. "No, sir. They own and operate The Bouchard Hair Emporium. It's a barbershop and beauty parlor. My parents are Bubbles and Billie Bouchard. You may have heard of them. They used to be singers, like Ashford and Simpson and Peaches and Herb."

He nodded. "Although they were more in my parents' era, I do remember them. I didn't know that they still performed."

"Yes, they do. In fact, my parents have several new CDs on the market. Their recording contract is with Alex-Mont Productions. That's the company of Roger and Ryan Montgomery. If your parents or you want to hear my parents live, they sing at shows at the Greenfield Community Center and in our family barber and beauty shop in Baylor Plaza Park. You should come by sometime."

"I may just do that." Quentin was beginning to see that, to their credit, the Alex-Mont family had close friends in many walks of life.

"Very good. I'll take that, Chester." He collected Quentin's single piece of luggage and laptop. "This way, sir."

Quentin nodded and shook hands with Mr. Dillard before following Mr. Bouchard into the side entrance, where a receiving line waited.

"I'll put this in your room, sir. It's the same one you used several weeks ago."

"Thank you." He moved up in the line, shortly reaching the hosts.

Chuck Montgomery extended his hand. "Welcome back, Quentin. We're glad that you could join us."

He took Chuck's hand and then moved on to Judge Alexander Montgomery, who hugged him as a way of greeting. He was introduced and then passed on to the grandparents, Bernard and Sylvia Benson Alexander, and then Steven and Harriet Jackson Montgomery. As he moved on down the receiving line making introductions and small talk, there were a bunch of Alexanders and Montgomerys he hadn't met before, but none of them was Samantha.

The receiving line dumped into a wide hall with snack and beverage stations throughout. He remembered that when he first came to Alex-Mont Ranch, he passed through this anteroom on the way from the helicopter pad to the interior of the great room. It was a good thing that the ceiling was high and wide as the hall began to fill with excited voices.

Over the din, he heard his name and turned to see his brother striding straight and tall toward him. He almost didn't recognize Samuel. A broad smile covered his face. He looked youthful, and his eyes didn't show any signs of pain. His thick hair was freshly braided, tied at the nape of his neck with a bushy tail that stopped at the middle of his back.

"Samuel?" his voice awed.

Samuel nodded, his eyes bright and going moist. "I can see by your face that I must look noticeably different to you. I can tell you that I haven't felt this good since I was in my teens. The fact that I can actually walk without feeling pain is nothing less than miraculous."

"I apologize for not making it out to the hospital to see you often, but I can't believe it. You do look like an almost completely different person."

Samuel shook his head, brushing away Quentin's apology. "You called every day, so I know you were thinking about me. The bone infusion treatments were painful. You didn't need to see firsthand how difficult it was to infuse calcium into my skeleton and the process to cause healthy bone mass to start generating. Dr. Montgomery has me on an exercise routine and healthy diet to perpetuate further bone density. He wants me to do resistance swimming for athletic and therapeutic purposes as often as possible or other low-impact exercises. It's not a cure, but I'm going to be all right, Quentin. This respite and treatment have been exactly what I've needed. So, enough about me. Paulette told me about the new condo and the interior design she helped to create. She's very excited about it."

Quentin recognized that Samuel's emotions over his renewed healthy appearance would overflow if they continued that conversation. He found himself becoming emotional, too. It was something that was rare for him since he often thought that he and Mr. Spock were from the same gene pool. So, he let it go. "She's right. She and Samantha did a great job."

"Paulette told me that you even cooked a couple of meals."

He frowned. "I actually liked it. I found it relaxing."

"She said it was good, too, and she showed pictures to me. I couldn't believe how much style and comfort were built into the bedroom décor. Speaking of style, I've never seen you wear something this fashion-forward. You look great. Did Paulette help you pick out new threads?"

"No, Mr. Dillard helped."

Samuel's brows drew together in surprise. "Your driver?"

Quentin nodded. "I've had quite a day," he began as they went to one of the tall tables and filled plates with finger foods and glasses from a variety of drinks. He took his brother through his day, including his encounter with Ms. Jenkins. That alone had Samuel laughing out loud. His laughter was infectious, and Quentin found himself laughing, too.

It occurred to Quentin that he and his brother never bonded like this before, and he wondered why. Of course, there was the age difference, and they never seemed to have anything in common. Nevertheless, he decided that they would find other occasions just to enjoy each other's company. Perhaps, Thursday night with Simon, Vincent, and maybe Brian would be a good opportunity. He was looking forward to it.

CHAPTER 23

"Are we ready?" Geneviève asked no one in particular, though a number of her siblings and in-laws surrounded her.

Everyone cast their eyes around the expansive ballroom and nodded.

"Okay. Lights. Camera. Action!" After her twin, Vincent's announcement, each of the Montgomery young adult and adult siblings wearing circus or other character costumes went to the array of double doors. With the chime of six bells, the doors were opened, and their guests began to swarm into the ballroom. The music played while people gaped at the birthday balloons and streamers anchored throughout the room. Each person's name was captured in an inflated balloon. The tables were dressed in festive primary colors topped with party favors. The children of guests oohed and ahhed and ran helter-skelter from one display to the next. It was a carnival-infused wonderland on steroids.

Once everyone was in the ballroom, the ceiling lights lowered, and Linda and Brian stood on stage with twin spotlights on them.

"Welcome, boys and girls and kids of all ages. We welcome you to the November birthday celebration. I'm Linda Montgomery Hamilton."

"Hi, all. I'm Brian Montgomery, and we're here to introduce our honored guests for the evening."

"Yes, first we have Laura and Laurel Montgomery, who will be thirteen on November third," Linda finished with a flourish as the girls came out.

They wore face paint, wigs, and costumes reminiscent of Anna and Elsa, the characters from *Frozen*. With the spotlight on them, they grinned from ear to ear and took their turn around the ballroom touching guests with their magic wands.

As Linda and Brian alternated with the introductions, each child came out wearing a costume of his or her favorite character. There was a creature or person from *The Lion King, Cats, Aladdin, Harry Potter, Mulan, Toy Story*, and *The Wizard of Oz*. However, little Sammy King came out wearing tennis whites and swinging a tennis racket with a ball tethered to it so that he batted it back and forth like a yo-yo. He moved as if he was actually playing the game. His hair was braided, but extensions were added for the desired effect of a bushy tail like the one his father wore. All of the children received roars of approval from the crowd, but Quentin thought that Sammy might have received extra high decibels.

When he looked at his brother in the darkened room, Samuel's tears glistened as they flowed unchecked down his cheeks while he grinned, enthusiastically applauded his son, and yelled, *"Bravo!"* People standing nearby patted his back or acknowledged him in other ways as they clapped. Although people knew Samuel King to be ranked as the top tennis player globally, no one intruded on his enjoyment of his son's shining moment.

The children assembled at the front of the room and took well-deserved bows for their creativity. Then a drumroll quieted everyone. The lights lowered more, and people dressed in fluorescent circus outfits and clown costumes danced into the ballroom, wheeling tables containing birthday cakes with lit candles for each child. The crowd began to serenade the children with an upbeat, happy birthday song. The children made their silent wishes, and then the candles were extinguished by the youngsters using long-handled snuffers.

When the lights grew brighter, the party was on amid energetic shouts. There were food stations in tents all around the ballroom, with everything from fish and chips to barbecue, hot dogs, hamburgers, steaks, and chicken. Banners were anchored on the front of each tent, advertising all of the different offerings, including the blooming onions hot from the cooker. They were in high demand, as were the hot-from-the-oven giant pretzels.

In all of that chaos were games like Pick a Duck, Water Coin Drop, Balloon Pop, Gone Fishing, Dino Dig, Bean Bag Toss, Spin the Wheel, Find the Ball, and Lollipop Pull. There was a giant bouncy castle with wings where the children could crawl from one chamber to another. An incredibly tall inflated slide stood against the back wall and accommodated four abreast on separate tracks. Children, and some adults, climbed up and, with war whoops, slid down twenty feet to the bottom. A train circumnavigated the room, taking on or dropping off little people at preassigned stations on its route.

Quentin had never seen anything like it. Above the crowd were zip lines, makeshift hot-air balloons which bobbed up and down, the solar system, and shooting stars with strings those on the zip line could try to grab for a prize at the end of the ride. All of it seemed to delight and fascinate the guests. He and Samuel found a tall table and bar stools where they could sit, eat, and take it all in. "This is amazing."

Samuel nodded. "It reminded me of a time when I was Sammy's age, and we were doing a sleepover at Samantha's home at the Georgetown house. Her mother woke us up at midnight and took us to watch the circus train unload the animals and equipment. We stayed and watched the elephants walk from the train to DC Armory near RFK Stadium. The next day, she took the bunch of us to the UniverSoul Circus. It is a single-ring circus, established by Cedric Walker, an American man of African descent. He had a vision of creating a circus with a large percentage of performers of color. He found people from all around the world with incredible talents and now has performers from at least twenty-four countries.

"It was the first time Paulette and I had ever seen the animals up close or been to a circus. There were people riding horses, elephants, and tall bicycles. Trapeze artists swung through the air, big cats jumped from stand to stand or balanced on balls, and dogs jumped through hoops on a track." He looked up and around in awe. "This brings back some of that magical time." He sorrowfully shook his head. "After all the embarrassment I caused Samantha and her family, they still opened their hearts and home to Sammy and me. How can I ever thank them?"

"I don't remember much about them back then because I didn't hang around if I had to deliver or pick you up from their home. Most of the time, they would pick you two up from school on Friday for the weekend and then deliver you and Paulette to school on Monday morning. I gather that they would be kind to people regardless. Just look at the number of health-challenged, abandoned, and/or orphaned children they have rescued and incorporated into their family. I don't think that they're looking for payback."

"You're right. They wouldn't look for payback, but maybe I can pay it forward by teaching youngsters from financially-challenged homes to play tennis. I know how expensive it is to play and to compete on the circuit. I can establish a foundation to help with those costs for children who show promise."

"I think that's the kind of thing the Montgomerys would appreciate. Just to see what lengths they go to for a November birthday party staggers the imagination." Quentin frowned. "I never went to the circus or even a carnival when I was young. Come to think of it, I don't remember doing anything as a kid that was considered *fun.*' Certainly nothing like this."

"The best times I recall were always when Paulette and I visited Samantha's home."

"Speaking of whom," Quentin said when he spotted Sammy and Paulette making their way through the crowd.

Sammy squealed, "Did you see? Did you see, Daddy?" and leaped into Samuel's open arms.

"I saw you! I am so proud of you, son."

"We did it just right. We didn't even have to practice much. You've gotta come get some of my birthday cake. I picked chocolate and vanilla, and Mr. Wesley and Mr. Isaac made it with my name on it. It's a really big cake, too. You gotta see. It looks like a checkerboard inside. I don't know how they did that, but you gotta see it, Daddy."

His excitement was infectious, thought Samuel. He put his free arm around Paulette, who wore a clown costume, and squeezed her. "Thank you," he whispered.

She nodded and returned the squeeze. "Now, you two hurry and get some cake. Bring some back for me and your Uncle Q, Sammy. Okay?"

Sammy nodded enthusiastically and, while still in his father's arms, pointed the way to the cake station.

"*Whew!*" Paulette breathed, plopping down on the stool her twin vacated. "This is the first time I've been able to sit…" She trailed off and stared at her brother. "Wow, Quentin, you really look fantastic!"

He looked down at his clothes and shrugged. "Is it lit?" he joked.

"On steroids!" she gushed as she looked him from the bottom up. "I can't get over it! You're styling, big time! You even let the hair grow a bit on your face. You don't even look anal retentive!" she joked.

He laughed. "That bad, huh?"

She shook her head. "I mean, I understood why you had to dress a certain way for business. It's not like you didn't look nice in your suits, but you always looked as if the suit wore you. Now you look like you enhance the clothes you're wearing." She grinned. "You certainly didn't change your look for Miranda Bazemore. I wonder who—?"

"Okay, enough already," he interrupted and looked around. "By the way, where is Samantha?"

Paulette stood on the bottom rung of the stool to see above the heads of the guests. "She's over there at about three o'clock. She's wearing a black catsuit."

Quentin stood and bobbed and weaved until he spotted her through the crowd. He would have made his way toward her, except a tall man put his arms around her lifting her off her feet.

"There you are, pretty girl," Dr. Paris McAlister said as he lifted her into a hug.

"Hi, Paris, when did you get home?" Samantha hugged him around his neck and kissed his cheek before he lowered her to the floor.

"Yesterday. I got a massage as soon as I got home. I heard from Sofee that you were already back from your tour. I apologize for not doing a better job of scheduling." He kept his arm around her shoulders.

Samantha snaked her arm around his waist and squeezed. "Not a problem. We were pushing it as it was. By the time we knocked down my exhibit, got it loaded in crates and on its way to the airport, we would have had only about an hour to get together. How did your lectures go?"

He nodded as if pleased. "There are definitely some school systems here in the states which are interested. I focused on the most economically-challenged cities and counties to begin my lecture tour. There are also school systems abroad that are interested in doing pilot programs that mimic our program here in the states. It's the cultural differences that are hard to sell. The idea that children go to class year-round and have two-week breaks every six weeks means a sea change for some cultures. Not everyone can afford to be off work for two weeks every six weeks to take care of their children or hire a child care specialist. The fact that the children may be away from home for six weeks wasn't as hard to sell." He laughed. "That, the parents and educators found appealing."

"Were there any educational systems that signed on?"

"Yes, so far, eleven signed on for a pilot program. Your pal, Adam Hawkins, signed on for The Full Monte, so to speak, and the largest program to be instituted for Seychelles. Thanks for the heads-up that Adam might be interested. Since your grandfather is here and he created the educational system, I was just speaking with him about it. Hawkins is heading up a program called Operation Uplift for his father's BlackHawk Foundation. His father, Jake Hawkins, is the U.S. Ambassador to the Republic of Seychelles. They're working with Dr. Noah Mikasi. You know him, I think."

They both looked up as two kids zipped overhead, squealing and smiling. "I know of him, but we haven't met. My cousin, Whitney, worked with him when he was still with UNESCO. She was the first one to tell me about him. Earlier this year, my sibs did a dive off Seychelles with him and our cousin, Cecile Dixon."

He nodded. "I didn't know that you and Dr. Dixon are related. I signed on to dive with Scripps Institution of Oceanography at UC San Diego during my next break between rotations. You should come with me and your sibs who will join the dive. Scripps has one of the world's largest academic research fleets. I hoped it would be during one of Dr. Dixon's dives, but her schedule wasn't set yet."

"She and her husband, my cousin, Donald Dixon, are here. They had to be in the area on business and brought their children to town with them for the party. I have her number. I'll get in touch with her and have her call you. How does that sound?"

He kissed her. "Like you're the best pal a guy could have."

Across the room, Quentin's eyebrow rose at the sight of the tall man, still hugging Samantha and kissing her.

CHAPTER 24

"Wow, I'm beat," moaned Roger as he and his siblings lounged near midnight in one of the salons while still wearing their costumes. "Two parties in one day."

"I'll say, but that's not a record for us. Still, we pulled both the baby shower and the birthday party off and survived," offered his twin, Ryan, as he slouched spread eagle in a chair, his eyes closed.

"I think everyone had a good time at both events, though we had to scramble to bring the birthday party inside." Geneviève yawned as she sat on the floor with her head on Simon's lap and her legs across her twin brother's back. "Who could have guessed that we'd get this much snow so early in the season."

"I did. I told you that the Farmers' Almanac predicted a big snow event early in the fall season." Vincent lay face down with his head pillowed on his stacked hands. "Hey, don't stop," he told his sister.

Geneviève huffed but lifted her legs and continued massaging Vincent's back with the heels of her bare feet.

Dena yawned, pulled off the fire engine, red clown wig, and scratched her head with both hands. "I sure am glad that the December birthdays don't want a circus."

"No, they're older. They want a Rave," Samantha offered and sighed. "The question is where to have it. I vote for the barn." She held up her hand as she lay with her head on one leather armrest and her legs dangling over the other.

"I second that emotion," offered Linda with her arm raised. She was sprawled on a sofa with her legs across her husband, Will's lap.

"I think we should draw straws to see who has to stay up all night to chaperone."

"Hey, Roger and I can handle it if you old folks need your beauty rest."

"Who's going to chaperone you and Ryan?" Linda wanted to know.

"Over twenty-one, remember?"

"Yeah, by about a minute." Dena joked.

"What time do we have to start dismantling the props?" Will asked. "It's beyond midnight now." He stretched with his long arms up over his head. Then he went back to massaging Linda's feet.

"Aren't there any elves around to bribe into doing that?" Dena joked.

"Andrew, Darren, and Spencer," they chorused and broke into unbridled laughter.

"They did a lot of the setup work and then had to operate the games all through the party," offered Samantha. "They each had dates and couldn't spend time with their friends."

"They may be making up for lost time now by taking the young ladies home." Roger looked at his watch.

"Not likely," yawned Dena. "They'll be back before one o'clock."

"How can you be so sure?" Simon wanted to know.

Vincent raised his head and balanced his upper body on his forearms. "The parental units let us determine what time to come in from a date, but if any of us was out past one in the morning, by four in the morning we were roused out of bed for extra duty work in the kitchen, setting up for breakfast at six. It didn't take rocket science to figure out what that was about."

"How would they know what time you got in?" Will raised his head. "This place is so large that I can't hear anything once I close the bedroom door."

"Trust and believe that Charles and Vivian Alexander Montgomery had parental radar and tracking devices on every one of us," sighed Dena. She didn't mention the security connection made by the gold neck chain they wore, which read **FAMILY**. Most people mistook it as just a piece of pretty jewelry, but it was much more. "Their first clue was that we had to badge in at any gate we used for entry to the ranch. They told us that there was nothing new under the sun when it came to our dating habits. They had been there, done that, and written the book chapter and verse."

"Yep, if we wanted to be treated like people with working grey matter, we knew how to behave," Vincent added.

"I, for one, wouldn't want to go back and do it all over again because those were some hard lessons." Roger stood, retrieved bottled water and passed it out to those who raised a hand.

"Speaking of do-overs. Did anyone notice Quentin King in his new threads? I almost mistook him for a much younger guy." Ryan popped the top of his water bottle and guzzled. "He came up with his nephew to play the bean bag toss game I was manning. I actually did a double-take when I recognized him."

"I saw him, too, and talked with him and his brother for a while. We're scheduled to hang out next week, and Samuel is going to join us," Simon commented.

"Makes a body wonder what made him change his look." Dena raised her head and eyed Samantha.

"Ignoring you over here," Samantha crooned. "I have absolutely nothing to say on the topic of Quentin King's wardrobe."

"I think he was a little miffed because Paris was giving you a great deal of his time and attention," Linda sang.

"Oh, for pity's sake. Not you, too. Sofee sings his praises every time she gives me a massage. Everyone knows that Paris is a flirt and more like a big brother to me and all of us. He stuck to me like glue because there were two women on his trail like rump rangers. He didn't want to get tangled up with either one of them. They're the single mothers of several of his students. So, he helped me get the kids safely up and down that huge, high rubber slide. I think Patty

Cake climbed up that thing fifty times," Samantha laughed. "He has absolutely no fear."

"Not hearing a change of subject are we, little sister?" Roger averred.

"Still ignoring you and the topic of the King clothes." However, she had seen Quentin and marveled at how good he looked, wondering whether she had actually influenced him to change his style.

"Hey, why is everyone still up?" Andrew entered the salon, followed by Darren and Spencer.

"See, I told you. I should have put money in the game on that bet." Vincent groused.

Everyone laughed, except Andrew, Darren, and Spencer, who looked confused.

Quentin heard music and laughter coming from one of the salons. *There are so many rooms and social areas in this mansion; there should be maps posted to the walls that indicate where you are in relation to the rest of the universe,* he thought. *A person could easily get lost and not ever be found.* He asked one of two teens in costume where he could find Samantha and was pointed in the right direction. When he stuck his head in, he was surprised to see Chuck and Vivian with a group of people, but not Samantha.

It looked like a nightclub with a long mahogany bar and barrel-back stools, a dance floor, and comfortable looking club chairs and cocktail tables. Several people were dancing, while others lounged or stood talking at the bar. There were remnants of a buffet and wine or beer glasses on some of the surfaces. The lights were just bright enough to see the caricatures of famous faces in pictures hung on the walls. Before he could back away, Vivian, who was dancing with her husband, motioned to him.

"Quentin, why don't you come in and join us?"

"I don't want to intrude."

"Nonsense." She laughed, went to him, and inserted her arm in his, drawing him further into the lounge. "It's the shank of the evening. Everyone, this is Quentin King V, President of King Advertising. Quentin and his twin siblings, Samuel and Paulette, attended the same school as Chuck's and my posse.

"Quentin, I think you already know the brothers Greenfield and their wives, Isaac and Carla Allen Greenfield and Wesley and Roselyn Hunter Greenfield."

He shook hands with Isaac and his wife, Carla. "I haven't met you before, but I'm familiar with your bakery and shops. Wesley, it's good to see you again, and it's nice to meet you in person, Roselyn."

Vivian continued making the introductions. "Here we have Nico and Tina Justice Collins. Tina and I were in undergrad together at Spelman College."

"I watch the Sweet Justice show and the Economic Empowerment Network."

"It's always good to know that we have an audience." Nico shook Quentin's hand. Tina did as well.

"Next are Peter and Cheryl Lawrence Brock. Cheryl is another Spelman alum. They're both lawyers, so be careful what you say around them. Their firm Brock, Brock, and Associates is a winning team."

"She's the smart one." Peter nodded to his wife while shaking Quentin's hand.

Vivian continued. "Next to them, we have Ashton and Kristen Bryant Marshall. We called her KC back in the day at Spelman, but they call her Judge Marshall these days. People who are in serious legal trouble call Ashton in the fervent hope that they can avoid going before KC in court."

"I believe your mother is the former governor of Oregon?" Quentin accepted Ashton's hand.

"That's correct. She and Kristin's father married several years ago. They were in law school together at Howard University. Now that they're retired, they're away on a world lecture tour. I believe they know your parents, Quentin and Ashante King IV."

"I'll mention your parents to mine."

"Then we have the sisters, both Spelman alum, with their husbands, Roderick and JaiHonnah Hawkins Baylor and Jefferson and LaiLoni Hawkins Logan."

Both Roderick and Jefferson shook his hand, as did the sisters JaiHonnah and LaiLoni. "Wesley mentioned that he had met with you," said Roderick, also known as JRock, the basketball phenom. "You bought a property through us, I believe."

"I did, and I'm very pleased with the possibilities."

"That's good to hear, Quentin. Let us know if there is anything else we can help with."

"I'll do that, but Wesley seems to know exactly what I want. I'm looking forward to working with your team."

"Next to them are Jeff's brother-in-law and sister, Nathan and Savannah Logan Flack."

"A pleasure to meet you, Mr. Ambassador, and you, too, Dr. Flack. My sister, Paulette, is a patient of yours."

"Of course. I thought the name was familiar. I saw Paulette here at the baby shower earlier and then at the birthday party with her nephew. It's good to meet you."

"The twins are my cousins with their wives, Donald and Cecile Jordan Dixon and James and Janice Adderly Dixon."

"We're not Spelman alum," deadpanned Donald Dixon, which brought on a spate of laughter since everyone knew that only females attended Spelman College. "Harvard in the house!"

"Times two," Jefferson Logan added, raising his glass of wine in a toast.

"Times three," Nathan piped up, giving Jefferson and Donald exploding knuckle bumps.

"Hey, UC San Diego, in the house!" Cecile and Janice chorused animatedly.

"Don't get them started," Chuck interrupted, laughing. "We'll be doing college roll calls half the night." Then in a deep baritone, he belted, *"Boston College in the house!"*

Tina Justice Collins approached and offered her hand again. "King Advertising? Are your parents Howard University alums?"

Quentin nodded and offered the year of his parents' graduation. "My ancestry dates back to when Howard University was chartered in 1867."

"Ah, yes, my father, Redmond Justice, and grandparents, Reverend Ellis and Anna Lettie Outlaw Justice, are Howard alums as are Peter's, KC's, and Cheryl's parents and grands. Though we didn't attend Howard, Peter, KC, Cheryl, and I all come from a long contingent of Howard grads. They all grew up together on the same block on Chicago's South Side. For many generations, Howard was the only historically black university in the country."

"Although my parents met at and graduated from Howard U, our ancestry doesn't go back beyond that. I wouldn't be here if it weren't for that Howard connection," Vivian joked, then turned to Quentin. "What would you like to drink?"

He looked around to see that most were drinking either wine or beer. "Red wine would be fine, but I'll get it."

"Good. Help yourself to that and the buffet."

"Thank you. I will."

As the conversations continued, Quentin recognized that he was in the midst of some of the nation's most influential people. Yet, they were casually dressed regardless of the billions in resources they controlled. They all had children in the same age groups as the Montgomery's posse. They came together to celebrate a baby shower and a birthday party for Chuck and Vivian's children and charges, which included Sammy.

It was a surprise to know that most of them knew of his parents, but apparently, none of them or their parents regarded Quentin and Ashante King IV as friends. Certainly, none of them were clients of King Advertising.

Moving from one conversation to another, getting to know them better, he began to realize that though they were celebrities in their own right, they were down to earth interesting people to know. They didn't flaunt their bona fides, though they were prominent. He found that he was thoroughly enjoying himself and them.

Vivian stepped out of view and placed a call. Shortly thereafter, Samantha walked into the room, confusion on her face. Her siblings followed her. She and they were about to break up and head to bed when her mother called.

When Samantha looked up, she saw Quentin standing at the bar, conversing with a group of their family friends. *Well, now, I wonder how that happened*, she ruminated.

"Oh, now there's a party in the house!" Vincent called out as he cranked the music before taking KC Bryant's hand and leading her to the dance floor.

That's all it took to pump up the dance marathon before the party was on!

CHAPTER 25

"Well, fancy meeting you here." Samantha eased up to the bar and took a seat across from where Quentin stood.

Most of the others were on the dance floor, and she had to lean in to be heard over the music.

He smiled and nodded. "Actually, I was down here looking for you. One of the fur-clad creatures from the circus said you were down here."

"Ah, you didn't go quite far enough. I was in the staging room doing a post-mortem on today's events with my partners-in-crime. We were also tossing around ideas for the December birthday party. We were about to shut down and go to our rooms when I was summoned to come here."

"Your sibs move as a group?"

She laughed. "If any one of us gets summoned, particularly at this time of the morning, we immediately start thinking we're in trouble. It's a nice surprise to know we weren't in hot water for a change." She took a sip of his wine. "Is there any more of this behind the bar?"

He lifted the half-full bottle and poured some into another glass for her. Then he refreshed his own drink.

"You and your partners certainly pulled off a spectacular birthday party."

She nodded and sighed. "More them than me. I was participating in the planning while I was away on tour. We had to scramble, though."

"Why? Did something go wrong?"

"It snowed on our plans. We were going to hold the circus outside on the back lawn, but it's still covered with snow. We had to bring it inside and fit as many activities as possible into the ballroom space. The only other place large enough to hold it without having to change our plans would have been the gym. However, we didn't have a reception hall for guests outside the gym. As you know, it's located on the opposite side of the house next to the barn garage. Logistically, it would have been a hot mess trying to pull this off. So, we had the party rental company set up inside the ballroom. In any case, usually, it's where we hold big events."

"It worked. I've heard nothing but good things about the events. Who did your costume?"

She looked down at herself and laughed. "I made it and a few others. The catsuit was easy. It's one of Linda's full-body dance leotards. With a tail, ears, paws, and face paint, I was good to go. It was the clown outfits that were a little time-consuming. I had to make those from scratch to fit different body sizes. Did Sammy enjoy himself?"

Quentin took a sip of his wine to wet his throat and then nodded. That catsuit fit her subtle curves like seal skin. It was a good thing he was standing behind the bar.

"He had a great time. He ate so much chocolate cake that I'm not sure his tennis whites will ever be white again. We appreciate your family for including him in the festivities."

She nodded. "We enjoyed having him. He's such a joy. He'll be missed when you leave on Sunday."

"He's made friends among your family members. I believe that he'll want to keep in touch."

"That's doable. When will Samuel, Paulette, and Sammy leave for California?"

"Just after Thanksgiving. I plan to go with them for a few days. I've never been to San Diego."

"It's beautiful there. Despite its southern location, San Diego rarely gets hot. Temperatures over one hundred degrees Fahrenheit are not normal there as it can be here in the south on the Eastern Seaboard. Indeed, the city averages only one day a year when the thermometer might reach ninety degrees. Warm weather is a year-round occurrence there. A day of eighty degrees can happen in any month but December. So, people tend to have a lot of outdoor activities. The summers are short, warm, arid, and clear, and the winters are long, cool, and partly cloudy. Over the course of the year, the temperature typically varies from fifty degrees Fahrenheit to seventy-seven degrees Fahrenheit. It's rarely below forty-four degrees Fahrenheit or above eighty-four degrees Fahrenheit.

"To know the climate that well, you must have spent a great deal of time in San Diego."

"I did. I went to college and grad school at the University of Washington-Seattle. The weather gets cold there, but if I didn't go skiing at Stevens Pass Mountain Resort in Skykomish, The Summit at Snoqualmie in Snoqualmie Pass or Crystal Mountain in Enumclaw, I would spend long weekends or short holidays at my uncle Benny's condo in San Diego or at my uncle Kenneth's homes in Santa Barbara or San Francisco."

"You should come to San Diego with us. You'd know all of the best places to visit and have good meals."

She laughed. "I'll give you a list. If you're going to be on the left coast for a while, I can highly recommend a road trip on the Pacific Coast Highway, also called the PCH. It is one of America's most famous highways, probably second only to Route Sixty-Six. It stretches from the southern tip of Baja, California, to the top of the Olympic Peninsula."

"The Olympic Peninsula?"

Samantha nodded. "Yes, it's the large arm of land in western Washington that lies across Puget Sound from Seattle and contains Olympic National Park. On the west, it's bounded by the Pacific Ocean. On the north by the Strait of Juan de Fuca and on the east by Hood Canal. Cape Alava, the westernmost point in the contiguous

United States, and Cape Flattery, the northwesternmost point, are on the Peninsula. The entire Olympic Peninsula is stunning and breathtaking.

"As I was saying, the PCH is about five hundred miles long. A drive from San Diego to the Redwood National Forest, San Juan Capistrano, and Big Sur are great trips for a boy Sammy's age. I can also highly recommend the Napa Wine Valley and San Francisco for the adults. Then, of course, for those who enjoy theme parks, there's Disneyland less than one hundred miles north."

"Obviously, your siblings aren't the only ones who are wanderers."

She smiled at that. "Contrary to the kiddy song, Dad and Mom always say that it's a big world after all, and they encourage us to see as much of it as humanly possible. They don't want us to live a little, confined life. Rather, they want us to explore the gift that life and living it gives all of us. We know where home is, and we know that we can always come home again, but they don't want us to have what they call 'small minds' that come from seeing life through only a single window."

"That's why your younger siblings are fearless when it comes to traveling halfway around the world to do a scientific dive in Seychelles."

"That's true. We all enjoy traveling. We learned so much from those types of experiences. It was more meaningful when I studied a subject if I got the chance to go to the actual location. Those are experiences I will never forget. What were you doing when you were their ages?"

He shook his head. *"Ha!* Certainly not diving in Seychelles. As I recall, my parents took me to the King Advertising offices and put me to work with the print shop employees to learn the business from the ground up. By the time I left for college, I had spent all of my spare time working in the business. I spent school holidays working and applying what I learned at UPenn and Wharton in my business and econ classes to King Advertising's best practices."

"When did you have fun?"

He shrugged. "I was on the UPenn swim team. We participated in the NCAA's Ivy League Conference tournament play and did very well. You already know that since your brother played NCAA lacrosse, and I don't think your family missed any of his home games."

"We didn't, and, if we could, we tried to make his away games, too."

"Did you play tennis while you were in college?"

"No, I used my extra time volunteering at a homeless shelter or traveling." Uncomfortable with questions about her years immediately following high school, she turned to regard the people on the dance floor as another body-challenging song started.

Quentin immediately recognized his mistake. They had an interesting conversation, and he asked her about playing tennis in college. That question was tantamount to throwing a bucket of ice-cold water on their tête-à-tête. She excused herself, got up from the barstool, and joined the line dance in progress.

CHAPTER 26

Early on Saturday morning, Quentin made his way down to the pool for a swim. He had become accustomed to the Alex-Mont household routine, which fit so nicely into the daily habit he'd adopted since he was a boy of Sammy's age. He also took advantage of the sauna and steam rooms. The fitness areas were outfitted as well as his private club. When he lived at King Manor, he'd take advantage of his men's club membership to get in his daily swim. Now, all he had to do was go downstairs to the Watergate's lower level, a heated indoor pool, with three-lap lanes, and a dedicated aerobic area to get in a good workout. It wasn't quite as homey as the Alex-Mont lagoon and fitness facilities, but nothing could be.

Quentin fully expected to find people already there and wasn't disappointed. However, although more people were getting in their exercise than he'd anticipated, the space didn't seem crowded. The view through the glass was still pitch black, without even fingers of the dawn's light coming up in the east.

He recognized Samantha's grandparents, Bernard and Sylvia Benson Alexander, Vivian's parents, and Steven and Harriet Jackson Montgomery, Chuck's father and step-mother, an interracial couple. He had met them in the receiving line at the start of the weekend festivities. Samuel was sitting with them, talking, and having a pre-breakfast snack. However, Quentin didn't expect to see Kenneth Alexander, Vivian's brother, and his wife, California Senator JeNelle Towson Alexander, climbing out of the pool. They had a large family, too, with three sets of twins and one set of triplets. Samuel pointed out the older two sets of twins the night before, the ones Samantha said were working together to take leadership roles in CompuCorrect. However, they hadn't seen the parents.

Kenneth was the former very successful, two-term California governor. After his years of public service, he resumed his prior position as the head of CompuCorrect Global, a Silicon Valley telecommunications firm. He originally started the company with two partners, shortly after his time in grad school and several years in corporate America. The firm was well known for its specialties in aerospace design, hardware and software computer technology, telecommunications services, security systems, internet, intranet, and social media platforms. In addition to an enviable list of prominent corporations, Kenneth also had certain government agencies under contract, including, but not limited to the National Security Agency, the Pentagon, and the Defense Advanced Research Projects Agency, as clients. Rumor had it that the CIA, FBI, and the Homeland Security Agency also used CompuCorrect's services. He watched as Kenneth and JeNelle joined his parents, who were also in swimwear, at the table where Samuel sat.

JeNelle Towson Alexander, a very influential and popular U.S. Senator, championed women's issues, particularly those in the military. With allies and cohorts such as her sister-in-law, Admiral Stacy Greene Alexander, and newly appointed Senator Veronica Henderson Wilde, Simon's mother, they were like the female version of The Three Musketeers. Senator Alexander had a reputation for introducing and seeing that legislation got passed that protected women from abuse in the home and workplace. She worked on legislation to give law enforcement greater authority to prosecute criminals who perpetrated crimes against special victims like women and children. Quentin knew that her legislation was geared to provide greater authority for those in the forced-labor sex trade, including the CIA, FBI, and local law enforcement officers.

When Samuel stood, he offered his chair to JeNelle. That's when he spotted Quentin, and Samuel joined him by the door. Quentin put his things on a chaise, preparing to take a swim.

"How are you feeling this morning?"

Samuel nodded and sat on an adjacent chaise with Quentin following suit. "Pretty good. When I put Sammy to bed last night, Dr. Montgomery suggested that I rest. He didn't want me to overdo it on my first few days out of the hospital. So, I spent a little time researching the San Diego area. There are several properties for sale that I believe would be ideal to set up as a school. However, I don't know anything about real estate in San Diego and what would be a good buy. From what I found, it's an expensive real estate market. I also don't know anything about running a business. I ruined my life and hurt my best friend because I didn't want to go to college. Instead, I wanted to become a tennis pro. Now, I may have to go to college or at least a business school after all to learn the things I should have learned when I was still a kid. I also want to set a good example for Sammy." He laughed at the irony and shrugged. "I told Samantha's grandparents, Bernard and Sylvia Alexander, about my plans. They suggested that I contact their son Gregory."

"Alexander the Great?" questioned Quentin, surprised. How did he not remember that one of Samantha's maternal uncles was a premier basketball icon? He and her uncle were about the same age. He'd followed Gregory Alexander's career in college, in the Olympics, and in the NBA until he retired at the top of his game in his early thirties with several championship rings to his credit. A year after Gregory retired from professional basketball, he started a semi-pro league made up of both all-male and all-female teams. The mid-Atlantic states of Virginia, Maryland, and North and South Carolina were where he began building the league. He used his extensive connections, in the basketball industry and business relationships developed through his New York City Wall Street firm, Compliant

Trading and Investment. He spread the concept nationwide to places in those states that don't have major professional or big university sports teams. They currently have ten leagues now across the country and the U.S. territories. Their headquarters are in second cities or what's better known as cities outside of the top one hundred.

Gregory started a real trend. He put together business people in Annapolis and Baltimore, Maryland; Norfolk, Richmond, and Roanoke, Virginia; Greensboro and Wilmington, North Carolina; and Columbia, Charleston, and Myrtle Beach, South Carolina, who were interested in grouping together and sponsoring the semi-pro, basketball teams. The fact that it's also a lucrative business seemed to be a nice by-product.

Not to mention the fact that Gregory opened a bank, which is one of the major sponsors of the leagues. Although he created the leagues and acted as the chairperson of the association, he didn't also own a team in contention. Yet, he controlled the addition of new franchises to the leagues nationwide.

Quentin knew that these semi-pro teams were being highly publicized and getting a great deal of attention. These were essentially farm teams the NBA used to find talented second-string players. Highly-talented, amateur ballplayers were coming in from other countries to get a chance to display their skills and abilities in ways they may not have had an opportunity to do otherwise. That sparked an idea for Quentin.

"You know, Samuel, you might consider starting an amateur/semi-pro tennis league, in addition to or in lieu of starting your own school. You could have a greater impact that way. You wouldn't be limited to youngsters in the San Diego area. You could branch out and start with kids in the most economically challenged areas of this country."

Sam looked into Quentin's eyes, frowning. "A league? I don't know how to start a business, and you want me to consider starting a national tennis league?" His laugh was mirthless.

Quentin nodded, smiling. "Yes. If you want to help indigent youths have an opportunity to play, you have the means to do it. You've made contacts throughout your career that would jump at the opportunity to find and promote young talented athletes. Gregory Alexander's league business model may prove beneficial to reaching the goal you set for yourself."

Quentin watched as his brother's countenance began to change as he considered how the concept could work.

"You're serious, aren't you?"

Quentin nodded. "You have instant name recognition, which could open a number of important doors for you and this plan. Were I you, I'd definitely get in touch with Gregory Alexander and see what guidance he could offer."

"You really think I can do this?"

"Yes, I do. You'd know the people to tap to work with you on this type of undertaking. This gives you something to consider."

"I do know people, but I trust you. Would you work with me…I mean, I know King Advertising takes up the majority of your time, but you're the one who graduated with an MBA with honors from UPenn's Wharton School of Business."

"Yes, I'll work with you. We'll talk more about this next week at home."

"Home. You say that word and, although I haven't even seen the place yet, it feels like a home to me." He reached for Quentin and exchanged a manly hug.

"I'm looking forward to it, too. We'll start making family memories regardless of where we are."

Samuel nodded. "We've got a lot of time to make up for, but I feel like I've been given a new lease on life. This time, I want it to be all about my family—you, Paulette, Sammy, and me. If our parents don't want to conform to the new normal, then we'll move on."

"Agreed. Now, I need to get in some time in the pool." He rose to his feet, Samuel following suit.

"I've got to shower and change. After breakfast, I'm taking Sammy to one of the barns to meet Brian. Sammy doesn't know that we're going there to see the puppies. Then tomorrow, we'll select one to take home with us. He is going to be so happy. Are you sure it's all right to bring an animal to the Watergate?"

"I'm sure. I had my assistant, Ms. Carmen, check on the pet policy of the places she found for me to consider. I confirmed that the Watergate allowed pets before I signed the lease. They have a kennel and other pet services should they be needed. We'll get all of the things we'll need before we go to the condo tomorrow."

Smiling, Samuel nodded and headed out of the door, while Quentin headed for the pool for his thirty-minute workout.

Samantha was about to go for a swim when she noticed Samuel and Quentin in conversation. Instead of going in, she turned around and headed for the gym. About midway there, her mother's challenge, that she was hiding from Quentin, stopped her in her tracks. Was her mother right? Was she hiding from Quentin and, if so, why? She didn't know the answer to those questions. Yes, she was attracted to him, but why was that the case? He wasn't the type of man she was generally attracted to, though there hadn't been that many. Her mother got her to admit that she wanted to "fix" Quentin or to loosen him up. Was that true? Did she want to shave off some of the stiff personae he exhibited? Even more troubling was the thought that she might want to exert a little payback of her own. Maybe to even the score on how the Kings treated her and her mother.

No, no, her parents taught her and all of her siblings to be better people than that. They did not seek to exert revenge because whatever goes around comes around. She wasn't that type of selfish or insecure person. She was taught to face whatever came at her head-on, and even though she did not know why Quentin King mattered to her, she wasn't afraid to face him or her future with or without him in it.

Without hesitating, she turned around and headed back the way she came. When she walked into the moist enclave, Samuel was gone, and Quentin was doing laps in the lagoon. He had a smooth routine, she noticed, as she took off her cover-up and went to the other side of the pool away from him. Swinging her arms over her head, behind her back, and shaking her legs and hands, she limbered her muscles to warm up. Diving off the board, she continued down the ten feet to the bottom and then speared up until her head cleared the water. With strong kicks, she moved effortlessly through the water, ignoring Quentin as she swam. Her concentration was on getting in a good exercise.

She was considering whether she should accompany her siblings and Paris McAlister when they went to Seychelles with her cousins, Donald and Cecile Jordan Dixon and their children, for a Scripps Research Institute dive. She wasn't a scientist, but she loved to dive. She'd have to give it serious thought since the trip would come up early next year in February. The weather there would be in the eighties and nineties during that time of the year.

Samantha pushed it for one more lap before she flipped over and did a lazy backstroke to the other end of the pool. She didn't notice that Quentin sat with his feet in the water, waiting for her to finish her swim.

He watched Samantha, enjoying the view until she flipped over and surfaced. "Good morning." He noticed her hesitation before she boosted herself up to sit beside him.

"Good morning." Samantha squeezed the water from her hair and picked up her towel to dry it.

"I meant to ask you last night or rather this morning what you were doing for Thanksgiving."

"We usually go home to Summer County, South Carolina, for Thanksgiving. The day after, the men in the family take the youngsters and teens skiing in Vail, Colorado, for the weekend. On Friday, the women go to Atlantic Beach, South Carolina, to the outlet malls in Myrtle Beach to shop for Christmas gifts until we drop. Then, on Saturday, we pamper ourselves with the full works at a McCoy Resort and Spa, located right on the beach. Our great grandaunt Hanna Ivy Benson has a big oceanfront Victorian tea house. On Sunday, we have high tea and buy special teas from her gift shop. Why did you ask?"

"I was going to invite you to join us, Paulette, Samuel, Sammy, and me for Thanksgiving dinner. I've decided to cook some of the food…not all of it, of course," he hastened to add. "I've ordered a stuffed turkey from Mountain Fresh. I think I can handle the baked ham. I looked online for what constitutes a traditional Thanksgiving Day meal. I wanted to show you what I've learned."

She didn't know why she was even considering attending a dinner with Quentin. Still, she shrugged, interested to see firsthand the results of her interior decorations and his handiwork in the kitchen. "Well, actually, Geneviève is having dinner with Simon's family in Alexandria, Virginia, at Ye Come Back Inn, a restaurant owned by Simon's father's family. Later that day, after dinner, they plan to fly to South Carolina. If you're planning an early meal, I could attend and then catch a ride with Geneviève."

"I can do that. If we eat as a brunch or late lunch, would that work for you?"

She nodded. "Sure. I'll let my sister know that I'll need to fly down with her and Simon. Do you need me to bring anything?"

"No, I think I have everything covered. I'm not into baking desserts, so I've ordered pies and cakes from Greenfield Brothers."

"You're right. You seem to have all of the bases covered. Still, I don't want to come empty-handed. If you'll allow me to bring the wine and Sparkling Cider, I'd feel better."

He nodded and joked. "Yes, please do. As the consummate host-in-training, I want you to feel comfortable."

"Touché." She inclined her head. "Okay, how many adults and children will be there?"

"It will be only the four adults and Sammy. I'll invite my parents, but I'm not sure that they'll attend."

"Are you still at odds with them?"

"Yes, but it doesn't bear discussion. How are you planning to spend your day today?"

She didn't want to belabor the issue about his parents' behavior toward her and her mother, so she allowed him to change the subject. "After breakfast, a bunch of us are going riding."

"You ride bikes in the snow?"

Samantha laughed. "Uh, that's an interesting challenge, but, no. We do ride horses, though, even in the snow. Most of the snow has melted through the bridle paths, but it may be a little muddy. There are bridle paths through the ranch and into the state-owned parkland. A few of the paths lead over to the equestrian center at Havenhurst Estates. In addition to our own, we board horses here for residents of the Havenhurst community."

"Horses?"

"Yes. Do you ride?"

He shook his head. "Uh, no."

"Okay, let's try this. When was the last time you did something for the first time?"

He shook his head again. "Oh, no. I'm not going to let you maneuver me into riding a horse. The last time you asked that question, I ended up going grocery shopping, something I still don't like to do on my own."

"However, you also learned to cook meals for yourself as a result of that shopping trip. Paulette tells me that you even enjoy it."

"Yes, but you're accustomed to riding. After all, you live on a ranch in the middle of nowhere. I live in a city where they don't have horses anywhere."

"Oh, but there are horses in Rock Creek Park and Baylor Plaza Park, pal. So, you can keep learning new things and finding ways of adding them to your life experiences."

His sigh was long and heartfelt. He had a feeling that he wasn't going to be able to avoid learning to ride a horse. The maniacal laugh Samantha released cautioned that he hoped his health insurance was up to date and all-inclusive.

CHAPTER 27

"Okay, Quentin, this is Smoky Joe. He's one of Dena's four-year-olds and doesn't like to run. Smoky Joe, this is Quentin King V, and it's his first time on a horse, so you be gentle with him, okay, big guy?" Samantha rubbed the horse's long neck and smiled mischievously at Quentin. "Now that you've been formally introduced, place this blanket on Smoky Joe's back and put the saddle on top of the blanket. Yes, that's the way. Very good. Now, reach under the horse and pull the buckles and fasten them the same way you do a belt, but pull them really tight."

"He's a really big horse. How am I supposed to do that?"

She grabbed the reins, stooped down, pulled the buckles from the other side of the horse, and helped Quentin tighten and cinch up the saddle to the horse in no time at all. "Like that. Lesson One: A saddle girth is made of leather, canvas, woven horsehair or woven grass. It's essential to ensure your safety that this task is performed with precision." She continued checking the saddle for safety. Then she backed the horse up to a three-stair step. "Now, up you go and fit your boots in the stirrups. Okay, your legs are longer, and this isn't an English riding saddle.

"Lesson Two: In the Western world, there are two basic types of saddles used today for horseback riding. They are usually called the English saddle and the stock saddle. This is a stock saddle. The best-known stock saddle is the American western saddle, followed by the Australian stock saddle. Now, if you hold the reins, I'll adjust the stirrups to fit your long legs and then you'll be ready to ride."

Once she completed her task, she mounted a big, beautiful, butterscotch-colored horse with a blond mane and tail without the aid of the steps. She simply grabbed the saddle horn, stuck her booted left foot in the stirrup, and effortlessly hoisted herself onto the horse's broad back in one fluid motion. She wore a long western duster that skimmed the ankles of her cowgirl boots, matching well-worn gloves, and a leather baseball cap turned backward on her head.

Quentin simply shook his head in wonder. He noted that, no matter what she did, Samantha seemed to have a high confidence level now, which she hadn't possessed as a youngster. He remembered her as shy, almost timid, except when she had a tennis racket in her hand. Then she was all business and skill on the tennis court. However, off the court, he could hardly get a word out of her. He was continually surprised at the dichotomy between then and now. Using only the reins, she turned her horse one-handed with a practiced ease to come up next to him.

"Okay, I'll ride beside you. We're only going to walk the horses. Get comfortable with the center gravity of your body so that you don't tilt to one side or the other as Smoky Joe moves. Otherwise, if you tilt too far to the left or the right, you'll fall off the horse, and it's a long way down off of the horse's back to the ground. Just try to remember to maintain your center of gravity." They left the barn trailing a long line of horses and ponies.

"What's your horse's name?" Quentin tried to get comfortable, but it was a little tricky with his nuts resting against the hard leather saddle with his thighs spread wide. He wondered how Brian did it so easily with his son, Cord, strapped to his chest.

"Aces High. He's a three-year-old and loves to run. He and Smoky Joe are pals. They came from Tina's horse ranch in Argentina."

"Tina mentioned last night during the party that she and her husband have wild horse farms. Brian told me that he goes down to Argentina twice a year, to see what she has and to buy horses from her."

Samantha nodded. "She has over five hundred horses in different herds there and on her property in the upper peninsula of Wisconsin on Lake Superior west of Houghton. When the herds get too large in Wisconsin for her acreage, she thins them by bringing several herds to Argentina. Her acreage there is much larger than in Wisconsin. I've gone with Brian and my cousin, James Dixon, several times to both locations. James buys horses for the Alexander Dixon Consortium in Summer County. I found Aces High at Tina's ranch in Argentina, and it was love at first sight." She commented absently but kept an eye on Sammy as he'd been on a pony only a handful of times. His father and Paulette were experienced riders and trailed Sammy as he rode a black-and-white pony named Spot On. She wasn't concerned about her siblings. They were put in the saddle when they were Patty Cake's age, just as Brian was doing with his son. Even their young sister, Teresa Angelique, who is Sammy's age, was experienced enough to ride a horse but opted to ride one of the ponies beside Sammy. *Samantha noted those two tended to chatter away*, much the way she and Samuel did when they weren't much older than Sammy and Teresa Angelique.

Quentin sensed that he didn't have Samantha's undivided attention. He never knew exactly what to say to keep a woman's interest, particularly if they didn't have anything in common. He didn't have a gift for gab or an ability to glad-hand in a crowd of people. He really needed to step up his game and expand his horizons. Samantha wasn't the type of woman who would drop at his feet over a few kisses. She was an interesting woman and had so much going for her that she wouldn't subject herself to a mundane existence or relationship.

Despite the fact that she was knitting when he saw her in the Madrid airport, a rather sedimentary task, she clearly has a zest for life and living, which she banked. He imagined the type of man who would interest her had to be several steps above exceptional. He didn't know whether he had what it took to measure up, but he would give it his best effort because getting to know her was worth it.

He leaned forward, maintaining his balance, but giving his balls some relief. With Samantha's interest clearly elsewhere, it allowed him an opportunity to look around and pay greater attention to the scenery. The deciduous trees were bare, but some evergreens perfumed the cold air with the scent of pine. To his left, off the path through the woods, stood a beautiful, picturesque, timber-framed cabin where workers were beginning to clad a large addition to the exterior with lumber. Their hammers were ringing out against the nails. Drills and saws were the only noise that disturbed the absolute peacefulness of the woods.

The deeper they went, the more the path twisted and turned, skirting frozen ponds and brooks where waterfalls formed ice sculptures. Icicles glistened in the dappled sunlight, and the foliage seemed to envelop them with a tall canopy of trees. The sound of the construction faded the further they advanced through the woods. Overhead, there was a village of birds' nests visible through the bare branches. Instead of hearing birdsong, the youngsters were singing something about "this old man, he played one, he played knick-knack on my drum. With a knick-knack paddywhack, give a dog a bone, this old man came rolling home." He half-listened to the next stanza of their song while relaxing into the ride. Fortunately, he didn't have to do much more than stay centered on the horse and hold the reins. Smoky Joe continued to plod along with his head up and his tail swishing side to side, following the other horses. He controlled his position as the horse's movements rocked him side to side. Obviously, this was a well-traveled path through the woods.

Thirty to forty minutes later, they came out of the woods onto what appeared to be a golf course. The trail continued beside a golf-cart path between the tee-off points. Shortly after, someone yelled, *"Fore!"* Smoky Joe suddenly began galloping at breakneck speed across the snow-covered fairway.

"Whoa! Whoa!" Quentin shouted while trying to hold on to the saddle horn for dear life. He dug in his knees to the horse's broad

sides and his feet in the stirrups to maintain his balance, but his balls were getting the brunt of the abuse from the hard-leather saddle repeatedly slamming against his open thighs. *"Maintain your center of gravity,"* Samantha had told him, and that instruction stuck in his head. He couldn't look away from what was in front of him, but he sensed that there were riders on this flank trying to catch up.

"Quentin!" Samantha shouted, coming closer to his left side. *"Slowly pull back on your reins,"* she quickly instructed. *"You're doing fine, but you need to bring Smoky Joe to a gradual halt. Don't jerk the reins or you'll go flying over his head or he'll rear up and dump you on your butt. Just slowly and steadily pull back. That's good. You're doing fine."* As she cantered alongside him, she leaned over, placed her gloved hand over his, and slowly pulled back on the reins, bringing them closer to his body.

When the horse slowed to a trot, Samantha's fisted hand was lodged between the saddle horn and his hardened ridge. She may not have been paying close attention, but despite the jarring discomfort between his thighs, her fisted hand against his manhood conjured a different type of uneasiness.

Dena rode up beside him close to his right side, reached over, and grabbed the reins as Samantha had. Smoky Joe came to a stop. "Are you okay?"

"I'm okay. I don't know what happened. All of a sudden, he just started galloping."

Dena shook her head. "Smoky Joe was hit on his rump hard by a golf ball. I heard someone yell 'fore' just before the red ball hit. We're lucky that no one was hit in the head. Wow! I've ridden him for years, but I've never seen him run that fast. Are you sure you're okay?"

Quentin nodded. "I'm fine, Dena, but I may have to sit on a pillow for the rest of the ride."

Samantha and Dena chuckled, breathed a sigh of relief, and with Smoky Joe and Quentin sandwiched between them, guided them off the fairway and back to join the others who waited on the bridle path.

He wasn't joking about the pillow, but somehow with the chill in the air, the sun bright in the azure, blue sky, out in the open, riding through five or six inches of snow, it was exhilarating.

When they reached the Havenhurst Estates, a Baylor and Baylor Design and Developers championship golf community situated on thousands of acres, there were large mansions, human-made lakes, and an equestrian park. The scenery was breathtaking. Other people, families, and young children were out on horseback riding the quarter-mile track or traversing the different bridle paths surrounding the golf course, forests, and lakes. They raised their hands, acknowledging the arrival of the Alexander-Montgomery contingent of family and friends.

Linda, Dena, Kenny, and Brian rode chaperoning the younger ones, including Sammy, on the ponies several times around the track while Will, Simon, Quentin, and others looked on.

Later, a starting gate was brought onto the track, and eight horses and riders lined up in the stalls. Right out of the gate, Dena was in the lead and won by a full horse length with Kenny on her heels. Samantha made a decent showing at fourth. As that race finished, another group of eight lined up, and off they went flying around the track. Quentin thought it was fascinating to watch the Alex-Mont kids race on the track with their faces wreathed in smiles and joyous laughter. They exhibited levels of confidence and skill he would not have expected from young people. It spoke well of the type of self-reliance their parents infused them with.

After the races, they rode up to the back of the Foxes Lair Restaurant at the Havenhurst Country Club, where they dismounted and hitched their horses to posts where the horses could drink and feed. Stable hands tended to the horses and ponies for a cool-down session. Instead of going inside, the riders spread out at tables and chairs on the restaurant's terrace near a large, stone fireplace surrounded by pots of burning fragrant wood. The terrace overlooked the tennis courts and a closed and covered outdoor pool. After the food was ordered, everyone got up to tend to their needs and wash their hands.

As they were leaving the men's room, Quentin got Brian's attention and whispered a question to him.

Brian smiled and leaned closer to Quentin as they started toward the terrace where trays of piping hot loaded nachos were being served. "It is necessary for males to wear a cup in a cup-jockstrap and then wear-tight fitting compression shorts over it all to hold everything firmly in place and tight against your body. I apologize. I thought, because Samuel and Paulette are experienced riders, that you were, too.

"Look, if you'd rather, I can have someone pick you up here and take you back to the ranch. Dad is there. He can check you out; make sure that you haven't done any permanent damage."

Quentin shook his head. "No, I want to ride back with the rest of you. I'll chalk this up as a lesson learned for the next time."

Brian shrugged. "Okay, good, but you're going to be sore from the experience. You're tougher than I thought, but if your nuts get too painful, get an ice pack from the kitchen or from my dad. I'm glad that the runaway horse experience didn't sour you against riding."

"I actually hadn't thought of riding as something I wanted to learn to do. However, your sister challenged me to do something I hadn't done before. Despite this experience, I'd like to learn to ride."

Brian nodded. "I suspected that my sister had something to do with your sudden interest in learning to ride. Trying to learn about things she's interested in are moves in the right direction. If, as you told me, you want to be around her, there's an equestrian park at Baylor Plaza Park or when your schedule permits, I can teach you here at Havenhurst Estates or at Alex-Mont Ranch. Here you would have to become a member of the country club, but it's like a resort with guest accommodations and great amenities. I'll tell you, though, that riding is one of Samantha's favorite things to do, so you can go riding with her and share one of her passions."

"Thanks, Brian, I'd like that." Quentin was surprised that Brian was willing to take the time to teach him to ride. He would make time in his schedule to learn. It would be good for him and provide another opportunity to share time with Samantha.

The seat on the bench next to Samantha was empty, so Quentin grabbed it before someone else did. He sat, gingerly, leaning up so that he didn't put undue pressure on his family jewels. He was greeted with a foot-high stack of something hot with meat and cheese oozing over it. He frowned. "Uh, Samantha, what is this?"

For a moment, she just stared at him. "Nachos? Haven't you had nachos before? I mean, you went to UPenn for undergrad and grad school. You can't tell me that you didn't hang out at the local rathskeller or greasy spoon?"

He shook his head. "No, I didn't. I didn't have time. Or rather, I didn't make time to do those types of things. I had honors classes, swim practice, and competitive races. I had to stay on a strict diet to compete. So tell me what it is."

She continued to stare and then she chuckled. "Uh, don't ask. Push up your sleeves, dig in anywhere, and just taste." When he seemed reluctant or unsure of how to attack the mountain before him, she pulled a hot, sticky section off the pile and placed it on a plate before him. When he started to pick up a fork, she shook her head, broke off a loaded section, and held it up to his mouth.

With his eyes on hers, he held her wrist, opened his mouth, and accepted the offering. Heat and unusual flavors exploded on his tongue. *"Hot. Hot."* He fanned and then accepted the glass of cold beer she held out to him, taking a long swallow. He wasn't usually one who liked the taste of beer, but it immediately cooled the burn of the peppers and heat.

"Wow, this is good." He dug in for more.

"It is, and the Foxes Lair makes really good Nachos Grande, too. It's tortilla chips, topped with ground turkey, ground beef, diced tomatoes, jalapeño peppers, refried beans, hot cheeses, nacho sauce, and just for giggles and grins, sour cream." She dug into the pile, putting more on his plate and then on hers.

"Is this stuff legal?" he joked as he scooped up more with his fingers.

The way he was enjoying himself made her smile at him, and he noticed. "What?"

She shook her head. "Nothing."

"No, tell me. What made you smile at me that way?"

She laughed. "You just did something else for the first time that you hadn't done before."

He thought about it and smiled at her. "You're right," he nodded and leaned over and kissed her on her cheek. They looked into each other's eyes and then went back to the treat, digging in with sticky fingers.

They were amicably chatting when someone said, "Hey, pretty girl, whatcha got there?"

Samantha smiled and looked up over her right shoulder. "Hey, good lookin' guy, come sit yourself down and share the load."

"Don't mind if I do." He squeezed in between Samantha and Andrew on the bench.

Samantha leaned back. "Quentin King, this is Dr. Paris McAlister, Dean of the Alex-Mont Academy."

"I'd shake your hand, but…"

"Not a problem. Are you related to Samuel King?"

"I'm his brother." Quentin recognized Paris as the man who spent most of the evening with Samantha the night before during the birthday party and wondered what their relationship was. He was a man who women would consider handsome. He was tall, slim, with a clean, clear complexion just south of a vanilla wafer. His eyes were a mossy green, but his braided hair was long and a rich dark brown.

"Ah, yes. I'm a fan of his," he nodded and then looked at Samantha. "Thanks for that hookup with Cecile Jordan Dixon, Samantha. I spoke with her today and she gave me her schedule for the dive. As it turns out, it works perfectly for me and one of my nature environmental classes. I'm putting the trip on the schedule, but for only two weeks. Are you going to make time to join me?"

She nodded. "I think so, if it's the dates we discussed."

"Great. I'll add your name to the group."

"You're going to dive?" Quentin questioned.

She nodded. "I'm going to join one of the Alex-Mont Academy dives with my sibs, Paris, and my cousin, Dr. Cecile Jordan Dixon. I think you met her last night in the after-hours spot. She's an oceanographer and one of the deans of the Scripps Institute of Oceanography at UC-San Diego."

"Yes, I remember talking with her. She's married to your cousin, Donald Dixon."

Samantha nodded. "Yes, that's her."

Paris poured beer from a cold pitcher into a mug and then dug into the nachos. "You did a late-night party after the circus?"

"You know my dad and mom are night owls when they have their friends in from out of town. I don't know what time they broke up the party this morning, but none of them showed up for breakfast. So, we brought their children on this ride with us." Samantha took a long swallow of her beer and wiped her hands before digging in again.

"I wish I had known. I would have stuck around. With Capri out of town with China, the place is pretty empty with just me and the twins in that big house."

"Capri is your wife?" Quentin hoped.

Paris shook his head. "No, she's my sister. She and her family live here in Havenhurst Estates. She's off visiting our other sister, China, her husband, and their children in New York City. She wanted to do some Christmas shopping in the Big Apple without the children so they wouldn't see what she bought. So, I kept the twins with me and brought them to the birthday party."

Samantha swallowed and wiped her hands and mouth before explaining Paris' family's connection to the Alexanders and

Montgomerys for Quentin's benefit. "Paris' sister, Capri McAlister Kennedy, is an attorney, a lobbyist with Kitt, Kenmore, and McAlister, a law firm where she's part-owner."

"Oh, yes, I've heard of her and her firm. David Carter, from your mother's former firm, recommended that I get in touch with her if I was considering adding a political ad component to King Advertising."

"She's a very good lawyer. She's also the wife of astrophysicist and astronaut Tate Kennedy."

"Ah," Quentin intoned. "Yes, the SPACEHOME PROJECT. Isn't your uncle Benny the pilot for that program, Samantha?"

"He is, but he didn't take the last flight up. Despite being an astronaut, he's still a five-star general in the Air Force. He selected one of his Air Force jet fighter pilots, Lieutenant Colonel Shawn Baxter Rodgers, to be vetted to take his place and fly this mission. Because my cousin, Whitney Ivy, Uncle Benny and Aunt Stacy's oldest daughter, is married and living in Germany with her husband, Uncle Benny and Aunt Stacy say that time is passing too fast. They are expecting, so he's spending more time at home in Japan with her and their other six children who are teenagers."

Paris nodded. "My brother-in-law, Tate, and Capri are also expecting. He's planning to stay Earthbound for a while when he returns from his current mission. He missed the birth of their twins because he was on SPACEHOME. When I moved here to accept the position of dean of Alex-Mont Academy, Tate and Capri asked me to move into their home because she and the twins are alone in their home while he's away. I help to take care of my nephew and niece. I'm only moments away from the campus, and my schedule is more flexible than hers. It is convenient for all of us. In addition to her law practice, she is of counsel to UN Ambassador Nathan Flack."

Quentin nodded. "Yes, I met Ambassador Flack and his wife, Dr. Savannah Logan Flack. I think my nephew, Sammy, introduced me to your nephew, Brody Richmond Kennedy, and his twin sister, your niece, Jamaica Charmaine Kennedy, at the circus last night. Sammy was pumped because Brody and Jamaica's father is an astronaut. Your nephew and niece are a little older than Sammy is."

"They are. They were nine on their last birthday in September. They're real extroverts like Sammy, though. I'd love to have your nephew enrolled at Alex-Mont Academy on a full-time basis. He's very bright and intuitive. When my nephew and niece called Sammy this morning and learned that he was going riding, they got me out of the house to ride our bikes over here to meet and visit while you have lunch."

"Will you take them on the dive with you?"

"I will. They're both in that class at Alex-Mont Academy."

"Hey, Paris. Sorry for the interruption. Quentin, could I see you for a moment?"

"Sure, Brian." Quentin wiped his hands on several napkins and then rose from the table, following Brian into the restaurant. When they were sufficiently out of sight of the others, Brian handed a shopping bag to him. When he looked inside, he had to laugh. "Thanks." He shook Brian's hand and hurried to the men's room to put on the cup and jockstrap Brian purchased for him. He had to make it quick because he didn't want to miss any conversation between Samantha and Paris McAlister.

CHAPTER 28

"So, I said to him, yuh lissen 'ere tuh me, yeah? Yuh mudda and yuh fadda, not be foolish and tink yuh be in school to be jokkin. Yuh behavior not gud. Yuh feel me, yeah? Yuh understand me? Yuh mudda and yuh fadda iz gud peoples. Dese peoples loves ya, bouyee, they be sad when dese gud peoples here dat you not be goin' wid us. That set him up fine and proper." Paris laughed.

Samantha laughed, too. "You are too funny."

"You're not American?" Quentin asked as he rejoined Samantha and Paris at the table and overheard part of his conversation.

"Oh, no, I am an American citizen. I was conceived in Paris, France, but born in Germany. My father and my mother are both military doctors. My father was born and raised in Maine. My mother was born and raised in Jamaica. They met and married in college when they were eighteen. Then they went into the military together and then medical school at Johns Hopkins. My sisters, Capri, China, and I were born while they were deployed to various military bases. Our parents recently celebrated forty years of marriage. Both sets of my grandparents are hale and hearty, as is my paternal great-grandmother, who is French and still lives in Paris. As a result, I speak several languages.

"I was giving one of our students a lesson in linguistics in Jamaica. He didn't understand how the large majority of the Jamaican people speak a form of English Creole, known as Jamaican Creole or Patois."

"Your dialect is spot on," Samantha commented. "Paris was just telling me about an expanded program for the students in language classes at the academy."

"How many children do you have in each class?"

"Twelve is the max for any class, but the average class size is about eight. However, there is no limit on ages. We have pre-adolescents in classes with teens. It all depends on each child's level of proficiency in any course of study. We don't hold our students back if they are mature enough to handle higher levels of learning."

"It's an interesting program. Brian told me about it and that his grandfather, Dr. Bernard Alexander, actually designed the educational system."

Paris nodded. "He did, yes, and I've been traveling to conferences and meetings to share the benefits of the program with other educational school systems."

"Paris and I almost hooked up while I was on my last tour while we were both in England, but we couldn't get our schedules to mesh."

Hooked up? That set Quentin back a step or two in his thinking. Was there something going on between Paris and Samantha? Paris is undoubtedly a charismatic character, likely the kind of man Samantha would find intriguing. Before his thoughts could take him further in that direction, they were summoned. Everyone had finished eating a hearty lunch.

"Let's head 'em up and move 'em out!" Brian shouted to the family and friends assembled on the terrace. "Let's go. We're burning daylight."

Everyone began to stand while the waitstaff filed in to clean the debris and rearrange the tables and chairs. The kids started to sprint toward the barn where the horses were tethered. Quentin made his way over to the maître d' and picked up the tab for the luncheon.

As he hurried to catch up, he noticed Paris McAlister in a tight embrace with Samantha. Intense curiosity knotted Quentin's gut. He didn't know what jealousy felt like. He hadn't cared enough about the women he dated to have intense feelings about any of them. However, with Samantha, it was different. He considered himself to have a great deal of self-confidence and very little if any insecurities.

He had to be to take over the leadership of King Advertising, and he'd been successful early in his role, driven by ambition to build upon the company which had been handed down to him through many generations. He hadn't harbored any insecurities from the very beginning, but in his private life, outside of his business personae, he faced concerns about missteps where Samantha was concerned. His attention was diverted as Brian intercepted him.

"You didn't have to do that, Quentin. Alex-Mont Ranch has an account here to cover our use of the facility."

"Maybe not, Brian, but I'd appreciate it if you'd let me do this. You and your family have done so much for us. I know that you're not looking to be reimbursed, but my siblings and I just want to express our appreciation in this small way."

Brian shrugged. "Okay. Thank you."

"No, thank you. This has been another good experience…despite the racehorse regatta."

Brian smiled and nodded. "I agree. Your nephew is doing very well, learning to ride, too. Samantha had her eyes on him to judge how well he was handling the pony. Paulette plans to put him in a riding program in San Diego."

Now it dawned on him why he didn't have Samantha's undivided attention. She was evaluating Sammy's proficiency in the saddle.

"Come on, Quentin. You're holding up progress." Brian jokingly called to him.

He acknowledged him and moved as quickly as his gap-legged walk would allow. He was definitely going to have to soak once he got back to the Alex-Mont Ranch, but the cup and compression fit already felt better on his balls.

"Samuel?" Gregory Alexander hailed as he and Quentin were leaving their suites on the third floor of the mansion.

The brothers turned in the wide hallway and waited for the much taller man to reach them. He was formerly the top basketball player in the world and stood six feet, ten inches tall. He reached out a hand to shake each of theirs.

They began to move toward the staircase. "I was on my way to see you. My parents mentioned that you're looking at starting a business venture and that you might need some guidance."

"That's correct. I've been thinking about opening a school in San Diego to teach tennis. Quentin suggested that I consider starting a league."

Gregory nodded. "Both good suggestions. Do you have time to talk now?"

Samuel and Quentin looked at each other and nodded. "Sure, we were just going down to the game room."

"Let's go to the computer lab. It might be a little easier to see what's going on in San Diego and evaluate the properties you're considering."

Quentin frowned. "There is a computer lab here at Alex-Mont Ranch?"

Gregory nodded, smiling. "Oh, yes. My brother, Kenneth, designed it. The family uses it to design programs for games or apps. My nephews, Roger and Ryan, are our technology whiz kids. They create stuff that only Kenneth understands." They moved down the stairs to the level where Samantha's studio was located, but they moved in the opposite direction.

Quentin was impressed with the number of support systems this home contained. There were studios for things like Samantha's workshop, an adult after-hours club, and an in-home movie theatre. There were also a ballroom, a music room complete with an audio and video recording studio, and a fully-equipped gym. A swimming lagoon, individual sports facilities like the racquetball courts, and who knew how much more he hadn't found existed on the Ranch.

They worked steadily for over an hour in the computer lab. Gregory pulled up the site locations Samuel mentioned on a big screen monitor and used CompuCorrect's satellite transponder to evaluate each area.

"Okay, this one seems to be the best of the ones we've seen so far." Gregory had a collage of the locations grouped together.

Samuel stood and moved closer to the monitor. "Why do you say that?"

"According to the City of San Diego's ten-year master plan that I found here online, this section of the city is slated for renewal. The price for acreage in this area hasn't started to rise yet, but it will the closer the city gets to its plan. Speculators will begin moving in and buying these old shopping areas. If you get in on the ground floor now, your investment will double and triple in the next ten years."

Samuel pointed to other sites. "These other two sites look to be in more stable communities."

"You're right, they are, and you'll get a great deal of pushback from the homeowners' associations in those areas because of the increase in property taxes and traffic your tennis center will create. That means you'll spend more time, money, and resources trying to locate there. You need to look at the long view as well as the short view of what is happening in the area. You'll want to not only do a population study, but also do a cost-versus-benefits evaluation on each of the sites that interest you. If you're going to make tennis a viable sport for disadvantaged children, you'll want to locate on or near thoroughfares where there are easily accessible public transportation systems.

"The vacant land that you found is zoned for estate-sized homes. That's why the price for the real estate was so inordinately high. What you need for your school is an area where there are already several businesses or areas zoned for business construction.

"Now, you can take the school outside of the City of San Diego into San Diego County and have a greater number of choices for your location and for less per acre. However, locating there would make it more difficult for certain people to access. As of the last census, the population was over four million, making it California's second-most populous county and the fifth-most populous in the United States. Its county seat is San Diego, the eighth-most populous city in the United States. So, you'll have a large pool of potential clients for your operation."

"I didn't realize that I would have to know so much about an area when considering where to locate the school."

Gregory nodded. "Based on this demographic, along with your name recognition and your brother's marketing expertise, my firm, CTI, would be willing to finance up to eighty percent of your expenses. We'd take an equity interest and provide you with the management team you would need for the first five years of operation. If, after five years, you believe you're on a firm footing and can handle all aspects of the business model we'll offer you, then we back out no questions asked. If you want to continue with our assistance, we sign contracts at five-year increments. There is no early prepayment penalty."

Samuel leaned back, dazed at the opportunity being offered by Samantha's uncle. "This is huge. Why would you do something like this for me?"

Frowning, Gregory looked at Samuel perplexed. "I don't understand. Why wouldn't I offer you this opportunity? This is the kind of thing that CTI does every day. We stand up fledgling businesses that have the potential to be successful. We make money for our investors and for our business. We've done thousands of deals with far greater risks than I see here. You're putting skin in the game with your twenty percent investment, and I feel you'll work hard to make it a success. You'll have your team of engineers, lawyers, accountants, planners, and architects through CTI to assist with anything that comes up."

Samuel shrugged. "I thought that because of what happened between me and Samantha and how my parents have treated your sister, you wouldn't be agreeable to work with me."

Gregory shook his head. "Okay, now I understand what you're referring to, but that's not how this family operates. You see, we live by a set of twelve principles that have been passed down through generations of our family. Those principles direct our interaction among us and with others. Just because you acted as you did doesn't require an equally adverse reaction from any of us. What was done is a part of history and cannot be undone or changed. Hopefully, you've learned never to behave that way again. Samantha is my niece, and I love her fiercely, but she would not condone retribution for past hurts. She's not built that way, and neither is my sister. I have a son who I'm teaching to abide by the family principles. Angelique and I plan to have more children, and we will teach them the same thing that I and generations of my family learned and still practice.

"I've given you a great deal to consider, Samuel. There is no hurry. Take your time and talk it over with your family. Take a look at our clientele, speak with any of them about how we operate and consult your own legal counsel. My offer of assistance is open-ended." He rose and extended his hand to Samuel and then to Quentin. "You're welcome to stay in here, use the equipment, and go over what we've discussed. However, beware that my family members could invade this computer lab at any time." He laughed.

"I have to go now to check on my wife and son, Clayton. He's a toddler and very energetic. Angelique and I are expecting another baby, and she tends not to get the amount of rest she should with Clayton around. If you want to talk more about this or the possibility of creating a league, tag me. A tennis league with you at the helm will fit in perfectly with the football league Nico Collins is starting; the baseball league Will Hamilton is starting; the lacrosse league my nephew, Brian, is considering, and the basketball league I've already started. We're going to co-locate the leagues in the same cities, namely those cities located outside the top one hundred. We're talking with JRock and JaiHonnah about designing and building the facilities we'll all need so that we can provide year-round activities in indoor arenas."

They agreed, and Gregory left.

CHAPTER 29

Bright and early on Sunday morning, Samantha strolled through one of the horse barns, following Patrick and holding a basket of sweet-smelling hay. The toddler went to each horse stall to have an earnest conversation with the horse and to feed each one a fistful of hay. She had the video rolling, recording his romp. When he heard the children's laughter, he made a surprisingly fast beeline in their direction without stumbling on short legs. Still recording, Samantha followed until they came upon Teresa, Angelique, and Sammy King rolling in the hay with ten or so black Labrador puppies crawling all over them. Brian, Samuel, and Quentin stood outside the stall, taking pictures of the children and puppies, and looked at her as she approached.

"Out for your daily constitutional?" Brian teased. He had his son strapped to his chest, but the boy was fast asleep.

"Patty Cake found me after breakfast and made it clear that he wanted to go for a walk outside. So, we got on our coats, hats, and boots, and here we are. He decided that it was time to feed the horses. I couldn't find any apples, so we settled for hay."

"Our sibs and the other children fed the horses and ponies all of the apples left in the bin. I'll have to buy or bring more down from Pennsylvania or up from South Carolina."

She nodded as she watched the three youngsters and the puppies at play. When Patrick joined in, she began recording again.

"Sammy is having such a good time that he hasn't taken time to figure out which puppy he wants to take home with him."

Samantha smiled at Quentin, who had moved closer to her. "I'll say. He has quite a large array of puppies to choose from. Does he realize what he will have to do to take care of the puppy he chooses?"

"Brian explained everything to us. Samuel and Sammy have worked out a schedule. Since Sammy will be back in school as of tomorrow morning, they will walk the dog before he leaves for school. The Watergate has a dog-walking service. So, they will come in the early afternoon…and I would like to see you again. Maybe you'd let me take you out for dinner or we could go to the theatre?"

She laughed at his abrupt change in topics from the dog training to going out on a date. "Which is it? Dinner or the theatre?"

"Both or either. Whatever your schedule would permit." He held his breath as she seemed to be contemplating his date offer.

She shrugged. "Okay, dinner at Angelique's Place on Tuesday at seven?"

He nodded and reached for her hand. "Should I send a car for you or pick you up?"

"No, neither. I'll drive into town and meet you at the restaurant. Let me make sure we can get a reservation. Otherwise, we'll be relegated to eating in the kitchen at the employees' table." She pulled her cellphone from her pocket and sent a message to her Uncle Gregory's wife, her friend and aunt. Moments later, she got a thumbs up emoji from Angelique confirming the reservation.

"Is it a date?"

"Yes. Angelique confirmed it." She keyed the date and time into her schedule. When she finished her phone beeped. After checking the message, she got Brian's attention, letting him know she had to leave. "You've got Patty Cake?"

Brian nodded. "You go ahead. I've got him."

She nodded and waved to those in the barn.

"You're leaving?"

She looked up at Quentin. "Yes, I have a class starting in about fifteen minutes. I'll see you at lunch before you leave."

He nodded, but he was reluctant to let her go.

"Okay, everyone. Let's start wrapping up," Samantha called out to the twelve young female teens and their twelve adult sponsors. "Lunch will be served in about thirty minutes."

There were groans from all who had spent the last three hours learning to sew. Each young girl was designated as "at-risk" of dropping out of school, getting involved in the drug culture, and/or becoming pregnant. This was a relatively new group of girls who had been selected by the mentoring program, which had been in place for several years, started by attorney Cheryl Lawrence Brock. She enlisted the aid of her close friends to provide one-on-one female guidance for the girls. They met with the group of twelve every other weekend to do something together. This weekend, Samantha agreed to give a sewing lesson.

"Thanks, Ms. Samantha," the girls chorused as they finished clearing up and filed out of her studio space.

"You're welcome, ladies." She smiled and waved.

Paulette moved to help put away big, heavy fashion books that held clothes patterns. "WOW! That's a handful."

Samantha nodded. "It is, but it's worth it. I'm pleased with the amount of creativity these young teens show for making clothes. It's a rather lost art, but it can lead to careers as seamstresses or as designers. What we're trying to do is to open their lives to lucrative careers they may not have considered before. The top and skirt they made today are rather simple, but each girl could feel a sense of accomplishment for what she did in the space of a few hours. They can now show off something they made with their own two hands to their friends and families. They have the extra benefit of the outfit being something they can wear. If any of them shows real promise as seamstresses, Bill Chandler said he would offer her an opportunity to work in his fashion house. He's found several outstanding fashion designers in the groups he hired for *Risqué* and *Stallion* clothing lines and features in his magazines. Since Bill's manufacturing arm is in Summer County, South Carolina, it's an opportunity for the girls to get out of an environment that may not be good for them and to live in a safe place."

"Where did they get the fabrics? Did Bill provide them?"

"Each girl's sponsor took her charge to a fabric store to find something she liked. It's all a part of the mentoring project. The sponsors act as big sisters to the girls and spend time individually with the teens one-on-one. We come together as a group every two weeks. Of course, I've been away, so my mom filled in for me. I'll have to swear you to secrecy, though. If the press and news media were to find out that Mom is one of the sponsors, the teen's life would be inundated. We don't want to do that to any of the girls."

Paulette nodded. "I won't mention it, but I think it's a wonderful thing you and the other women are doing. I just don't know where you get all of your energy."

"I find a way to invest my time and energy in things that are important to me."

"I hope my brother is someone you can invest your time and energy in."

Samantha frowned and looked squarely at Paulette. "Why would you say that?"

"It's no secret that he's very interested in you, and you've made certain positive changes in his life. Samuel and I haven't ever been as close to Quentin as we are now. We attribute the change to have come from your influence. We like what we're experiencing with him, and we hope that you two will continue to grow closer."

"Paulette, I like your brother, but I can't promise that what we share now will grow beyond friendship."

She nodded. "No, I understand, but he's been under a great deal of pressure from my parents to conform to their edicts. I think you're the reason he's able to smile more. He even leaves work at a decent hour these days. He turns on music when he comes home, gets comfortable, and whistles while he makes dinner. Believe me, this is not the Quentin King that I knew before we ran into you in Madrid."

That was a lot to think about, Samantha considered as Paulette and she left her studio to join the others for lunch. She didn't want to be responsible for anyone's happiness. If Quentin felt good about himself or his life in general, that was all for the better, and something she could add to her counted joys. The rest she wasn't quite sure about—until she sat with her family after lunch and watched the Sunday magazine show, *Let's Talk About It*.

It was raining fairly hard when Samantha stepped out of her SUV under the *porte cochere* and relinquished it to the valet. She hurried to the front of The Runway, the bar adjacent to the restaurant, Angelique's Place. Just inside the front door, Quentin King stood waiting and, for the first time, he was dressed in fashion-forward casual attire Samantha admired. Moreover, he didn't have a cell phone plastered to his ear.

"You're early," she said by way of greeting and smiled.

He took her in his arms and kissed her mouth. Then he sighed. "Ah, that's what I've been impatiently waiting fifty-three hours and twenty-three minutes to do." He had yet to relinquish his hold on her when he smiled. "I didn't want to be late for our first official date."

"When you called me and asked that I meet you at The Runway instead of inside the restaurant, I was a little surprised. Then when you told me the reason, I was more apprehensive about an open display of a relationship between us like this."

"Yet, you agreed. I appreciate that. This is a statement I want to make for all to see."

"I believe that you did that already during your interview on *Let's Talk About It*. I don't think you could have made it more clear that there is no marriage in the works for you and Ms. Bazemore and that those rumors of an engagement between you are false. You were kind, but direct."

"I wanted the world to know, but more importantly, I wanted you and your family to know that I'm not involved in a duplicative relationship."

She laughed. "Well, after the interview, there is no question about that."

"The question is, Samantha Montgomery, are you willing or not to let the world know that you are the woman I was talking about in that interview?"

"Yes, as long as you understand that I'm not ready to jump into an intimate relationship."

He nodded. "I understand. I think that we will both know when we're ready for that next step or whether to add sex to the equation. For now, we're officially dating, and it is not at this point an exclusive relationship. Agreed?"

She nodded. "Agreed." She took a deep breath and smiled at him. "Okay, let's do something for the first time that neither of us has ever done before."

Quentin smiled at her, nodded to the man holding the ropes to the stage curtains, and stepped forward. Camera lights flashed and music played as arm in arm they proceeded along the elevated runway stage to the cheers of other patrons already in the bar. They were met at the end of the runway and shown to available cozy seating. They stayed in the bar until they were called to the restaurant for dinner.

Angelique's Place restaurant was chic, having a style that immediately welcomed you in to relax and enjoy. Although he had never been there before, he liked the ambiance. The ambient lighting was perfect and the live music filtering in from The Runway didn't overlay or prevent conversation to flow at a normal volume. Nearly every table was filled, and other people came in after he and Samantha were seated.

At precisely seven-thirty, to the sound of melodic strings and harp, gauzy tents with hooped skirts descended from the high ceiling surrounding the individual tables, and the lighting lowered. The atmosphere gave an illusion of privacy in a sheltered garden setting to each table through the thin fabric. People could be seen in the tents, but mostly only in silhouette. A three-tiered candle arrangement burned in the center of the gaily-decorated, round table. Somewhere, it seemed off in the distance, a waterfall tinkled, and a brook soothingly bubbled.

Quentin appreciated the generously-sized, high-back chairs with padded armrests that didn't make his six-foot, five-inch, two-hundred-pound body feel cramped and uncomfortable.

He was intrigued over there being no restaurant menu. Apparently, everyone had whatever the chef decided would be on the menu that day, from soup to nuts. No substitutions except to avoid food allergies. Warm, peppermint-scented hand towels were distributed and removed before three wines were served in an awesome array of stemware. Gleaming flatware was already on the table in rigid formation and precise order. A basket held a generous grouping of small loaves of fresh, warm breads with flavored butters, cheeses, jams, and seasoned oils. It was a delightful surprise to see what was coming next throughout the delicious seven-course meal. Though the portions were not overly large, they were extremely filling, and each dish was beautifully presented and complemented by a different wine.

Waitstaff served and cleared after each course as efficiently and as unobtrusively as brain surgeons ply their trade. At the end of the meal, over an exceptional coffee and aperitif, Quentin declared the food lived up to the incredible ambiance. He paid the tab without paying close attention to the bill and added a generous tip.

A smattering of applause started and grew in intensity as the tents rose to the ceiling again, and the lights grew brighter. Quentin and Samantha stood and added their accolades to others who appreciated the meal and pageantry in which it was served.

"I supposed you've experienced this many times."

Samantha nodded. "I have, yes, but it never gets old. It's hard to get a reservation most of the time, so, as I said before, I end up eating in the kitchen at the employees' table. Still, I'm glad that you and I could enjoy this experience together for the first time."

"I am, too. I thoroughly enjoy doing things with you that I've never done before. Will you be all right heading home at this hour?"

"It's still raining hard. There will be minor flooding on my route home, so I think I'll stay in town."

"At the Watergate?" he grinned.

"Yes." She smiled at the glint in his eyes.

"Then, if I can catch a ride with you, I won't have to call for my car service."

"Samantha's Car Service is available for your convenience." She smiled broader with a bit of mischief as the valet brought her car under the *porte cohere*. At the Watergate, they kissed as they rode in the elevator. On the seventh floor, Quentin stood watching as the elevator doors closed on a smiling Samantha Montgomery. This had been a helluva great evening. With his hands in his pockets, he whistled as he walked the halls to his condo door.

CHAPTER 30

On Thursday evening, Quentin could hear the music before they reached the front door of Café Citron. Simon, Vincent, Samuel, and he had a great meal and time at the bar and restaurant, Déjà vu. Since the Salsa club wasn't far from Déjà vu, they decided to walk the few blocks.

Brian wasn't able to make it, but Paris McAlister planned to join them at the club. Over dinner, Quentin learned more about the McAlister family and their connection to the Alexanders and Montgomerys. For example, Paris' sister, China McAlister Goins, used to be the comptroller for JRock Baylor's company before she went into business with Vivian's brother, Gregory, at Compliant Trading and Investment. Vivian was JRock's attorney back then, and the families were still the best of friends. So, Paris wasn't just the dean of the Alex-Mont Academy; he was a close and trusted family friend. This information added to his learning curve about people in Samantha's sphere.

Quentin couldn't recall whether he ever walked the streets with a group of guys or with his brother. It was a chilly night, but Georgetown's streets were still teeming with people going in and out of popular bars, restaurants, and clubs. The four of them carried on a lively conversation and laughed at jokes as they walked. Groups of women flirted with the four handsome men on the street as they passed by. This was something else Quentin hadn't done before.

When they arrived at Café Citron, they checked their coats and then headed into the thick of the club. The place was pleasantly packed, and the dance floor held many energetic partners. They were led to seats on the second tier at a booth. Once settled, they ordered drinks and turned to watch the pageantry of those who were obviously skilled in the Latin dance forms.

Vincent craned his neck and frowned. "Simon, aren't those your sisters, Catrina and Lanae, on the other side of the dance floor?"

Simon stood and grinned. "They are, and they're with my beautiful fiancée, your other sister, Samantha, and Quentin and Samuel's sister Paulette." He laughed at the irony that so many siblings would run into each other at a Salsa club on a Thursday evening.

Vincent stood, too. "I thought they had some type of meeting tonight about the plans for the bridal shower."

Simon nodded. "That's what Geneviève said before she left home today. They were planning to have dinner at Angelique's Place."

Quentin and Samuel were curious, too, and stood. When the music ended and Geneviève was heading off the dance floor, Simon called her cell phone. When she answered, she turned around, searching the crowd until she spotted them waving at her. She waved back, got the other women's attention, and headed around the dance floor in the direction of the booth.

"Well, coincidence, much." Geneviève kissed Simon's mouth and then smiled at the group at large. "Catrina and Lanae Wilde, you know my twin brother, Vincent, but these are the King brothers, Quentin and Samuel."

Catrina reached out a hand. "Yes, we haven't met before, but I know Quentin was just on *Let's Talk About It* on Sunday. Wow, was that a blockbuster interview! The ratings for that show are through the roof."

Lanae accepted Samuel's hand while flashing a purely sensually winning smile at him. "Of course, there isn't anyone in the known universe who doesn't know the back-hand tennis phenom, Samuel King. I saw your final match in Madrid, Spain. I'm a devout fan."

The moment was pregnant with carnal awareness. Lanae was a strikingly beautiful young woman with deep blue eyes and long, curly, midnight black hair. It was clear that Simon, Catrina, and Lanae were closely related.

The moment was broken when someone called out to Samantha. When she turned, she was surprised to see Cameron Diaz, the co-pilot from her recent tour, striding toward her. "Cam?" she grinned and briefly hugged him. "Why didn't you tell me you were going to be in town? Are Glen and Fredrick with you?"

He shook his head. "I came to town to train for my captain's bars. Glen and Fredrick are on other flights in Europe. I thought I spotted your friends, the Kings, when I came in."

"Are you here with someone?"

"Oh, no. I was just out walking and heard the music. I'm staying at a McCoy Hotel near here. I don't know anyone in the Washington, D.C., metropolitan area…except you, that is."

"How long will you be in town?"

"My training will be over on December 1st. Then I'll head back to Texas."

"Then you'll have to join us."

He shrugged. "I don't want to interfere with your evening."

However, Samantha noticed how Cameron's eyes kept straying in Paulette's direction.

"We'd enjoy having you join us." Taking the decision out of his hands, she looped her arm through his. "Everyone, this is Cameron Diaz. He was the co-pilot on my last tour." She introduced him to everyone, including the King family members, who he had already seen on the trip from Spain to the United States.

Once the introductions were completed, Vincent smiled. "I didn't know you were going to be here, sis."

Samantha nodded and kept an eye on Cameron as he and Paulette conversed. "The bridesmaids met with the club's owner to decide whether we wanted to hold Geneviève's bridal shower here. All of the bridesmaids except Linda and Dena met for dinner at Angelique's Place. We completed the guestlist for the shower. Next, we have to decide whether to add The Runway to the potential list of venues. When we finished there, this is the second choice on the list. We have three more places to consider."

Just then, the chief medical examiner for the District of Columbia, Dr. Mervyn Lorenzo, a tall, slim man of Caribbean good looks, strolled up grinning with Paris McAlister.

"Hola, cómo estás?" Dr. Lorenzo greeted as he shook hands with the men in the booth, and introductions were made. "I didn't know you were going to be here tonight, Eve."

Geneviève grinned. "I took tonight off from work because my bridesmaids wanted my advice on where to hold my bridal shower. It was strictly supposed to be business in preparation for my bridal party. After the meeting with the owner, we decided to stay and enjoy the music for a while."

Dr. Lorenzo took Geneviève's hand and twirled her as the music began again. "Come, dance with me, *Chica*. They're playing our song. You have a lifetime to dance with this *sujeto*," he teased, nodding at Simon.

"Oh, no, *hombre*." Simon stood, took Geneviève's hand from Lorenzo's, twirled her into his arms, and smiled into her eyes before he kissed her. "I get the first dance with my *hermosa mujer*."

"Come on, pretty girl." Paris took Samantha's hand. "Let's show 'em how it's done."

Samantha grinned and let Paris lead her to the dance floor. He smoothly swung her into his arms, and they immediately matched steps to the music. Although Simon, half Irish and half Scot, learned the Salsa syncopation rhythms, Paris's mother was Jamaican, and he learned the dance from the time he learned to walk. So, his skill came through the blood. Samantha learned from Vincent and Geneviève and their maternal grandmother, Sylvia Benson Alexander. Samantha was surprised when she noticed Samuel putting a grinning Lanae through her paces. She was pleased to see Cameron patiently teaching Paulette the steps. Along the sideline, Lorenzo had another novice,

Catrina, learning the steps. When two women danced around Paris, she abandoned him and went to the table where Quentin sat alone.

"All right, pal, you know the question." She grinned at him and held out her hand, palm up.

He sighed. "When was the last time I did something for the first time? Is that the right question?"

She beamed a megawatt smile at him as if he was a favorite student, and she was the teacher.

He slid out of the booth and took her to the dance floor. However, instead of her having to teach him the steps, he swung her into his arms, molding her body to his as they moved expertly to the music.

"Well, well," she crooned, as she locked one arm around his neck and matched his steps. She moved in closer. "Obviously, this isn't your first time."

"You didn't ask whether I could dance the Salsa. I haven't done it in quite a while, but I'm not a complete social misfit. My parents forced me to take dance lessons so that I could escort the daughters of their friends to cotillions and other social gatherings. I can also do traditional ballroom dances and other Latin dances, like the Mambo, Cha Cha Cha, Bachata, Merengue, Rumba, Tango, Samba, Conga, and if forced, the Macarena, but only if forced." He noted the gleam in her eyes and shook his head. "No, absolutely not even for you."

She laughed and continued to precisely follow his steps.

He loved to see her smile at him and was enjoying having her in his arms. "How did you learn to dance?"

"Well, my parents certainly didn't force me and my sibs. Parties or even social gatherings around our homes with family always involve song and dance. You've heard of the French Mariah?"

He snorted a laugh. "Of course, who hasn't. She's the toast of Europe, Asia, and Africa, as was the phenom Josephine Baker."

"The French Mariah is my and my sibs' grand aunt."

He stopped dancing as the music was ending. "You're kidding me."

"No, I'm not. She's my maternal grandmother's sister, my grandaunt. So, as you can imagine, there is always music in our home."

Instead of going back to the table, they began dancing again as the next song started. "I learn more and more interesting things about you that I didn't know before."

"What do you think of what you've found out so far?"

"I think that you've become one of the most fascinating women I've ever met. I love your zest for life and living. Nothing seems to be beyond your reach."

She shrugged. "You said as much during the Wilde Star Media interview that aired on Sunday at one."

Quentin made sure that Samantha saw it by enlisting the aid of Brian, Will, and Simon. "What I said during that interview is true. I want to live in your world."

"As far as I know, we get only one chance at living. I want to live while I'm young enough to enjoy it. I want to help people enjoy life too. What do you want to do with your life?"

That question caught him off guard. He had never thought of his life as something where he had a choice. He was always going to head King Advertising. That was a foregone conclusion from the day he first drew breath. What would he do if he had been given a choice? He didn't know the answer to that question.

Samantha felt that she had asked a question which Quentin was having difficulty answering. "Let me know when you figure it out." She grinned and continued following his lead.

It was late when Samantha and the Kings entered the elevator in the Watergate. Paulette pushed the button for the seventh floor, and Samantha pushed the button for the eleventh floor. She decided to stay in town overnight rather than driving out to the ranch. She checked her parents' schedule to ensure they were not in town on a date night and spending the rest of the evening alone in the condo. She found that they were on an overnight trip to Philadelphia to go to a book launch event and signing for the new novel of one of

Derrick's nieces, Adelaide Jackson. It was on her schedule, too, but the bridesmaids' timetable to work on the bridal shower was also tight. Brian stayed at home with the family while she went out.

When the elevator opened on the seventh floor, Samuel and Paulette stepped out and waved goodnight. Quentin stayed behind and rode to the eleventh floor with her. He took her hand and walked with her to her door.

"I had a nice time tonight with Simon and your brother, Vincent. I think Samuel enjoyed it, too."

"I've been to Déjà vu. It's a nice restaurant."

"I enjoyed the other part of the evening, too, with you. You're a good dancer, Samantha."

"You're not so bad yourself."

When they reached the condo door, she inserted her electronic key and then keyed in her security code. "Would you like to come in?"

"Yes, I would, but I won't because I wouldn't want to leave. However, I do want to meet with you for purely business purposes. You see, I've purchased a property in the city. It's an old fire station, and Baylor and Baylor Design and Development is going to renovate it for me as they did for your uncle Gregory in his home in SoHo."

Her eyes widened in surprise. "A fire station? You continue to surprise me. That's usually a lot of space as it is in my uncle's home. It will certainly make for a fashion-forward home in D.C."

"It is; about seven thousand square feet on three levels, two thousand square feet each level and a thousand square feet for a partial basement."

She nodded. "Okay, yes, that's a great deal of space. What is it that you want me to do?"

"I want you to work with me on the interior design and décor. You have an excellent eye for these things, and you have an uncanny ability to understand what it is I like and would enjoy."

Surprised, she studied him for a humming moment, her eyes searching his. "Okay, but I'm not an interior designer."

"Still, you've done that type of work before. I'm starting with four blank walls on three and a half levels. I like what I saw in a video of your uncle's house. I'd like to see it in person because it's what I'd like to see in the home I'm planning."

She had to admit that what Quentin described would be an intriguing challenge. Generally, she came in after every wall was up and staged the interior to suit the client's taste. That wasn't even her primary job. She designed what when into the building. Of course, she had the skill to function in several capacities. Her work had form and function, but for the most part, it was considered a type of art. However, to be in literally on the ground floor of a project of this magnitude…seven thousand square feet…wow, that would be incredible, and she'd never had this type of *carte blanche* access. When she focused on Quentin's face again, she found herself nodding yes.

A broad smile grew by degrees on Quentin's face before he leaned in, and, without otherwise touching her, kissed her so thoroughly that her toes actually curled in her high-heeled ankle boots.

"Goodnight," he whispered a breath away from her mouth and then smiled before walking backward for a short distance. Then he turned, stuck his hands in his pockets, and whistled a tune as he headed down the wide hallway out of sight toward the elevator.

Samantha sighed, opened the door at her back, and entered the condo. She leaned against the door, closing her eyes, and calling to mind the way Quentin held her in his arms, her body flush against his as they danced. His need and heat were evident in the vertical ridge she felt against her. His kisses were becoming an aphrodisiac and causing an involuntary increase in her sexual desire. She was beginning to want to experience what she understood sexual pleasure could bring. That sensual haze left a lot to think about, but for now, she needed to sleep. So, heading to her old bedroom, Samantha disrobed and crawled into bed. It was a long time before the memory of Quentin's kisses would let her sleep.

CHAPTER 31

The stuffed turkey was in a warming drawer along with the ham, London broil, and stuffed baked fish. Samantha took the steaming hot, creamy mac and cheese from the oven and placed it on the sideboard in the round drop-in chafer, closed the lid, and then lit the Sterno. She returned to the kitchen to transfer the collard greens from the pot into a bowl before placing them in the dining area. She and Quentin had a routine going—transferring the hot food from the kitchen area to chafers on the sideboard while Paulette and, surprise, surprise, Cameron Diaz set the table and lit the candles. Everyone wore aprons with bibs, which Samantha made for the occasion. They were humming to music and dancing a bit. Samuel and Sammy took his dog, Samson, out for a walk and allowed Sammy some time to play on his skateboard. They were having a grand time.

"So, you like the fire station?" Paulette picked up the cloth napkins Samantha also made as gifts, along with matching placemats. The gifts complemented the décor she worked into the open-concept space. Paulette began to set the dinner table for the six who would share the Thanksgiving meal.

Samantha nodded. "I do, yes. It's a massive amount of space, and obviously it's going to need a lot of work. Still, now that it's been gutted and cleaned out, I can see that it's got real potential to become a unique home. It's in a prime location with the rear access to what could be a four-car garage. From the rooftop, Quentin will have an enviable view of the city skyline. If he decides to add the four-season garden and swimming pool on the roof, that will be awesome."

"Quentin said you took him to New York on Monday to see your Uncle Gregory's home, which is similar to what my brother is looking for. He was impressed with what could be accomplished in the fire station here."

Quentin nodded. "I was more than impressed with Gregory's home in SoHo. I really appreciate that he let you show me around his place while he and his wife are at their winter retreat. So, it's full steam ahead to get the plans finalized."

Paulette opened a chafer for Samantha to insert a clear glass bowl of seasoned stuffing. "Are you going to be able to work this project into your schedule?"

Samantha headed back to the kitchen to pour the giblet gravy into a bowl. "I've already started working on some preliminary plans for the main floor. That will be fairly simple. It's all open space much the same as my uncle Gregory's home is laid out. It's sturdy because it's where the fire trucks were kept. Wesley's structural engineers are thoroughly checking the place before the framing, wiring, plumbing, and HVAC systems are installed. Then he'll have the heating elements installed in the floor before he pours the finished concrete. I'll work with the architects to infuse their plans with what I know about Quentin's needs and tastes."

Paulette smiled. "That cute kid, Marcus, followed you around the whole time you were there. Who is he?"

"Oh, Marcus Greenfield is one of Wesley's three sons. He's always had an interest in construction."

Paulette frowned. "His son? Did he have a different mother than Wesley's wife, Roselyn? I mean, I know Roselyn. We're members of the same sorority. Marcus doesn't resemble Roselyn or Wesley."

Samantha nodded as she placed the hot bowl of Green Beans Almondine with thin slivers of garlic in another round chafer. "In a way of speaking, yes. Cole, Marcus, and Simone were adopted when they were very young by Wesley and Roselyn. They are half-siblings, and when their mother died in an automobile accident, their fathers weren't in their lives. Wesley and Roselyn were friendly with one another back then. However, they didn't want to see Cole, Marcus, and Simone separated and placed in foster care. So, Mom represented them in court and helped them jointly adopt the children."

Quentin stopped and stared. "That is an incredibly unselfish act. That couldn't have been easy for them to manage."

"They're incredibly unselfish people, as were their parents. They knew Cole, Marcus, and Simone's mother and cared about her children. They didn't have any other relatives, but later they found Cole's deceased father's sister. She's a wonderful woman who owns and operates a working farm and lives in Pennsylvania near Pittsburg. Before he died, her brother didn't know that he had fathered Cole, whose legal name is Coltrane.

"Wesley was the head of the community center, and Roz was the principal of the neighborhood elementary school the children attended. They lived and grew up in the same neighborhood together with JRock and their cronies. Their parents were friends. Wesley and his brother, Isaac's father, owned the local bakery and ice cream shop in their old neighborhood. He was the one who taught them how to cook and bake. Roselyn's parents are dentists and, although retired now, come back from North Carolina several times a year to provide free dental services. Their old office was in the same location with the bakery. So, Wesley and Roselyn grew up together and were both single when the children were orphaned. For them, it was a no-brainer. They married just so that they could adopt the children jointly as a couple.

"My mother was still practicing law back then, and JRock Baylor, the former superstar basketball player, was one of her clients. Wesley's best friend is JRock Baylor, and JRock asked my mom to represent Wesley and Roselyn in court. Of course, Mom was very familiar with the adoption process, since she already had Derrick Junior and the eleven of us. She agreed, and Cole, Marcus, and Simone legally became Greenfields. Then the most wonderful thing happened. Although they started out as just friends concerned about the children, Wesley and Roz fell in love. Since they married, they've had two more children; Elizabeth, who we call Lizzie, and Hunter. I was still in my teens when this all happened. I don't think many people remember that Cole, Marcus, and Simone were adopted."

Samantha went back to the kitchen for more hot food dishes. What the Greenfields did endeared them to her, just as her parents' open hearts brought health-challenged, abandoned children into their home. For her parents, it was a no-brainer, too.

Cameron nodded as he placed the silverware on the napkins. "This is true of so many Latins who take in the children whose parents have been deported to countries where they have never lived before, never to return. My own parents have taken in children whose parents were rounded up in raids and deported. Some have been sent to places where their families were not from. My ancestry lived in Texas before it was a state and still, sometimes, the police force me to prove that I am an American." He remorsefully shook his head. "Sometimes, I want to ask them to prove that their ancestors lived on the North American continent longer than mine have."

They all laughed with Cameron, but it was a sad state of affairs to be questioned about your right to be in America. Samantha noticed that Paulette gave Cameron's arm a comforting rub before everyone went back to work, setting up for the early meal. They seemed to be spending a great deal of time together after they met at Club Citron while he was in town for training. She eased the candied yams, followed by the mashed potatoes and corn pudding, into separate chafers.

Quentin used mittens to take the bread out of the lower oven. "This cornbread smells great. I've never seen it like this." He began to remove the small loaves of cornbread from the baking pan. "What's in it?"

"I use Mexicali corn and creamed corn to keep it moist. Those are red and green peppers and a little onion and garlic in it. too."

Cameron came to the kitchen island, smiled, and patted his heart, making everyone laugh. "This is good, like how my mother makes it."

"Wow! This place smells great!" Samuel came into the condo with Sammy and Samson on a leash. "When do we eat?"

Sammy beamed. "Yeah, I'm hungry."

"We're almost ready." Quentin nodded. "I need to put the mint jelly and cranberry sauce in bowls and get the Waldorf salad and Ambrosia on ice on the buffet."

Paulette raised her hand. "I'll do that."

Cameron stepped up. "What's next?"

Thoughtfully, Quentin looked around. "We could make a fresh, field-green salad with pecans, Mandarin oranges, cranberries, and raisins. Everything is on the counter beside the refrigerator, including the salad dressing."

Cameron headed in that direction. "On it."

Samantha stepped forward. "What can I do next?"

"I'll transfer the steamed cabbage into a bowl. You could help by putting the hot dinner rolls and buttermilk biscuits into the heated tray with the cornbread."

She nodded. "Done."

"What can Sammy and I do?"

"Wash your hands, give Samson something to eat and drink, and then you two can pour the water and drinks."

"Yes, my captain," Samuel and Sammy saluted, making Quentin laugh until the doorbell rang. He frowned. He was not expecting anyone else and was concerned because whoever it was, was not announced by the Watergate security. "Answer the door, would you please?"

"Sure," Samuel nodded and followed his son to the door.

Paulette, Cameron, and Samantha were singing to a popular song while they worked when five people filed into the open-concept living area. Except for the music, everything stopped and seemed to be held in a tableau vivant of suspended animation.

"Father, mother, Mr. and Mrs. Bazemore, Miranda?" Quentin frowned, stepped forward, and acknowledged the group while drying his hands on his apron. "Why are you here? Is something wrong?"

"You invited us to Thanksgiving dinner, didn't you?"

"Yes, father, I did, but you didn't acknowledge the invitation. I presumed that you weren't coming. How did you get in past security?"

"That's not important. We're here now. You can have the help serve." Ashanti looked down and kicked at the dog that was sniffing her feet. "Get that filthy animal out of here!"

"*No!*" Sammy railed, grabbing the puppy into his arms.

Samuel went to his knees to gather Sammy and Samson into a hug. "Mother, that was uncalled for!"

"Don't tell me how to behave…" The vitriol began and escalated.

Samantha felt eyes on her, but she ignored them and went to Quentin, turning her back on the argument unfolding as Paulette joined in to chastise her mother.

Samantha took his hand, and he looked down into her eyes, frowning. "Quentin, they're your parents. Simply invite them to join you for dinner."

He frowned. "There isn't enough room for them to be seated, and I'm not sure about the amount of food…"

"Not to worry. It will work out just fine. There's plenty of food. I planned for enough to have leftovers for another day."

Nodding, he squeezed her hand comfortingly.

She leaned in closer, and he bent to hear her. "By the way, is this the Manerva Bazemore, the woman you were dating?"

Grinning at her, he nodded. "Maranda, not Manerva. Yes, she is, but I promise. I broke off my relationship with her. She and her family were not invited by me to attend today's dinner. I invited only my parents."

"I believe you, Quentin. This is an obvious ambush. Please don't let it throw you. The important thing to consider at the moment is that Sammy is impressionable. He doesn't need to hear a family feud."

Quentin nodded and desperately wanted to kiss her, but she made a frog face at him, making him smile down at her. He sighed and launched into the melee. "Okay," he raised his voice to get everyone's attention. When that was accomplished and everyone was quiet, he smiled at his nephew. "Sammy, if you would put Samson away, then you and your dad can get washed up for dinner. We still need water poured and the drinks arranged on the table. Paulette, if you would show everyone where to hang their coats, we can…"

Ashante huffed and held her coat out to Cameron. It would have fallen to the floor if he hadn't caught it. "Let the help handle these menial tasks. That's what they are paid to do. Girl," she motioned to Samantha with a flick of her hand, "You there, fix a glass of wine for my guests and me. You can serve when I tell you to do so."

"Stop…" Quentin began and felt Samantha's restraining hand in his. "Oh, no, I won't tolerate this disrespect to my guests. Not even for you, Samantha," he shook his head and then raised his eyes to the group at large. "Let's make introductions so that everyone is clear that there are no servants here. The gentleman is Lieutenant Captain Cameron Diaz, a pilot with Adventurer Executive Airlines and a friend of Paulette, Samuel, and mine. The lovely lady beside me is my very special guest and co-host for dinner, Samantha Montgomery, head of Alex-Mont Textiles. She is responsible for making the festive aprons, placemats, and cloth napkins." He moved on to introduce his parents and the Bazemores. When he finished, the silence was deafening.

Into the void, Samantha stepped. "Paulette, I believe we're going to need to add leaves to the table and to add five more chairs. Everything should be in the storage room. You may also want to show your guests to the powder room and closet."

Cameron grinned and gave Samantha a thumbs up as he followed Paulette and the others. He would get the leaves and extra chairs to elongate the dining table for the additional guests.

As they were leaving the living area to store their coats, Samuel returned, frowning. "I hope inviting them won't turn out to be a colossal mistake."

Samantha reached out and touched his arm. "How is Sammy?"

"He is shaken up, but Samson wasn't hurt, so I think he'll be okay. We put Samson in his playpen with food, water, and toys. Sammy will wash up and be out shortly. Thank you, Samantha, for intervening. Now, what can I do to help?"

"If you and Quentin will unlatch the dinner table and pull it apart, we can insert the additional leaves when Paulette and Cameron bring them out of the storage area. We will need five more chairs from the storage room. This table is designed to serve twelve for a sit-down dinner, and there should be more than enough food."

"Clever." Quentin leaned down and kissed her mouth, and she grinned at him. "What did you do that for?"

"Just because…"

Samuel laughed. "I would have done the same thing, but I don't relish another hospital visit because my brother broke my newly forming bones."

Samantha snorted a laugh and, after turning, looked right into the malevolent expression on Miranda Bazemore's face. She turned back and patted Quentin's chest. "Your turn. I'm going to help Paulette and Cameron complete the setup. I'll get the additional dishes, silverware, and stemware. I made enough placemats and napkins for everyone. Come on, Samuel, let's do this."

Quentin watched Samantha and Samuel move to help set up and noticed the others checking out his condo, scrutinizing the art, touching the fabrics, and observing the view from the array of French doors, which led to the wrap-around balcony. He imagined they had inspected his private space, his home office, sitting room, bedroom, and bathroom, too. He wasn't surprised when Miranda approached and knows she would have embraced and kissed him if he hadn't stepped back.

"What are you playing at, Quentin?" she demanded in a low but strident voice.

"I'm not playing at anything, Miranda. I care very much for Samantha. We're dating."

"Isn't she your brother's girlfriend?"

"She and Samuel dated in high school. Now, they're not in high school anymore, and they're not dating."

"Your parents forbade you from communicating with her or her family. Yet, you defy them and put her in my rightful place? You made a spectacle of yourself at the club Runway with her. It was in all of the newspapers and even on television."

"You and I are over with, Miranda, regardless of my parents' dictates—or did you miss my appearance on *Let's Talk About It*?"

"Yes, I saw it! You humiliated me on national television!"

"You seem not to be able to catch a clue. You circulated false rumors among people I know that you and I were engaged. What, exactly, did you think I would do to clear my name and salvage my reputation and my relationship with someone I care deeply about?"

"She's not for you, Quentin. She doesn't even have a name or heritage among our people. She's got European blood in her body!"

"You think I care one whit about that because why?"

"You're the head of King Advertising!"

"Yes, I am, and she's the head of Alex-Mont Textiles. So, your point would be what? That we're not professionally suited?"

She shook her head. "You're such a colossal disappointment! All you men care about is a female who is light, bright, and damn near white with big tits and ass! At least with me, you know that when I spread my legs for you, your brother wasn't there before you!" So saying, she stormed away.

When everything was set, Quentin took Samantha's hand and guided her to stand behind the seat beside his at the head of the table.

However, defiantly, Ashante moved to stand behind the seat at the opposite end of the table. "Junior, you move and let your father sit at the head of the table. You can find a seat elsewhere. Now, Miranda, you sit next to Junior and—"

"Mother!" Quentin's voice held censure. "This is not King Manor. You may sit anywhere you want except at the head of my table. Either Samuel or Paulette will sit there."

Again, the silence reigned, but Quentin had established his position as the head of his household. Slowly everyone, including his mother, shuffled, finding a chair to stand behind.

Quentin looked around the table and nodded his approval. All eleven seats would be occupied. The space for the twelfth seat was to Samantha's right side. That was fine with him. "Sammy, would you say grace?"

The little boy beamed a smile, put his palms together, and closed his eyes. He repeated a short prayer of thanksgiving and then said enthusiastically, "Bless the cooks! Let's eat!"

Quentin smiled. "We will let the guests go first, and then we can serve our plates."

Sammy frowned. "Why come, Uncle Q?"

"Because you're the host with me, your daddy, your aunt Paulette, and Ms. Samantha, right?"

"'Kay," he sighed, his tone exasperated and barely placated, making some laugh.

Well into the meal, Samuel was talking about a recent meeting he had. "Will Hamilton and I met on Monday when Quentin, Samantha, and I flew to New York for the day. He plans to franchise a pro/am baseball league in the same cities where Gregory is creating the pro/am basketball teams for his new league. Their friend, Nico Collins, has finalized the details for creating a pro/am football league. He was at the meeting, too. We met at the offices of the CTI Wall Street firm with the team assigned to assist me for the next five years. I signed the papers for my new venture, King Academy of Tennis or KAT. Paulette has signed on as my director of marketing." He smiled at his twin sister.

"That's intriguing," Mr. Bazemore grinned. "Maybe you should be the one to get the ad contracts for all of these pro/am sports leagues for King Advertising. When you come on board, your notoriety will open a lot of doors for the company."

Samuel shook his head. "No, sir, that's not my intention. I've discussed this with Quentin and Paulette. We won't take advantage of the relationships we've been privileged to form through the Alexander-Montgomery family. I have a different agenda planned for my next career objectives. Of course, I've contracted with King Advertising to create my marketing campaign. Paulette will take the lead on that." He smiled at Samantha, who nodded in return. "In a few days, Paulette, my son, and I are moving to San Diego, where I've purchased a warehouse building as my place for the school. Cameron has agreed to fly us there on an AEA charter flight on his way back to his home in Texas."

Cameron lifted his glass of water to take a sip. "I remember him, Will Hamilton, I mean. He was called The Hammer when he played professionally. He was a hero to those of us who had dreams of being like him and bringing home baseball trophies. I played third base as a kid."

Samantha recognized Cameron's comments as an effort to keep the conversation from turning contentious. Mentally, she applauded his efforts and winked at him when he smiled at her. *Yes, Cameron didn't come down with yesterday's rain. He is swift*, she thought, *even-tempered and not easily offended.*

Mr. Bazemore nodded. "I remember him, too. He was among the greats. I also remember Nico Collins. He was a high-profile football player who retired at the top of his career. He's now the head of the Financial Empowerment Network. I've watched several of his television shows about investments and establishing portfolios of certain stocks and bonds. He's married to one of the wealthiest women in the world, Constantina Justice. She is the head of Sweet Justice Productions. Her parents are Howard alumni. I wonder why they don't use King Advertising? Do you know them, Quentin?"

Quentin IV nodded. "Yes, I know her father, Redmond Justice, but he married some chick he picked up on the street, a Latina or some such. Redmond is in the trash business. King Advertising doesn't need to be associated with that type of rabble."

Mrs. King nodded and chimed in. "He's one of a whole passel of kids. His father is one of them jackleg preachers who married a redskin…"

Samantha had heard enough. "Actually, Mrs. Justice, Redmond's wife, Margurite Alonza Dela Vega Justice, is Spanish royalty. However, it is true that Redmond and Margurite did indeed meet on the street. She was new to the U.S. and the streets of Chicago. She came to America to attend nursing school at Chicago Med. On her first day of classes, she plowed her car into the rear of Redmond's first refuse collection truck. It's a bright red behemoth truck that you can't miss seeing, but somehow Margurite did. That story has become folklore in the Justice family.

"Margurite's father, Rafael Alonzo Dela Vega, is a diplomat. Redmond's father, Reverend Doctor Ellis Justice, is married to Anna Lettie Outlaw. She is Indigenous Chippewa and American of African descent from the upper peninsula of Wisconsin on Lake Superior. They have a proud heritage in that part of the country. I've been privileged to participate when Reverend Justice and his family feed, clothe, and help to shelter hundreds of needy families in Chicago during every religious holiday, including Kwanzaa. They've saved the lives of hundreds, probably thousands, over the many years they've been providing aid where needed.

"Working with Ambassador Jake Hawkins and Ambassador Emeritus Jefferson Logan, Redmond Justice recently provided, free of charge, five refuse trucks to each of several African nations to help with their waste management efforts. Those nations were so appreciative that they awarded him and Justice, Inc, their highest medal of valor…as did the president of these United States, for his service. Not bad for a man who made a career out of collecting refuse for a living. Did I mention that one of Reverend Doctor Ellis Justice's five brothers, Ned Justice, is the Chicago Police Commissioner?

"Also, in addition to Tina Justice, she has six older brothers; Miguel is vice president of Justice, Inc. Juan is a medical doctor. Keenan is a Chicago Police Lieutenant. Tyson works for the CIA. Diaz is a captain in the U.S. Coast Guard, and Bouchard is the head chef of his own trendy Miracle Mile restaurant. Yep, quite a success story for someone from the Southside of Chicago who built an incredible business on picking up someone else's trash, wouldn't you say?" She rose from her seat and smiled winningly at Mr. and Mrs. King and Mr. and Mrs. Bazemore. "Please help yourselves to the buffet, as Quentin has provided plenty of food for this Thanksgiving feast."

Silence fell over the room as Samantha returned to the buffet to replenish her plate.

Cameron followed and whispered, "Way to go, Samantha!"

Paulette stifled a laugh and stepped into the silence. "Samuel is considering starting a tennis league in addition to KAT," Paulette proudly offered. "I think that Quentin should consider a swim league. JRock and JaiHonnah could design and build the facilities."

Mr. Bazemore looked up the table toward Quentin. "Really? Quentin, do you think that you have time to lead King Advertising effectively and manage a pro/am swim league, too?"

Ashante bristled, slamming her napkin down on her dinner plate. "Of course not! This is all such foolishness! Samuel, now that you've decided to stop traipsing all over the place playing silly games, you should take your rightful place at King Advertising. Moving to San Diego is a preposterous idea. You have no idea what you're doing. You should move back into King Manor with Paulette and start establishing roots in the community where you were born. It's your responsibility—"

Samantha returned to the table. "Anyone for dessert? I believe there is deep-dish apple pie, pumpkin pie, carrot cake, and homemade cherry and pistachio ice cream."

"*Me! Me!*" Sammy piped up, raising his hand and bouncing excitedly in his seat.

"Okay, pal-of-mine. Why don't you help me figure out what everyone wants, and we can serve them?"

He nodded gleefully, popped up from his seat beside his father, and took Samantha's outstretched hand. They went to the dessert table, where Samantha retrieved a serving tray.

"Do you remember how we did this at Alex-Mont ranch?"

"Uh-huh," he eagerly nodded as his eyes got bigger and bigger as he looked at the array of desserts. Then he grinned up at her.

It made her laugh, and she caressed his face in her hands and then kissed his forehead. Then she loaded an array of offerings onto the tray. With his tongue stuck between his teeth at the left corner of his mouth, Sammy carefully balanced the tray and walked slowly to each person. After the selection was made, Samantha followed, pouring hot, aromatic mint and chocolate coffee into each person's cup.

The conversation moved to more neutral territory, Quentin noticed. Each time it appeared an argument would ensue, Samantha would say or do something to get everyone onto a different track. She seemed to be working harder than anyone else to make the Thanksgiving dinner a cordial event. He appreciated her efforts but feared that her level of tolerance wasn't bottomless.

When Mrs. Bazemore spoke to him, it took his attention away from his thoughts. "I apologize. What were you asking me?"

"I asked who catered this meal? It's very good. I'd like to consider them for upcoming events my husband and I are planning."

Quentin laughed. "I'm afraid that Chez King isn't available for future engagements."

The woman's brows narrowed. "I don't understand. Are you saying that this meal was not professionally catered?"

"That's correct," Samuel nodded and held up his glass to toast Quentin. "Samantha took us grocery shopping yesterday, and we prepped most of today's dinner before eight last night when we ordered pizza to celebrate. Then this morning, Samantha's brother, Brian, delivered the Mountain Fresh stuffed turkey and dressed ham with pineapple, cherries, cloves, and brown sugar glaze, to which we added the London broil and seafood stuffed fish from Alex-Mont Farms. We prepared the rest of the meal ourselves with Samantha's guidance, except for the desserts, which I picked up from Greenfield Brothers Bakery."

"Well! I never expected that overnight the King legacy could be brought down to mere cooks in a kitchen! Our reputation will be forever tarnished if this gets out. I can understand such behavior from a low-life like that chit of a girl," she flicked her hand at Samantha. "She is not fit to lick the dirt from my shoes, and that whore of a mother of hers is no better!"

"Get out!" Samuel railed, standing and pointing toward the door. "Take that filthy mouth of yours and nasty attitude and get out of here!"

"Sam!" Samantha stood and shook her head. "Don't! It's getting late, and I have a flight to catch." She turned to Quentin, who had stood beside her and was seething with anger. "I'm fine. If I don't have an opportunity to say so, have a happy holiday season."

Quentin frowned. "What do you mean? You're coming back after your visit to South Carolina, aren't you?"

She shook her head as she began to move toward the front vestibule. "No. After the Thanksgiving holiday, I'll head to New York to do a Christmas holiday installation of a window at McCoy's Department Store. I have other commitments before I join my family in Monroe County, Pennsylvania, for Christmas. Then I'll be back for only a short time for my parents' annual New Year's Eve party before I head out again.

"You keep up the good work and continue to do something for the first time that you haven't done before." She grinned. "You're really getting good at it." Then she turned and bade everyone a Happy Thanksgiving and holiday season before heading to the front door.

Ashanti intercepted her. "You're a cool one. You're the reason my children are acting like fools. You think you're something, but you're still some stinking whore's bitch. You were found in an alley with the rest of the dregs of low-class society. You spread your legs for one of my sons, and now you're after the other one. Well, you can take your money-grubbing, no class, social-climbing behavior out of here and leave my children alone!" Her hand went up and was caught an inch from Samantha's face in the younger woman's grip.

With her eyes drilling into Ashante King's, Samantha hissed in a deadly quiet whisper, "I don't know who died and made you God, but she wasn't my God? You have a right to say and think whatever you want, Mrs. King, but your rights end at my ears. You want to talk about my parents? Go ahead. Their reputations will stand up against anything you have to say about them. They have the respect, love, and trust of people who matter to them, including me, and that's all they need or want. Your rhetoric doesn't matter to them or to me.

"You're right. I have no idea who my biological egg and sperm donors are, but ask me if I give a damn. Whoever they are, I hope they aren't as shortsighted and mean-spirited as you are. It says something about you that you would put on this shameful display in front of your impressionable grandchild. You have a problem with me, tell it to someone who gives a damn about what you think." She pushed Ashanti's hand away, eyeing her for a humming moment before she continued to the door.

Quentin followed, angry at his mother. "I apologize for my mother's behavior. I've never seen her act that way." He stopped Samantha while she was in the act of putting on her coat, hat, and gloves. "Please wait, Samantha. I don't want you to leave like this."

"I'm not angry with you, Quentin. However, I want to make one thing crystal clear. Samuel and I never had sex together. However, if he and I had continued, we likely would have. I was prepared to make love with him after the prom, but you know what happened there. So, thankfully, it never happened. Still, if we had, I wouldn't be the person I am today, and I like the person I see in the mirror each day. I don't wake up with regrets." She squeezed his hand and was about to leave when Sammy grabbed her around the waist. She knelt to hug him, kiss his cheek, and then she left.

CHAPTER 32

Geneviève piloted the Cessna 425, Corsair eight-seat turboprop twin-engine light aircraft with Samantha sitting next to her in the co-pilot's seat. Simon sat in the cabin with Bill Chandler, Esquire, going over their notes for the upcoming meeting about the film *Rising Eagles*.

"So, how did it go?"

"Not great, but Cameron Diaz was there. He was a nice addition to the party. He has a great personality, and he's a knowledgeable conversationalist. He's really quick on his feet, too. Wicked smart. Paulette invited him to dinner."

"I thought there might be something percolating between them the night he joined us at Café Citron. He spent the majority of his time teaching Paulette to dance the Salsa. That's nice for them. He seems like a really great guy."

"I believe you're right. He comes from a nice middle-class family and has eight siblings. They are all college graduates and are apparently very close. His parents take in needy foster children. They've had more children in their household than we have in ours."

"So, what didn't go well? Did the food not turn out to be palatable?"

"No, the food was surprisingly good. In fact, one of the guests thought the food was catered."

"'One of the guests?' Who was there in addition to you, Cameron, and the King family?"

"It doesn't bear repeating."

"Samantha, we have another hour of flight time. I've told you all about dinner with Simon's family. Stop making me dig for scraps of intel. What went wrong?"

Samantha relented and told her sister about the unexpected guests for Thanksgiving dinner and what transpired.

"She did *what?* She actually tried to slap you?" Outrage hummed through Geneviève's tone of voice. "She must not have known that you're a Sandan, a third-degree martial arts black belt."

Samantha snorted a laugh. "It didn't come up in my conversation with her. Some time ago, Mom alluded to the fact that Mr. and Mrs. King are racists, but I believe that Mrs. King's behavior surprised even Quentin, Samuel, and Paulette. They were outraged. I think her husband was somewhat shocked, too. I could see that Mr. and Mrs. Bazemore were intimidated into silence, but not their daughter Miranda."

"Miranda Bazemore? This is the woman Quentin is said to have been engaged to? I remember her name from the television interview."

Samantha nodded. "I believe that she still thinks Quentin is available to her. I don't think that Quentin noticed that she wasn't wearing a coat when it's as cold as a witch's tit in D.C. The others were bundled for the extremely cold weather, and the Watergate security office did not announce their arrival. When Quentin asked how they got in through security, Mrs. King deflected the question. Quentin didn't follow-up on it because the situation was quickly going to hell in a handbasket. I was trying to placate the combatants because Sammy was already upset by his grandmother kicking at his puppy."

"You think this Miranda lives in the building?"

"Yes, I do. I don't know whether she moved in after him or already lived there. I believe it's unlikely that Quentin would have moved into a building where he knew his former lover lived."

"So, you think it's the former. She moved in after he did to continue to pursue him."

"That's my thinking."

"Do you believe that this is some kind of fatal attraction syndrome?"

"I don't know, but I'm glad that Sammy will take Samson with him to California and out of harm's way soon. I wouldn't want to see that puppy end up in a pot of boiling water."

"Do you want me to run a background check on this Miranda Bazemore or Mrs. King? I mean, no one missed your appearance as a couple at The Runway. That was shortly after Quentin made it abundantly clear in his interview that Miranda Bazemore was yesterday's news and that another woman, namely you, is vitally important to him. Of course, Quentin didn't give your name during the televised interview, but he did everything except that to identify you. I quote, 'she is the personification of Maya Angelou's phenomenal woman,' unquote, and that he had known this person most of her life."

Samantha shook her head. "Well, that was a stretch. I really didn't *know* Quentin during those early years. I don't think that I noticed him much. He seemed like such a nerd to me back then, but I wasn't particularly outgoing either."

"Well, I didn't pay attention to him or his parents either, back in the day. Though we are in the same age group as Samuel and Paulette, they were more your pals than Linda's, Dena's or mine. From what little I remember about him, Quentin certainly has changed. That's not to say he's not highly intelligent because he is wicked smart. Simon, Vincent, and Will like him. Andrew, Darren, and Spencer believe he has potential. Brian is coming around to the same opinion because Quentin has done so much to try and appeal to you. So, he gets the seal of approval from them. However, say the word, and in twenty-four hours or less, I'll know everything about these two women down to the type of toothpaste and tampons they use."

Samantha knew her sister was serious. Geneviève, a homicide lieutenant, in the D.C. Police Department's Major Crimes Division, had a squad of detectives and police officers under her command. This is just the kind of thing her detectives investigated *after* the fact.

"No, I think it's up to Quentin to handle his business. We agree. He's not stupid."

"As long as they know that if anyone comes after you, it will be like bringing a knife to a gunfight. No one lays a hand on my sister," she boasted without heat.

Bill appeared in the doorway. "Samantha, come talk with me and Simon a moment."

She unstrapped from the co-pilot's seat and stood to follow Bill back to where he sat next to Simon. She picked up a short bottle of water from the refrigerator before sitting at the table across from them. "What's up?" She regarded them, uncapped the water, and took a healthy swig, all while continuing to eye both of them.

"We're going over some of the plans for the movie. We noticed that King Advertising submitted a bid to create and produce the ad campaign for the movie. We wondered whether this has anything to do with your relationship with Quentin King."

"You mean, whether he's involved with me to get the advertising contract?" She shook her head. "I don't think so. When did the company submit the bid?"

Bill frowned and looked through the heavy binder. "It looks like the company's bid came in when the movie was announced." He looked up at her.

"Uh, no, that's before we met at the airport in Spain. I hadn't heard from any of them since Samuel dumped me on prom night."

"Is it possible that the meeting at the airport was contrived?"

She grinned and took another sip of her water. "Anything is possible, Uncle Bill, but in this case, it's unlikely. You see, they were scheduled for a different AEA flight that was delayed because of heavy weather in Brussels. Frederick, the steward on my flight, delayed *our* flight because the company contracted to deliver the provisions was late. The company gave him additional meals because they were responsible for delaying our departure. Ten minutes one way or the other, and the Kings and I wouldn't have connected. I waited to board the flight until Frederick got everything loaded. Otherwise, I would have been sitting on the plane, and I wouldn't have even seen the King family. If you can make something out of what appears on the surface to be happenstance, more power to you."

Bill nodded. "Okay, if you don't think that Quentin King is advancing his bid for the ad campaign through you, then we'll leave his company in the mix."

"Do that. If you don't think that Quentin could be interested in me because of my sterling personality," she batted her eyes at him and grinned, "I don't have an opinion one way or the other. We're just friends at this point. However, at dinner today, Samuel made it abundantly clear that he will not take advantage of his connection to our family to benefit King Advertising. I take him at his word."

Bill looked skeptically at her. "You did see Quentin's appearance on *Let's Talk About It*, right? It's clear to me that he has an interest in you that's not benign."

She laughed. "As apparently did millions of others. However, the bottom line is whether I think that Quentin is using me to get the contract for the movie, right?"

"Right."

"That's a definite no. I don't believe that the King family knew the connection between Sweet Justice Production company, Simon, and the Alex-Mont posse. In fact, if today's Thanksgiving dinner at Quentin's condo is any indication, I'm positive they were unaware of how close we are to the Justice family."

"You may be right, but if I find out otherwise, they'll be permanently out of consideration. We believe that we can have a three-movie deal once Simon completes the last novel in the trilogy."

Samantha looked at Simon and grinned. "Goody! That means I get to design the sheets and comforters for Bill's bedroom scenes in the next two movie releases. Write in some really steamy hot and sexy bedroom scenes for Bill, please, Simon." She gave Bill a salacious wink.

"Cut it out, imp."

Samantha just grinned and finished her water. Bill could pass for a better version of Matt Bomer. He had unbelievable sex appeal and often posed nude for gay trade magazines, including his own magazine *Risqué*. Though he claimed to be bisexual, she always felt that Bill had a dangerous edge about him, a type of city quickness that enhanced his sex appeal. He would be an excellent James Bond character with his suave and debonair persona.

However, Bill wasn't all good looks, a great body, and no brain. On the contrary, he was among the top sports and entertainment lawyers in the world. He had clients all over the globe and traveled extensively. In addition, he was among her mother's best and most trusted friends. He helped raise them after Derrick's death and even after her mom married Chuck. If his schedule permitted, Mom and Chuck would allow him to pluck up any of the Alex-Mont posse and take them with him to exciting destinations.

To the world, he is known as the cunning legal expert, mega movie star, impressive businessman, and the world-class supermodel, Chandler. To all of the Alex-Mont posse, he is simply their beloved Uncle Bill.

CHAPTER 33

After the Thanksgiving weekend, Samantha waved goodbye to her sister, Linda, her husband, Will Hamilton, their two toddler boys, and Will's brother, Drew, as they headed toward the exit of the New York City LaGuardia Airport AEA terminal. Then she turned to wait for the airline attendant to retrieve her luggage and smiled when she rolled it toward her. "Thanks, Ginny."

"You're welcome, Samantha. Have a good holiday…" she frowned, stepped to the side to look behind Samantha, and then her smile broadened, her voice dropping to a near breathless level. "Well, hello, Captain Kennard. Fancy meeting you here."

The woman preened, batting her eyes. Samantha turned to see Glen leaning his butt against the back of a waiting room chair, hands in his pockets so that his coat opened, revealing a beautiful sweater which did justice to his flat abdomen, pronounced six-pack, and beautiful pecks. His long legs and booted feet crossed at his ankles. She almost didn't recognize him in casual clothes. He was handsome to the extreme, and when he released a polar-ice cap-melting smile, he was drop-dead gorgeous.

"Hello, Ms. Swinson." He acknowledged with a nod, but his eyes were only briefly on the flight attendant before they landed on Samantha again. He stood to his impressive height and moved forward. "Hello, Samantha."

She grinned. "Hi, Glen. I didn't expect you to be here so soon."

He reached for her luggage with one hand and her free hand with the other. "My charter came in last night, but we have only a few days before my schedule requires that I fly him and his group to Germany. It all depends on how well his meetings go."

Samantha accepted his hand and walked shoulder to shoulder with him dodging the oncoming crowded terminal toward the exit. "Then, we'll have to make the best of the time we have."

"You're scheduled to dress one of the ground-floor windows at the McCoy Department Store?"

She nodded. "I am, yes. I have to complete it by the weekend. The reveal for all of the holiday season windows is on Sunday."

"Do you know what theme you plan to use?"

"Yes, love, charity, and peace."

They stopped beside a waiting AEA Ground Transportation car. Still holding one hand, he took her other hand and drew her closer. He grinned down at her. "Love, charity, and peace? Why am I not surprised? I can't wait to see what you've come up with, but I also can't wait another moment to kiss you."

She smiled, leaned up on her toes toward him, and laid her mouth on his. With their eyes open on one another, they shared their first kiss while smiling at each other. Samantha was determined not to make any comparisons between kissing Quentin and kissing Glen, but there was definitely a difference. It was as if Glen's eyes smiled throughout the joining of their mouths, and they both sighed.

The driver placed Samantha's luggage in the trunk while Glen opened the back door and followed her in.

"Okay," he placed his left arm around her shoulders and drew her closer. "I didn't know what you've already seen on Broadway, but I do know that you like to eat at Angelique's Place. So, I was able to secure reservations for dinner tomorrow. Is there any show you haven't seen on Broadway that you'd like to see?"

"Riverdance."

He inclined his head. "Good choice. I haven't seen it either. I'll see to getting the tickets. Where would you like to go for dinner tonight?"

"Jazzabelle's. It's a dinner club in SoHo. It serves Louisiana cuisine and usually has an excellent jazz band for entertainment. Are you game?"

"Yes, it sounds great. Perhaps we can walk around the area afterward? I haven't spent any time in SoHo."

She nodded. "Good idea. What else do you have planned for us?"

"Oh, all manner of interesting things which we will manage to enjoy around your work schedule. We'll begin with a jog around Central Park at five-thirty, breakfast at the McCoy Café at six, and then I'll leave you alone until I bring lunch to you at one o'clock. Then, dinner at seven at Angelique's place. We'll plan to have an early dinner and go to the theater the next night."

She nodded her approval. "Then, after you leave me alone to toil in my solitary space," she teased, "I have a surprise for you."

"Really? What is the surprise?"

"You think I'm not going to make you wait until tomorrow to receive it?"

"Uh, Samantha, we're not talking about something intimate, are we?"

She shrugged nonchalantly, a Mona Lisa smile on her mouth.

"You're killing me."

She laughed as the car pulled under the *Porte-cochere* of the McCoy Grand. Valets opened their car doors. They got out and went into the hotel holding hands.

Later that evening, Glen opened the door to Jazzabelle's and stepped in behind Samantha out of the icy cold rain. He helped her out of her winter poncho and handed over his coat and umbrella to the hostess in the cloakroom. Then he stepped back and appraised her from the bottom up. A smile grew broader on his face. "Before we go any further, please let me tell you that you look absolutely stunning." He stepped to her and kissed her mouth.

She grinned. "Oh, this old thing?" she teased.

He shook his head. "No, that couldn't be that old. What you're wearing is too fashion-forward."

"Haven't you heard that what's old is new again?" she sang.

He harmonized with her, "*Dreams can come true again when everything old is new again. Get out your white suit, your tap shoes, and tails. Put it on backward when forward fails. Better leave Greta Garbo alone. Be a movie star on your own.*"

The dining room hostess smiled at them when they finished. "Wow, are you two performers?"

They laughed. "No," Glen shook his head. "We saw the show in London not long ago. We've been singing those lyrics ever since then."

"You're terrific together. I hope you can bear with us for a few moments. We have only one table coming up. It shouldn't take long. Maybe ten minutes. Do you mind waiting?"

Glen and Samantha regarded one another. "I don't mind, if you don't, Samantha."

She shrugged. "It's fine with me. We're not in a hurry. The food and entertainment here are well worth the wait."

"Thank you, and by the way, Miss, that's an incredible outfit you're wearing. If you don't mind, did you buy it somewhere here in SoHo?"

Samantha shook her head. "Uh, no, I made it during a class I held to teach a bunch of teens the basics of sewing."

"Really? This fabric is beautiful. I haven't seen anything like it before. It moves and changes colors as if it's sealskin. You did a great job on the design."

"Thank you."

Glen took her hand in his. "So, how did the rest of your day go after we had lunch?"

"I think it's a good start. I have everything laid out in the positions where I want them to be. I need to work on the guy-wires tomorrow. I need some like we use on our boat. They are stronger tensioned cables designed to add stability to a free-standing structure, and I have ten heavy canvases that I want to hang. I need thinner ones like the ones that are used commonly in ship masts, radio masts, or wind turbines."

"The lighted ones you had didn't work?"

She shook her head. "No, they aren't strong enough for what I need, but I'll wrap the guy-wires with the lights. I wanted the wires to look invisible, but that's not happening. Instead, I'll make the lights seem like icicles dripping off the canvases. That should give it a nice holiday effect with the music of strings and harp on an invisible carousel."

"Members of my family are in the boat building business here in New York City; Peter and Joyce Montgomery Callaway. Peter went to UVA with my uncle Gregory. Joyce is my dad's youngest sister. I called Uncle Peter to ask if he had guy-wires that might work on this project and seem invisible. He's bringing over samples for me to look at in the morning."

Glen laughed. "You have family and friends in interesting places. I want to be one of your friends."

Just then, the door opened, and another couple rushed in out of the blowing wind and icy rain. Glen put his arms around Samantha to block the wind. When the couple looked up, Samantha and the woman laughed.

"Satarah? Oh, my, and Douglas."

"What in the world, Samantha!" The woman hugged her tightly, as did Douglas.

"I can't believe this. Glen Kennard, this is my cousin Satarah and her husband, Douglas Johnson."

Glen shook Satarah's and then Douglas' hand. "A pleasure to meet both of you."

"Same goes." Satarah winked at Samantha.

"I was just telling Glen about members of my Montgomery family. What got you two out of Summer County?"

"We brought the children up to see New York at Christmas. We're going to see Linda's show, Goodwill, on Broadway, visit Rockefeller

Center, and do many other things tourists do in The Big Apple at Christmas. This excursion is a part of our holiday gift to our children. We'll be here for the rest of the week. However, between you, me, and the fence post, this trip allows us to have the floors sanded, re-stained, and polyurethaned in The Summer House while we're away."

Samantha and Glen laughed. "Does Linda know you're here?"

"We didn't mention it to her or to Gregory when all of you were there for Thanksgiving. We closed The Summer House after everyone left and prepared to come here. The kids wanted to stay in a hotel in the center of the city. So, we're at the McCoy Grand."

"Well, hell, so am I. I've contracted to do one of the windows at the McCoy Department Store."

"Pardon me," interrupted the hostess. "Your table is ready." Then she turned to Douglas and Satarah, "We have about thirty-minute wait times to be seated."

Glen took Samantha's hand. She knew what he was asking with that gesture, and she nodded perceptively to him. "Will the table you're preparing for us fit four?"

When the hostess nodded, Glen turned to address Douglas and Satarah. "Would you like to join us for dinner?"

Douglas and Satarah looked at one another, and then Douglas nodded to Glen. "Sure, we'd like that if it's not an imposition."

Samantha smiled. "Great! Then it's settled."

The hostess smiled, too, retrieved four thick menus in leather binders, and wine lists, handing them over to the waiter. "Table 1," she offered, and then to the couples, she nodded, "Enjoy your evening."

The restaurant's walls were filled with painted caricatures of a hundred years of Jazz greats. Charlie Mingus, John Coltrane, Herbie Hancock, Miles Davis, Wynton Marsalis, Dizzy Gillespie, and Thelonious Monk, among others, were displayed there. As Glen looked around the restaurant, his eyes landed on the songstress Alicia Keys and her family. Other notables, like the actor Robert DeNiro, were there as well.

Glen seated Samantha and then looked up at the waiter. "By the way, who is performing tonight?"

"Los Angeles percussionist Bruce Carver."

Samantha smiled. "Oh, we're really in luck tonight. He's a master of advanced Bodhrán techniques and rhythms."

The waiter nodded in agreement. "His next performance will begin at nine. What can I get for you to drink?"

After the foursome gave their dinner orders, the couples settled in to chat over cocktails.

Satarah turned to her right toward Glen. "So, you're a pilot, Glen?" Satarah asked, turning toward him.

"Yes, a captain. I've flown for Adventurer Executive Airlines for quite a while."

"So you know that Samantha's mother owns the airline and ground transportation system. Vivian and I grew up together in the same community."

Amused, he nodded. "Yes, I know who Samantha's mother is and that she was born and raised in Summer County, South Carolina. Samantha speaks of Goodwill, South Carolina, and her parents quite often."

"Really? Have you two known each other very long?"

"Satarah, in her not so subtle way, is being a mother hen. She is trying to find out whether she can include you as my guest for our Juneteenth Family Reunion." Samantha laughed.

"I'm available if you need a plus one."

Samantha placed her hand on top of Glen's hand on the dinner table. "Uh, I warn you, Glen, that in our family, it's not that simple. The annual reunion is a ten-day event around June 19. We hold educational and career counseling classes during the morning hours, group games in the afternoons, and parties every night, some until the wee hours of the morning. There is food and elaborate meals galore at all times of the day throughout the reunion. For us, it's a multicultural holiday. It includes performing dramatizations of the Emancipation

Proclamation, singing traditional songs, such as 'Swing Low, Sweet Chariot' and 'Lift Every Voice and Sing.' We read works by noted African-American writers, such as Ralph Ellison and Maya Angelou. Our celebrations often include picnics, rodeos, a county fair, and cook-offs. Did I mention the food?"

Satarah grinned. "There are historical reenactments, blues festivals, and Miss Juneteenth contests. Strawberry soda is a fundamental drink associated with the celebration. It's among my favorites."

"Mine, too," Samantha giggled. "The Mascogos, the descendants of Black Seminoles, who have resided in Coahuila, Mexico, have joined us before to celebrate Juneteenth. We have lectures that teach our family members about African-American heritage, exhibitions on African-American culture, and our connections to the Indigenous People. We perform plays and retell stories passed down through many generations of our ancestors."

Satarah picked up the conversation. "We promote voter registration efforts and ensure that every person eligible to vote is registered in his or her home state. Did we mention that the holiday is also a celebration of soul food and other food with African-American influences? Barbecue cooking competitions are the centerpiece of most Juneteenth celebrations."

Samantha nodded. "Then on the last Saturday are the weddings spaced two hours apart. Each wedding is uniquely different. We're planning for my sister Genevieve's wedding to writer Simon Wilde at the next Juneteenth celebration. He's from close-knit families that are Irish and Scottish, which are as large as the Alexanders and the Montgomerys. This wedding promises to be larger than any we've had so far."

Glen laughed. "Let me guess: there is an abundance of food during each wedding reception?"

"There you go! You're spot on!"

Douglas laughed. "That's for sure. You see, Glen, when one of the Alexander members brings a date to the Juneteenth Family Reunion, it's tantamount to announcing your engagement."

Glen laughed. "Considering this is our first official date, I don't think we're ready to pick out our China patterns quite yet…are we?" He grinned at Samantha.

She shook her head and smirked. "Definitely not. It's entirely too soon. We'll pick the stemware and silverware patterns first, after our second official date."

Glen nodded. "That will give me time to pick out your engagement ring before our third date." Everyone laughed. He looked between Douglas and Satarah. "Is that what happened with you two?"

Douglas smiled. "No. I came to Summer County because my son, Donovan, was in a school bus accident on his way to Florida. It was during the worst snowstorm in recorded history in South Carolina. I was a firefighter in Richmond, Virginia, when I got the word about the accident. A trip from Virginia to South Carolina that would have ordinarily taken three or four hours took nearly half the night. Little did I know that the head of the emergency room nursing staff saved my son's life." Douglas took Satarah's hand and smiled at her. "I fell in love with that registered nurse who happens to be this wonderful woman. I married her the following year during the reunion. I ended up staying in Summer County because Samantha's grandmother, Sylvia Benson Alexander, has Svengali tendencies. I now believe it's a trait that runs throughout the Alexander clan, so be aware. I'm currently the County's Fire Chief. In my opinion, it is the best accidental meeting ever. I have a snowstorm to thank for my happiness and six children."

"Speaking of that event, Satarah, have you heard from Mary Ella recently?"

"Contact with her or Mark Brooks is spotty at best."

Samantha took a sip of her wine and turned to Glen. "Mary Ella Baker is Satarah's cousin. She, like Satarah, is a registered nurse. Mary Ella is with Doctors Without Borders."

"Yes, we're best friends and cousins on my father's side of the family. Mary Ella and her guy friend, Dr. Mark Brooks, are somewhere in the Middle East, Asia or North Africa. I never know where she is at any given time. She's been away for nearly four years. However, every so often, I'll receive a call or a text message from her or Douglas will hear from Mark."

Douglas nodded. "Mark and I were in the Marines together."

"I imagine that working for an NGO, like Doctors Without Borders, is challenging." Glen sat back while the waiter served the meals.

Satarah placed her napkin in her lap. "Were you in the military, Glen?"

"Uh, no."

"How did you learn to fly?"

"I'm a graduate of Baylor University in Waco, Texas. I hold a Bachelor of Science and a Master's degree in Aviation Science. I took courses in aeronautics, mathematics, and physics, which allowed me to graduate with a commercial pilot's certificate and degree. When my career as a pilot ends, I should be able to pursue a career in the aerospace industry. With my math and science background, along with aircraft pilot training and upper-level course content in aviation, I should be able to go into operations, management, or logistics. Worst-case scenario, I can open a flight training school and teach."

Samantha looked up from her meal and frowned. "You're not planning to make that switch anytime soon, are you, Glen?"

"No, oh no. I have quite a few milestones I want to reach before I stop flying."

She grinned. "Good, because I don't want to lose you before my next tour begins."

He shook his head and squeezed her hand, which he still held on top of the table. "That's a definite no. You're my primary concern on your next tour. There is no chance of you losing me."

They bowed their heads while holding hands as Douglas offered a short prayer of thanksgiving before they began to eat.

After the show, the audience stood enthusiastically, applauding Bruce Carter's performance. He rewarded them with an encore before they would allow him to leave the stage.

Satarah smiled at Samantha. "So, should we visit the ladies' room before we leave?"

"Sure." Samantha had a feeling that she knew what this trip to the restroom was all about. She wasn't wrong.

"So, who are Glen Kennard's people, Samantha?"

Samantha snorted a laugh. "I haven't compared DNA samples or done a full genealogy search on him, or myself, yet, to determine whether we're related or compatible. AEA does a complete dossier and vets their employees, so I know he's not a criminal."

Satarah laughed, too. "You know what I mean, girl. He's a walking, talking wet dream. He looks like a well-packaged gift to womankind. How come some enterprising woman hasn't snapped him up?"

"I have absolutely no idea."

"Well, you need to find that out and who his people are. You need to know where he came from."

"Satarah, I don't know where *I* came from," she deadpanned.

"Chuck, Derrick, and Vivian. That's where. The biologicals aren't a consideration. It's nurture over nature unless you find a DNA match between you and Hunkamania."

Samantha laughed until she actually had to rush into one of the bathroom stalls. After tending to her needs, when she returned to Satarah, they linked arms.

"Oh, by the way, I want a copy of that shit-sharp outfit you're wearing."

Samantha laughed. "Size eight?"

"Size ten. I've had two babies in the last four years, and I'm consistently and actively nailing Douglas to any surface to work on a third. My hips are as wide as a Mack truck."

"Geeze, Satarah, you already have four teenage boys and two toddler daughters. Six isn't enough for you?"

"How many siblings do you have?" she teased.

Samantha nodded. "Enough said."

After seeing Douglas and Satarah off in a car service, Samantha took Glen's arm as they snuggled in under the wide umbrella and walked in the pouring rain. They talked as they skirted the seventy-three acres SoHo community bordered by West Broadway, Crosby, Houston, and Canal streets. They never tired of conversation or the adventure. They came to Battery Park, a twenty-five-acre green space, bikeway, and promenade. Samantha pointed out where the park included, on one end, Hope Garden—a memorial to AIDS victims—and on another, the ferry to Ellis Island, the Statue of Liberty, and several other memorials and monuments scattered in between. They walked on past the Shrine of Elizabeth Ann Seton and an area where clipper ships used to dock. She explained that, in the 1800s, ships would dock there, and Black stevedores would sing their sea songs, called shanties, to earn extra money.

"My mother's family, the Alexanders, were originally seamen who were privateers from Alexandria, a small principality in Egypt." Eventually, they came to a wide expanse of land where several soccer fields were installed.

"You know a great deal about your family's history. I don't know a lot about mine. When I see a soccer field like this, I have vague memories of my father teaching me to play."

A few stores were still open. So, they took the opportunity to get in out of the rain. A Cast Iron District gallery was rich with pictures, memorabilia, and artifacts from the colonial period. Samantha pointed to an old hand-painted map. "When part of the SoHo area's former farmland was granted to freed slaves of the Dutch West Indies Company, this was the site of the first free Black settlement in Manhattan."

For Samantha, the gallery was a shopper's paradise. She purchased the map and many other pieces she could use in her interior designs and had them shipped. The gallery owner was delighted with her and gave her a more than fair discount on her purchases and promised more should she decide to come back. The area was full of other retro galleries, upscale international clothing and accessory stores, and one-of-a-kind boutiques.

"I'm enjoying this walk and your running commentary of facts about SoHo, but are you okay? The outfit you're wearing can't be keeping you but so warm. It's getting colder out here this close to the water."

"I'm fine. I love walking in the rain, but we'll go this way." She pointed to the right. "I know of a place where we can have a nightcap before we return to the McCoy."

A few blocks more, they reached a retrofitted building. The rain was pouring like Niagara Falls. While Samantha keyed a code into a wall plate, pressed her right hand against the plate and her eye to a scanner, Glen held the umbrella over their heads. When the door popped open, Glen shook the water off the umbrella and folded it closed. Interior lights automatically came on. Once the door was closed and locked, Samantha keyed in a security code. He placed the umbrella in a bucket by the door and then hung their coats in a walk-around closet. Together, hand-in-hand, they walked up the wide, floating, thick, teakwood steps to the main level.

At the top of the stairs, Glen just stood and stared. "Is this your home?"

"No," Samantha was in the act of turning on the gas fireplace when her cell phone chimed. "It's my uncle Gregory and aunt Angelique's home. Hold on a moment, please. Hi, Uncle Gregory. No, I'm secure. My safe word is Patrick." She waved her hand in the air. "You can turn off the cameras. I was out on a dinner date with Glen Kennard at Jazzabelle's. We ran into Douglas and Satarah, and they joined us for dinner. Afterward, Glen and I walked all around SoHo, but it's raining hard here and getting colder. We just stopped here to get warm." She laughed at something he said and looked up at Glen, who was looking at the art on the walls. "Thanks, Uncle Gregory," she whispered, "but I'm not quite ready for that stage in my life yet. So, no, I don't need confirmation that the guest room sheets are fresh. Yes, much love and many hugs to you and Angelique, too. Goodbye."

She went to the bar and poured two globes of Amaretto, which she heated before handing one to Glen. "To the conclusion of a successful first date." She touched her glass to his, and they drank.

"Agreed. I'm looking forward to many more dates." He wandered around the nearly three thousand square foot main level. "This was once a fire station?"

She nodded. "Yes. The fire trucks and other emergency vehicles were parked on the ground level. Uncle Gregory parks his vehicles there now. He uses part of the space to recondition old, vintage cars. He gives each of us, his nephews and nieces, one of the cars for our sixteenth birthday. His wine cellar and hydroponics garden are on that level, too. On the back, on that level, he has a basketball court and exercise gym and equipment. The space on this level is the common area. The next level up is where the guests' sleeping quarters are located, with part of the space used as a game room. Above that is the master bedroom level. My uncle had the rooftop level added to accommodate a year-round indoor-outdoor garden, swimming pool, and sunroom."

"This is nice, but it's so large that it needs its own zip code."

That made her laugh. "My uncle doesn't like small, compact spaces. After all, he's six feet ten inches tall. He and my aunt, who is five-ten, have a toddler son and a daughter on the way, so they need the open space. When all thirty-plus of my siblings, parents, and grandparents descend on our uncle and aunt, we don't feel as if we're bursting at the seams."

"He's away?"

"Yes, he and Angelique—"

"Ah, the supermodel and Le Cordon Bleu chef?"

She nodded. "Yes. They are at their winter retreat in Atlantic Beach, South Carolina."

"You have an amazing family." He pointed to a wall-sized picture of people filling up what looked like an entire center section of bleachers in an indoor gymnasium. "This plaque at the bottom indicates that this is a photograph of last year's Alexander family Juneteenth reunion. This is your mother's side of your family?"

"It is. Actually, as the oral history goes, the original members of the colony were from Alexandria, a small pharaonic town founded by Alexander the Great. Hence the family name that survived through the many generations of my ancestor's family. An ancestor from Alexandria, Egypt, on the Mediterranean Sea, was a privateer, and he and his five sons owned ships that raided slave ships, freed the captives, looted, and then stole or sank the vessels. They hunted in packs.

"One of the sons spotted an English Man of War vessel attacking a passenger ship off the coast of Barbados and attacked the British galleon. My ancestor lost his own ship and got separated from his father's and brothers' ships in the battle during a hurricane. He and his crew weren't much more than nineteen at the time, but he managed to save the Barbadians and their ship. Among the passengers was a girl of only about fourteen or fifteen. Her father was sending her to a wealthy Greek merchant in exchange for horses and other livestock. Though they couldn't speak a word of each other's language, my relative fell instantly in love with her.

"Because the Barbadian ship was severely damaged in the battle and swept nearly two thousand nautical miles off course, they had to sink her off the coast of what is now known as South Carolina. The Egyptian sailors and Barbadians had to hide from other British ships that were hunting for them and other pirates in the area. They went into the deep woods and swamp and formed a colony living in harmony with the Indigenous Americans in the area and then intermarrying with them. The Egyptian and Barbadian sailors never saw their homelands again but lived there in isolation avoiding slavery and helping enslaved people escape their captors. The Underground

Railroad made a path through the dense woods and great swamp to the colony and then moved north or west from there. Some of the escaped enslaved stayed in the colony and raised families, intermarrying with the Barbadians, Indigenous Americans, and the Egyptian sailors. Many years later, around the late eighteenth or early nineteenth century, that colony became Summer County.

"Most of the people who live in Summer County descended from those early settlers and the Indigenous Americans who inhabited these lands before they were invaded."

"That's fascinating. Is that true for both sides of your Alexander family?"

"Only my grandfather's side, not my grandmother's. My grandmother's family, the Bensons, originated in the coastal area around Charleston, South Carolina. It's an area known as Goose Creek, Saint James. Her people didn't escape slavery the way that Granddad Bernard's did. Ancestors of my grandmother, Sylvia Benson Alexander, worked in the rice patties and made indigo ink. They descended from the Gullahs on the Sea Islands. The many times great-grand Benson grandparents and great-grandparents left the Islands and were entertainers. They traveled Europe with the great Josephine Baker and lived there until the war chased them home.

"Further back in my grandmother's ancestry, her many-times great grandfather never took to working for somebody else's welfare and not his own. He had seen his own grandfather and father trying to survive on little or nothing while the Europeans invaded and claimed the land that rightfully belonged to the Indigenous Americans. Still, the European who stole the land lived lavishly and took any one of my enslaved ancestors' female children to his bed. The Europeans even fathered children with the enslaved people with no regard for the girls or young women he assaulted. Because the European didn't often sleep in the same bedroom with the woman he legally married, every night he took a different woman, sometimes two or more women, to his bed as bed warmers and other things I shouldn't have to explain. It didn't matter whether the woman was already married or mated with a man or how young she was. He took the younger girls when they were as young as ten or eleven.

"My grandmother's great-great-grandfather was disgusted with what he had witnessed his father and grandfather suffer. As soon as he could, when he grew up and married, he took his wife and children away from the Islands where his parents and seven brothers and sisters still lived and brought them to the mainland.

"He started working in the bars and hotels singing with his wife, and at times all of their children sang on stage. They had a regular vaudeville show going on. Along the way, my mother's great-grandfather and great-grandmother met in the theatre, married, and had many children while on the road traveling from place to place to perform. They were very talented singers, dancers, and musicians. Eventually, there was a cast of twenty-two performers.

"One day, someone who knew the famous Josephine Baker told her about the Benson family troupe, and she sent for them to come to see her. They did, and when they performed for her as they say, the rest is history. Ms. Baker was a huge hit in New York. Because of what the Benson ancestors were subjected to, they were their own rainbow coalition of skin tones. It was still hard for people of color in that society. So, they went to Paris, France, where they were readily accepted. Ms. Baker opened in La Revue Nègre at The Théâtre des Champs-Élysées. She and her troupe, which included the Benson ancestors, gained instant success for the erotic, nearly-nude dancing they did. Some of the Bensons learned to work in other backstage trades and capacities, like costume design or set construction. They were a complete ensemble of touring actors, singers, and dancers. They toured all over Europe with Ms. Baker and sometimes on their own to standing-room-only crowds every night. When they returned to France from one tour, they opened with Ms. Baker at The Folies Bergère."

Glen was fascinated. "Is it true she performed the Danse Sauvage, wearing only a string of artificial bananas?"

Samantha nodded and grinned. "It is, yes, and she was the toast of Paris and much of the European and North African continent. Ms. Baker was born in Missouri in 1906 and died in 1975 in Paris, but her name is still spoken with reverence in France. Like my mom, who initially adopted eleven children, Ms. Baker fostered twelve children.

"As you know, my grandmother Sylvia's sister, Mariah, still lives in Paris and owns the restaurant and jazz club where we had dinner, and she performed especially for us. Her floor show is terrific and still very popular. I think it is reminiscent of the ancestors' shows and Ms. Bakers.' People have to book weeks in advance to get a seat in the restaurant and the show. She's known as The French Mariah and has starred in foreign films, stage, and British music television shows. She has toured Europe, Asia, and Africa to perform. She's the only one in the Benson family so far who is still in the entertainment business.

"When they came back to the United States just before the war, though they were very popular in Europe, they weren't favored here. Ms. Baker returned to France to work for the French Resistance. My grandmother's family settled back in South Carolina in Goose Creek, Saint James, outside Charleston, and built other careers."

"How did your grandparents meet?"

"My grandmother's parents and grandparents saved quite a nest egg after being in Europe all of those years. When they returned to the United States, they didn't trust the banks. Because of their suspicions, fortunately, they survived the Great Depression. They made sure all of their grands and great-grands went to college. My grandfather and grandmother met on the campus of Howard University. He played basketball on scholarship while in college and was in graduate school for a degree in education. My grandmother was in nursing school. After they graduated, they married and moved to Goodwill, South Carolina. My grandfather began teaching in the Summer County school system, and my grandmother began working as a private-duty nurse. Later, after Granddad Bernard earned his doctorate, he became the high school principal, and my grandmother became the head of a new nursing school at what is now Summer County Academy. Granddad Bernard is a State Senator representing Summer County at the state capitol in Columbia, South Carolina, and Grandmother Sylvia is the head of nursing at the Summer County Medical Center."

"That's interesting. You really know your family history."

"Actually, I don't know anything about my biological mother or sperm donor or their ancestry. Vivian and Derrick Jackson adopted me when I wasn't much older than a toddler. Five years after Derrick's death, my mom married Chuck Montgomery. There were twelve of us, and Chuck adopted all of us. We've heard the history of the Alexanders and Bensons all of our lives. It feels real and natural to my siblings and to me. My parents have offered to help us find our biological families." She shrugged. "I've never been interested in finding out who they are."

He pointed to her face in the large picture. "That's you right there."

She nodded. "Yes, there are a lot of us, and I love them fiercely. I've talked a great deal about my family tonight. How about you?" They moved to sit on one of the comfortable sofas.

He shrugged. "I have a sister, Kaitlyn. I think she's still a reporter for a television station in the Dallas-Fort Worth area. My brother, Dion, is an actor. He's currently shooting a movie in Ireland."

"Are you close?"

"No, not particularly. In fact, I haven't seen either of my siblings in the last four or five years. We'll call one another on birthdays, if we remember. However, we don't get together for holidays or any other event."

"How about your parents?"

"Both are deceased." He took a deep breath and another sip of his drink. "My mother and father weren't married. They were the offspring of New Agers. They lived together until my mother came home to find my father in bed with his long-term lover. She shot and killed both of them and then killed herself." He took another long drink and looked into Samantha's eyes.

"I'm sorry for your loss."

"Thank you, but it was a long time ago. I think I was nine at the time. I'm thirty-three now. Our paternal grandfather raised my siblings and me. My grandmother left him to be with another man after she gave birth to my father. My grandfather was a minister who believed in spreading his love around to the female members of his congregation biblically. Though he is deceased, it is known that my siblings and I have many aunts and uncles among his former parishioners. Our mother's parents were never in our lives. They rode with one of the bike gangs and died in a road accident."

"Are your siblings married?"

He snorted a laugh. "Uh, no, and no offspring."

"Why? Don't you or they plan to marry and have families?"

"That's a definite no. We're too dysfunctional for that. The only reason they or I would marry is to procreate. However, none of us want to have children, so Dion and I both had vasectomies. I believe my sister had a tubal ligation when she was twenty-one." He looked into her eyes. "I imagine from your cousin's conversation this evening that you want to marry and have children in the future?"

"I do, yes, but certainly no time soon."

"That puts me at a competitive disadvantage over other men you may be interested in."

"Other men?"

"I spoke with Cameron to coordinate our schedules. He mentioned that he had Thanksgiving dinner with you and the King family. He didn't know about my interest in you and mentioned that you and Quentin King have been dating.

"I don't play games, Samantha, and I know that you don't play games either. You're the most honest and forthright woman I've ever met. I thoroughly enjoy being with you. Your intellectual prowess thrills me. I want an exclusive, intimate relationship with you. I would love it if you would relocate to Texas, but, if not, I'd be willing to move anywhere that would be convenient for you. We could even buy or lease a place together if you want, but I felt that you should know that I don't want to marry or have children. If this doesn't fit with your plans, you only need to let me know. I'd be sorely disappointed, but no harm, no foul. You're a special person, and I want to remain in your life even if it's only as good friends. However, if we take this relationship to another level and become lovers, I can pledge fidelity for as long as we can make our connection last.

"Now, it's getting late. If it's okay with you, I'll call for a car to pick us up."

She shook her head. "No, you don't have to do that. I'll take one of my uncle's cars. If you're ready, I'll tidy up and we can be on our way."

At the hotel, Glen walked Samantha to her door and kissed her. "I know I've given you many things to consider. Take your time, but I'd still like to see you again before I leave."

She lingered over the kiss she gave him and then hugged him tightly before letting him go. "In the morning, after our run, check your mail at the concierge desk." She grinned and then slipped inside her hotel suite, leaving him with a perplexed expression on his handsome face.

CHAPTER 34

Glen and Samantha were laughing when the door to The Runway was opened for them by the doorman. "You really surprised me with the couple's massage at INDULGENCES this morning after our run. When you hinted at something intimate, my thoughts went in a completely different direction."

Samantha grinned. "I made sure that you got the full treatment, didn't I? If I couldn't put my hands on your body, then I could do it through a surrogate."

He laughed. "I don't think Sven's touch could be as invigorating as yours."

"Still, you enjoyed it?"

"I did, yes. It was a wonderful and unexpected holiday gift. I also enjoyed meeting your sister, Linda, the renowned prima ballerina, the Black Swan, and her husband, the famous baseball player, Will 'The Hammer' Hamilton. However, I felt like I was going through an even more intense Spanish Inquisition than your cousin, Satarah, gave me last night."

She grinned. "You survived and passed with flying colors. However, expect that whenever you meet members of my family, you'll have to put on your big boy pants and be prepared."

"I will, because it's clear to me that you're precious to your family. They love you very much. I'm not offended that they put me through my paces, but I know that you've probably had people interested in you because of your family's wealth and notoriety. That's not why I'm interested in you."

She shrugged. "It's happened a few times with people who figure out my family connections."

"Yes, like that really pushy guy in England. He was a character."

"Yes, like him, but not so much with people I've known for most of my life. You, Cameron, and Frederick weren't impressed when we met for the first time and started traveling together. All of you treated me like a little sister."

"Well, my thoughts about you did stray beyond familial bonds a time or two."

"Mine too." She grinned.

"Ms. Samantha?" the tall, stately-looking black man questioned, as he approached, extending a hand.

"Hello, Mr. Conway." She took his hand as they kissed each other on both cheeks. "Glen Kennard, Mr. Conway is Angelique's head of security for the New York bar and restaurant."

The two men shook hands. "Welcome to The Runway."

Glen nodded. "Thank you."

"How is your wife, Mr. Conway? I was at Uncle Gregory's house last night, but it was late, so I didn't stop by to see her."

"Janie is just fine. The boys are out of the house now, so it's just the two of us."

"Janie is my uncle Gregory's housekeeper, and she manages a condo building for him on the same street where he lives. Until recently, he mentored Janie's grandsons, Dijon and Keaton Joyner." She turned back to Mr. Conway. "Both boys are in college now, right?"

"That's right, and they're both doing well. They'll be home for the holidays in the next couple of weeks. Your uncle is still their mentor."

"Please tell them and Janie that I'd love to hear from them."

"I will certainly do that, but they keep up with your travels just as your immediate family does. We have linens from your collection in our home. We know how busy you are."

"I'm never too busy for my friends."

"Thanks, Ms. Samantha. Now, Mr. Kennard, is this your first time here?"

"It is, yes."

"Ms. Samantha? How do you want to do this?"

She turned toward Glen. "What Mr. Conway is asking is whether we want to enter the club on the runway entrance or through a less public display."

"Oh, I see. I imagine the stage entrance comes with lights and cameras."

"Absolutely, for about forty feet and the music of your choice. It's a real runway."

He grinned. "Oh, hell. Let's give them something to talk about."

She shrugged. "Okay, Mr. Conway, you can have someone cue the music."

He did, and Glen and Samantha danced onto the runway, singing to the lively applause, bright lights, and photo shots.

"Wow, that was surreal," Glen joked as they were seated.

"I'll arrange for you to receive a copy of our entrance. You got some loud whistles from the females."

"My younger brother and I look alike. They must have mistaken me for him."

"You always do that."

"Do what?"

"You downplay how truly handsome you are."

He sighed and shook his head. "I didn't have anything to do with my appearance. My brother and I both look like our father and grandfather. They weren't men of good character, and, at least in my father's case, he came to a bad end. My brother, on the other hand, is following in their footsteps. I see pictures of him in trade magazines and on entertainment shows with one woman after another all the time." He looked earnestly into her eyes. "That's not who I am, and you're the first woman who has looked beyond the façade to see me as a person. That's one of the many things I like about you, Samantha."

"You make it easy, Glen. Yes, you're very handsome, built like a Greek god, and wicked smart, but one of the many things I like most about you is you're so down to earth."

"So are you. You're beautiful, intelligent, and adventurous. However, one of the many things I like about you is that you knit."

Samantha frowned. "I knit?"

Glen chuckled. "Yes. You're energetic, but you have the ability to sit still for long periods of knitting. You block out everything and everyone and have the most serene expression on your face. However, I can see the wheels turning in this beautiful head of yours. It's clear to me that you have inner strength and control. You're an amazing dichotomy."

She shrugged and smiled warmly. "I suppose that's my maternal grandmother's influence, my Nana Sylvia. She taught my sibs and me to knit, to settle down, and let our brains relax while we did something productive." She giggled. "She taught all of us needlepoint, knitting, crocheting, and sewing. My brother, Vincent, is a pediatric surgeon. He says our Nana's lessons got him through medical school. He makes the most incredibly beautiful graphgans for wall art. Another one of my brother's, Spencer, likes to Macramé in his spare time. Me? My Nana is the reason I began a career in the textile industry."

Glen touched her chin and smiled at her. "That's the face I enjoy looking at the most. When you talk about your family, you have this incredible glow about you. Your eyes shine when you smile, and I'm hooked on that smile."

The waiter came to the table, and they ordered drinks. Their dinner reservation wasn't until seven, so they relaxed and enjoyed each other. They got up to dance several times and cheered and whistled as others came into the club via the runway.

The next morning at six, after their thirty-minute run in Central Park, they entered the hotel and headed to the café for breakfast. One of the desk clerks got Glen's attention and handed a note to him. He sighed after he opened it and read the message.

Samantha sighed, too. "Is it what you expected?"

Visibly disappointed, he nodded. "Yes, I have to file a flight schedule for two o'clock today to Germany." He looked up at her.

"You wouldn't want to fly with me, would you? I have a two-day layover in Rhineland-Palatinate, Germany."

She shook her head. "I wish I could. My cousin, Whitney, and her husband, Tucker Cavanaugh, live there. She's an attorney, and he's a Marine medical doctor at the Landstuhl Regional Medical Center, but, no, I can't go with you. I have to complete this contract. I also have a Women's Empowerment panel discussion in Harlem to participate in with my sister, Linda, on Thursday at one. My aunt JeNelle Alexander arranged it." He looked so perplexed that she took his hand and guided him to the café.

After Glen seated her and sat across from her, he took her hand. "When will I be able to see you again?"

"From here, I'll likely head to my family's home in The Poconos to prepare the decorations for Christmas. Then I'll return to Maryland for New Year's. In February, I'm going to dive for a few weeks in Seychelles with some of my family members and friends. In late March to early April, I should be set for my spring tour."

"What about your schedule?"

"I'm booked solid until your tour starts, except for mandatory crew rest periods."

She squeezed the hand she still held across the table. "It's always going to be like this, isn't it?"

He sighed and nodded. "I'm afraid so. At least for the next seven to ten years. That's one of the reasons I suggested that we move in together. I would have you to come home to for mandatory crew rest periods. If you had free time, you could always fly with me." He looked into her eyes. "It's hard to maintain a relationship when I have a flight schedule as unpredictable as mine. If I flew for the commercial airlines, I might have overnight layovers, but for the most part, we could have breakfast together, and I'd be back home by dinner time."

"Yes, but you wouldn't enjoy it half as much as you do flying the private jets to interesting destinations."

"You're right about that. These flights are never routine. I've been to places in this world I never would have seen flying for the public airlines. It's always a new adventure. We have time, Samantha. Let's see what the next few months entail. Do you know who is flying you to Seychelles?"

She shook her head as the waitress served coffee to them and took their order for breakfast. "I don't know."

"I'll check and find out, but we'd be back to an employee/employer relationship. So, no kisses." He teased.

"The hell you say," she joked. "If you can exchange flights, bring Cameron and Frederick along as your crew. I still want to see Freddy in a speedo. I'll kiss Freddy, and he can kiss you for me."

Glen laughed. "You're wicked." He leaned forward and kissed her across the table. "That could work, though. Just don't slip Freddy any tongue."

She burst out laughing at his cross expression. They continued to talk, hashing out their concerns.

Quentin waited for the last possible moment to leave the balmy San Diego weather and catch a red-eye private jet to Washington. The flight landed at five in the morning. It was a short ride from the airport to the Watergate, but it was long enough to know that it was frigid in the city. Quentin closed his front door at his back and continued to his bedroom suite. Putting his luggage on the bench at the foot of his bed, he opened it and began to toss clothes into the laundry basket. Stripping, he got out his shaving kit, toothbrush and toothpaste, and went into the adjacent ensuite. He turned on the shower, and the instant hot water felt good as it soaked his skin.

He was able to sleep on the flight with visions of Samantha as they danced at Café Citron in his head, but he wasn't tired. Instead, he was eager to get back to work. He passed on his daily swim so he could get into his office early. He'd swim after he returned from work, make dinner, and then relax with a good book and a glass of wine. Maybe he'd be able to catch up with Samantha. She answered his text messages with short responses or funny emoji, but they hadn't spoken since she left his condo on Thanksgiving Day. He was curious to know how her date went with the pilot, Glen Kennard.

As he shampooed his hair, he recalled that it had been a good and productive ten-day trip to San Diego, California, for his family and him. Members of the CTI team Gregory Alexander put together were on hand to assess the warehouse structure and the area. Wesley Greenfield was on hand, too, but JRock and his wife couldn't be there. Still, they arranged for JaiHonnah's cousin, Fiona Lizette Lowry, a very talented, young architect and structural engineer, to meet with them in San Diego. With her were her father, Alroy Lowry, and her twin brothers, Peter and Paul Lowry. They were all in the construction industry in Bay County, Maryland. They held meetings in the building for three days, and everyone came away with a feeling that this new venture would be a roaring success.

Inside the warehouse, once it was retrofitted and remodeled, Samuel could accommodate four tennis tournaments and games going on simultaneously with bleachers at the head and foot of each court. Outside, he could accommodate sixteen courts to play on clay courts, hard courts, grass courts, and carpet courts. It wouldn't be as big as Wimbledon, the U.S. Open, the Australian Open, or the French Open, yet. However, Samuel would be able to host Grand Slam Events in the next three to five years.

They felt that the tennis club wouldn't have to compete with the Pechanga Arena that accommodated all kinds of sporting events and concerts, or the Omni La Costa Resort & Spa in Carlsbad, California, or the Coronado Community Center in Coronado, California. His club would be devoted to the game of tennis all the time. He also had space to add handball and racquetball courts. Samuel was also interested in introducing the game of Jai alai to American audiences.

They were able to identify an established residential neighborhood not too far from the warehouse that had excellent private schools for

Sammy. They found the home on five acres of land with a clay tennis court, swimming pool, and ample fenced yard space for Samson to run. It was an older home, so they enlisted Fiona's expertise in the remodel potential. The price was high, and it was more extensive than what they needed, but it was in a private, gated community with all of the amenities, including a golf course and country club. It even had a skateboard park. That sold it for Sammy

After Fiona confirmed through a thorough professional inspection and appraisal that it had good bones, Samuel purchased the property. They would take possession in fifteen days, and remodeling would begin as soon as they got the keys. It would take four to five months to complete, but it would fit their needs with five bedrooms and five and a half baths. There was also a separate pool house complete with two bedrooms, two baths, a kitchen area, and a combination living and dining area. Paulette was eyeing that space for her she-shed when working with Samantha on interior designs.

The four-bedroom, four-and-a-half bath, bi-level condo in the Harbor Towers that Samantha arranged for Samuel to lease for six months from her uncle Benny Alexander was in a perfect location. Along the dock, there were great clubs, shops, and restaurants convenient to the Harbor Towers. It was fully furnished and had spectacular terrace views of the Pacific Ocean, San Diego Bay, the U.S. Naval Base, and the city of San Diego. They learned that the base is the second largest surface ship base of the U.S. Navy. It's the Pacific Fleet's principal homeport, consisting of over fifty ships and over one hundred ninety tenant commands, all within walking distance of the Harbor Towers.

Sammy was so fascinated by the sight that they usually ate the meals they shared at home on the terrace so he could watch the big ships as they entered or left the base. However, the Olympic-sized indoor/outdoor pool and lagoon in the building were a sight to see. They captured much of their attention at least once a day. One of the twin towers housed mostly families, while the other tower was full of singles. There were many social areas in the buildings, and Sammy met children his own age. Some also attended the private school where Sammy would be enrolled in January.

One morning, when Paulette had a salon appointment, and Samuel and Sammy took Samson to a veterinarian, Cameron and he joined a charter to dive at La Jolla Cove. The dive spot was located on the west end of a six thousand-acre protected marine sanctuary. It was accessible from a small beach at the base of the sea cliffs and an underwater paradise.

Cameron, an excellent diver, was into underwater photography. The shots he took were fantastic and could be considered art. Quentin and Samuel thought him to be a great guy. He obviously liked Paulette because most evenings they went out alone to explore the places Samantha recommended. He had flown them from Washington to San Diego. Still, he could stay only five days before returning to Dallas, Texas, to begin flying the charter routes for Adventurer Executive Airlines.

After he dressed and was groomed for the day, Quentin sent a text to his driver. Then he left his bedroom to go to the kitchen to brew a cup of coffee. When he turned on the light, he was brought up short with the sight of the devastation in the common areas of his condo. The furniture was shredded, the murals were a soggy paint-splattered mess, and all of the dishes were destroyed. There wasn't anything recognizable about his home. He stood amid the wreckage and wondered who could do such a thing.

CHAPTER 35

Geneviève Montgomery stood with her arms akimbo, feet apart, and frowned at the spectacle that was Quentin King's demolished condo. CSI techs were swarming all over the place with the Watergate security team and D.C. Police Department's Chief of the Robbery Division on their heels. When the call came into the department from Watergate security, some enterprising soul in dispatch recognized the name Quentin King and the connection to Geneviève's sister, Samantha. Because of Quentin's stature in the city, the Chief of Police was notified, who then, in turn, notified the head of the Robbery Division.

Geneviève was about to go off duty, on time for a change at seven o'clock, when she was given a heads-up, too. She was looking forward to going home and getting Simon naked, but that would have to wait. Anything which concerned her family, even remotely, would get her undivided attention.

The head of the Robbery Division came and stood, much as did Geneviève, regarding the chaos. "So, Eve, what's your take on this crime scene?"

"Captain Reddick, I think someone has it in for Quentin King."

He nodded, offered a stick of gum to Geneviève, which she dismissed with a shake of her head, and shrugged and folded it into his mouth. "Yeah, I get that. Big time. Actually, this is a really nice space. I've never been inside the Watergate before. I couldn't afford a paper napkin in here. We don't get calls from places like this. The security here is top of the line. I guess that's why these rich muckety-mucks pay up the wazoo for digs like this." He angled his square chin, pointing toward the head of the Watergate security. "I guess, when I grow up, I'll be able to wear thousand dollar suits like that guy."

"That *guy* is Joseph Proctor, also known as Stonehenge or Stoney, a former Marine. He is battle-tested and earned medals for bravery and honor. I think he's earned the right to dress for success."

"Hey, I'm just sayin', Eve. Don't get your bloomers in a twist." He was talking to her back as she walked away. *I wish I could throw a hump into that fine ass of hers, but the last police captain who tried it ended up working in the evidence locker room. I don't have an inclination to make a career-ending decision by putting my hands on her. Uh-uh, she is entirely too well connected and rumored to have broken a guy's jaw with her bare hands.* He sighed. *I really have to put in work to solve this break-in—and fast.*

When Samantha rushed to Quentin's door, she was barred from entering by two police officers. "I'm Samantha Montgomery. Would you tell my sister, Lieutenant Eve Montgomery, that I'm here?"

"Hold on, Miss." One of the officers opened the door and shouted, "Yo, LT, you've got company."

Shortly, Eve appeared at the door and, upon seeing her sister, invited her in.

Samantha released an audible gasp, her eyes going wide at the sight. "Eve, where is Quentin?" she demanded. "Are you sure he's all right?" She couldn't move any further into the room or take her eyes off the destruction. It was as if she was nailed to the spot.

"I promise, Samantha. He's okay, just royally pissed. I sent him to Mom and Dad's condo. They're with him now. You should go up…"

"Yes," she turned and briskly walked out of the devastation. In the elevator, she paced like a trapped animal and, when the doors opened, barely restrained herself from sprinting up the long, wide hallway to the door. She jabbed the security code into the panel so fast that she entered the wrong numbers. Having to take a step back, she took a deep breath before entering the right code more slowly. When the door opened, this time she did sprint in, calling Quentin's name.

Quentin heard the panic in Samantha's voice before he saw her face. He put down his cup of coffee, quickly rose from the sofa, and had her securely in his arms, his face buried in her hair. Then he searched for her mouth and was rewarded when her mouth fused to his. Her arms banded around his neck like a vice.

Moments later, she broke the kiss and knuckled away her tears. Looking up into his face, she frowned. "Are you all right? Were you hurt?"

He smiled wanly at her and, palming her face, thumbed away her tears. "I'm fine, Samantha. I wasn't there when this happened. I came in from California early this morning. It was still dark out, but I didn't turn on any lights until I got to my bedroom. I showered, got dressed, and was about to make coffee when I saw the damage."

Searching his eyes, she frowned. "Quentin, do you think that Minerva is capable of doing this?"

He smiled and shook his head. "Miranda, not Minerva."

"*Whatever!*" she snapped, her voice testy.

"I don't know, but your sister asked the same thing. Miranda is being questioned. Apparently, she moved into the building sometime after I did."

Samantha nodded and sighed. "I know."

Quentin's brows drew together. "You knew? How?"

"She wasn't wearing a coat when she came to your condo for Thanksgiving dinner. Your parents and hers were in heavy weather gear, but she wasn't."

He searched her eyes. "'A coat?' From that, you deduced that she lived in the building?"

She shrugged, annoyed. "I'm a woman. I notice such things. Either she is a tenant or she's impervious to the cold."

He shook his head and kissed her. "You're a wonder. I didn't even notice what she was wearing. In any event, my parents and hers were strategizing in her condo this morning. They were all there when the police, including Eve, knocked on her door."

"The interview must be over because Eve is in your condo."

He shrugged unconcernedly. "I'm sorry that this upset you, but I can't say that I'm not glad you're here. Your parents…oh, I apologize," he shifted so that Samantha could see her parents sitting on the sofa wearing their nightclothes. "When Geneviève told them what happened, they invited me up to sit with them until the police finished. Since my condo is a crime scene, your parents have graciously offered the opportunity for me to stay here in one of the guest rooms until I can return to my home."

Chuck sat with his arm around his wife's shoulders, shrugged, and toasted his daughter, and the man who would likely become his son-in-law, with the mug of coffee in his free hand. "Oh, don't mind us. We're enjoying the show."

"Hi, Dad, Mom." Samantha smirked as she leaned down to hug and kiss each of them. "You spent the night here?"

"Your mother's office had its holiday party last night in the ballroom here in the building. It shut down around two in the morning, so we decided to stay here instead of going out to the ranch."

Vivian yawned and looked at her watch. "You made good time getting here. Where were you when you got the word?"

"I was at home at POV when Geneviève called me."

"POV?" Quentin questioned, frowning.

"Uh, Point of View. It's what Mom calls our winter retreat in Monroe County, Pennsylvania. It's in the Pocono Mountains where Dad was born and grew up."

Vivian sighed as she took a sip of her terrible cup of tea. "Actually, Quentin, they should change the name from Monroe County to Montgomery County. You can't roll a bowling ball in that county and not knock down ten Montgomerys. You'll come up and have Christmas with us." She peeked over into Chuck's cup and inhaled deeply. "Couldn't I have just one sip of your coffee?"

Chuck shook his head and downed the rest of the coffee in his cup. "Nope."

Vivian pulled a mean face at her husband before she stood, went to the kitchen, and poured the rest of her tea in the sink. "I'm going to shower and dress." She put her cup in the dishwasher, all while giving Chuck a meaningful look, hugged her daughter, and then Quentin before she sashayed out of the living area.

Chuck stood, kissed his daughter, and hot-footed after his wife.

Samantha sighed and went to the coffee bar to pour a cup for herself. "Who would do this, Quentin?"

"I have no idea. I don't have enemies personally or in business that I'm aware of. I've been trying to figure this out since I found my place wrecked at six this morning. Initially, I thought that someone hit the wrong condo. Still, that didn't make sense either because none of the bedrooms or bathrooms were touched. All of the destruction is centered in the common areas. It's all open space so I could see everything at a glance when I turned on the light." His jaw knitted. "All of your hard work ended up trashed."

Samantha could hear the barely controlled anger in his tone. She reached for his hand and squeezed. "They're just things, Quentin. There's nothing I can't recreate."

"Except for the one-of-a-kind pieces you created."

She shook her head. "Maybe not, but for you, I'll try."

Mindful of the coffee in her hand, he drew her to him with the hand she still held. Leaning down, he kissed her and then released her hand to wrap his arms around her body, drawing her closer.

"Knock, knock," Geneviève's voice intruded.

"Go away, sister mine," Samantha grinned up into Quentin's eyes. "I'm busy."

When Geneviève cleared her throat, Samantha and Quentin both frowned, turned, and regarded the people who stood just inside the living space.

Slowly, Samantha and Quentin untangled. She put down her cup of coffee and turned to face the crowd.

Quentin came forward, holding Samantha's hand in his. "What have you found, Eve?"

"It's not my investigation, Quentin. This is the Chief of the Robbery Division, Kurt Reddick."

The chief reached over and clasped Quentin's hand, the whole time eyeing Samantha from the bottom up. "You're the LT's sister?"

"One of them. What have you found out?"

Her cool tone wiped the salacious grin off his face. "Well, um," he nervously cleared his throat. "It doesn't appear that anything was stolen, just utter destruction. CSI will give me a report on their findings. It's a B & E; I mean, it's a case of breaking and entering, except whoever came in had code access. So, technically, there was no breaking." His joke fell flat. He cleared his throat again and hurried on. "From what we found, nothing seems to have been stolen. The safe in your office does not seem to be disturbed. There is no damage done to the bedrooms or baths." He produced an electronic clipboard. "If you will sign here, Mr. King, I'll provide a report you can give to your insurance company. The report has the case number on it. We'll be in touch once we have more."

Once Quentin signed the document, the clipboard spit out a paper report. Captain Reddick handed it over, shook Quentin's hand, nodded at Samantha, and gave her another quick once-over before turning to Geneviève. "I'll keep you in the loop, Montgomery."

"I'd appreciate that, Captain."

He nodded and was gone, leaving a heavy silence. However, as soon as the door closed, Miranda stormed toward Quentin and Samantha.

"You would dare to sic your dogs on me?" She demanded, but Geneviève's quick action became a barrier between the distraught woman and Quentin.

"Step back, Ms. Bazemore." Geneviève's tone was quiet but deadly. She left no room for the woman to advance another step.

Miranda gave Geneviève a scathing appraisal but ultimately stepped back.

Quentin frowned. "I didn't 'sic' anyone on you, Miranda. The Friday after Thanksgiving, I had a conversation with the chief of security here in the building because you were not announced. He told me that security wasn't aware that there was a problem because you're a tenant in the building. When I reported the break-in to him this morning, he notified the police. He reported my earlier conversation with him to them. If you have a problem with the way you were treated, take it up with him, not me."

"Then your whore had something to do with it, I'll bet. Her damn sister is a cop. She came into my condo big as brass this morning while I was having a breakfast meeting with my parents and yours."

Geneviève frowned. "Look, lady, you were the one who wanted to speak with Quentin to ensure that he wasn't harmed. That's the only reason I permitted this meeting. As you can see, he is perfectly fine and unharmed."

Joseph Proctor stepped forward. "Ms. Bazemore, it appears that you were not truthful when you applied for residency here. You were specifically asked in the application whether you were acquainted with any other resident. I've reviewed your application, and it's clear to me that you were less than truthful. As you're aware, telling a lie on your application is a basis for eviction. I will have papers prepared to confirm the revocation of your residency application. You have ten days to leave or you will be forcefully evicted."

"This is outrageous! I simply forgot that Quentin lived here. He and I are lovers…"

"Ten days, Ms. Bazemore." The security chief's demeanor bode no argument.

Ashante stepped forward. "Junior, stand up for your fiancée!"

"No matter how many times you say it, Mother, Miranda, is not now, nor was she ever my fiancée. I'm not in love with her, but I am in love with Samantha."

Ashante's heated gaze landed on Samantha, and the vitriol ensued.

Chuck and Vivian rushed into the area, frowning. "What is going on here?" Chuck stepped forward.

"See! See! That's what I mean! This white man steps onto the scene, and everything turns in his favor. Then he brings his slave whore with

him. Look at her! She's pregnant with another of his seeds. I'll bet you didn't put up a fight to keep him from knocking you up, did you?"

Vivian snorted a laugh. "I certainly did not fight him off. Are you kidding? Look at him. He's a fine example of mankind and can bring it between the sheets. I nail his fine ass to any flat surface often and continuously."

"*Harlot!* You're no better than a prostitute, spreading your legs for any Tom, Dick, or Harry! You're a disgrace to all peoples of color when you lay down with the likes of those who enslaved us for generations. First, it was that no count from the Philadelphia ghetto, and then as soon as he died and made you rich, you go chasing after a white man. You think you're too good for a decent black man."

"Oh, hell no! You will not disparage my wife and the name of our best friend in his home! You will never know a finer man, a finer human being than Derrick Jelon Jackson! Yes, he was born into an economically challenged Philadelphia neighborhood, but *the ghetto,* as you perceive it, was not born in him! He was my best friend, my brother! Many times we fought back-to-back against white men who wanted to jack him up or black men who didn't think I had a right to be in his neighborhood. We fought together to ensure that there was no more injustice to people like George Floyd, Ahmaud Arbery, Breonna Taylor, Rayshard Brooks, or a multitude of others like them.

"Do you think for a damn moment that Vivian doesn't make every effort to bring justice to those who deserve it in court? Have you read any of her legal opinions? She is neither conservative nor liberal in her deliberations. She speaks the twelve principles that have been passed down through the generations of her ancestry. Her black ancestry, who on her father's side, were never enslaved. It is obvious on her mother's side of the family, the women were raped repeatedly, but her mother continues to work for the common good. Those principles are what we teach our children regardless of the color of their skin or ours. I am proud of Vivian and honored to be her husband. I thank my Creator and all the ancestors every day that she allowed me to love her to distraction. I am equally proud of the rainbow collection, who are my children and Vivian's. So if you think that I will tolerate even an unkind word about her or any of our children, you've got another damn thought coming!"

Vivian placed a restraining hand on her husband. "Chuck, this isn't about what you or I did or didn't do." She looked directly into Ashante's eyes. "This is about a shameful history once practiced in the black community. While shadows of colorism may still exist within the culture of African-American fraternities and sororities, there was a point in which it was blatantly clear that certain organizations took the hue of one's skin into account before giving a person a chance to pledge. We have all heard stories of the practice of fraternities and sororities, allowing only members with skin color lighter than a brown paper bag to gain admission into their bonds.

"One may think that these destructive practices have been overlooked as a simple fact of life, but apparently, they weren't. In 1928, Edward H. Taylor, a sophomore at Howard University, published an article in 'The Hilltop' student newspaper that accused fraternities of 'splitting the various classes into groups of different shades—yellow, brown, and black.' According to Taylor, 'The light-skinned students were sought after by the fraternities and sororities, particularly the latter. The dark ones were passed by, so they formed their own cliques. The blacks are left in the cold.'

"I once read that 'there is nothing in a white skin to gloat over and nothing in a black skin to be depressed about. It is character, intelligence, and virtue that count. Millions of morons, cretins, and degenerates have white skins and straight hair while a long list of able Negros, from the Kings of Ethiopia who once dominated the civilized world, to Askia of Songhai, to Tshaka the Zulu Napoleon, Mosheh the nation builder, Karma of Bamangwate, Sir Apollo Kaggwa, Prime Minister of Uganda, and to Roland Hayes and Nathaniel Dett have been dark as the night.'

"This is the basis for this harassment my children and I have been subjected to by Ashante King. You see, my dad was a popular basketball jock on Howard's campus. He was sought after by many young college women, but he had eyes for only one young nursing student, Sylvia Benson. He is a brown-skinned man, but Sylvia could pass the brown paper bag test, though those issues meant nothing to either of them. However, one of the young freshmen women was enamored with my dad. Because he wasn't interested in her, she started a vicious rumor that he was color struck and interested in the nursing student only because of her skin color. The nursing student is my mother. It wasn't true, but because of his popularity, it caused a chasm to grow on the campus among the students.

"My parents told me years ago that young woman is Ashante Gilmore, now King. You see, she was caught in the middle, not quite light enough to pass the brown paper bag test or dark enough to fit comfortably in the opposite camp."

Everyone in the room turned inquiring eyes on Ashante, who turned on her heels and strode away. Her entourage slowly followed her out.

Once everyone was gone, Geneviève frowned. "Mom, why didn't you ever tell us the whole story?"

Quentin turned to face Vivian. "Because she didn't think it was pertinent, and she was trying to spare me, Samuel, and Paulette the truth. She held onto that secret when she could have let it corrode the friendships my brother and sister had as children with Samantha."

Geneviève frowned. "Is that it, Mom? Is that why you never said anything?"

Vivian nodded. "It is, yes, and it really wasn't my secret to tell. It was up to your grandparents, but I couldn't stand here and let what I see developing between you, Samantha, and you, Quentin, be torn apart by something that started more than a hundred fifty years before you were born.

"Howard University opened its doors in a time of turbulence. It's clear that even today, some of that negativity could rear its ugly head and impact my family." She shook her head before she turned toward Quentin. "I apologize to you for springing this on you. This is likely hard for you to understand. Racism among peoples of color is less prevalent than what you experience practiced between the different races of humans. People with light skin were viewed as a race unto itself. They were neither white nor black. White people didn't consider them white, and Black people didn't consider them black. Still, they are your parents. I trust that you'll try to find a way to reach out to them and understand their generation's dynamics versus your generation. It's worth a try."

She sighed and kissed her daughters; Chuck followed suit. "I'm proud of you both, but it's past time for me to be in my good government office at the U.S. Supreme Court. Quentin, find a way to work for the common good." She hugged him and took her husband's outstretched hand. "Now, if you don't want to sleep alone, City Cowboy, you'd better find a better type of hot tea for me to drink." They left the condo laughing.

EPILOGUE

Quentin leaned his outstretched arms against the marble walls of the shower and let the water beat down on his tired body from several directions. He had quite a day on the ski slopes trying not to kill himself. There were parts of his body that hurt so badly that he didn't think they would operate ever again. He swam daily, thank Christ, so he got in regular exercise and had good muscle tone, but nothing prepared him for slapping two pieces of wood on his booted feet and making a kamikaze run at break-neck speeds straight down a mountain range with miles and miles of snow. Of course, the Alex-Mont kids had no trouble skiing around him just as they ice skated around him yesterday, doing pirouettes on the frozen mountain lake.

Well, they did have a bit of excitement when Brian's wife, KiLe, and Vivian gave birth on the same day, Christmas Eve. Fortunately, Vivian's mother, Sylvia Benson Alexander, a registered nurse, was on hand to help with both deliveries, as was Chuck, an emergency room doctor. Up close, Mrs. Alexander did resemble the iconic songstress Phyllis Hyman. He could see why Vivian's father, Dr. Bernard Alexander, had eyes for only her back in the day. However, Dr. Alexander looked like the actor Sir Sidney Poitier in his youth. Quentin learned that Dr. Alexander's roots began from a many times Bahamian great-grandmother and an Egyptian many times great grandfather. After only a few conversations with the man over a game of pool and a game of chess, Quentin could understand why his mother, Ashante, was enamored back in college with the man.

Then there was also on hand, Vincent, Chuck and Vivian's son, a pediatrician and newly minted pediatric surgeon to tend to his new baby nephew, Kyle, and new baby brother, Edward Aaron Montgomery, already known as Eddie. Quentin smiled to himself. They seemed to have all the bases covered. Both mothers and sons were pampered throughout the day's festivities. The grandparents, and in the case of Brian's son, great-grandparents Stephen and Harriet Jackson Montgomery, claimed first rights to hold the newest additions to the family. Quentin admitted to himself that he never experienced such unadulterated joy and excitement during the holiday season. He was learning a number of new things, like how to let go and get into the swing of the controlled chaos that is any time he was with the Alex-Mont family.

They inspired him in other ways as well. Samantha challenged him to work for the common good in his neighborhood. She told him, "*You shouldn't behave like some petulant child defiantly running away from your parents. They are your parents. They gave you life and deserve your respect. The silent treatment doesn't work. Talk with them, not at them. No threats. When you were a child, you spoke as a child. You understood as a child. When you became a man, you put away childish things.*" These days, those words were his mantra.

When he called Wesley to ask whether he knew of anything he could do to help in the city, he told him to contact the Police Boys and Girls Club. Geneviève knew exactly who to contact and personally made the introductions. Before he knew it, he was signing on as one of the swim coaches for the teenage boys' team. He didn't know it before, but the community center with the pool was within walking distance of the Watergate. It was in an economically challenged neighborhood. However, with Wesley's help, the newly formed King Advertising Foundation would adopt the community center as an urban improvement project.

He left work early two days each week on Tuesday and Thursday for practices and made time on Saturday for swim meets. His driver suited up to learn along with the boys' team. What was surprising was that he, and some of his account executives, were enjoying the challenge his sixteen boys presented.

In January, he would have to start working with them on their academics and preparing them for the possibility of college-level competition. Seven of the teens showed real promise. If they showed improvement, he'd arrange to take them to Seychelles in February to dive. He was determined that his boys would have an opportunity to grow and develop into productive young men, like Andrew, Darren, and Spencer Montgomery.

When they returned from their rotation at MIT with Dena, he elicited their help with the team, and they readily agreed. They had been early for each practice session and worked well with the teens. He believed they were only half air-breathing mammals as they loved the water as much as he did.

There was other good news. Geneviève actually was the one to solve the break-in at his condo. One of the housekeepers with code access to the condos was away for the holidays. She didn't know that her badge had been stolen by a woman who lived in the condo building. The woman was single, delusional, and off her meds. She was carrying on a fantasy romance with Quentin from the time he appeared on *Let's Talk About It*. She imagined that he was in love with her until she saw pictures of him online with Samantha. She stole the badge to go to him to profess her undying love and to offer him her body. When she found that he was away, she believed that he was with Samantha and destroyed the common areas. She didn't touch the master bedroom because she imagined that she and Quentin would be together there when he returned and didn't want to make a mess. How Geneviève was able to narrow down the list of suspects was a mystery. Still, the woman was now in a hospital receiving the care she needed. She no longer had a home at The Watergate, and the housekeeper didn't lose her job because of the loss of her badge. In his mind, all's well that ends well.

When two hands reached around him, he jolted. He looked over his shoulder and into Samantha's smiling face. He turned back, placed his forehead against the wall, and closed his eyes. "Please tell me that

I'm not dreaming and that you're really standing naked in the shower with me."

Samantha reached down and captured his member in her hand, exercising him slowly.

"Uh, okay, that's not a figment of my imagination. I'm going to turn around with my eyes closed, and I hope with all that is holy that you're still there touching me when I open my eyes." So saying, he turned, opened his eyes, and looked into Samantha's grinning face.

Soaping her hands, she continued to look up at him while she washed his body. "So, Quentin, first, I want to tell you how proud I am of you for taking on the community center project in your neighborhood."

"I can't take credit for that. Initially, I was going to throw money at the project and call it a day. However, you made me a better person. You made me get out of my cocoon, out of my own head so that I could see out of more than only one window. I've reached out to my parents in the hope that we can begin to heal the broken parts of our family. I've learned so much from you and your family about how you all work together for the common good."

She nodded. "Good. Now I have a few questions for you."

"Okay, yes, to anything you want and no to anything that you don't want. Next question."

"Can you make babies?"

He looked skeptically at her and down at his member, which she was exercising with her hands. He looked up into her eyes. "Like right now? Immediately?"

"Or any time in the future."

"Uh, yes, as far as I know, I understand how the process works, and if you keep touching me like this, I'll demonstrate what I know for the next lifetime."

"How many babies do you want?"

"I'll keep it up for as long as you want. Just tell me when you're ready to start and stop."

"Do you want to marry me?"

"That's a definite yes. Just tell me where and when."

"Okay, now here's the big one. Did you know that I'm a virgin?"

He closed his eyes and swallowed hard. "You're killing me. No, I didn't know, but if you keep up this sweet torture, you won't be a virgin an hour or two from now."

"Would you take me to bed now?"

"Yes, but only if this is the start of an exclusive, long-term relationship, probably leading to marriage."

She nodded. "It is. I had a long talk with Glen Kennard and let him know that he and I had irreconcilable differences. He understood, but we will remain friends. Can you deal with that?"

He nodded. "Yes, I can deal with that. I know that when you make a commitment, I can trust your word."

"Good, then we'll see how far we can go. Just so you know that if you're really good at the sex part of the relationship, I'm going to want regular sex with you."

"We'll learn together until we get it right."

"Okay, can we start tonight?"

"Yes, please, but I didn't bring condoms with me."

"That's okay because I did. However, we really won't need them unless you have health concerns."

He shook his head. "No, I've been tested since I was last with Miranda months ago, and I haven't been with anyone else. I'm negative. Why?"

"I had an IUD inserted and my hymen broken by my gynecologist. It's good for the next four years. By then, we should know whether this relationship is going to work between us, and, if so, I won't have another one inserted because we should be ready to have babies by then, agreed?"

"Agreed." He lifted her wet body in his arms, and she wrapped her long legs around his waist.

"So, is this when we get to the good parts of our evening discussion?"

"I'm not sure, Samantha. My brain is in my other head, concentrating on the steps and stages necessary to make you repeatedly orgasm." He kissed her mouth as they sank into the king-sized bed. "I'm in love for the first time in my life."

"I'm in love for the last time in my life."

About the Author

Ann Jeffries, the critically acclaimed author of the Family Reunion—Wisdom of the Ancestors Series, is a native of Washington, DC. As an only child, she enjoyed the benefits of a private school education at Allen in Asheville, North Carolina, and a public education at the University of Maryland. Ann began writing fiction for her own amusement.

Ms. Jeffries is the recipient of many awards for leadership and public service. A keynote speaker at colleges, universities, conferences, and conventions, she has extensively traveled the North American continent, Asia, and Europe. Among other endeavors, she is an entrepreneur, an avid supporter of public television, a genealogist, and a voracious reader.

Her pride and joy are her family, particularly her Fabulous Four grands. She lives in Maryland and South Carolina.

Follow Ann on her website: www.annjeffries.net, on Facebook @Ann Jeffries, on Twitter @AnnAnn Jeffries and her publishing house site: www. newviewliterature.com. Inbox: annjeffriesauthor@ gmail.com. Her novels are available in both e-book and paperback. Her autographed copies can be found through annjeffries.net. Also un-autographed on Amazon.com, barnesandnoble.com, and IngramContent.com for retail bulk sales. The Family Reunion— Wisdom of the Ancestors series is also available in audiobook format at Audible, iTunes, and Amazon.com.

www.ingramcontent.com/pod-product-compliance
Lightning Source LLC
Chambersburg PA
CBHW030759200726
48285CB00013B/303